SONG

OF

BLOOD

&

STONE

SPECIAL EARTHSINGER EDITION
EARTHSINGER CHRONICLES BOOK ONE

SONG

OF

BLOOD

&

STONE

SPECIAL EARTHSINGER EDITION
EARTHSINGER CHRONICLES BOOK ONE

L. PENELOPE

ST. MARTIN'S GRIFFIN NEW YORK

First published in the United States by St. Martin's Press, an imprint of St. Martin's Publishing Group

SONG OF BLOOD & STONE: SPECIAL EARTHSINGER EDITION. Copyright © 2018 by L. Penelope. All rights reserved. Printed in the United States of America. For information, address St. Martin's Publishing Group, 120 Broadway, New York, NY 10271.

www.stmartins.com

Book design by Steven Seighman

The Library of Congress Cataloging-in-Publication Data is available upon request.

ISBN 978-1-250-30689-0 (trade paperback)
ISBN 978-1-250-14808-7 (ebook)

Our books may be purchased in bulk for promotional, educational, or business use. Please contact your local bookseller or the Macmillan Corporate and Premium Sales Department at 1-800-221-7945, extension 5442, or by email at MacmillanSpecialMarkets@macmillan.com.

First Edition: May 2018
First St. Martin's Griffin Edition: July 2019

10 9 8 7 6 5 4 3

For my father, who wanted me to live a happy life

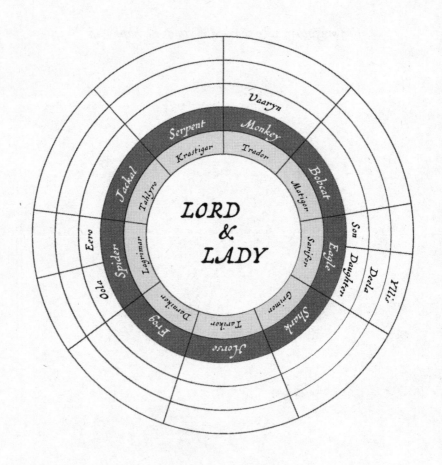

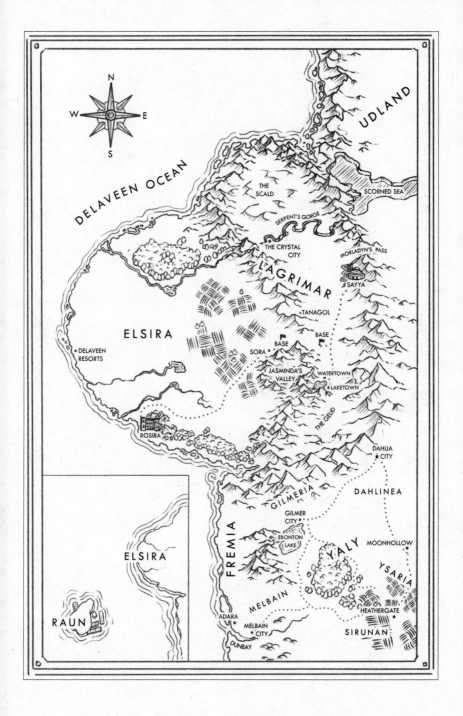

SONG

OF

BLOOD

&

STONE

SPECIAL EARTHSINGER EDITION
EARTHSINGER CHRONICLES BOOK ONE

PROLOGUE

In the beginning, there was silence.

The melody of life and breath and heartbeats and change lay locked in a noiseless hush. No green shoots worked their way out of rocky soil. The parched earth was sterile, yearning for change.

The folk had long since shunned the scalding rays of the sun, instead choosing to burrow inside the mountain they called Mother.

And too far away to fathom, another world shattered and died, expelling two refugees who found their way to our shores. The arrival of the Lord and Lady pierced the quiet—their resonant Songs brought to life the hidden power of Earthsong. They were the Firsts.

They sang the grass and seeds and trees into being. They swelled shriveled streams into rivers, and stymied the will of the desert.

Curious, the folk came out of their caves, little by little, to bear witness to the rebirth of the land. Some were suspicious of the newcomers, but others, the young especially, were awestruck by a magic so different from their own.

And it came to pass that the Lady bore the Lord nine children, each as different from one to another as sea is to soil. Each with a Song rivaling the beauty and power of their parents. And they were the Seconds.

These children took wives and husbands from among the folk of the caves, now brought into the light. The fruit of these unions was plentiful, some bearing rich and varied Songs and some harmonizing the echoes of the caves. And they were the Thirds.

The Lord and the Lady ruled their brood with steady hands and hearts overflowing. And all was well.

For a time . . .

—EARTHSINGER CHRONICLES

CHAPTER ONE

A young man beseeched the Mistress of Eagles, How may I best honor my ancestors?

Eagle replied, You could carve your history into the side of a mountain to hold the tale longer, but only those standing before it may read. Or you could write your history on the waves of the ocean so that it may carry your story to all the lands of the world.

—COLLECTED FOLKTALES

Jasminda had wished for invisibility many times, perhaps today she'd finally achieved it. To the best of her knowledge, Earthsong could not be used for such a thing. But when she'd walked into the post station ten minutes ago, the postmistress had promptly disappeared behind the curtain. Now, the clock on the shelf ticked on. Jasminda's fingers drummed in time on the scarred wood of the countertop.

The bell above the door interrupted the duet. Jasminda's back was to the newcomer. A sharp intake of breath greeted her, and she didn't bother to turn around.

Not invisible, then.

The open door let in the sounds of horses and carts rumbling down the tightly packed dirt road, before closing, leaving the shop in silence once again.

With the arrival of the new customer, the postmistress reappeared, smiling warmly, while at the same time shoving an envelope and a large parcel wrapped in brown paper to Jasminda without even looking in her direction.

According to the postmark, the letter had traveled all the way from Elsira's capital city of Rosira on the western coast. The return address was a solicitor's office. Not the piece of mail she was expecting.

"This is it?" Jasminda's voice pitched higher with each word. She held up the envelope. "Everything since last month?"

"It's all that came in," the postmistress said brusquely. Jasminda sighed, her body deflating.

Out of the corner of her eye, she noticed the rigid way the new customer held herself, leaning her entire body away at an awkward angle. The woman was graying and stooped with age, which made the contortion act all the more laughable. She'd pressed herself into the corner of the small shop, carrying on as though she were sharing the space with a rabid animal and not a nineteen-year-old girl.

Unable to help herself, Jasminda closed her eyes and focused on the well of power within her. By itself, her Song was nothing but raw potential, a match waiting for a strike. But when the rush of Earthsong swept over her, the match caught fire, burning bright.

She extended her arms and scrutinized the deep, rich tone of her skin, so different than everyone else in the town, than just about everyone in the entire country of Elsira. The energy rippling through her gave her a deeper connection to her body. She became even more aware of her skin, how it knit together over muscle and bones. Silently, she sang a spell to shift its color to match the muted, less vibrant shade of the astonished women before her.

"Better?" She looked up, wearing a sweet smile as a mask.

The older woman made a sound like a cat struggling with a hairball and stumbled back, grabbing at the doorknob several times before catching hold.

"*Grol* witch," she muttered, then wrenched the door open and fled. The little bell jingled mercilessly.

The postmistress shot her a murderous glare and backed away, once again retreating behind the curtain separating the front area from the back.

Jasminda's brittle smile crumbled. She released her hold on Earthsong, and her skin changed back to its natural hue. She really shouldn't have wasted her power; she was weak enough as it was. There was no telling what she might meet on the journey home, and she couldn't afford to exhaust herself.

Frowning, she ripped open the unexpected letter from the unknown solicitor. She scanned the text, but the words inside were so formal she could barely make sense of them. A telephone exchange and number were printed on the letterhead. Jasminda had never phoned anyone before—hadn't had anyone to call—but the legal language on the page was gibberish, and she needed to have someone decipher it.

The letter and documents included must have something to do with the tax lien against the farm. Could this be the good news she'd been hoping for? Perhaps the tax bureau had turned the case over to the lawyers for her appeal. She didn't know how these things usually happened.

"How do I phone Rosira?" she called out. The post station had installed a public telephone kiosk six months before. Jasminda approached it warily.

The postmistress fought the dividing curtain in her rush to the front. "Who does someone like you have to call in the capital?" Her deep-set eyes narrowed.

"How. Is. It. Done?" Jasminda pressed her lips together, forming a barrier against other, harsher words she longed to say.

The woman paused, hands on her hips, before relenting. "Pick up the handle and click the lever a few times until the operator comes on. She'll tell you how much it'll be."

"Thank you." Jasminda smiled tightly and followed the postmistress's instructions. The operator's staticky voice announced that the call would be a haypiece. Jasminda dumped five tenthpieces in the slot then waited long minutes for the call to be connected.

Once through to the solicitor's office, she had to wait again to be directed to the man named on the letter she'd received, a Mr. Niqolas Keen.

"It's really very simple, miss." His tone was clipped as if he was in a great hurry. "You sign the paperwork in front of a witness, alert us, and forty-thousand pieces will be wired into your bank account."

"But, why? What's the money for?"

"Your discretion. Your maternal grandfather, Marvus

Zinadeel, has recently decided to act on long-held aspirations of running for public office. He's a wealthy merchant with good prospects, you know." Jasminda did not know.

"However, if news of his late daughter's . . . er, unfortunate marriage were to be discovered, that would substantially harm his chances of electoral success."

Jasminda swallowed the rage building inside her. "So you want me to sign these papers, which say that my mother was not my mother, and then be *discreet* for how long?"

"Forever. You would not be able to reveal your maternal parentage for the rest of your natural life."

A cold emptiness spread inside her. Forever? Tell no one of her mother's kind eyes and gentle touch? It wasn't as if she had anyone to tell anyway, but the idea chafed. "And the price my grandfather is willing to pay for changing history is forty-thousand pieces?"

"That is correct."

Jasminda stared at a spot on the wall, a crack in the paint, just an insignificant blemish. At least for now. Things like this started small, like a cough or a bout of dizziness easily hidden. Then they grew, expanding without warning, narrowing vision, causing periodic vertigo. All of which you assure your loved ones is nothing, a mere inconvenience. Until one day you are caught with such an attack while on the second floor of the barn loft, doing an activity you've done for many years, and fall to your death before anything can be done to save you.

The paint on the wall wasn't ruined yet, but it could be, just as easily as a mother's life.

"Miss, are you still there? Have we been disconnected?"

Jasminda nodded, knowing he couldn't see her. Her voice was small when she spoke. "And if I don't?"

Papers shuffled around on his end. "I understand that you owe a substantial amount in back taxes on the property that is still deeded in your mother's name. Mr. Zinadeel's funds would certainly take care of that expense, would they not?"

The icy sensation seeped through her pores to numb her skin. If her appeal had been rejected, her only option was to petition the board in person—in Rosira. Impossible. This offer could be her last chance. She owed twenty-thousand pieces she did not have. "Yes," she said through gritted teeth. "But—"

"Very well then. Once we have word the paperwork is in the post, the money can be yours the same day. An easy way to solve your problem, true?"

Easy? To sign a paper and suddenly, as if by magic, have no mother. At least not legally. Jasminda didn't know all the implications of such an action, but her heart told her it was wrong. And yet how could she face losing the farm?

She told the solicitor she would consider signing the papers and ended the call. As soon as she stepped out of the booth, the postmistress was there, wiping down the handset and receiver with a cloth smelling of cleaning solution.

Jasminda wanted to smear her handprints on every surface, daring the woman to scrub her presence away. Instead, she scooped up the wrapped package on the counter, cradling it to her chest. The books inside were precious, an escape from the drudgery and loneliness of farm life and the affronts of her rare visits to town. They were her only way to experience the world.

While the postmistress was busy cleaning, Jasminda left coins on the counter to pay for her delivery. The only crime she'd ever committed thus far was being born, she would not add thievery to the imaginary list the townsfolk had created.

With a silent curse at the jolly bell, she left the shop, exiting onto the main street.

Her steps were heavy as she approached the blacksmith, whose shop was at the end of the short row of buildings in the tiny town. She entered the warm space and rested her parcel on the counter. Old smith Bindeen turned from his forge wiping his wrinkled brow, and smiled at her. Against her wishes, her heart unclenched. Bindeen had been the closest thing to a friend her papa had made in town and was the only one who didn't make her feel like a five-legged dog.

"Miss Jasminda, it's been a long time."

"As long as I can make it," she said with a crooked grin. She gave him her order, and he gathered the supplies she needed: nails, an axe head, shotgun shells, door hinges.

"Weather's turned a bit cool, true?" he asked.

"You feel the storm coming?"

He patted his bad hip. "Old bones speak mouthfuls."

She nodded, peering out the shop's front window at the rocky peaks standing guard over the town. "A bad one's brewing. Should hit the mountain tonight. It probably won't make it down here at all, but best be careful."

"How bad d'ya reckon it'll be?" He avoided her eyes as he spoke, but his limbs held as much tension as hers did.

"As bad as two years ago." Her voice was quiet and steady, but her hands clenched into fists involuntarily. She didn't want to get lost in the memory of that last terrible storm. Of searching the mountain paths for Papa and her brothers. Of never finding any trace of them. Mama had been gone for nearly seven years. Papa and the twins for two.

Jasminda cleared her throat to loosen the hold of the past and peered at the old man. He'd lived in this town his whole life, perhaps he knew something she didn't. "Do you remember my mama ever talking about her people?"

Bindeen scratched his chin and squinted. "Not that I can recall, why?"

"No reason." Her voice sagged along with her shoulders.

Mama's family had disowned her for marrying Papa. Now they wanted Jasminda to disown *them*. People she hadn't even met. She didn't think she could get more alone than she had been the past couple of years. But she was wrong.

The old smith pursed his lips and gathered her purchases. "That'll be fifty pieces."

Jasminda frowned. She'd always trusted Bindeen, unlike most in town.

"I'm not tryin' to cheat ya, young miss. The price of everything's gone up. Taxes, too, especially on what comes imported. It's the best price I can give."

She searched the man's face and found him sincere. Using Earthsong would have confirmed his intentions, letting her feel the truth in his heart, but she didn't bother, instead counting out the money and placing it in his hand.

"If ya have any of that magic cream of yours, ya can make some of this back, eh?" He flexed his empty hand, thick with muscle from working the forge for decades, but gnarled with arthritis.

"It's not magic—just goat's milk and herbs." She fished around in her bag and dug out a jar, handing it to him and pocketing the money he gave back to her.

"Works like that magic of yours is all I know."

She held the blacksmith's eye. "You're not afraid of Earth-song like everyone else. Why?"

Bindeen shrugged. "I fought in the Fifth Breach. I've seen the power of those *grol* witches." Jasminda flinched at the epithet, but Bindeen didn't appear to notice. "I been in sandstorms in the middle of a wheat field, pelted with rocks and hail and fire. It's only by the Sovereign's sweet mercy it can't be used to kill directly. Even so, that Earthsong of yours . . . there's plenty of reason to fear it. But I've also seen your father put a man's bone back in its socket and heal it up good as new without ever touching him."

Jasminda swallowed the lump in her throat. Her papa's Song was so strong. He'd been a good man, bearing the insults and scorn of the locals for decades with his head high.

Bindeen's eyes crinkled. He patted his good hip. "This joint he fixed is the only one on me that doesn't ache." His voice thickened. "Most folks hate easy and love hard. Should be the other way around, I reckon."

"Hmm." Jasminda placed her newest packages into her overstuffed bag, unwilling to dwell on what couldn't be.

"Get home safe now," the man called.

"Thank you. May She bless your dreams."

"And yours, as well." He bowed his head with the farewell as Jasminda left the shop.

The sun was hours away from setting, and the journey home would last straight through the night. She knew the steep mountain paths well enough to negotiate them in the dark; her main worry now was beating the brewing storm.

Something about the scent of snow in the air gave her an ominous foreboding. Had the bit of her axe not been worn to a nub, she wouldn't have risked a trip to town so close to the storm at all.

She'd reached the edge of the street and was just heading onto the path leading up into the foothills, when approaching hoofbeats made her turn.

A huge, black Borderlands pony rode up to her, the county constable astride. "Jasminda, have you been causing trouble again? I just got an earful from that woman what runs the post station about you."

The constable was a jovial, red-faced man whose great belly laugh seemed to echo off the mountaintops. He treated Jasminda like a mischievous child, but at least on most days seemed to realize she was not a criminal.

"No trouble, sir. I just picked up my mail and made a phone call." She willed patience into her bones. She could not handle the opinions of one more Elsiran today.

The constable snorted then raised his eyebrow. "Best show me your papers." At her involuntary eye roll, he held up a hand. "I know, I know. You were born and raised here. Sovereign knows I remember when you were just a wee thing scampering about your mama's skirts, but rules are rules." He shrugged.

Hands shaking with impotent fury, Jasminda pulled a small leather booklet from the pocket of her skirt. Inside were her birth and citizenship papers. Proving that no matter what she looked like, she was, in fact, an Elsiran.

She'd never seen anyone else in town ever asked to show their papers. No one but her and Papa.

The constable barely glanced at them before handing them back. They did this dance each time he happened upon her on her increasingly rare trips to town.

"I believe the magistrate wanted me to remind you about the auction next week. You'll need to be out of that cabin of yours by then. Make way for whoever the new buyer will be."

"I still have seven days to pay the taxes, sir." The wobble in her voice shamed her.

He straightened the bill of his cap, chuckling. "Well, that's right, missy. I suppose you can magic up twenty thousand just like that." He snapped his fingers, and his laugh deepened. "If that witchcraft can spin straw into gold, then we've been fighting on the wrong side of this war all these years." His sizable belly shook, and the pony tossed its head, appearing amused as well.

Jasminda narrowed her eyes. "Thank you for the reminder, sir. I really do need to be heading home now."

"We don't want things to get ugly now, missy. Just clear out like you're supposed to, and everything will go real smooth-like."

She wanted to rage. Where exactly was she supposed to go? What was she supposed to do? But pride kept her lips sealed and good sense kept the heat out of her expression.

"Well, on with ya then," he said, shooing her before turning the pony around. "The sooner you leave town, the sooner these old hens will stop worrying me to death with their nattering."

As horse and rider sauntered away, Jasminda took her first full breath. Once they were out of sight, she turned on her heel and marched up the path leading home.

Still her home, at least for a few more days.

She'd only been walking for a couple of hours when something laying in the path made her stop short. At first she thought a discarded pile of rags had somehow blown up the mountain.

Then she realized it was a man.

Jack had found himself in a great many hopeless situations in his life, but this one was the grand champion—a twenty-two-year record for dire occurrences. He only hoped this wouldn't be the last occurrence and sent up yet another prayer that he might live to see his twenty-third year.

The temperature had dropped precipitously. His spine was assaulted by the rocky ground on which he lay, but really that was the least of his discomforts.

His vision had begun to swim about an hour ago, and so at first he thought the girl looming above him was a mirage. She peered down at his hiding spot behind a cluster of coarse shrubbery, her head cocked at an angle. Jack went to stand, years of breeding kicking in, his muscle memory offended at the idea of not standing in the presence of a lady, but apparently his muscles had forgotten the bullet currently lodged within them. And the girl was Lagrimari—not a genteel lady, but a woman nonetheless—and a beautiful one, he noticed as he squinted into the dying light. Wild, midnight curls floated carelessly around her head and piercing dark eyes regarded him. Her dress was drab and tattered, but her smooth skin was a confectioner's delight. His stomach growled. When was the last time he'd eaten?

Her presence meant he was still on the Lagrimari side of the mountain range bordering the two lands and had yet to cross the other, more powerful barrier keeping him from his home of Elsira: the Mantle.

The girl frowned down at him, taking in his bedraggled appearance. From his position lying on the ground, he tried his best to smooth his ripped uniform, the green fatigues of the Lagrimari army. Her confusion was apparent. Jack was obviously Elsiran; aside from his skin tone, the ginger hair and golden honey-colored eyes were a dead giveaway. And yet he wore the uniform of his enemy.

"Please don't be scared," he said in Lagrimari. Her brows rose toward her hairline as she scanned his prone and blood-ied body. Well, that *was* rather a ridiculous thing to say. "I only meant that I mean you no harm. I . . ." He struggled with how to explain himself.

There were two possibilities. She could be an opportunist who would turn him in to the squad of soldiers currently combing the mountain for him, perhaps to gain favor with the government, or she could be like so many Lagrimari citizens, beaten down by life with no real loyalty to their dictator or his thugs. If she was the former, he was already dead, so he took a chance with the truth.

"You see, I was undercover, spying from within the Lagri-mari army. But now there are men looking for me, they're not far, but . . ." He paused to take a breath; the effort of speaking was draining. He suspected he had several cracked or broken ribs in addition to the gunshot wound. His vision swirled again, and the girl turned into two. Two beautiful girls. If these were his last moments before traveling to the World After, then at least he had something pleasant to look at.

He blinked rapidly and took another strained breath. His mission was not complete; he could not die yet. "Can you help me? Please. I've got to get back to Elsira."

She stole an anxious glance skyward before kneeling next

to him. Her cool hand moved to his forehead. The simple touch was soothing, and a wave of tension rolled off him.

"You must be delirious." Her voice was rich, deeper than he'd expected. It eased the harsh consonants of the Lagrimari language, for the first time making it sound like something he could imagine being pleasant to listen to. She worked at the remaining buttons of his shirt, pulling the fabric apart to reveal his ruined chest. Her expression was appraising as she viewed the damage then sat back on her haunches, pensive.

"It probably looks worse than it is," he said.

"I doubt that."

Jack's chuckle sounded deranged to his own ears, so it was no surprise that the girl looked at him askance. He winced—laughing was a bad idea at this point—and struggled for breath again. "The soldiers . . . they're after me. I have to get back through the Mantle."

"Shh," she said, peering closely at him. "Hush all that fool-ishness; you're not in your right mind. Though I'll admit, you speak Lagrimari surprisingly well. I'm not sure what happened to you, but you should save your strength."

She closed her eyes and suddenly his whole body grew warmer, lighter. The odd sensation of Earthsong pulsated through him. He had only experienced it once before and it hadn't been quite like this. The touch of her magic stroked him intimately, like a brush of fingers across his skin. The soft vibration cascaded over his entire body, leaving him feeling weightless.

He gasped, pulling in a breath and it was very nearly an easy thing to accomplish. Tears pricked his eyes. "Sovereign bless you."

Her expression was grave as she dug around in her bag. "It's just a patch. You must have ticked someone off real good. It'd take quite a while to fix you up properly, and the storm's coming. You need to find shelter."

She retrieved a jar filled with a sweet-smelling substance and began spreading it over his wounds. The Earthsong had turned down the volume of his pain and the cream soothed him even more.

"What is that?"

"Just a balm. Helps with burns, cuts." Her hand paused for a moment. "Never gunshot wounds, but it's worth a try."

He laid his head back on the ground, closing his eyes to savor the ability to breathe deeply again. "A quick rest and I'll be back on my way. Need to keep moving, though. Need to get back."

"Back through the Mantle?" Her tone vibrated with skepticism. "And away from the Lagrimari soldiers chasing you?"

"Yes." Her palm met his forehead again. She thought he was delusional. He wished he was. Wished the last few weeks had been nothing but the imaginings of an impaired mind.

"The Seventh Breach ended five years ago." Her voice flowed over him, along with another tingle of Earthsong, cool and comforting. "We've had peace since then. No way to cross the Mantle from either side."

He shook his head, aggravating the hole in his upper chest, inches from his heart, where the inconvenient bit of metal was still lodged. "There are ways."

A crunch of boots in the distance set him on alert. He grabbed the girl's wrist to halt her while he listened. The soldiers were near.

He opened his eyes and looked into her startled ones. "Shh, they're coming."

Her head darted from side to side, and he saw the moment she realized someone was indeed coming. Jack couldn't let her be found helping him. Having seen firsthand what these men were capable of, he couldn't let her be found by them at all. The Lagrimari army was filled with men unfit even for Elsira's prisons. This girl had been kind, a trait his people didn't believe the Lagrimari even possessed, but he knew better and felt the need to protect her. He wrestled himself to a sitting position, ignoring the daggers of pain impaling him with every movement, but her strong arms prevented him from standing.

"Hide here, and I'll draw them away," he whispered and motioned for her to crouch down. "They will find me anyway, but it's best they don't see you." Her gaze darted back toward the sound of approaching footsteps.

As he agonizingly made his way to his hands and knees, the pain flared hot, threatening to blind him. With a tug on her arm, he pulled her behind the shrubbery and half crawled, half dragged himself back onto the narrow, rocky path. Her head stuck up over the grouping of rocks and shrubs, and he motioned for her to get down as he put a little distance between them.

The footfalls grew closer. He turned to face them, not wanting to draw any attention to the girl hiding only a few paces away.

Six Lagrimari men appeared from around the bend in the path. The sergeant spotted him, and a hard smile spread across the man's narrow face. Jack only had time to feel a small amount of satisfaction at the purple bruise around the sergeant's eye before a foot to his midsection stole his breath. A kick to the head stole his consciousness.

CHAPTER TWO

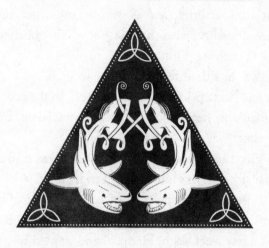

A poor man said to the Master of Sharks, Though I am in need, I fear I am not worthy to receive.

Shark responded, If a waterfall withholds its flow from the pool below, then it ceases to exist. To give only to the deserving is stagnation.

—COLLECTED FOLKTALES

Ella removed the fabric draping her customer with a flourish, then stepped back, holding her breath. The sounds of the beauty parlor faded in her ears as Berta inspected herself in the oval mirror, turning her head from side to side.

The woman pursed her lips, her expression giving nothing away. Ella feared she may pass out for lack of air.

Finally, the corners of Berta's mouth lifted. Her smile

spread until her face was as radiant as the sun. "I love it! It's perfect!"

Breath escaped Ella in a rush, and she laughed shakily in relief. "It's low maintenance as well. I know you don't have time for a lot of fuss with the new baby." She touched a curl in the back, tucking it into place.

"Thank you, Ella. I feel like a new woman."

Beaming, Berta paid her bill and was off. In the next station, Doreen shook her head. "I don't know how you do it, Ella."

"Do what?"

"You give the woman a trim and she makes it sound like you've transformed her into the Queen herself!"

Ella chose to ignore the trace of jealousy that had infected the other hairdresser's voice. "Berta gave birth to her third child just a few weeks ago. Her husband wanted to do something special for her and sent her here. Sometimes it's the little things that make a big difference in someone's life."

Doreen shook her head and went back to organizing her curlers. Why else become a hairdresser if you didn't want to bring a little beauty and confidence into the world? Ella shrugged. She liked making people feel good about themselves, and just wished she understood what was stuck in Doreen's craw. Maybe it was the fact Ella was a foreigner, maybe because she was the newest girl here.

Instead of worrying on it, she swept up the hair clippings around her chair, humming along with the tune played by the fiddler busking out on the corner. The shop's front door was propped open, letting in the breeze along with the sounds of the city. Outside, a woman shouted rapidly in a language Ella didn't understand. Horses and carts rattled along the cobblestone streets, and automobiles chugged along belching smoke into the air. And further, the lapping of waves against the hulls of giant vessels, the cursing of dockworkers as they struggled loading or unloading cargo from a trading ship. Ella soaked in all the sounds, loving the melody of the neighborhood of Portside in the capital city, Rosira.

The shop was slow today. Only one hairdresser had anyone in her chair and the wash girls sat at the front counter, folding and re-folding the same towels over and over. One of them looked out of the window and gasped. "Oh no! It's Anneli!"

The other women murmured in dismay.

"Who's Anneli?" Ella asked.

"This deranged old woman who hardly ever leaves her house," the nail girl said.

"Except for twice a year to get her hair cut," another girl said, shivering.

Doreen snorted. "I heard that her husband died in their flat decades ago and she mummified his body like some savage Udlander and keeps it at the dining room table."

Ella frowned. The people from Udland didn't mummify their dead, but she didn't bother to correct her. Instead, like everyone else, she watched the slow progress of an old, stooped woman shuffling down the sidewalk. A tangled mass of silver hair flowed to the middle of her back.

The woman, Anneli, crossed the threshold of the shop and stood there, waiting. Suddenly everyone was very busy, organizing bottles of shampoo, putting away brushes and scissors, or wiping down their chairs. No one would look the woman in the eye.

Ella stood there for a moment in disbelief. Then she stepped forward. "Hello, can I help you, mistress?"

Doreen shot her a shocked glance.

"Need a haircut," Anneli said gruffly.

"Well, you've come to the right place. Have a seat."

Anneli shuffled forward and sat. Her dress had been patched many times over and one of her boots had a hole through which you could see a stocking-clad foot. But far worse was the state of her hair. Thick and greasy and matted. Did she not wash it between twice-yearly visits to the salon?

Ella took a deep breath and grabbed a wide-toothed comb.

"The day's not too warm for you is it?" she asked pleasantly and received only a grunt in return. "It's summer's last hoorah, I think. Just so we remember her once autumn is upon us."

She began at the ends of Anneli's hair, combing it out with great patience, loosening one knot and then another.

"Are you from Elsira?" No response. "I'm Yalyish myself, from one of the smaller commonwealths. It gets plenty hot there around this time of year. No ocean breezes to cool you off, either." She was content to hold a one-sided conversation. Maybe eventually Anneli would join in.

"I married an Elsiran man, my Benn. That's him there." She pointed to their wedding photograph propped on the counter. Benn stood, back straight, staring intensely into the camera, while Ella grinned widely, showing all of her teeth. He looked so gallant in his uniform—every bit the dashing soldier who'd swept her off her feet.

Her heart panged and she swallowed, throat suddenly thick. Her Benn, deployed so far away.

Anneli must have seen the change in her expression in the mirror. "Handsome fella," she offered.

Ella forced the melancholy back with practiced ease and

managed a smile. "Yes, I'm very lucky. My, you have thick hair. Mine's so fine and thin, always breaking off if I'm not careful. Yours is quite strong. I'm not hurting you am I? You've let it get quite tangled."

"Doesn't hurt."

And so she worked while chatting aimlessly, sometimes getting a one or two word response, most times not.

"So what kind of cut are you looking for today?"

"To my shoulders."

Ella leaned down, as if about to tell her a secret. "Would you like to try a bob? It's all the rage these days." She patted her own short, sandy-colored hair, curled to just under her ears. "It would be quite fetching."

"I'm too old for all that," Anneli said, waving a wrinkled hand.

Ella laughed, shaking her head. "You're only as old as you feel. My grandpa taught me that. Besides, you have such lovely cheekbones and striking eyes." She'd noticed their bright green color, not dulled with age as she would have expected. Those eyes marked Anneli as foreign to Elsira. "I think a bob would highlight your best features. You'll be beating off the men with a stick."

Anneli snorted, but the ghost of a smile crossed her lips.

"And this color," Ella went on, "you don't need any help there. It's a perfect silver. Never let anyone convince you to dye it. I hope one day to have hair this color. A sign of wisdom I always thought."

The woman's smile deepened, and she shook her head. "Fine, fine. Do what you want, just don't prattle on about it."

Ella's grin split her face and she bounced up and down.

"Trust me, you'll love it!"

———

When Ella removed the drape and spun Anneli around she expected a reaction of some kind—a small gasp or cautious smile. But the tears in the woman's eyes made her own begin to burn.

"By the saints," Anneli said, eyes wide. "If only my Henrik could see me now." She stared in the mirror, entranced by her appearance. The cut really did make the woman look decades younger, and even with her drab, patched clothing you could see the echoes of her former beauty.

Their eyes met in the mirror. Anneli reached out to grab Ella's hand. "Thank you." She seemed unable to say anything else. Ella squeezed her hand gently and wiped her eyes with her free hand.

"What do I owe you?"

They settled the bill, and Anneli walked out of the shop her back a bit straighter, her gait a bit surer.

Ella could feel the gazes of the others in the shop on her as she counted the coins, but didn't look up. She hadn't charged Anneli anything extra for the additional time it had taken to work on her hair. She just hadn't had the heart.

The shop remained quiet, like a blanket of wonder had been laid over it. The hush was interrupted by a newcomer in the doorway.

"Zorelladine Farmafield?"

Ella stood. "That's me."

A young boy walked over, yellow envelope in his hand. "Telegram fer ya." He spoke with the accent of the Elsiran street youth who filled Portside. Some earned their money as messengers, some as pickpockets, some as lookouts or thieves or worse. This one wore a billed cap with the logo of the telegram company, though his clothes were grimy and ragged.

"Thank you," Ella said, parting with a hundredthpiece as a tip. The boy gripped the hunny like a lifeline and headed off.

Ella ripped open the telegram. Her heart nearly stopped at the words.

APOLOGIES FOR LACK OF CONTACT, BUT I NEED YOU. DESPERATE. AT TEMPLE IN SORA, BORDERLANDS. COME NOW. THE YOKE OF MAN IS THE YOLK OF MAN. YOURS, KESS.

Ella turned over the paper wishing there was more. As it was, a telegram of this length would have cost her sister dearly. Kess had given up any chance of wealth when she'd joined the Sisterhood and dedicated her life to the Elsiran goddess. She'd also given up her family, though in reality, that had happened many years earlier.

From what she recalled, the town of Sora was located in the county that was home to both the eastern army base and the only temple of the Followers of the Queen Who Sleeps that far east.

Ella's hand shook as she stuffed the message in her pocket. She looked up, once again everyone was staring.

"I, um . . . I need to take the rest of the day off." She grabbed her purse and ran out before anyone could question her.

The little bodega on the first floor of her apartment building held the only public telephone booth for eight blocks. Fortunately, when Ella got there, there was no one waiting to use it. She slipped inside and fished in her change purse for enough coins to make the call out east—after they'd plinked into the slot, all that was left in her purse was lint. Then she waited long minutes for the operator to connect her.

"High Commander's office," a familiar voice said. "Lt. Ravel, speaking."

"Benn, it's me."

"Ella," her husband's voice filled with joy, "I was just re-reading your last letter. But—What's happened?" Trepidation there at the end. She was not due for a call for another few days yet.

Benn's latest deployment had lasted nine long months and fourteen days so far. Much as she would have loved to hear his voice more often, they could not afford frequent calls.

"I received a telegram. From Kess."

Soft static filled the line. Ella's only sister was ten years older, and the two had never been close. They'd grown up in the Commonwealth of Sirunan, a tiny farming state in Yaly, Elsira's southern neighbor, on the plantation her parents were the administrators for.

Ella remembered her sister as headstrong and fierce, a battering ram of a girl who drove their parents to distraction. At eighteen, Kess had left the farm, vowing to travel the world. She'd eventually settled in Elsira. They'd only seen one another a handful of times in the past two decades. Kess had even missed Ella's wedding.

Benn's voice crackled over the line. "Is she all right?"

"I don't think so, no. She says she needs my help. Her note was . . ." Ella pulled the folded paper from her pocket. "Troubling." She read it to him.

"Benn, I need to go to her."

"Ella, no." She could imagine him shaking his head on the other end of the line. "No, it's too dangerous. Leaving Portside without any papers, you could be arrested. Deported."

Portside not only separated Elsira's capital of Rosira from the Delaveen Ocean, it separated Elsirans from the undesirable influences of the rest of the world. The busy port welcomed not only ships and goods, but merchants, visitors, and workers from far and wide, but they could stray no further than Portside without citizenship papers or some special exemption.

She'd had a two week vacation pass when she'd first come to Elsira as a university student to visit one of the famed resorts in the north. There she'd met a broad-shouldered, handsome soldier and had never looked back. But even married to a native born Elsiran, she would need to wait another four years to be eligible for citizenship and the ability to travel within the country.

Kess needed help now.

"She's my sister."

"And you've had almost no contact with her since you were children. When was the last letter you received?"

"I think she congratulated me on my wedding."

"Six years ago? Ella, it would be such a risk for you."

She nodded, conscious he couldn't see. "I know, but . . ."

She thought of the phrase Kess had included. *The yoke of man is the yolk of man.* It was a maxim of St. Siruna, the patron of their commonwealth. She was the champion of mothers and families, invoked to remind believers of the strength of those bonds.

"One of my clearest memories of Kess was when she used to read to me at night. She tried to help me understand the teachings of St. Siruna. Our yokes—those things that weigh us down and burden us—are our yolks—the meaty part of the egg that feeds us. Our nourishment. What we need to get through. She included that phrase in the telegram so I would know the message was truly from her."

And though Ella was fairly sure that St. Siruna had abandoned her as completely as her parents and sister had, she could not find it in her heart to do the same.

"I have to do this, Benn. I can't just turn my back on her."

Benn sighed deeply. "I don't want you putting yourself at risk. I'm not sure she would do the same."

The statement stung, but Ella couldn't disagree. "It doesn't matter."

"You're going to go regardless of what I say, aren't you?"

"Yes?" She phrased it as a question and his dry chuckle sounded defeated.

"I really wish I could stop you."

The line clicked indicating that she would either need to insert additional coins or the call would end in another minute.

"So what's your plan?" he asked.

"I could dye my hair." Ella grasped at her wheat-colored strands. Not red enough to pass for Elsiran. "Maybe then no one will ask for my papers?"

Benn was quiet for a moment, and his voice was all business when he spoke. "There's a noon bus from Portside, daily. An express that many of the soldiers use to get back and forth to the capital. I know a fellow at the depot who owes me a favor and should be able to get you aboard without having your papers checked."

"Thank you. Sora isn't so far from the base, is it? Maybe you could find a reason to stop by?" Hope crept into her voice. It felt like an eternity since she'd last laid eyes on her husband. He had been due for leave weeks ago, but then it was mysteriously cancelled.

"I . . . I hope so. The High Commander is away and I've been tasked with babysitting this researcher here doing a study. She's quite a handful for an old woman." He sighed. "You'll be so close . . ."

"Close as raindrops."

A beeping started, the countdown to the end of the call. "I love you, sea-monster," she said softly.

"Love you, too, seashell. And be careful. Don't draw any attention to yourself. If they find out—"

But the line clicked off.

Ella held the earpiece for another few moments, willing the tears not to come. Finally she placed it back in the cradle and hugged her arms around herself, trying to remember the exact feel of Benn's embrace.

Then she straightened. Threw her shoulders back, scrubbed at her eyes, and exited the telephone booth.

The crowded bodega was full of familiar faces from the neighborhood. Many called out to her in greeting. Young mothers whose children she'd babysat, dockworkers who'd labored alongside Benn's father and brother, foreigners like her restricted from leaving Portside, but not really wanting to. This neighborhood may be poor and crowded and dirty, but it was home. More home than anywhere else she'd known.

And she didn't want to leave. But how could she turn her back on her own flesh and blood?

She pulled out Benn's old pocket watch, the one she used to count down the minutes until he was home. Now it told her that the express bus would leave in under two hours. Which would put her in Sora in the wee hours of the next morning.

Kess. What kind of trouble have you gotten yourself into?

And how was Ella going to be able to help?

The first snowflakes began to fall as Jasminda crept down the mountain. She followed the lantern light of the men who'd dragged away the unconscious Elsiran, staying a few dozen paces behind. While she'd thought his tale fantastical, there was no doubting the six Lagrimari soldiers who'd appeared, or their viciousness toward him. She'd winced as they'd continued to strike him, long after he'd passed out.

He was an odd one, surely—his manner, his clothing, his perfect Lagrimari speech and accent. She'd never heard of an Elsiran who could speak the language. Even her mama had never been able to master it. And with his talk of crossing the Mantle, of course she'd thought him deranged. The magical border between the two lands followed the mountain range. The Mantle had stood for five hundred years and had only been breached seven times, each resulting in months or years of war.

Her papa had come over during the Sixth Breach. He'd been one of the soldiers stuck in Elsira as prisoners of war when the gap in the Mantle closed. After their release from prison, they'd been unable to obtain citizenship or find jobs, so the Lagrimari had formed settlements, shantytowns really, and eked out a meager living with the help of the Sisterhood. But Papa had met Mama and built a life with her. He never talked much of home or said anything about wanting to go back.

Jasminda had asked him about it, over and over, always afraid that as soon as the chance came, he would disappear into the mysterious country of his birth, just over the mountains. He would reassure her that he wasn't going anywhere—sometimes with a chuckle, sometimes with an exasperated sigh, and occasionally with a haunted look in his eye that made her stop the questions.

The Seventh Breach took place the summer of her fifteenth year. The fighting had ended before her family even heard about it, isolated as their valley home was. Jasminda was glad they didn't find out until the breach had closed. She believed Papa's words that he would never leave her—believed them until two years ago when he'd been proved a liar.

But now her own two eyes bore witness of Lagrimari soldiers on her mountain. The odd Elsiran had been convinced he was still in Lagrimar. That meant he'd crossed the Mantle without even knowing it. Was this the start of another breach war, or something else entirely?

If she'd believed the Elsiran, she would have drained her Song to heal him more. His injuries were beyond her limited abilities, but she'd selfishly only given a little of her power to ease the worst of his pain. She'd wanted to leave a bit in reserve for her long journey. Could she have helped him avoid the men? There was little she could do for him now, not against six armed soldiers, but guilt made her follow them anyway.

It made no sense; he was nobody to her. Just another Elsiran. Except . . . He had not stared at her or been cruel.

He had, in fact, shielded her from those men, put himself in their path so they would not find her. Why would he do such a thing?

As the men took wrong turn after wrong turn, she stayed on course, though the direct route she'd planned to take would have had her home and warm in bed by now.

Dawn poked its head over the jagged peaks, and with its arrival came the crowing of a rooster. The soldiers stopped short at a fork in the path. Jasminda knew that crow all too well.

The men conferred for a moment and chose to follow the crowing. The mountain made the sound seem closer than it really was, but the sign of civilization could not be mistaken. Her relief to be headed out of the storm battled with alarm— these strangers were now on a path that led only one place.

Her home.

The Elsiran had regained his senses, and instead of being dragged behind the men like a sack of beets, he stumbled along, his hands tied in front of him. The men climbed down the mountain, leaving the storm behind bit by bit. The snow and ice would grow worse over the next few days, but it would stay at the higher elevations. The valley where her home lay would remain lush and green, protected from the harsh weather either by the mountains surrounding it, or some lingering spell of Papa's, or perhaps a little of both. But there would be no way out. These men would be trapped in an area that was only a two-hour walk from end to end. They would find her cabin; there was no way to avoid it.

She doubled back and took a shortcut she usually avoided, though it had been a favorite of her brothers. It involved a very steep climb, required scaling several large boulders, and brought her far too near one of the caves that peppered the mountain. She ignored the yawning black opening and focused on beating the men to her cabin.

Awake now for over twenty-four hours, she pushed herself far beyond exhaustion. Snow made the rocks slippery, and she lost her footing and slid down an embankment, skinning her hands and forearms. She picked herself up, ignoring the injury, and raced to her cabin, confident she had at least twenty minutes before the soldiers arrived.

She hurried to the barn, where she found the goats already awake, agitated and jittery, no doubt because of the storm. They were like her, craving peace and quiet. Any interruption to their routine or change in the weather troubled the sensitive creatures. She checked their food then barred the outer barn door to keep them from wandering.

Her next stop was the cabin, where she set down her bag and retrieved her shotgun. She carried a pistol with her on trips to town, but the shotgun was her favorite. It was almost an antique but shot straight and true. She loaded it with the shells she'd purchased from the blacksmith, then sat on the porch steps. Waiting.

Do what you think you can't. That's what her papa had always said. It was a mantra of his. When he'd repeat it, one of her brothers would often make a face, crossing his eyes and mouthing along. But with them all gone now, it became her own incantation, chanted inside her head at moments like these.

This was her home. The only thing she had in the world. No tax man nor enemy soldier could take it from her. She would do whatever she must to protect it.

It wasn't long before the telltale clomp of boots announced the men. She hadn't gotten a good look at them in the dark, but the cool, morning light revealed dirty uniforms and even dirtier faces. All except for their leader, a man of skin and bone, his narrow face overshadowed by both a giant, curling mustache and a blackened eye. He was clean and well-groomed, hair parted and shining with pomade.

She stood as they approached, shotgun dangling almost casually from the crook of her arm. The Elsiran, barely standing, was held upright by a soldier. All her healing work had been undone by their brutality.

The leader spoke first. "Pleasant morning to you, miss. I am Tensyn ol-Trador, Honorable Sergeant of His Majesty the True Father's royal army. My men and I are in need of food and shelter. We must speak with your father or husband." His voice was high and nasally, like a human rat.

"This is *my* home."

His eyebrows shot up, and he glanced back at his men, his mouth twisting into what perhaps was meant to be a smile. "You are alone?"

"I want no trouble here," she responded. The Elsiran's head popped up; he frowned and squinted at her, his bruised face freezing once he recognized her. Astonishment and sorrow settled across his features. His shoulders slumped.

Nerves caused her to struggle to catch hold of Earthsong. The power skittered out of her grasp.

"We have been caught in the mountains by the storm and cannot make it to the capital until it passes. We are tasked with transporting this spy to face the True Father's judgment."

"An Elsiran spy? In your uniform?"

"Yes, he had been spelled to look like one of us. I witnessed it wear off with my own eyes, miss. There are traitorous souls infecting our land, working with our enemies. The Singer responsible for this spell is soon to meet the World After, I think. But that is a matter for the True Father to sort out."

The soldier holding the Elsiran kicked at his legs, causing him to crumple, face-first, to the ground. His upper body heaved as he drew in jagged breaths, but he did not cry out. Jasminda held her breath, keeping her face rigid to hide her horror. The prisoner rolled awkwardly to his knees, then slowly struggled back to his feet. The soldiers beside him snickered as he wobbled before finding his balance. His head shot up defiantly.

Her breath escaped in a rush. The man she'd met the day before on the mountain had been somewhat peculiar, but also gentle. Even with the uniform, he'd struck her as a painter or poet who had fallen upon thieves or been mauled by an animal. She hadn't truly believed him to be a soldier. But now, the sharp lines of his face had turned savage. With his sculpted cheekbones, decisive chin, and that cold power in his eyes, she wondered how these soldiers ever thought they had him cowed. How could she have thought him anything but a warrior?

She forced her gaze back to the sergeant who looked at her expectantly. He'd been speaking, but she hadn't been paying attention. "Excuse me?"

"May we shelter here?" His tobacco-stained smile sent a cold chill rolling through her.

"You and your men may stay in the barn. I will bring you food and water."

A collective grumble arose from the other soldiers. Sergeant Tensyn's grin fell away. "The barn? You must be joking."

"The cabin is quite small, as I'm sure you can see. Plus, I am not in the habit of inviting strange men into my home."

He took a step closer to the porch, bringing his eyes level with her chest. Though his gaze reached her face quickly, she did not miss the route it took. "Miss . . . ?"

"Jasminda ul-Sarifor." She spat out her name as if it tasted vile.

"Miss Jasminda. As the True Father says, it is your duty to aid his representatives to the best of your ability. I'm afraid the barn will not do. For the prisoner, perhaps, but my men have been marching for days with little food or rest." His cajoling tone turned darker. "We have already learned there are traitors among us. Would not a loyal citizen answer the call of our great leader?"

As she had suspected, these men also believed they were in Lagrimar. If they thought her Elsiran they would likely kill her. She closed her eyes briefly and finally connected to Earthsong. With the energy pulsing into her, she could sense emotion and mood. It was not her strongest skill by far, but these men were easy to read.

Danger rolled off them, impatience, barely reined-in malice. And determination. She would not be able to keep them out. Her best chance was to go along with their assumption of her loyalty, be vigilant, and bide her time. Though she knew little of her father's homeland, being a Lagrimari may save her life, so that is what she would be.

She released her connection, adjusted her shotgun in her hands, all while glaring at the sergeant. "You may wait here for the storm to pass, but listen to me clearly. I will kill any man who touches me."

He swallowed. The others shifted where they stood. Finally, Sergeant Tensyn bowed. "I give you my word on the

True Father that none of my men will harm you in any way. Food and shelter are all we ask."

Her raw palms burned from gripping the metal of the gun, and her heart stuttered in her chest. The Elsiran looked on, an apology written on his face. She was sorry, as well.

"Well, come in then."

CHAPTER THREE

Said a stonecutter to the Mistress of Frogs, How may I complete my work and feed my family, though I am lame?

To which she replied, A stone needs only a trickle of water, unceasing in its focus, to create a groove. If you are the water, take your time to do the work. If you are the stone, best roll out of the way before you are split in two.

—COLLECTED FOLKTALES

It was not in Jack's nature to despair. He'd been through his share of hardships, to be sure—well, less than most but more than some, he suspected. The Seventh Breach in particular came to mind. Ninety-nine days of misery that had felt like a thousand. But even then, he'd been full of righteous rage, which had kept him from sinking into the depression so many of his men had succumbed to.

There was a desolation that sank into the hearts of people who'd lived through war. He saw it in the old-timers who fought in the tail end of the Fifth Breach, a war that lasted seventy years. But he'd also seen it in the faces of Lagrimari children in the villages the squad had passed through on his spy mission. Before his bloody disguise had worn off.

Now, a kind of melancholy he was not used to threatened to overtake him. He was back where he'd started—captured— and worse, the girl he'd tried to protect had been hauled into this mess. But he couldn't allow himself to sink too far. Giving up was also not in his nature, not while there was breath in his body.

He wasn't sure how many breaths he had left, though. Each one was more difficult than the last. He'd been trained to work through pain, to put it in a box in his mind, then put that box into another box until he had as many boxes as he needed to keep moving, keep fighting. He had lost count of his boxes, and they'd long stopped helping. Pain was all he knew, but even that meant he was alive and still had a chance to escape.

The brute to his left, a lout called Ginko, squeezed a brawny hand over Jack's arm and pulled him forward, toward the girl's quaint cabin, which sat under the shade of several tall trees. A barn stood off to the side with a chicken coop beyond it. Rows and rows of carefully tended plants stretched out on either side of the house, interrupted every so often by thickets of trees.

Most of Lagrimar was desert wasteland, but in the very far west the climate was more pleasant, almost like lush Elsira. He would have imagined that most of the country's population would live in this tiny region, but it was not the case. Aside from the two western Lake Cities, the people were spread evenly across the barren country with many living in the capital city of Sayya, far to the east.

Jack's travels during his undercover mission had kept him mostly in the west. But he had never been inside a Lagrimari home before and found himself surprised at its warmth and coziness. He had thought they would all look like the tenuously built mud-brick huts of the poor villages, but this was a proper home for a family. Quilts covered overstuffed couches and chairs. Colorful rugs hugged the floor, though they were currently being sullied by the mud tracked in on the soldiers' boots. The mantelpiece featured children's drawings, wood carvings, a cuckoo clock, and a photograph of several people that he couldn't make out from this distance.

The girl, Jasminda, pointed out two bedrooms and a washroom on the main floor for the men to use. Just beyond the living room was the entrance to the kitchen, through which a squat woodstove was visible. A staircase in the living room led up to a closed door that she indicated belonged to her. When he looked back to the mantel, the photo had been turned facedown.

"And what of communications, Miss Jasminda?" Sergeant Tensyn asked. "Our radio equipment is badly damaged, and we've had no contact with our regiment."

"No electricity. No radio or cables here."

Tensyn looked ready to continue his questioning when she broke in. "Sergeant, you hope to bring the spy in alive, yes?" She had not looked at Jack since that moment of recognition outside, and she did not glance at him now, yet he felt her attention on him all the same.

Earthsong moved across his skin like the lips of a lover.

When Darvyn had cast the spell to change Jack's appearance before leading him through the crack in the Mantle into Lagrimar, it had felt so different. Less personal, less invasive. But thanks to Jasminda's continued ministrations, finally, the pain could fit in a box. He fought the desire to fall to his knees with relief.

"There is a reward for the return of this man," Tensyn said. "Alive."

Jasminda wrinkled her nose. "He stinks of infection. Why has he not been healed?"

Her words caused a spike of fear. He'd seen many a man die of untreated infection from wounds more minor than his.

"All of my men have already given tribute to the True Father."

"And their Songs have not returned?"

Jack's gaze snapped to her, and Tensyn's expression sharpened. "Tributes are irreversible, as I'm sure you know, Miss Jasminda. Once your Song is gone, it cannot be returned."

All of the men were looking at her now, but her expression did not change. Her eyes flashed for a moment—perhaps with fear or anger—but it was gone so quickly Jack could not be sure.

"I had heard sometimes they did, that is all. This man will die in days if the infection continues." She spun away and stalked into the kitchen.

Was it possible she was more than just a sympathetic Lagrimari? Her ignorance of the True Father's tributes could mean she was a Keeper of the Promise like Darvyn. They often stayed in isolated places like this, free from the dictator's edicts.

"Can you keep him alive?" Tensyn asked.

"Yes." Her voice was clipped.

A cautious hope welled within Jack.

She slammed a basket of fruit on the kitchen table and retrieved more food from the pantry, still clutching her shotgun. The other soldiers, except for Tensyn and Ginko, sat and began eating without ceremony. Jasminda grabbed a bowl, filled it with water, and gathered towels and a knife.

"Back porch. The floors in here are already filthy." Her words cracked like a whip.

"My apologies, miss." Tensyn lowered himself into a bow. "I'll have my men be more careful with the state of your home."

The sergeant motioned to Ginko, who pushed Jack forward. His injuries screamed, but he remained silent. Jasminda's lips pursed and she spun around, leading the way out the back to the porch. She motioned to the top step with her chin. Jack was pushed down until he sprawled across the stairs, gasping for breath.

"Untie him," she said, staring at his lashed wrists. "I need to check his wounds."

Ginko pulled a knife from his boot to cut the rope. The sharp edges of the pain had been bound by whatever spell she'd sung a few moments before, but the weakness in his limbs couldn't be ignored. The lack of food and water, the days of walking and hiding, had all left him teetering on the edge of his endurance. She, too, had deep circles under her eyes, and he wondered what she'd been doing up on the mountain.

As she settled next to him, his awareness of her pulsed like an extra sense. She smelled of cool mountain air, pine, and something light and feminine that he couldn't place. He closed his eyes and inhaled her nearness, allowing it to soothe and calm him. He imagined himself far away, in the bar-

racks he'd called home since childhood or maybe even farther away, floating on his back in the Delaveen Ocean, the
sun warming his face.

The vision faded when her fingertips grazed his forehead.

"Does that hurt?" Her whispered voice stroked his cheek.
He opened his eyes to find her very close. Unable to find his
voice, he shook his head.

"Take that off." She pointed to his shirt. He had the absurd desire to chuckle. How many times had he longed to hear
a woman ordering him to take off his shirt? What he'd felt of
her touch so far had been very soft . . . She must be soft all
over. He'd never imagined a Lagrimari girl could be so lovely.
The coils of her hair called to his fingertips and—

"Has your tribute day been scheduled?" Tensyn's oily voice
broke through Jack's musings. He and Ginko stood in the
doorway, and Jack hated having anyone at his back. That kind
of sloppiness had literally been beaten out of him. He blamed
the pain and the fatigue.

His bruised fingers faltered on the tiny buttons as he
shrugged awkwardly out of his shirt. Once again, Jasminda
assessed his injuries impassively, though he suspected things
were quite a bit worse than yesterday when she'd seen him.

"No," she answered Tensyn.

"And your family?"

"Dead." Her unexpressive mask slipped for an instant, and
Jack glimpsed a cavernous well of grief in her eyes.

"May they find serenity in the World After," Tensyn said,
his voice grave.

Jasminda repeated the blessing. Jack's eyes met hers briefly
before she looked away. "Lie back," she told him.

She dipped a cloth in the water and ran it across his chest, cleaning away the blood and grime. He suppressed a groan at the incredible coolness of the water on his skin, relishing in it until she stopped suddenly. He craned his neck down to see what had caught her attention. The bullet wound was far worse today, the skin black with infection, blood and pus seeping out.

The screen door slammed. He looked up to find the two of them on the porch alone.

"What is your name?" She pitched her voice low, speaking directly into his ear in perfect Elsiran as she continued cleaning his chest.

He took hold of her wrist, stilling her hand. How had she been able to learn Elsiran when no one in Lagrimar spoke the language? She shook free of his grip and continued cleaning his chest and face. Inside, the soldiers chortled, ensuring they would not be overheard.

"Jack," he whispered, scanning her face desperately. "Are you a Keeper of the Promise?"

Her brow wrinkled in confusion. She darted a look at the door. "No. I don't know what that is."

"How can you—"

"This is not Lagrimar." The door opened again, and Ginko emerged, taking a stance with his arms folded while he chewed on a stick of jerky.

Jasminda switched back to Lagrimari, speaking quietly. "I need to cut away the dead flesh from the wound. Otherwise the infection will kill you."

He nodded faintly, still trying to process her last words. If they weren't in Lagrimar, that meant they had all passed through the Mantle without knowing it. He'd been on home soil the whole time. That must be why she'd acted as if he were deranged.

Escape was so close. The despair threatening to pull him under faded away like mist in the sun.

"My Song is not strong. I can't both stop the bleeding and dull the pain."

He met her worried gaze and smiled, though the action reopened one of the cuts on his lip. Her expression said she thought he was delirious again. Perhaps he was.

"The only way to the other side is through it," he said. She blinked, staring at him blankly before the corners of her mouth rose a tiny fraction. He hadn't seen her smile yet, and even this hint of one lightened him. She closed her eyes, and once again the warm buzz of Earthsong poured into him like a fizzy cola. He opened the largest box he could to tuck away the pain.

Elsira. He was home. That meant all hope was not lost.

Ella jerked awake at the creaking of the bus doors. She was surprised she'd fallen asleep at all during the long, bumpy ride. Shakily, she stood, clutching her frayed carpet bag, certain that some of her bones had been jarred out of their sockets on the trip.

The only other passengers remaining after the bus's few stops were the dozen or so soldiers who allowed her to pass first, their familiar brown uniforms making her yearn for Benn. She climbed down the narrow stairs where the darkness of the town swallowed her.

A flickering lantern hung on the wall of the tiny bus depot before her, but the rest of the street was swathed in the night.

Just as Benn had promised, no one had asked for her

papers when she'd boarded in Portside. Still, she'd avoided her natural inclination to chat with the other passengers. She spoke perfect Elsiran, and had long ago learned to mask her accent, but fear of discovery bristled her skin to the roots of her newly russet-colored locks.

An even more uncomfortable looking military vehicle waited for the soldiers. Ella glanced at it longingly, knowing it could take her to Benn. Then she backed into the shadows, hoping to remain unnoticed as the area cleared of all life. When the bus drove off and the soldiers left, the street was quiet as death. Worry over her sister deepened the gloom.

Fortunately, the moon revealed itself, illuminating the buildings and causing the largest structure at the end of the street to glow. Ella sucked in a breath. The temple was beautiful. A rectangular structure of gleaming white marble with a half-dozen columns along the front. The domed roof was covered in gold stamped with some kind of print or etching she couldn't make out.

The devotionaries of the saints in Yaly were bigger and more ornate, but the simplicity of this structure was breathtaking. She found her feet moving toward it of their own accord.

As she approached, wondering how she would gain entry at this time of night, the bobbing glow of a lantern grew closer. Once she was near enough, the lantern's bearer became visible. She was a short, rather stout woman of middle years. A Sister, wearing her hair in their signature topknot with robes of royal blue.

"Are you Zorelladine?" the woman asked.

"Yes, please call me Ella, though."

"Oh, thank the Sovereign. Kess told me to expect you. I

wasn't sure how you'd arrive, but the express bus was a good guess. Sorry I wasn't able to meet you there. I'm Serra by the way. Please hurry," the woman rushed out, her words tangling together. "Your sister is in labor."

Ella froze then rushed to catch the woman who was marching into the building through a plain wooden door located on the side.

"In labor? Kess is pregnant?"

Serra shot a look over her shoulder. "Aye. Her water broke yesterday morning. That's when she bid me to send the telegram." She hurried through darkened hallways and up a flight of stairs.

Struck dumb with shock, it took a few moments for Ella to respond. "Well, I thank you."

"Never worry. No thanks are needed."

They turned a corner to see a light shining at the end of a dark hallway. "She's just in there."

This was the residential section of the temple. The small room she entered held only a bed, washbasin, and two chairs, with several blue robes on pegs on the wall. Ella took it all in with a sweeping glance before focusing on the woman on the bed.

Kess looked much the same as she had at eighteen. Though her hair, several shades darker than Ella's natural color, had some gray streaks in it now, and her face bore the footprint of the years. Still, the sight of her was a punch in the gut.

Ella stood frozen in the doorway until her sister let out a pained moan, making her rush in. Two other Sisters were already in the room, another middle-aged woman, wiry with strong features, along with a young and startlingly attractive woman with a feline gaze and blazing golden eyes.

"These are Sisters Heleneve and Gizelle," Serra said motioning to them respectively. "This is Ella."

Ella nodded.

"Sister Heleneve is the midwife," Serra said quietly as the woman in question bustled around with efficient movements. Ella tried to stay out of her way.

"H-how far apart are the labor pains?" she asked.

"About three minutes," Sister Gizelle responded, her bright eyes regarding Ella curiously. There was something familiar about her, but she couldn't place the woman.

"What do you need, Kess?" Heleneve hunkered down at the foot of the bed and Ella settled at her sister's side. Kess held out her hand and Ella grabbed on, grimacing when her bones were crunched as another contraction took hold.

Their gazes locked. Ella had forgotten that they both shared their mother's dark brown eyes. Looking at Kess was like looking in a mirror of the future.

"Just . . . for this . . . enormous child to be . . . born." She was pale and wan, in labor already for nearly a full day. Her spirits seemed low. Ella dug a handkerchief from her pocket to wipe Kess's brow.

"You've gained . . . weight."

Ella smirked. "So have you." Kess huffed a laugh. "Is this your first child?"

Kess nodded. "What about . . . you?" she rasped. "Any children?"

Ella firmed her lips and shook her head. Nor were there likely to be. She'd been married six years already with no hint of a child. But she didn't have long to wallow in self-pity. Another pain hit Kess like a train; she moaned and cursed.

"Just think of how nice it will be to hold the little one in your arms," Ella said, brushing damp hair off her sister's face. "This will all be a distant memory once you look into that tiny mewling face." Instead of rallying as Ella had intended, Kess wilted at the mention of the baby.

Heleneve's face betrayed no emotion, but when she instructed Kess to push, Ella did her best to cheer her sister. "Let's have another good push, then, all right? Give us one more."

Kess gathered her strength, tightened her face and pushed with a war cry.

"The little one is crowning," Heleneve called out. Serra exclaimed with joy, but Ella didn't like the tone of the midwife's voice. Shouldn't she sound more relieved and not so . . . cautious?

As the minutes passed, the midwife's skin took on a gray pallor.

"What's happening? What's wrong?" Ella asked.

Heleneve straightened. "The baby's shoulder is stuck." Her voice was calm and even. "If it won't come out, we'll have to make a cut to widen the way. I'll need matches. More towels and water. Needle and thread."

Serra stared at her blankly.

"Now." The midwife's voice didn't raise but her tone spurred Serra into action. The Sister blinked, then picked up her skirt and ran. Heleneve bent to unfurl a leather pack she'd produced from somewhere. Inside, the metal of several sharp instruments gleamed in the lantern light.

Ella sucked in a breath, and Kess's grip on her hand tightened. If she thought St. Siruna was listening, she would send up a prayer. Dash it, if she thought Kess's Queen would intervene she would give that a try as well—Ella would pray to any deity in any faith she could think of, if it would help.

She looked from her older sister's pained face to the midwife's grim one. And wished she still had faith.

In the end, Kess gave birth to a very small, very slippery, baby boy.

Sister Heleneve wrapped the infant in a towel and handed him to Ella while she dealt with the cord and waited for the afterbirth.

Ella stood, rocking the baby, admiring his tiny scrunched face.

"He'll need to be cleaned off," Gizelle said brusquely, pulling the child from her arms. Ella was too shocked to protest as Gizelle carried him to the wash basin. The Sister may be uncommonly beautiful, but her manners left much to be desired.

Warm water revealed soft-looking, creamy skin and a tuft of hair, already thick and full, and completely white. Shockingly, ghostly white.

The room was silent.

The baby wasn't crying. Heleneve retrieved him once more to check his airways. She pronounced him healthy and after a tap on the back, the infant coughed and finally released a sputtering cry. Ella fought tears, allowing a smile to come to her lips.

"Do you want to hold him, Kess?" Heleneve asked.

Kess looked up wearily, her eyelids fluttering. But she did not answer and made no move for her son. Heleneve passed the babe back to Ella, bypassing Gizelle's outstretched arms.

Ella moved to the foot of the bed and could not suppress a gasp. A torrent of blood had begun to gush from Kess, soaking the towels and bedding.

Heleneve looked over and shook her head slowly. Ella wanted to protest—wasn't there anything that could be done? But the midwife's precise movements had spoken of long experience. Ella had grown up on a farm, the complications of birth were not unfamiliar to her. She knew very well that all the skill and experience in the world was not always enough.

Gizelle abruptly left the room, and Kess made a sound of anguish.

"Kess?" Ella moved back to her side.

"Ellie," she whispered, her voice raspy. "Do you have a hair pin?"

The strange request had Ella frowning. She didn't want to hold her own child, but she was concerned about her hair?

"When you're feeling better, I can curl it for you. Would you like that?"

Kess shook her head impatiently and pushed out her open palm in demand. With a sigh, Ella balanced the bundled infant in one arm, reached into her hair, and pulled out a pin then passed it to her.

Instantly, Kess grew calmer. Though her fingers still trembled as she began picking at the coating covering the pin, peeling it away to reveal the sharp, metal point underneath.

"What are you doing?" Ella asked.

Kess ignored her until she'd finished with the pin. The action seemed to have exhausted her. She dropped her arm to the mattress, took a deep breath, then began whispering.

"I can't hear you sweetheart, speak up." Ella leaned down

toward Kess's mouth, but her sister wasn't speaking to her. She was chanting something in a language Ella didn't understand.

The sounds were rough and guttural. Short, choppy words but strung together in a way that sounded almost musical. Kess's eyelids fluttered and Ella wondered if she was having some kind of fit.

She glanced at the midwife whose arms were slicked with blood. Kess made no indication that she was in any pain, she just kept up the string of whispered words, which caused a shiver to descend Ella's spine.

Finally Kess reached out for her child. *Good, this is good,* Ella thought, *she wants to hold the baby.* Ella placed him in Kess's arms and watched her sister unwrap him just enough to reveal a tiny arm.

He must be so soft. He still needed a proper bath. Ella wasn't enthused about touching whatever still coated his body, but the velvety texture of newborn baby skin called to her. As she reached out to touch him, Kess swatted her hand away, still chanting.

Ella drew her arm back, surprised. Then, quick as a tick, Kess took the hair pin and scratched her baby's arm, drawing blood.

"Kess!" Ella yelped. "No!" She pulled the towel back around the child to cover his arm and took him from his mother. Maybe the strain of labor had deranged her. Kess must not know what she was doing.

The baby wailed. The poor thing had just been injured by his own mother. On Kess's lips, the strange words died and an even stranger foreboding grew within Ella. She *did* recognize something about that language. Vague memories haunted her of PawPaw chanting, sitting on a cushion in the corner with a strange, white knife. Blood on his arms and legs.

Other images came. Mother and Father yelling, fear and disgust in their eyes. PawPaw packing his things. Ruffling her hair on his way out. Whispering something that sounded like, "Everything has a cost, even love." Mother saying her father was not welcome in their home unless he could act like a civilized person. He hadn't come back again for years.

"What did you do?" Horror laced her tone.

Kess lay motionless for a long time, clutching the hairpin. Heleneve had stilled, staring at both of them. Then she blinked and focused back on the towels and the blood and trying to keep Kess from bleeding to death.

"I asked you to come because I need your help. I need you to promise me something," Kess whispered. "Vow by all the saints that Syllenne Nidos won't get her hands on my son."

Heleneve froze for a moment, her gaze flicked up to Kess, then to Ella.

The baby fidgeted; she shifted his bundled form in her arms. He had quieted after his initial outburst. "All right, Kess," she said slowly.

"I'm serious," her sister croaked.

"All right! By all the saints in all the lands I vow it." She had no idea who Syllenne Nidos was, and given Kess's mental state, wasn't quite certain it was even a real person.

Ella leaned in close enough to whisper in a tone no one else in the room would hear. "Was that a blood spell?" It was the only thing that made sense, but where had she even learned such a thing? Blood magic was a dangerous, forbidden, and arcane bit of craft. With a few exceptions, the people of Yaly had largely left magic behind, especially such a primitive, brutal form of it.

Kess didn't answer. Her dark eyes were red-rimmed. "I'm so sorry, Ellie."

Heleneve cursed softly. Tears stung Ella's eyes. Her sister's time was looking short, and there was one other very important thing they hadn't discussed. "Who's the father?"

Kess shook her head, looking away. Her face was drawn; she shuddered. Squeezed her eyes shut.

"Kess, there's so much I don't know."

"Just keep him away from Syllenne." Apparently, that took the last of her strength and she passed out.

Tears streamed down Ella's cheeks. She gripped her sister's hand, willing her to wake up again, but Kess never regained consciousness.

The sun was streaming through the window when Ella looked up. Kess's eyes were glassy and still. Her skin already cold. She had passed beyond the Veil.

The other Sisters and the baby were gone. She didn't even remember them leaving.

Ella convulsed in wracking sobs, burying herself in her sister's side. There hadn't been enough time. Not nearly enough. She had so many questions. So much to say.

After a while she straightened and stared at Kess's motionless form, unsure of what to do. Back home they would invoke St. Phelix, champion of the mystery, and perform the rites of the dead, but she wasn't familiar with the rituals of the Followers of the Queen. She didn't want to risk blaspheming her sister's corpse, so she simply drew the bed sheet up to cover the body.

Standing, she rubbed her aching arms. Hours of tension had turned her muscles to stone. An involuntary yawn captured her, and she wiped her cheeks.

Sister Serra appeared with a mug of some steaming liquid and a covered plate. "I thought you might be hungry. You've been at your vigil a long while."

The smell of the food turned Ella's stomach, but she accepted the coffee. A typically weak Elsiran brew, but she wouldn't complain.

"Where's the baby?"

"Sister Gizelle took him for the Book of Records. It's how we—"

"Yes, I know." She was aware of how the Sisterhood liked to record everything. They kept detailed genealogies and chronicled all sorts of aspects of their citizens' lives. But so much was unknown about the child. What would the records call him? He didn't even have a name.

Ella turned, avoiding looking at the body on the bed behind her.

"Serra, do you know who Syllenne Nidos is?"

The woman lowered her head, speaking quietly. "Of course. She's our High Priestess. The head of the Sisterhood."

Ella swayed and dropped back into her seat. She spilled coffee on her skirt, but barely noticed.

CHAPTER FOUR

Bobcat and Horse raced to the river to see who was fastest. Bobcat fell behind on a turn in the path, and Horse began to gloat. But when he approached the riverbank, he was shocked to find Bobcat leisurely bathing.

How did you beat me? Horse cried, angry.

Bobcat replied, When the path curved, I stayed straight. A road is not enough to throw me off my path.

—COLLECTED FOLKTALES

Jasminda lay awake in bed, straining to hear any movement in the house. Dull moonlight filtered in through Mama's frilly curtains. It was several hours to dawn. Exhaustion hollowed her bones. She'd depleted her Song helping Jack. It would have been wise to keep some in reserve to better monitor the soldiers, but the Elsiran's wounds were severe. Though her

Song was too weak to effect a complete healing, the infected flesh was gone, and he would live another day.

Her muscles tensed. She held her breath, listening. Tiny frissons of unease burrowed under her skin.

Gripping the shotgun she'd taken to bed in one hand, she reached under her pillow for her father's hunting knife. Another, smaller blade was already strapped to her thigh.

She rose, seized with the desire to check on Jack. The men had left him tied to the porch, saying even the barn was too good for the likes of him. She wrapped herself in a robe, hiding the shotgun in its folds, and slipped down the stairs. Snores rumbled from behind the doors of both bedrooms. Pushing down the anger at having strangers around her parents' and brothers' possessions, she crept through the kitchen to peer out the window.

Jack lay on his back shivering, hands bound in front of him, feet tied to the porch railing. She doubled back to the main room to grab a quilt, then went out and draped his shuddering body. He didn't appear conscious, but when she began to move away, he grabbed her hand.

"Thank you," he said in Elsiran. She cast a glance into the quiet shadows hugging the porch.

"They didn't feed you, did they? You must be hungry," she whispered, drawing the quilt closer around his neck.

"Mmm." He groaned, leaning his cheek against her hand. His skin was cold and clammy, face drawn and gaunt. She brushed his forehead and ran her fingers through his short hair. He did not flinch from her touch, but sank into it. His hair was like the soft bristles of a brush, his expression serene as she stroked his head. The fierceness in his face had once again been replaced by a soulful calm.

Such a contradiction, this Elsiran. Neither her skin nor her magic frightened him, yet he had more reason than most to hate Lagrimari. Of course, she wasn't Lagrimari, but she wasn't truly Elsiran, either. She pulled away.

"I'll be right back."

"I'll be here," he said, a small smile playing on his lips.

She rooted around the dark pantry to produce a tin of jerky and some dried fruit. She returned to give him a few strips of jerky, then pulled up a loose board in the floor where she could hide the food.

"You can get to this when no one's looking. You'll need to build up your strength."

"We are truly in Elsira?" His accent was lilting and formal, and it put her in mind of her mama's, a good deal more refined than those of the townsfolk.

"We are."

His forehead crinkled in confusion. "But you are Lagrimari?"

"My papa was a settler; Mama was Elsiran. She was in the Sisterhood. That's how they met."

"I've never heard of such a pairing."

Jasminda chuckled, a dry and empty sound. "She fell pregnant, and her family disowned her. Papa found this place and built a home for them." She stroked the board beneath her feet, cut and nailed with her father's two hands, a structure that proclaimed a love that never should have been. That even now, twenty years later, was not accepted. The thought of losing the place Papa had built for his family made her chest constrict.

Jack laid his hand on hers, and her skin tingled at the contact. The intensity in his expression dissolved her creeping sorrow, bringing instead a pang of yearning. She did not touch people. She barely even spoke to people. She was either here alone with no one but the animals as audience, or in town armoring herself against the cutting stares. The tingle in her hand turned into a warm heat that threatened to spread. With great effort, she pulled away from the impossible temptation of his touch.

"How far is it to—"

He paused as a floorboard inside the house groaned under the weight of heavy footsteps. Jasminda froze as another board creaked. She grabbed her shotgun, scooted away, and crept down the steps into the yard. The moonlight cast heavy shadows, and she crouched beside a cherry tree, holding her breath.

Two soldiers darkened the doorway before stepping onto the porch. One nudged Jack with his foot, and Jack moaned, pretending to be asleep. The men chuckled to themselves and leaned over him.

"You're sure the sergeant is out?" one of the men said. Ginko, she thought his name was.

"Thank the Father for thick walls and a soft bed. He sleeps like he's in his mother's arms," the second man said. Based on the outline of his large, misshapen head, Jasminda thought this was the one called Fahl. He'd eaten the last of the boiled eggs earlier, before she'd even had one.

Fahl squatted down and ran his hand across Jack's body. The action took an impossibly long time, and Jasminda's stomach hollowed. When he moved to loosen his own belt, she fought back a gasp. They were going to whip Jack.

"The bitch is upstairs. Are you sure you wouldn't rather . . ." Ginko said.

"I'm thinking the sergeant has her in his sights. Besides, she looks like she's got a mean scratch. No. I'll make sure this one won't make a peep, and who's to care what state he's left in? What Tensyn don't know won't hurt him." He snickered, and Ginko scratched his meaty head, looking back toward the house, appearing uncertain.

Understanding dawned on Jasminda like a blow to the face. She had worried for herself, expected trouble from these men seeking *her* out in the middle of the night, but she'd never considered Jack's vulnerability. Never considered how depraved these men might actually be. She could not sit by and allow him to be violated, though she was not sure what could be done to stop it.

They'd said the sergeant wouldn't approve. Maybe if she woke him, he would stop this. But she couldn't be sure, and going into his room at night could put her in the same predicament. She gripped her shaking hands and prayed to the Queen Who Sleeps for a solution.

The soft bleat of a doe rang out from the barn. The storm on the mountains was still making the goats uneasy. An idea took hold. What she needed was a distraction, and quickly.

Jasminda crouched, setting her shotgun down at the base of the tree, and felt around for a stone or branch. After finding a good-sized rock, she threw it with all her might. It sailed across the yard to hit the chicken coop. Once the men turned toward the sound, she raced around the front of the house, taking the long way to the barn.

The first distraction bought her a minute, but now she needed something larger to really draw the men away. She slid open the well-oiled barn door. Instead of nestling on the floor sleeping, many of the goats were awake and stumbling around, agitated. She hoped that, for once, the stubborn animals wouldn't need much cajoling. Luckily for her, the buck was eager to be out of doors and the does were of a mind to follow him. Grabbing the shovel, she nudged the herd along, increasing the pressure on their backsides until they bleated in disapproval.

The goats operated almost as a hive mind—when one was upset, they all were—so Jasminda continued poking and prodding at them, pushing them from the barn. Their discontent grew louder. Whines and cries pierced the night air. She'd often cursed the herd's fickle temperament, but tonight it was a blessing.

She couldn't see the back porch from where she stood, but an oil lamp flickered on inside the house. The goats' racket would awaken the soldiers, leaving Fahl and Ginko no opportunity to hurt Jack.

Jasminda slipped into the garden shadows as the front door opened and the smallest soldier, Wargi, stumbled out. The sergeant's voice carried over the yowls of the animals as he barked orders. The remaining two soldiers, Pymsyn and Unar, followed Wargi out to investigate what had spooked the goats.

She stifled a laugh at the way the men floundered, chasing after the scattering herd. They wouldn't get much sleep trying to track down each animal. If they asked her in the morning, she'd say she slept through it. She'd been listening to them her whole life, after all.

When she returned to the backyard, she retrieved her shotgun and found Jack as she'd left him. He opened his eyes and the moonlight made them sparkle. She knelt and pulled the blanket down from his chin to check him out, not sure what she was even looking for.

"Are you all right?"

"What did you do?"

She shrugged. "A distraction. Have they . . . harmed you?" She grimaced at the foolishness of her question. "Further, I mean."

He shook his head, his face a mask. Warrior Jack was back.

"But they will . . . when they can." The braying cries echoed in the distance.

She gathered up the hem of her robe and nightgown, and reached for the band holding the knife in place around her thigh. Jack's eyes widened. Her face grew hot as she hurried to remove the blade and put her gown back in place. After prying open the same loose floorboard as before, she hid the knife beside the tin of food.

As she laid the board back in place, his hand covered hers. "Thank you."

She flexed her fingers under his palm, ignoring the tingles sparking once again on her skin. "I'm sorry I didn't believe you yesterday."

"You thought I was mad." His mouth quirked. He must have been in a great deal of pain, but it hardly showed. Perhaps he was a warrior jester—fierce one moment, jovial the next.

"I still might."

He snorted a laugh, then winced.

Guilt tightened her chest. "I'm sorry. You shouldn't laugh."

"I'd rather laugh than cry. Wouldn't you?"

She couldn't even remember the last time she had something to laugh about.

"Is this a new breach?" she asked.

He sobered. "Not yet, but soon. There are cracks in the Mantle. Places where people can slip through, either knowingly or accidentally. But a breach is coming. The Lagrimari think they've found a way to tear it down permanently."

"Permanently?"

He nodded. "The True Father has never been able to cross during a breach, not while any part of the Mantle is intact. But without it . . ."

"Without it, he could cross. What would that mean?"

His grip on her hand tightened. "The end of Elsira."

The True Father was the most powerful Earthsinger alive. He had ruled Lagrimar for five hundred years, stealing more and more of his peoples' magic through the "tributes" to keep him alive and in power. But the magic had never been enough. Each breach had been an attempt for him to expand his influence.

Though her relationship with the land and its people was tenuous at best, Elsira was her home. She could claim no true allegiance to the Prince Regent or the structures of society, but she wasn't so naive as to believe even her isolated home would be immune to the fall of the country. "Could nothing stop it?"

"There is—" At a sound from inside, his lips snapped shut.

Jasminda whipped her head around. She strained to listen, and felt that same uneasy sensation that had awoken her. Jack was safe for the moment, but something was still not right— something in addition to the six enemy soldiers who'd overtaken her home.

Slowly, she backed away from Jack and crept to the door. It was past time to go back to her room, she couldn't afford to be caught here.

She looked over her shoulder to find Jack's gaze locked on her. The two sides she'd seen before—soulful Jack and warrior Jack—merged before her, giving a complete picture for the first time. She took in a jagged breath and shivered, though she was not cold.

Her feelings a riot within her, she pulled open the door to the kitchen and slipped inside.

A warbling bird landed on the porch railing. Early morning sunshine stole the chill from the air. The blade hidden under the knotty floorboard called to Jack. *Freedom.* He could cut his ropes and head west for home. But it was doubtful he'd make it more than a few hundred paces in his current state. His wound was no longer infected—yet it hurt to breathe. A full day of rest had helped, but also brought into focus just how severe his injuries still were.

He awoke to the healing tingle of Earthsong; Jasminda was doing all she could, and leaving now would only increase his chance of recapture. He needed to bide his time until he was at least well enough to walk without aid.

But time was steadily running out. Jack had witnessed the Lagrimari army amassing far too close to the border. Whispers of the True Father's rapidly increasing strength had spread through the countryside like a plague. Word was, tributes were being taken from whole towns at a time. Not just adults but children, infants even, were being drained of their Songs to feed the god-king's unquenchable thirst for power. Darvyn had warned him as much, but Jack hadn't believed the former POW. How could *he* have known, having been trapped inside Elsira since the last breach?

But Darvyn knew a great deal, including the location of a crack in the Mantle. He'd led Jack through that place where the magic had weakened in order to allow Jack to personally gather the proof his Elsiran government would not accept from a Lagrimari. The two had agreed to meet in a fortnight to return to Elsira, but Darvyn's spell had worn off early, and Jack had been exposed, shot, and forced on the run before the appointed date. He rubbed his chest wondering, not for the first time, what had happened to the young man.

Jasminda appeared through the copse of trees behind the back garden, a full basket on her arm. Her dark eyes flashed as she scanned the area, always alert. A gentle breeze ruffled through her mass of tight curls. She moved like a stalking cat, with grace and purpose.

When she reached the porch, she paused, cocking her head to listen for the men.

Jack kept his voice low. "They do fitness drills first thing in the morning; they're all probably in the front yard going through their paces."

Jasminda tiptoed through the door to the kitchen, but was back in moments with a cup of water in her hands. "You're right. Their calisthenics are . . . interesting." She barely contained a smile.

Jack snorted, recalling the bizarre movements the sergeant insisted they all participate in to stay limber and strong. But when she brought the cool water to his lips, his humor faded as he quenched his thirst.

"Thank you."

She brushed off his gratitude and fidgeted with the sleeve of her dress, a frayed and faded creation that might once have been blue. "So what will you do? About the Mantle?"

He had been pondering just that thing while on the run from the soldiers, but perhaps the Queen had sent him the solution. Maybe being shot and captured was just what he'd needed. "There is a way to strengthen the Mantle. Prevent the breaches, prevent it from coming down."

She leaned in closer, bringing her scent with her. He breathed in her aroma—delicate and woodsy, both refreshing and fragrant—then cleared his throat.

"An old Lagrimari man in one of the villages recognized me, or rather my disguise. The Keepers of the Promise already had a spy embedded in this unit. Darvyn, the Singer who spelled me, simply switched me in for their agent and gave me his face."

Jasminda's eyes rounded. "I had no idea such power was possible. To change a person into someone else for—how long? Days?"

"Nearly two weeks."

"This Darvyn's Song must be very strong."

Jack nodded, pushing away the foreboding that built when he thought of his friend. One crisis at a time was all he could manage. He only hoped the young man was still alive.

"The elder passed on something for me to give to the Keepers." He motioned to his left boot and bent his leg to try and reach, then hissed as pain arrowed through his limb.

Jasminda stopped him with a hand to his thigh.

"Hidden in the lining of my boot."

She nodded and unlaced his ties with nimble fingers then slid the shoe off. From the lining she pulled a small, irregularly shaped shard of black stone, its surface smooth as glass, then promptly dropped it as if the thing stung her. It skittered across the wooden boards, landing a pace away.

"W-what is that?" Her lips were parted, eyes round. She shook out her hand. *Odd.* Touching it had not affected Jack in any way, nor had it the old man, though Jack was not a Singer, of course, and the elder had long ago lost his Song.

"He told me it was a map. An ancient one that is supposed to lead to the cornerstone of the Mantle."

Jasminda leaned down until her nose was only a few breaths away from the rock fragment. "The cornerstone?" she asked.

"The old man said the ancient Singers who built the Mantle reinforced it with a single cornerstone, hidden in the mountains. Over time it must have weakened, and now there are cracks in the magic. But it can be shored up, strengthened with Earthsong."

Her profound reaction puzzled Jack. She seemed horrified by the small stone. Jack grabbed it, feeling nothing but cool, polished hardness. Nothing to match Jasminda's aversion.

He rubbed his thumb across it. "Fortifying the cornerstone will stop the breaches and keep the True Father on his side of the mountain. I was planning for Darvyn to do it, but now . . ."

Jasminda met his eyes with skepticism. "And you believed some random old man with a rock? Where did he get it from, and why has no one heard of it before?"

Jack shook his head. "I don't know. The Keepers have a network of sympathizers hidden across the country. I didn't have long to speak with him before the others returned." He motioned to the house, meaning the soldiers. "But I did verify one thing, the stone *is* magic."

She wiped her hands on her skirt and swallowed. "Of that I'm sure, but I don't know that it's a map."

"What does it make you feel?"

"Bad. Wrong. It's bad magic." She shook her head and rose, backing away from him.

"Jasminda—" he whispered. Footsteps inside the house cut him off. He cursed under his breath, fisted the shard, and closed his eyes to feign sleep.

"Pleasant morning, Miss Jasminda. You certainly rise with the sun, don't you?" The sergeant's obsequious voice made Jack's skin crawl. Jasminda merely grunted. Jack cracked an eye to find her trying to get past Tensyn, whose angular form efficiently blocked the doorway.

"If you'll excuse me, I need to get breakfast started." Her shoulders were drawn as tight as her voice.

The man didn't move immediately, and a nasty foreboding caused Jack's fist to tighten until the little shard threatened to slice his skin. Finally the sergeant stepped aside allowing Jasminda to pass, then followed behind her.

Jack fought to bring his breathing back under control. He did *not* like the way Tensyn looked at Jasminda. He settled his weight protectively over the floorboard where she had stored the knife the night before.

He would find the strength he needed to get out of here. And he would have to take Jasminda with him.

CHAPTER FIVE

Jackal and Monkey stood at the edge of a wide canyon.
Monkey asked, If I leap and make it to the other side, was
that my destiny or merely my good luck?

Jackal replied, Our destiny can be taken in hand, molded,
and shaped, while chance makes foolishness out of whatever
attempts to control it. Does this make destiny the master of
luck?

—COLLECTED FOLKTALES

Benn sped over the rocky, dirt road, excitement threatening
to pound through his chest. His Ella was so near. Just a handful of kilometers away.

The early morning sunshine made the Elsiran countryside
look like something you'd see in a painting. Last month, when
his leave had been suddenly canceled, the rolling fields and

placid pastures turned into a tangled jungle full of insects and vermin. But now the sight made him smile.

He should be exhausted, considering he hadn't caught so much as a snore the night before. Only when the transport had delivered the soldiers to the base and Benn verified that a woman of Ella's description had gotten off in Sora had he taken his first deep breath. Now, with her image in his mind, he pressed the accelerator a little harder, willing the distance between them to narrow.

On the passenger seat, his radio beeped—someone trying to hail him. Benn was determined to ignore it. He'd given the army most of his life, it could do without him for a few hours.

At fourteen he'd enlisted, after recovering from the injury that meant he'd never join his father and brother as a dock-worker. Most called it a miracle that he'd lived, much less walked again, after being trampled by a runaway colt in the street just outside his apartment building. But even after all the hard work he'd done to regain the use of his legs, Benn would never be able to haul cargo on and off the freighters that docked in Portside from all over the world.

To his father, he was still broken. To his older brother, an oddity. He had the same burly build as the men in his family, but unlike them, he was quiet and bookish. The army seemed like the only way to prove himself. But though he could walk and march and carry a rifle, he was still deemed unfit for combat and sent to the Staff Corps. So if he had to be a pencil-pusher, Benn was committed to being the best pencil-pusher he could be. He had his eye on making Staff General, the highest rank in the Corps, earlier than anyone before him.

He'd already progressed far more quickly than anyone expected. Much of it was due to the High Commander, who'd taken a liking to him. He was not only personal assistant to the army's leader, Benn was in charge of logistics for the army base, and oversaw personnel and operations as well. He was expected to be easily reachable for all the various issues that came up on such a large base—especially with the Commander away.

The radio's beeping taunted him.

He thought of his wife, crossing the country without papers, in danger from the whims of any constable or citizen who suspected she was foreign. Ella understood his drive for advancement, didn't complain about his long absences though she had every right to, and by the Sovereign, she was only minutes away. He needed to see her.

The radio's tone increased in frequency, citing the urgency of the caller. Benn cursed and picked up the handset, swerving to miss a divot in the road.

"This is Ravel, go."

The radio hissed. "Lt. Ravel, this is Private Teraseen. The old woman got away."

"Got away?"

"Yes, sir. She was here one minute and then she told me she needed the privy. I turned my back while she set off behind a tree, and the next thing I know, she's stolen my vehicle and driven off. High tailed it out of here like a woman half her age. I'm sorry, sir."

Benn considered letting Zaura nyl Herrsen, the famous Fremian anthropologist and ethnographer, keep the vehicle and stay missing. She was nearly eighty years old, for Sovereign's sake. And yet he couldn't blame the private for being duped. The woman was more stubborn than a spoiled mule and wilier than a fox.

Apparently, Mistress nyl Herrsen was a friend of the Prince Regent's, and Prince Alariq had insisted on a military escort for her during her stay in Elsira. She should have been High General Verados's problem, but that would require the base's second in command to actually do some work.

Benn's chest grew tight as the fields on either side of him closed in. The town of Sora was less than four kilometers away. Ella was so close.

He pulled the vehicle over and slapped the steering wheel. Closed his eyes. Took a deep breath.

"What's your current location, Private?"

He couldn't have an old woman roaming around the countryside on her own. Not a foreigner, and especially one who was a personal friend of the prince. Borderlanders weren't like city dwellers, who may have at least come in contact with a few Fremian artisans or servants. Out here the people were rougher. Even more mistrustful of the unfamiliar. The abhorrent way they treated the Lagrimari settlers was proof enough of that.

With great regret, he turned his truck around and headed back the way he'd come.

He picked up Private Teraseen near a low hill at the intersection of the main road and a narrow trail leading to the foothills.

"She drove off that way." The private pointed east.

Benn turned down the trail, which was really two grooves worn into the grass, likely by wagon wheels. They bumped along, precious minutes flying by.

The tops of the mountains towering above were obscured by a whirling darkness. A bad storm raged at the higher elevations, though down here all was calm and peaceful. Except for inside of Benn.

The path turned north, putting the mountains on their right side. Both soldiers scanned the area for signs of life or of the stolen four-wheeler.

About a half hour later, he pulled up next to the missing vehicle. It was empty. Trees and dense brush surrounded them. The trail they'd driven on had petered out to little more than a walking path through the undergrowth, too narrow for a truck.

"Let's split up. You check down there," Benn ordered, pointing to the path. "I'll head up the hill."

The private nodded and marched off. Though it may seem logical to think that Zaura had continued down the path, Benn had a strange sense the foothills were her true destination.

The trees thinned, leaving the ground sparsely dotted with tough little bushes. A tall, rocky outcrop to the south caught his attention. Had he seen movement there?

Cougars and bobcats were more common further north, but some had been seen in this area in recent years. He palmed his sidearm, cocking the hammer of the pistol in case he came across any wildlife.

The breeze picked up, bringing with it the low hum of voices. Benn holstered his weapon.

As he approached the rocks, a weathered voice called out, "Lt. Ravel!"

A head of wiry, gray hair popped up from behind a boulder. The anthropologist wore her signature outfit: a highly unusual combination of men's knickers tucked into sturdy leather boots and a belted, leather corset over a white blouse. Perhaps it was the fashion in Fremia, but Benn had never seen a woman so oddly attired. Her hair was wrangled into a plaited bun but her usual derby was missing.

He exhaled deeply. "Mistress nyl Herrsen—"

"Zaura, please. It's shorter, and when you're my age there's no time to waste."

He bit back a smile. "Zaura. I would very much appreciate if you did not steal army equipment or vehicles again."

She shooed him with a leathery hand. "It's only stealing if you don't return it, young man. Now come quickly, I've made a discovery!" With alarming speed, she raced around the rocks, which jutted far over his head.

Benn followed, hoping not to lose her, given her pace. Oldenberry bushes grew at the base of the rocks, and Zaura crouched next to one of them, talking softly. Calming a spooked animal, perhaps?

As he drew nearer, the hair on the back of his neck rose.

"This is Lt. Ravel," she was saying. "He's a friend."

Benn frowned and peered over Zaura's head. A pair of blinking eyes stared up at him. Startled, he jumped back and pulled his sidearm. Zaura laid a hand on his wrist.

"No." Then to the eyes peeking through the bushes she said, "Come on out, now." She motioned gently, and the bushes rustled as two small children emerged. Their dark hair was matted and dirty, their clothes—oddly long tunics with thick leggings—were patched and worn.

"They're Lagrimari," Benn said softly.

"They certainly seem to be."

He blinked. The bushes were moving again. Two teen boys stepped out. Followed by an elderly woman. Then a younger woman carrying a baby.

These were not former prisoners of war trapped in Elsira

since the last breach. Benn swallowed turning wide eyes to Zaura.

"What is happening?"

Her eyes were wide and solemn. "I don't know. But these people need our help."

He took a step back and shook his head to clear it. A half-dozen Lagrimari had somehow made their way through the Mantle to stand on Elsiran soil.

He squeezed the bridge of his nose and pressed his eyes shut. Pictured his wife's sweetly smiling face and then her disappointment.

"I'm sorry, Ella," he whispered under his breath. Then he straightened his shoulders and faced the problem at hand, ignoring the pulsing agony of his heart.

Ella sat at her sister's bedside as the sun rose steadily higher. For quite a long time, she couldn't force herself to move. Turbulent thoughts raced through her mind. She'd have to send word of Kess's death to her parents—where were they now? Who else to tell? What else to do?

A sunbeam struck her face and she blinked, coming back to the present to stare out the room's small window. The mountains loomed impressive and daunting. Though the day had dawned clear, the peaks swirled with angry energy. Gooseflesh pebbled her skin bringing a sense of unease.

Her stomach growled—how long had it been since Serra's offer of food? Hours, she reckoned. And Gizelle and the baby had not returned. Ella stood, stretching her legs and aching back, then ventured out.

The hallways were silent and solemn with no windows or

overhead lighting to brighten them. Ella went back to grab the lantern from her sister's room then stepped into the hall, unsure of which direction to head.

The interior of the temple was like a marble encased icebox, cold and unforgiving. She chose to go left and moved quickly, seeking light and warmth. The quiet hallways were eerie, but eventually she came upon a set of stairs and at the bottom, sounds of life.

She entered a bustling kitchen, where three Sisters, including Sister Serra, were making the morning meal. Ella was relieved to see a familiar face.

"Oh, Ella." Serra's hands were coated with flour. She appeared to be baking the soft flatbread Elsirans loved so much. "Hungry yet?" Compassion and shared grief welled in the woman's eyes. She shook her hands out, then wiped them on a towel.

"If it isn't too much trouble," Ella said.

The other two women were on the far side of the kitchen and barely looked up at the newcomer's arrival. Serra opened a cupboard and began pulling things out.

"What can I do to help?"

"Oh nothing, nothing, dear. I could probably do this in my sleep." Serra organized her ingredients and began mixing the dough with practiced hands.

"Where is the baby?" Ella asked. "The measurements for the Book of Records can't possibly take this long."

"If the child has fallen asleep, then prayers are made for the Queen Who Sleeps to bless his dreams. Though you're right, those aren't lengthy." She frowned. "We don't often get a new birth around here. Perhaps Sister Gizelle is showing him around."

A newborn didn't need to be shown around. Especially around a cold, drafty building like this one. He needed his mother—and since that was impossible, he'd require rest, milk, a proper bath. Could the other Sisters be overseeing that?

Ella resolved to get something in her stomach, and then search the temple if she had to. "I'm surprised you get any births here at all. Is chastity not a part of your faith?"

Serra smiled. "Oh, no. The Queen does not require forbearance of that sort. Children are, of course, expected to arrive within the bonds of marriage—but that's a matter of practicality. And Sisters may marry, though most who choose that life end up leaving the order, as it is nearly impossible to manage our duties while caring for a husband. Men are so wearying, are they not?"

Ella wistfully thought of Benn. He was not wearying at all. He was simply absent most of the time. Perhaps she'd find him tiring if he were around more often, but she doubted it.

Serra went on. "I do know of a few Sisters who have been in Kess's position. Good girls who had their heads turned by shiftless men."

"What happened to their children?"

"The mothers took care of them. The other Sisters helped. Instead of living in the dormitories, they were given single rooms, of course. When the children are old enough, they're sent to a nearby school. When grown, they're free to choose the Sisterhood, or some other path."

They settled at a table in the corner with a spread of fruit, jam, and flatbread. Ella dug in, unable to recall when she'd last eaten.

"Are there men in the Sisterhood?" she asked around a mouthful of apricot.

"There are a few Brothers. All who hear the call of the Queen are welcome to join us."

Could the child's father be one of these rare men?

"Did Kess tell you who the father was?"

Serra shook her head slowly. "Kess and I had served together some years ago at one of the southern temples. But I had not seen her in quite a while. A month ago, she was transferred here. Came with nothing more than the clothes on her back. This post . . . well, those who are assigned here have generally run afoul in some way of the High Priestess. It is usually best not to speak of our transgressions."

She gave a significant look to the two women across the room, still working at the sizzling stove, then tapped her lips and ears.

Ella's eyes widened as understanding took hold. Though her experience was limited to university dormitory life, where gossip was its own industry. She lowered her voice. "But if you're not expected to refrain from . . ." she waved her hand around, "intimacy, could the father have been the transgression that led her here?"

"I don't know. I do wish I'd asked her about it now." She looked away, her face crumpling. "That poor child. Poor Kess."

Ella swallowed the lump in her throat. The bread, which had tasted delicious, grew leaden in her belly. Serra cleared her throat before standing and returning to the work table with her dough.

Ella ate in silence for several minutes. Discovering her sister had converted to the Elsiran faith and embraced it so wholeheartedly as to devote her life as a member of the Sisterhood had been a shock. She hadn't known what to think, and the only response she received from her parents was a

short note about letting people choose their own paths. The
Queen's path was largely unknown to Ella, but she'd hoped
her sister had found peace. Now, she was fairly certain there
was far more to this religion than their curious sleep rituals.

The two other Sisters left the kitchen, carrying a platter
of savory meat with them. Ella rose to stand near Serra.

"The High Priestess, why would Kess fear her?" Ella asked,
keeping her voice low.

Serra flinched, but didn't look up or answer.

Ella paced down the length of the kitchen and back, taking in the neatly organized shelves and equipment. Life here
was orderly, purposeful, calm. It probably never changed all
that much. Sisters must choose this life to avoid chaos—and
yet the terror in Kess's final words belied that.

She decided to take another tack.

"You all take turns cooking?"

Serra looked relieved at the change in subject. "In theory.
Though in practice those of us with the inclination generally
take on more shifts than the others."

"Growing up, Kess was never much of a cook."

Serra snorted. "That didn't change."

Ella chuckled. "She and I grew up on a farm, you know.
Barley, corn, soybeans. Twice a year the workers would get
together for a celebration—when the planting was done and
when harvest was complete." Ella leaned back against the opposite counter, casually, ankles crossed. "Some of the labor-
ers were local folk, but many were indentured. They weren't
supposed to gather together without permission and could offer nothing of their own for the feast. But since they'd worked
side by side with everyone else during the year, the local folk
shared with them.

"Our parents were administrators, they managed the plantation. University educated. Didn't want us mingling with the riff-raff. Books full of rules for us, my parents had." Ella smiled ruefully. "They turned a blind eye to the celebrations, though. Let the workers have their fun. And on those nights Kess would sneak out. I'd lie in bed listening to the music and singing. Smelling the roast pork or pit beef."

She sighed. "I was too young for her to take along, even if she'd been inclined, and not yet bold enough to sneak out like her. She would come back smelling of sweat and dirt and moonshine and be too keyed up to sleep. And she would dance. There in the dark in our small bedroom. I'd see her in the moonlight because I could never sleep on those nights. I didn't see her smile often, but when she'd come back in through the window . . . she couldn't keep the joy off her face."

Ella wiped the tears that had begun to fall. Serra sniffed and dabbed at her eye with the corner of her apron. She'd finished placing flat discs of dough onto large baking sheets and stood, hands on the counter, staring at nothing in particular.

After a long while, she spoke.

"Those who take the robe do so from a calling. Help the underserved, spread the word of charity, forgiveness, discipline, honor—the code of the Queen Who Sleeps. Power has no place in that. The betrayer sought power. His witchcraft doomed our Queen."

She looked up and held Ella's gaze. "To rule is dangerous. To love the act of ruling is tyranny."

A chill swept across Ella's skin as if an icy wind had blown in. She straightened and crossed her arms over herself. Serra slid her baking sheet into the oven, then began collecting ingredients to make another batch.

"Why would Kess think the High Priestess would take her child?" Ella whispered.

Serra's lips pursed. "Every High Priestess is chosen based on her embodiment of the attributes of the Queen. Every *previous* High Priestess. The last conclave was different . . . There were whispers and quiet accusations of some sort of treachery." Her gaze grew haunted and she shook it off. "The Queen's will is sometimes unknowable. In truth, I don't know what Kess was afraid of, specifically. I wish I did. But you would be wise to heed your sister's words."

She cut the butter into the flour in a large bowl with swift, economical movements. Ella looked around, determined to do something to help. She needed to keep her hands busy so her mind could work through this puzzle.

Then she froze, noticing two eggs in a small bowl at the edge of the table. One egg was whole, the other cracked and empty.

"Do you . . . need this egg?"

"Hmm?" Sister Serra looked up. "Oh no. Pulled out one too many." She smiled distractedly and kept mixing.

Ella couldn't move. One whole egg next to one cracked egg was St. Siruna's symbol. A message for when she wanted you to listen to her word and take action.

Ella turned away from the cooking table, heart racing. It must be a coincidence. This was a kitchen after all. St. Siruna didn't have more than a handful of believers in all of Elsira, and all of them were in Portside. The champion would not send a message now after so long a silence. Surely she'd forgotten Ella's existence since prayer after prayer had gone unanswered for years.

She rubbed a hand over her stomach and fought the desire

to crumple into a ball, right there on the kitchen floor. Somehow she made her way back to the little table, and sank into a chair.

After a minute of slow, deep breathing, she had gathered herself again. "I'm going to see if I can find Sister Gizelle and the baby," she announced.

Serra looked over, expression grim. She tapped her lips and ear again. Ella took it as a warning and nodded that she understood. The High Priestess may not be present, but her presence was strongly felt.

CHAPTER SIX

Monkey said to Jackal, I believe that luck is the master of destiny, for one cannot be ruled by that which one considers foolish.

Then he took a running leap over the edge of the canyon and disappeared into the setting sun.

—COLLECTED FOLKTALES

Six soldiers crowded around the table, devouring the morning meal Jasminda set in front of them. Their favorite pastime seemed to be making fun of the youngest and smallest: bespectacled Wargi.

"This one is more coddled than an Elsiran brat," Pymsyn said through a mouthful of eggs. "Came into the army straight from his mother's skirts, he did."

"Thinks he's better than the rest of us because he's not

harem-born," said Fahl. "Just because your mam didn't have to spread her legs for the True Father doesn't make you top shit."

"And doesn't make your mam any less of a whore than ours," Ginko grunted. The table erupted in laughter.

Jasminda had been paying close attention to the men's taunting and verbal sparring. She didn't want to make any more mistakes and cast suspicion on her Lagrimari identity. But she knew next to nothing of life in that land. Her father had been tight-lipped, and it wasn't as if any of her books had information on their culture or practices. Aside from the breaches into Elsira over the years and very limited trade with Yaly, their neighbor to the east, Lagrimar was cut off from the rest of the world. Mountains surrounded the country on all sides, with only a small flat area a few thousand paces wide on the Elsiran border, where all the breaches had occurred.

As the men continued to mock Wargi, the young soldier just smiled and laughed, appearing to take it all in stride. But his eyes remained brittle, and Jasminda almost felt sorry for the boy. His round face hadn't yet lost its baby fat; he couldn't be older than sixteen.

Soon enough, the sergeant called the table to order, issuing instructions for the men to split into pairs to explore the valley and monitor the progress of the storm. All the soldiers except Wargi and Tensyn himself headed out.

"Is there anything my men can help you with, Miss Jasminda?" Tensyn's stained smile verged on lecherous. She swallowed the bile that rose and forced herself to smile back.

"No, sir. Dishes are almost done. Once the spy gets his rations, I'll be back to my chores."

"Wargi, finish the dishes for the lady, then throw some crusts at that vermin outside," he barked.

Wargi stood and gently removed the dishrag from her hand.

"Thank you," she whispered to him. He looked embarrassed and began tackling the pots in the sink.

"Come, rest your feet a moment, dear girl," Tensyn said.

She could think of no way to refuse, and so took the seat offered, cringing as Tensyn slid uncomfortably close to her.

"Beauty such as yours should never have to look upon that filthy Elsiran. Wargi, find a bag to cover the pig's head with."

"Yes, sir."

Jasminda shot a quick glance toward the porch but couldn't see Jack from her position. Tensyn launched into a long and meandering tale of his valor during the Seventh Breach, of the vast number of Elsirans he'd killed and the accolades he'd received from the True Father. Every so often, he would twirl the tips of his mustache and pause to check her reaction. She'd never thought herself a good actress, but she strove to appear impressed.

He finished his story, and she bobbed her head enthusiastically, eyes wide as saucers to portray her awe. He then gave a great yawn and announced he was off for a nap. Jasminda slumped in her chair, exhausted, and noticed Wargi had slipped away at some point. She stood to retrieve the extra food she'd set aside for Jack before heading out to the porch.

He sat propped against the railing, looking like a discarded scarecrow with the sack covering his head. She knelt and uncovered him. He blinked at her, then frowned.

"I was rather enjoying the privacy."

She bounced the bag in her hand. "I can put it back if you like."

He yawned, stretching his shoulders as far as he could with his arms tied. His shirt remained open, revealing the bruises and wounds, but also the coiled strength of lean muscle underneath.

Silence stretched between them, and she realized he hadn't missed her stare. Her cheeks grew warm and she ducked her head, pushing the bowl of mashed turnips toward him. He picked it up and awkwardly shoveled the spoon into his mouth with his bound hands, then turned to her with raised eyebrows and a grimace.

"Those are the herbs," she said, voice apologetic. "They're bitter, but good for your healing." Her Song was nearly depleted. She would have to wait until later in the afternoon to be strong enough to help him again.

"I need your help," he said, only speaking once he'd fully swallowed his food, unlike the Lagrimari soldiers. "With the cornerstone."

She shook her head, recalling the vile energy coming from the tiny thing he claimed was a map. "I don't want anything to do with that rock."

"You don't have to read the map, that doesn't require a Song. I can do it. All it takes is a bit of blood."

Jasminda shivered. "Blood?"

"I tried it before. Just a drop and you'll see the path unfold in your mind. Landmarks, trails, the whole journey runs in your head like a photoplay."

Unease was an army of ants marching across her skin.

"But only an Earthsinger can fortify the cornerstone," he

continued. "And you are the only one available." His eyes were all earnestness, gently pleading with her.

But the soldiers, her home, the taxes, the constable. He didn't know what he asked of her. In less than a week, she would have to either accept her grandfather's terms or leave her home. Appealing to the Taxation Bureau in person would require traveling across the entire country, and she had neither the money nor the means to do so in time. There wasn't really a choice open to her, much as she hated to admit it. She would have to sign and return the paperwork before the auction and could not both journey through the mountains with Jack and meet the magistrate in five days.

"There has to be someone else. I can't—I have to . . ." A pulse of energy stole her breath. She shuddered and squeezed her eyes tight.

"What is it?" Jack asked, leaning toward her.

"I don't know. Magic, I think." The faint sensation was not dissimilar to the crawling unease that had overtaken her when she'd touched Jack's map. But this was different. This felt like it was coming from the house. She sucked in a deep breath, rose, and slipped back through the door.

The kitchen was empty, as was the main room beyond. Both bedroom doors were closed, but as she approached, voices rose from her parents' room.

"I don't believe I heard you correctly, mistress. Is that truly what the True Father desires?" Tensyn spoke softly. Jasminda strained to hear. "We have gone through much to recapture the prisoner."

"Do you question your king's commands?" A woman's voice, deadly and elegant, came from behind the door. Jasminda froze and used what was left of her Song to seek out the speaker. But the energy gave no clues. She sensed only one person in the room—Tensyn.

"No, certainly not. I just want to be sure that I understand my orders. I live to obey."

The woman scoffed. "Then follow my instructions. And when this tantrum he calls a storm clears, you and your men return to Sayya. You will be rewarded for your diligence, Sergeant. I will make sure of it."

"Th-thank you, mistress."

Jasminda rushed back to the kitchen, her mind a whirl. The soldiers had claimed their radio equipment was broken. Had that been a lie? But the woman's voice wasn't staticky like it was being sent over the airwaves. She'd been as clear and crisp as if she'd been standing in front of Mama's mirror, speaking directly into Tensyn's ear.

The sensation of bad magic had faded now that the conversation was over. Though the Lagrimari had all lost their Songs, it was obvious that some kind of spell was at work here. The sort that left a bitter taste on Jasminda's tongue.

What had the mystery woman's instructions to the sergeant been? The men had wanted to bring Jack back to the capital alive for questioning, but perhaps now that had changed.

If so, Jasminda needed to come up with a plan to save Jack *and* remove these men from her home. Before it was too late.

Ella walked along the edge of the large, open space that made up the temple's sanctuary, keeping to the smooth, white walls. There were no benches or seating as in the saints' devotionaries back home. But Elsiran temples were not the place to go for listening to speeches and sermons. Here, people came with pallets or blankets and pillows for one purpose: to sleep. It was said the Queen Who Sleeps came to her followers in their dreams, and the Dream of the Queen was highly sought after and seldom granted.

At least a dozen people were spread out on the floor, though it was midmorning. Some had their hands clasped in prayer, others were already asleep. A Sister sat on a raised platform at the front of the room, reading silently from *The Book of Her Reign*. A copy of the holy book sat unused on a shelf back at Ella's apartment, a gift from her mother-in-law.

She circled the room instead of crossing it and having to step over the prone worshippers, to reach the other side. Several hallways sprouted from the center of the building.

The first few doors she tried were locked. An unlocked one led to a dark stairway heading down. It was uninviting enough to not bear further investigation. At the end of the short hallway, she pushed a door open that led outside to a fenced garden. The sun warmed her quickly, a pleasant change from the chilly interior.

The garden was lush with flowers on one side and vegetables on the other. Just ahead, a woman stooped in the dirt, weeding.

"Excuse me," Ella called out. The gardener stood, brushing off her palms and knees and squinted at Ella. Instead of the blue robes of the Sisterhood, she wore a homespun gray dress. Her dark auburn hair hung in a long braid down her back instead of a topknot. She looked to be in her early thirties.

"I'm sorry to bother you," Ella said, "have you seen Sister Gizelle anywhere?"

The woman shaded her eyes from the sun with a hand on her brow. Her expression was entirely closed. "Can't say that I have."

"So you haven't seen a baby, either, I'm guessing."

The woman's brow rose. "Baby? In the temple?"

"Just born this morning." Ella tilted her head at the woman. "You're not a Sister."

"I tend the garden." Her tone was matter-of-fact, as if it hadn't occurred to her to say anything more.

"I'm Ella. I'm . . . visiting."

"Name's Lalli." She made no move to greet Ella properly.

Ella took another look around. "Your work here is magnificent. You've gotten popinjays to bloom quite late in the season, that is some trick." She grinned. "How long have you worked here?"

Lalli looked her up and down, her sun-toasted face carefully blank. "Few years."

"Well, I'm sure they're grateful to have you. And look, I don't think I've ever seen jack-a-dandies in quite that shade before." The fruit was a heavy, deep purple that almost didn't seem real. "That's amazing. Can you share your secret?"

Despite her wary stance, Lalli's shoulders pushed back a little. "No secret. Place a bit of ash in the soil with the seedlings, only from certain woods though. Walnut's no good. Beech is better."

Ella's eyes widened in genuine awe. "Fascinating." She leaned down for a better look at the plant. "I've always admired people who could coax life from the ground. I'd kill a cactus just by looking at it."

Lalli snorted, but her glare had softened a fraction.

Ella leaned in toward the tiny white buds of a kale plant

that had already begun to bolt. Its leaves were pocked with little holes.

"Cabbage worms," Lalli offered, disgust in her voice. "Soon as I get rid of them, more pop up."

Ella tsked in sympathy and spent a few more minutes admiring the garden under Lalli's watchful eye.

She wandered onto the flower side to sniff a vibrant yellow coneflower. "My sister, my blood sister that is, lived here. Her name was Kess, did you know her?"

"Don't mingle much with the Sisters, eh. I stay outside, do my work, go home."

Could this woman be one of the people Serra had warned her about? Or did she have no loyalty to the order she wasn't a part of? Given Ella had so few people to ask, she took a chance. "Have you ever met the High Priestess? Syllenne Nidos?"

This time Lalli's snort held derision. "She used to be the priestess here a few years back. Hard to forget."

Ella stepped closer, lowering her voice. "Why?"

"Why what?" Lalli raised a brow.

"Why is she so hard to forget?"

Lalli squinted at her again, and Ella held her breath, hoping the woman would answer.

The gardener inclined forward slightly. Ella leaned in as well. "Question you should be askin' is why I'd *want* to forget."

A door opened behind them and Ella jumped back, but Lalli didn't so much as flinch. All of a sudden, Sister Gizelle was there standing before them looking like she was cut from stone.

That's why she'd looked familiar. She reminded Ella of

St. Ysari, champion of artists. In statues and artwork, Ysari was depicted as an unattainable beauty, with a face known to make grown men weep. Gizelle was striking in a similar way, tall and graceful with sharp cheekbones and a delicate chin. Her cat-like eyes were such an unusual shade, it was a shame her gaze was frigid as the northern sea. In Yaly, such a woman would have become a fashion model or graced a stage somewhere. Ella wondered what had driven her to join the Sisterhood.

"Mistress Farmafield," Gizelle said, but she was looking at Lalli. Her openly hostile stare was met by a slight smirk from the gardener. "Please come with me."

Ella clenched her jaw and turned to Lalli. "Lovely to have met you. The garden is beautiful."

Lalli acknowledged the praise with a slight nod, the turned back to her weeding.

Gizelle entered the temple through a different door and set a quick pace down the hallway and up a flight of steps.

"Your help with your sister's birthing was much appreciated." Her voice was as sharp as her footsteps. "The room at the end of the hall is yours for the duration of your stay. Return passage to Elsira has been booked for you on the bus leaving in an hour. I request that you stay in the dormitory area until you leave so as not to disturb the running of this temple."

"Where is my nephew? I'm Kess's closest family. I'll need to take her child home with me."

Gizelle stopped so abruptly that Ella nearly ran into her. When she turned, her face was placid, but her eyes held a storm. "Kess was a Sister. *We* are her chosen family. Her child will be well taken care of. He's already on his way to Rosira so that we may oversee his care with the full force of our considerable resources."

Alarm bells rang in Ella's mind. Something in the Sister's tone sounded like a threat. "You sent a newborn across the country? With who? Why? I need to see my nephew!"

"That child is the nephew of every Sister now. When you take the robes, you leave your old family behind. We will all ensure he comes to no harm." And with that, she gave a curt bow and took off down the hall.

"Wait!" Ella called racing after her. But Gizelle was taller with longer legs that ate up the distance. She disappeared through the door at the end of the hall. When Ella reached it, she found it locked. She banged on it several times, then turned to run to the other end. That door was locked as well, effectively trapping her in this hallway.

The only room she could enter was the small bedroom at the end, which Gizelle had pointed out. Its window was far too small to fit through and didn't even open. Plus, she was three stories up.

She banged the wall in frustration and sat on the narrow bed. Losing her sister after so long without contact was a big enough blow, she could not fail Kess's dying request.

The Sisterhood was a powerful force, going up against them would be like a rabbit facing off against a bull. But no matter what it took, Ella needed to find her nephew.

CHAPTER SEVEN

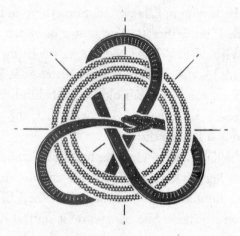

A boy, having accidentally stepped into a nest of vipers, cried out to the Mistress of Serpents for aid.

Serpent turned the vipers to glass and entreated the boy to leave the nest without breaking the glass. For it is you who have entered their home without invitation, she said. Why should they change their nature in their own home?

—COLLECTED FOLKTALES

Night had fallen, and the cool breeze sighed across Jack's heated skin. Raucous laughter swelled inside the house. Jack winced when something heavy crashed to the ground. Guilt for his part in leading these men to Jasminda's home had not waned. And now it sounded as if they were breaking the place apart.

He smelled Jasminda's presence before he heard her footsteps. She crept up the back steps to kneel beside him. Her palm slid across his forehead, and he pressed into the touch. Another loud *thunk* resounded from within the house, followed by rising voices.

"It sounds like a tavern in there," Jack said.

"It is."

He raised an eyebrow.

"They discovered my father's gin. They're three noses into the still."

There were few things crueler than a drunken soldier. Jack rolled his cheek back into her hand. "I am sorry for it." The men's intoxication would not bode well for them.

Jasminda's fingers skated across his scalp, soothing the dull ache in his head. The breeze picked up, whistling a warning in the air.

"How much longer will the storm trap us here?" he asked.

A shifting of clouds revealed the moonlight, illuminating her pensive expression. "Another twenty-four hours or so." Her vivid dark gaze drove into him. "Do you think you can walk?"

He rose onto an elbow, searching her inscrutable expression. "I believe so. Are we going somewhere?"

A knife appeared in her hand and with a snick, his ropes were cut. "They're all distracted now. I think we should try to get you out of here."

Shock momentarily froze him, but he shook it off and rose to his feet. She wrapped an arm around him, helping to support some of his weight. Jack was grateful for it; much as he hated to admit it, he needed the aid. His wounds and bruises complained noisily, but he ignored them, focusing on finding his footing.

"What's the plan?" he asked as they stumbled down the back steps.

"Stay alive." He wanted to grin at her response, but instead pursed his lips at the shooting pain that stabbed his chest. He boxed it away and concentrated on putting one foot in front of the other.

The two of them sank into the shadows cast by the moonlight, keeping to the tree line, and skirting the side of the house with quiet steps. Inside, discordant voices began a bawdy drinking song.

They had just rounded the corner of the house, when the front door slammed open. Jasminda's arm turned to stone around him. Jack held his breath. The moon blessedly chose that moment to sink behind a cloud, leaving the yard in darkness. It was too dim to identify the man who lurched forward, but he walked straight toward them, stopping a handful of paces away before a thick-trunked dogwood. If he'd looked to his right, he would see them standing stiff as statues trying to blend into the night.

The soldier unzipped his fly and began to piss. His stream was seemingly endless; how much gin had there been? Jasminda trembled.

Finally, the soldier finished and tucked himself back into his trousers. He turned toward the house, swaying on his feet. Jack exhaled slowly, ready to weep with relief, when the bloody moon broke through the bloody clouds, brilliantly illuminating the yard.

Yet, the soldier—Pymsyn he could see now—had his back to them, staggering toward the cabin. Jack swallowed. Just a few more steps. He counted them down as Pymsyn drew farther away.

On the porch, the soldier's hand met the door handle. From the corner of Jack's eye, he saw Jasminda blinking rapidly, watching the man's every movement. They dared not move, out in the open as they were. Once the Lagrimari was safely inside, they could regain the cover of the shadows.

But instead of opening the door, Pymsyn turned around.

A bone-deep chill took over Jack's body.

Pymsyn's eyes widened. His alcohol-soaked brain took several moments to process before the connection was made. Jack spotted the moment it did, as recognition and outrage crossed the man's expression.

In that split second, Jack reacted. He pulled the knife Jasminda had used on his ropes out of the front pocket of her dress, where she'd slipped it. At the same time, he adjusted his hold on her to appear menacing and lifted the knife to her throat.

The maneuver was swift and left him aching. But by the time Pymsyn raised his voice to shout, to all appearances Jasminda was at Jack's mercy. A hostage, not a savior.

"I forced you to do this," he whispered. She struggled against him, though he sensed she was not playing along, but rather rejecting his plan. It did not matter; her tussling would only reinforce Jack's story.

He held her tighter. The sweet fragrance of her hair filled his nose. He inhaled the scent as the soldiers streamed drunkenly out of the cabin.

Jasminda was wrenched away, taking her warmth and aroma with her. Blows from the angry soldiers came down thick and fast. Jack was sorry to have undone all her healing work—he hoped she would not be too angry with him over it.

The severity of the men's punches paled in comparison to

what he'd suffered when he'd first been discovered. A few days of rest and relaxation and several fifths of gin had turned the men soft.

"Is that all you've got?" Jack wheezed out during a break in the action. Once again a foot to his midsection stole his breath. A kick to the head stole his consciousness.

"Have you been harmed, my dear?" Tensyn asked, his eyes bleary and bloodshot.

"I'm fine." Jasminda fought to keep her composure. *She* was fine; Jack on the other hand had been dragged off back to the porch, insensible. She couldn't tell for sure, but he may have been as bad off again as he was when he arrived.

Tensyn grabbed her chin to peer down at her. He was trying to appear attentive, but she couldn't bear the touch of his skin.

"I assure you, he did not hurt me." She stepped back out of reach.

Tensyn's forefinger was bandaged. It hadn't been so earlier. She was surprised he hadn't asked her to come nurse him whenever he'd injured himself, though it was likely done destroying some valuable keepsake of hers.

She glared at him, holding herself back from railing against Jack's treatment. Tensyn's expression was loose and heavy-lidded. He did not seem inclined to kill Jack at this moment—he had ordered his men to stop the beating in an outraged tone—but Jasminda remained unsure as to what she'd overheard earlier in the day.

Something tickled at her memory, but skittered away when she tried to bring it into focus.

"I will post a guard at your door tonight, to ensure your safety. You are under my protection, after all." He bowed. It might have been more gallant if he hadn't stumbled halfway through and messily righted himself.

"That isn't necessary," she said, fear spiking in her veins.

"Oh, I insist." He glanced at the direction the men had taken Jack, his expression sobering for a moment. "*That* is a desperate man."

Jasminda shivered in the cool night. She was growing desperate herself.

She had no intention of falling asleep. Sitting upright on her bed, she kept her shotgun on one side and a long blade in her other hand. But her body ignored her intent, succumbing to exhaustion and its need for rest. Her eyelids drooped and nothing she could do kept them from closing.

The tinkling of wind chimes—the makeshift alarm she'd hung on her door—was her only warning. A figure loomed above her in the dark. A beefy hand covered her mouth, stifling her scream. Fahl towered over her, reeking of gin. He was strong and had an iron grip on her face, pushing her back into the pillow. The hand holding her knife was stuck underneath her head, and Fahl's other hand felt roughly for her nightgown and grabbed at the hem.

Jasminda kicked out, struggling, fighting with all her might, but Fahl was huge and heavy as he lay on top of her, fully immobilizing her. He eased up enough to continue pushing up her nightgown and then pawed at her thighs as she tried to clench them together.

The shotgun rolled off the bed, hitting the floor. Fahl

chuckled when he saw it, launching a blast of alcohol-infused air into her face.

"Keep fighting, sweetheart," he said. "It's been months since I had any, and I don't mind working for it a little."

Jasminda stilled, unwilling to give this man anything he wanted. She hunted for an escape.

He fumbled with his trousers, pulling and tearing at them until his squiggly, limp penis emerged. He made a sound of disgust, then started stroking himself while pinning her down, one hand covering her mouth. Jasminda strained to see what was going on down there—and thanked the Queen he wasn't making much progress.

The terryroot was doing its job. Odorless and tasteless, her herb dictionary listed its use for "wives wanting some peace from their husbands." Her mother had laughed heartily when a young Jasminda asked what that meant, telling the girl that she would find out when she was older. Since the soldiers had arrived, Jasminda had been liberally dosing their food with the herb.

Growling in frustration, Fahl kneeled up over her, angrily pulling on himself. Without his weight on top of her, Jasminda could now move her arm but didn't know if she would be quick enough with the knife. The moment of indecision cost her when he stood suddenly, grabbing her by the hair. She winced from the pain as he forced her down the stairs. Her side pressed against his giant chest, immobilizing her arm, but allowing just enough reach for her to slide the knife into her pocket.

"Ginko!" he whispered loudly. "Mate, where are you?"

An answering groan sounded from the living room. The door to one of the bedrooms hung open, revealing another soldier sprawled on the floor inside. Fahl pressed her onto the couch next to a groggy and very drunk Ginko.

"I've brought you a present, mate," Fahl said. His pants sagged and his flaccid penis hung out shamelessly.

"Eh?" Ginko replied, peeling open his eyes. He perked up when he noticed Jasminda. "What about the sergeant?" he slurred.

"Can't hold his liquor." Fahl grinned evilly, showing off his blackened, stinking teeth. His grip loosened for a moment, and Jasminda tore free with a shout, lunging off the couch toward the kitchen, jumping over furniture in her way. But Fahl and Ginko surprised her with their speed, catching up to her quickly and slamming her down on the kitchen table. She pulled the knife from her pocket and swiped out, slicing through a fleshy arm. A corresponding yowl rang out from whichever of them she'd cut.

She screamed a war cry and lashed out again, but a hand pinned her arm like a vise before the knife met its target. A blow to her face rattled her senses before her legs were pinned, as well. She kicked and flailed with all her strength, but it felt like immovable rocks held her in place.

Ginko clutched her legs, nudging her nightgown up. Near her head, Fahl hadn't stopped pulling at himself futilely.

"Perhaps this will go better if I stuff it down your throat." He released her arms to grab her hair and tilt her head back toward him. His grip was tight enough to make her vision blur, but she focused on her newly freed hands. A little closer and she'd be able to reach the two sensitive sacks behind his drooping manhood. She would rip off whatever she touched and bite off anything that came near her lips.

As Fahl drew closer and Ginko's hands slid toward her

panties, the back door crashed open. All movement ceased. Through watery eyes, she saw Jack standing in the doorway, the knife she'd hidden for him in his hand, his restraints dangling from one wrist. He leaped across the room and tackled Fahl, plunging the knife deep into the man's belly. Ginko sprang away.

Jasminda crawled off the table and dropped to the ground. She blinked, clearing her vision, and rose to see Jack duck Ginko's wide punch. The swing threw the Lagrimari soldier off-balance. He wobbled until Jack landed a vicious, crunching kick. Ginko crumpled, hitting his head with a loud *crack* on the kitchen counter before falling to the floor. Blood pooled around his head and he stared upward, unseeing.

Fahl, knife still lodged in his belly, had been leaning against the opposite counter, but when Ginko fell, he rushed Jack with a new burst of strength. He grasped Jack in a bear hug and wrapped his hands around Jack's throat, squeezing. Jasminda screamed and ran toward the hulking man, climbing on his back. The fingers of one hand sunk deep into his greasy hair as she pulled back his head, then in one swift motion slit the man's throat with the other, just as she'd do with a goat.

She jumped back and he fell, blood spurting everywhere, covering Jack with its spray.

CHAPTER EIGHT

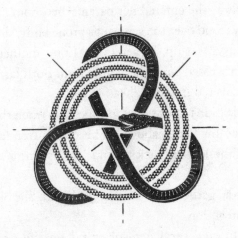

The Mistress of Serpents was asked to judge a dispute between two farmers.

This man has diverted the stream so I cannot water my crop, the first farmer said.

For years, this man has kept the stream to himself, the second replied. I am balancing the scales.

Serpent transformed the fields of both men into a magnificent lake. Now there is water for all, she said.

—COLLECTED FOLKTALES

The weight of what she'd done hit her. Jasminda had just killed a man. Nausea squeezed her belly. She released the knife from her shaking hand, startling as it clattered to the floor.

"Are you all right?" Jack asked. She turned to face him and caught sight of Wargi in the doorway. The boy was frozen, eyes on the carnage of his former squad members. And then he was gone.

"Wargi!" she shouted, taking off after him. Jack followed on her heels as she entered her parents' bedroom.

The boy stood over the sergeant's prone body, shaking him awake. Tensyn sat up, bleary-eyed. Long moments passed before he processed what was before him. Both Jasminda and Jack were covered in blood, head to toe.

Jasminda didn't know what to expect, so when the sergeant slowly raised his hands above his head in surrender, she was surprised. She looked back to find Jack training a pistol on him.

"Jasminda, gather the weapons," Jack said. She blinked and jumped into action.

An additional service revolver sat on the dresser. She grabbed it and opened the chamber to find it full of rounds.

She bent to check the ground, when a rucksack in the corner began to vibrate. That same uneasy feeling of bad magic returned, pulsing in time to the movement of the sack.

"What is that?" Her voice hitched.

Jack's brow was furrowed, but Tensyn stared at the bag, eyes wide, before turning away. The sergeant swallowed. The noise grew louder, more insistent.

"Answer her." Jack motioned with his gun.

"It's a speaking stone," Tensyn said through clenched teeth.

Jasminda had never heard of such a thing. The queasiness in her stomach grew with each rattle. Jack slipped his hand around her wrist, raising her weapon until it was trained on the two Lagrimari, then he turned to the rucksack and searched its pockets.

A bandana covering his fingers, Jack retrieved a small

brownish-red pebble, about the size of his thumbnail. The tiny object shook in his palm, unrelenting. Jasminda winced at the magic coming from it.

"A speaking stone." Wonder laced Jack's voice. "Why is it shaking?"

Tensyn firmed his lips, refusing to answer.

"The shaking must be how it alerts you to a communication." Jasminda could feel the insistence of the magic. She glanced at Tensyn and suddenly the bandage on his finger made sense.

"Blood," she said. Tensyn's eyes narrowed. She turned to Jack who nodded, understanding. He wiped some of the blood covering him onto the stone. It stopped rattling.

"I do not like to be kept waiting, Sergeant. Is it done?" The same imperious female voice Jasminda had heard before came through the stone.

"Who is this?" Jack asked.

A pause. "Who is *this*?" The voice was smiling. It was as though the woman already knew who she was talking to. "I suppose introductions can come later. Time and the True Father wait for no man. Ta-ta."

With a cry, Jack dropped the stone and shook out his hand.

"What happened?" Jasminda asked, but the speaking stone ignited like a match as it hit the ground. The flame instantly caught hold of the bedroom rug and raced across its length, impossibly fast.

As if possessed with some kind of intelligence, the fire leapt up the legs of the dresser. Before Jasminda could move, one of the oil lamps exploded, showering the room in sparks and flame. She screamed and ducked. Jack was on her in an instant, leading her out of the room, away from the blaze.

Wargi and Tensyn, coughing and sputtering, raced out behind them and disappeared through the kitchen. Jack pulled the bedroom door shut and stuffed the quilt from the couch in the crack at the bottom of the doorframe.

"Do you have a fire suppressor?"

His words scrambled in her head. "A what?"

"No, I suppose you wouldn't, all the way out here. We don't have much time. Save what you can." He dashed into the kitchen, leaving her staring at the door, still not believing what lay on the other side.

A coughing fit caused by the acrid smoke filling her lungs shook her from her stupor. Tears like acid stung her cheeks. Her house was burning. Her home.

She raced upstairs and replaced her blood-soaked robe with a dress and boots. Tossed items blindly into a sack. Some part of her was still in her parents' bedroom, watching the flames consume the walls. She stared at the bag in her hands, not remembering how it got there, not knowing what was inside, only that the tightness in her chest was not just smoke, it was the mouth of an endless river, a wash of despair sweeping her away.

She found herself in the living room again, standing in front of the cabinets. Had she run down the stairs? Is that why she was struggling to breathe?

No . . .

Everything here was precious. Sooty fingers skimmed each shelf, committing the feel of each object to memory. Her chest contracted. Was that her heart shrinking away to nothing?

Jack appeared next to her, carrying a basket stuffed with what remained of the pantry. "Give that to me." He plucked the sack from her grasp. She stared at her empty hands for a moment, then to Jack, and felt grounded by the firmness of his expression. His uniform was tattered and stained. She pulled out a set of her brothers' clothes from the cabinet and tossed them at him.

"These should fit—the boys were tall for their age."

Flames reached out from under her parents' door, the quilt having been eaten away. In mere minutes there would be nothing left of her life.

"Jasminda."

Time spun without her knowledge. She turned to find Jack changed and ready. He'd even pulled on Papa's old coat, the one the three children had saved up to replace over the course of a year. Papa had been wearing the new one the last time she saw him.

Tears formed and her throat began to close up. Jack said her name again. "We have to go."

She nodded, throat too thick to speak, and allowed him to take her hand and pull her from the house.

On the front yard, Wargi dragged Pymsyn's body, laying him next to the charred, motionless form of Unar. Tensyn sat on the ground, enthralled by the vivid flames. The reflection of them danced in his dark irises.

Jasminda's knees hit the ground as a crash sounded behind her. Heat crawled over her skin. Pungent smoke punched her nose. She could not bring herself to look. Jack wrapped his arms around her and pressed her into his chest. He whispered something she couldn't hear above the rush of blood in her ears.

Gasping, she worked to pull herself together, clutching at the coat Jack wore that had long since lost her father's smell.

Finally, she could breathe steadily. His arms were a cage of safety around her, but she still felt like her chest had cracked open and everything inside was leaking out.

"This is all I have. I have nothing else."

He held her tighter and rocked her gently, but she found no solace in his arms.

The cock of a hammer made Jasminda freeze. Slowly, she pulled away from Jack and turned around. Wargi held a pistol trained at them. He shook with fear and made little hiccupping sounds.

Jack raised his palms. Jasminda did the same.

"W-Wargi?" she said, voice shaking. "Please." The boy looked broken, so unsure.

His grip tightened on the gun and with his unsteady hand, she was afraid he might shoot them without even meaning to.

"There, there, my boy," Tensyn said, rising. "Give that to me, then."

With relief, Wargi gave the revolver to his sergeant. Jack's shoulder brushed against hers as they stood side by side. Jasminda closed her eyes on a long blink, then opened them to face her fate.

Tensyn glared at them. Soot covered half the man's face and his normally coiffed hair stuck out all over his head. Part of his mustache had burned off. He looked from Jack to Jasminda, taking in their close proximity, and snorted.

"You think this Elsiran will think twice about you when he no longer has use for you?" He sneered and lowered the gun, pushing forward the hammer and placing it in his waistband. "But by all means, run off with this scum and see for yourself."

His yellow smile gave Jasminda a chill. "Y-you're letting us go?"

The sergeant turned so his face was in profile. He affected a magnanimous expression and shooed them away with a flick of his wrist.

"I don't understand. Why would you do this?" Jack asked.

Tensyn tsked. "I've lost the bulk of my squad." He motioned to the dead men, the dwindling fire. "I doubt very much that Wargi and I could get you back to Sayya with our necks intact. Let us call it a tactical relinquishment. Now go, before I change my mind."

Suspicion had both Jasminda and Jack backing away. She fully expected the sergeant to shoot them in the back as they fled, but he paid them no attention. They walked backward to the tree line, then rushed behind a large trunk.

"What was that?" she asked.

Jack's face was drawn, worried. "I have no idea. I don't trust it."

"He wants us to leave. But why?"

Jack lifted his shoulders. "I think we have little choice but to go."

Jasminda forced herself to view the wreckage. The barn did not appear in danger from the rapidly dying flames. Some idiot had left the door unbarred, but perhaps that was for the best. The goats would be able to leave and forage for food. They were tough animals and too stubborn to die.

She led Jack through the grove of crab apples, deeper into the valley. Once they were a good distance from the ruined cabin, she stopped. Tears stung the backs of her eyes as the reality of the night's events sank down on her.

"What do you think Tensyn and Wargi will do?" Jack's voice cut through her self-pity.

"Go back. The speaking stone—that woman, I heard him talking to her before. She ordered him back to Sayya. I'd thought he would kill you first, but . . ." Her head was clouded from grief, and she couldn't connect all the dots clearly.

Jack bent over and breathed deeply. His face was ghostly pale and the energy that had been fueling him seemed to ebb.

"I need your aid," he said.

She rushed over to help him sit. "I'm surprised you're even standing."

"That is not what I meant. The cornerstone." His gaze held hers, and she couldn't look away.

"Jack, I want to help you, but in five days I will have no home." At his incredulous look, she went on. "This valley is so far out, so isolated, the Prince Regent didn't even know we were here for many years. But when the crown found us— found me—they determined I owed a small fortune in back property taxes." She took a deep breath. "I researched the stat-ues. By law, since we didn't get any notices for all that time, we can apply for something called safe harbor and not have to pay."

She blinked back her tears and sniffed. "I sent an appeal detailing everything, but it doesn't seem to have helped. Ac-cording to the magistrate, on Seconday of next week they will auction the land if I don't come up with the money."

Jack reached for her hand, threading his fingers through hers. The sensation calmed her, gave her something to hold onto.

"What will you do?" he asked.

She shrugged. "Renounce my mother and save my home. And then rebuild."

"Renounce your mother?"

She told him of her call with the solicitor and her grandfather's offer. The paperwork he wanted her to sign. "I don't want to, but I don't know what else to do."

Jack was quiet for a moment. He reached into the bag he'd slung across his back. The bit of silver he pulled out took Jasminda's breath away.

"I found it in the back of the pantry when I was gathering food. It was your mother's?"

The pendant hung on a slightly charred chain. Snaking lines of metal had been designed to curl in on themselves in a beautiful tangle. Jasminda smiled at the familiar necklace.

"The sigil of the Queen," she said, running her finger along the warm metal, tracing the endless curving line. "I haven't seen this in many years. All in the Sisterhood wear them. I always thought it looked much like a spider."

Jack smiled and tilted his head. "I can see that. Here . . ." He grasped the chain with nimble fingers. "Let me fasten it for you." She swept her hair from her nape and presented it to him. His fingers brushed her neck, leaving goose bumps in their wake. She swallowed as the weight of the pendant settled just below her collarbone.

Rubbing the silver charm between her thumb and forefinger was soothing. It was an action Mama had done several times a day. Jasminda used to wonder if the motion aided in prayer. The Queen Who Sleeps visited the dreams of some—a very rare few—though Papa was included in the number.

He'd never spoken of the words of wisdom received

during these dreams, so Jasminda could only guess. Her own dreams had always remained silent, though she prayed for a visit just as most Elsirans did.

Mama had described joining the Sisterhood and devoting her life to service of the Queen as the best decision she'd ever made. Even when she'd left the order to start her family. That hadn't stopped her generosity. She'd made up baskets for the sick, those who would have benefitted from Papa's healing but refused it out of fear. She was kind to those who shunned her, and even coolly polite to those who only accepted her and the twins—who all three appeared Elsiran and had no magic—not Papa and Jasminda.

Her mama had been too good for this world and was needed in the World After to spread her love there. At least that's what Papa had said. It was just a platitude to soothe grieving children, but as Jasminda grew older, she believed it more and more.

She released the pendant and spun around, the realization hitting her like a blow to the chest. "I can't sign those papers, Jack."

His eyes rounded with concern. "They burned, did they?"

She paused, thinking. "No, I never took them out of my bag. But I wish they had because I won't sign. Mama never distanced herself from me. She walked away from everything she knew and everyone just for us. I can't—I won't disrespect her memory by giving in to my grandfather's shame." She stood and paced, her boots rasping across the fallen leaves.

A nagging doubt had chafed against the back of her mind since her call with the solicitor. She couldn't put her finger on it, but her gut told her there was more to her grandfather's offer than what had been stated.

"You do have another option, you know," Jack said.

She stopped her pacing.

"The in-person appeal. Go to Rosira. Your grounds are sound. There's no reason why the Taxation Bureau won't listen." He reached for her hand and she gripped him. "I will help."

"You'll help me get to Rosira? I don't have any money, and"—she motioned to herself—"traveling across the country would be difficult for me." She imagined she'd be stopped every few steps by someone asking for her papers. The rest of Elsira would likely be far worse in their regard for her than those in the tiny Borderlands town.

Jack pursed his lips. "Yes. Of course I'll help you. I could even . . ." He bit back whatever he'd been about to say. "I will do whatever it takes to help you save your land so you can rebuild."

Her free hand found the pendant again, worrying the smooth silver. "All right. And I will help you with the cornerstone . . . as much as I can."

CHAPTER NINE

The Master of Bobcats stalked his prey through the dark caves, and the cold mountain peaks, and the dead grass of the plains. While his jaws remained empty, his tongue salivated for the forgotten taste of flesh. For what is hunger but survival and destruction locked in an endless embrace?

—COLLECTED FOLKTALES

The baby's cries shredded Ella's eardrums. The reverberation caused an ache to spread behind her eyes. A driving pulse echoed through her, shaking her bones. She stood in a darkened hallway, the wailing all around her. Suddenly, a light appeared. White, marble walls stretched out before her on all sides. The dim glow illuminated them to ghostly proportions.

A flickering, lucent image of Kess hovered mere steps away.

"Everything has a cost, even love," she said, shaking her head sadly.

The baby bawled. Kess's mouth was downturned in disappointment. Ella had nowhere to go, the smooth white walls were a prison.

A strong jolt jerked her awake.

She sat up, released from the dream to find herself once again on the bus. The adolescent soldier in the seat next to her was fast asleep. Ella fished out Benn's watch from her pocket, but it was too dim to see the hands.

Unlike her relatively speedy arrival in Sora, the trip back was taking many hours longer. Gizelle had not booked her on the express bus, but the local, which seemed to stop at every village and hamlet on the way to Rosira.

Ella held her head in her hands as the bus slowed yet again. Out the window, a large town took shape. The streets were empty, it must have been quite late at night, but a handful of travelers stood waiting outside the bus depot. A constable was among their number, gold buttons glinting in contrast to his blue uniform.

Ella's breath caught, and she shrank down in her seat. The newcomers clambered aboard, seeking out empty seats. Ella was grateful for the gently snoring boy beside her.

The constable meandered down the aisle, having a look at every passenger. Ella squeezed her eyes shut, feigning sleep, hoping the footsteps would pass her quickly. In the gloom, he would not be able to see any of the little differences that marked her as foreign. Eyes a dark shade of brown unknown to Elsirans. Forehead a bit too broad.

The man's steps slowed near her, and she held her body

rigid. Then he moved on toward the back of the bus and she let out a breath. She didn't open her eyes again until the driver called out, "Arriving in Rosira, our final destination. Last stops: Northside and Portside."

She clutched her carpet bag to her chest and watched the city approach. The bright lights were a beacon, and even the enormity of the sleeping ocean beyond was a comfort.

Most of the passengers, including the constable, got off in Northside. The remaining minutes of her journey were spent as most of it had been—wondering how she would find more information on the High Priestess.

Could she go to the press? The local Portside paper might be interested, but would the larger rags care about an immigrant's accusations of kidnapping against one of the most powerful people in the country? And was it even kidnapping? Should she consult a lawyer? How would she pay for it?

Her worries accompanied her to the final stop. The clock on the front of the depot read three fifteen in the morning. Ella yawned and stretched as the soldier beside her rose.

She stepped off the bus back to the familiar soundtrack of Portside, welcome after her time in the quiet countryside. Even at this time of night, the streets were alive. A tavern across the street was kicking out its final patrons. Street urchins, fishermen, sailors, factory workers, women of the night, and more filled the streets. She could blend in again, a foreigner in a place that accepted—if not welcomed—them.

If she were to fail, how would her nephew fare in the care of the Sisters? Would his shock of white-blond hair darken as he grew older? Who could his father have been to provide such a strange feature? The babe hadn't been an albino, his eyes were dark and his skin bore a golden sheen similar to

Kess's, but the child would stand out in a place where differences were distrusted.

And why did Kess believe he was in danger from Syllenne Nidos?

Ella turned toward home when her path was blocked by a wide figure.

"Mistress Ravel?" The deep voice was resonant. The man was dressed as a driver, black coat and billed cap on his head. His long, dour face resembled that of an undertaker. Ella took a step back.

"Who's asking?" she responded cautiously.

"Your presence is requested by the High Priestess at the Southern temple."

Her jaw dropped. She had expected for it to take days or weeks of agitation to get a meeting with the High Priestess. A summons in the middle of the night was alarming.

"I-I don't have any papers to travel outside the gate." Though she'd just been across the country without papers, it was a far greater risk to set foot the few blocks away from Portside to where the temple was located.

"That will not be a problem." The driver motioned toward the town car. "The guards do not stop the High Priestess's vehicle."

Still nervous, but eager to meet this woman face to face, Ella squared her shoulders and followed the man. He held the back door open like she was an honored guest and helped her inside, then drove the short distance to the temple. The guards at the gate did not even look twice at the car as it passed.

The Southern Rosira temple was a grand structure, much the same on the outside as the smaller temple in Sora, just on a larger scale. Its golden domed roof was visible from blocks away and deep shadows darkened the space between the many columns out front.

The driver pulled around the back into a narrow alleyway and let Ella out. Then he got back into the car and drove away without another word.

There was only one door near her, which was, fortunately, answered quickly when she knocked. A young acolyte, perhaps only nine years old, curtsied and led the way inside. Sweet saints, did they force children to work all night here?

As in her dream, the hallways seemed to close in on her. They were as dark and cold as in the other temple. The girl led her up a flight of stairs and then another and yet another. Were they to meet in the attic? Finally, the girl pushed open a door on a landing and led Ella to a balcony that overlooked the sanctuary below.

From this vantage point you could observe the hundreds of people sleeping on the floor, small as insects due to the distance. Each level beneath them featured a balcony with carvings decorating the railings. Images of strange creatures that Ella couldn't name, beautiful cities full of spires and needle-like buildings reaching high into the sky. People flying through the air on gusts of wind. Plenteous crops and celebrations that reminded her of the ones she'd told Serra about back home.

The acolyte had faded back into the shadows after bidding Ella to wait. And wait she did.

There was no chair in sight so she was forced to stand or sit on the polished wood floor. After sitting for so long on the bus, she really didn't mind standing, but her nerves grew more frenzied with each passing minute. She studied the carvings and the people below until staring so far down became disorienting. A wave of exhaustion hit her and she yawned. Her sleep on the bus had been fitful and grief made her ache.

"So sorry to keep you waiting."

Ella spun around. Standing before her, having crept up silently, was a woman strung like a bow ready to snap. Her lean face was deeply lined, silver hair shot through with hints of its former deep red, most distinctively at the temples, and pulled into the most severe top knot Ella had ever seen. A hawkish gaze tracked Ella as she approached.

"High Priestess?"

The woman bowed. Ella dipped into a curtsey, smooth and graceful after hours of practice in her university deportment class.

"Is it Mistress Farmafield or Mistress Ravel, I wasn't certain?" Her voice was silvery, shot through with music and an edge of iron.

"Women do not take their husbands' names in Yaly, so Mistress Farmafield is fine." She paused. "How should I address you?"

This seemed to please the woman, if a twitch of the eyebrow could be counted as pleasure. "'Your Excellency' is most common, though unnecessary as you are not a believer." The predatory gleam in her eye left Ella feeling hollow.

"I am very sorry for the loss of your sister. Kess was a valuable asset to our cause. A dream-touched woman with endless compassion and empathy. We are bereft."

Her words felt sincere, and Ella began to tear up. "Thank you." She couldn't bring herself to call the woman "Your Excellency."

Syllenne smiled brittlely. She moved to the railing and peered below. "So many souls seeking guidance. It is wise they should do so. To take a journey without having the proper direction is folly, don't you think?"

Though the priestess still looked down, Ella could feel her sharp perusal. She suspected Syllenne had eyes in the back of her head. "Getting lost can be part of the fun," she countered. "You never know where it might lead you."

"I suppose you are an expert. I understand you are a hairdresser now, but your employment history has been . . . colorful." Ella was on her sixth job in as many years, but how did the High Priestess know that? And why did she care to check up on her?

She carved a smile onto her face by sheer force of will, feeling exposed under the woman's scrutiny. "I've . . . been . . . exploring various options. Not everyone is as fortunate as yourself to find your true calling."

"Indeed." Syllenne sniffed then turned abruptly, her robe billowing. "Please, come with me so we may speak privately."

As far as Ella could see, they were alone, but she followed the woman back down the steps, all the way to the ground floor. Instead of discreetly circling the sanctuary and its worshippers, Syllenne set a path directly through them.

Though soft snores and heavy breathing indicated many were asleep, a great deal were awake and stood to pay homage to their High Priestess. She held out her hand to accept kisses and waved magnanimously at those too far away to touch. Though the praise was silent, many were awakened, perhaps by the changed energy of the room.

Ella followed behind, wondering if her lack of similar reverence for the priestess was construed as rude or inappropriate. Syllenne was obviously beloved by the people. Those she interacted with were left awestruck. Some even cried.

Finally, they'd crossed the room. Syllenne pushed open an elaborately carved mahogany door leading to her office. The interior was . . . shocking. Ella had come to think of the Sisterhood as valuing simplicity and humility. But the High Priestess's office space was luxurious. Detailed tapestries graced the walls, fringed with gold or silver. Leather chairs, thick, finely woven carpeting, shelves full of artifacts and sculptures. And in the center of it all a gleaming wooden desk with gold painted inlays. Syllenne sat behind it and bid Ella to sit in the straight backed chair with the embroidered cushion facing her.

The High Priestess clasped her hands on the desktop, long fingers tipped with sharp-looking nails. "When your sister first joined our order, I fast-tracked her citizenship. It is a lengthy and expensive process, one that I understand you are still undergoing?"

Ella remained silent, not confirming or denying. Syllenne obviously knew that Ella had been traipsing across the country without the proper papers. Could she have Ella punished after the fact?

"Elsira is a land somewhat afraid of change, I'm sorry to say. But I have found that fresh blood in an organization, other ways of thinking and looking at things can be most . . . beneficial." Her hands were clinched in front of her in a way that looked uncomfortable.

"I thank you for your obvious care and concern for my sister," Ella said. "But I would like to see my nephew. Do you know who the baby's father is? Will he be called upon to take responsibility for his child?"

"The babe is the child of all of us now." She spread her arms. "He will be loved as one of our own. Reared in the reverence of our beloved Queen to become a man that Sister Kess would be proud of."

Syllenne's subtle threats and digs had shaken her, but her sister's last words rang in her head. "Where is my nephew? Why can't I see him? He is my blood kin and I—"

"Blood is a rather inconvenient liquid, is it not?"

Ella shifted uncomfortably, the memory of Kess's whispered spell coming to mind. "I'm sorry?"

Syllenne leaned forward. "People act as if blood is steel or iron. Permanent and unyielding. But it is just a bodily fluid, not dissimilar from that which coats the inside of handkerchiefs or spittoons or privies. A man injects fluid into a woman's womb and nine months later you have a creature of mucus and vomit and blood."

Ella jerked back.

"These ties you imagine that bind you to Kess's child, were they not the same ties that allowed you to go seven years without seeing your own sister? Your *blood*?"

Ella's mouth opened, but no words came out.

"And what of your parents? When was the last time you saw them?" A small smile played upon Syllenne's lips as she watched her words take hold. The pain of being sent away by her parents had never quite gone away. At thirteen, Ella had been effectively dismissed by the people who were supposed to love her, shipped off to boarding school, and never welcomed back home. Her parents no longer worked on the plantation where she'd grown up. She wasn't sure where they were now; they were traveling auditors and difficult to keep up with.

She struggled not to let on how much Syllenne's words

affected her, blanking her expression as the woman kept speaking.

"Kess made provisions for the care of her son if the unthinkable were to happen. It is unspeakably grievous that she journeyed to the World After before her time. Give yourself the space to mourn. And never worry, we take care of our own, Mistress Farmafield, I assure you. Your nephew will lack for naught."

A sour tang filled Ella's mouth, but the knot tangling her tongue finally loosened. "But I cannot even see him? Ever?" she croaked out.

Syllenne smoothed her hand across the wood of her desk, brushing away imaginary dust. "At this time, so soon after the loss of his mother, we feel it's advantageous for him to be in our exclusive care. It really is for the best."

"But . . . I . . . I don't . . ." Anger and sorrow and fear tripped her up. This was unacceptable. But she had no leverage. No power. Even her voice was daunted in the presence of the High Priestess.

"I understand that you are grieving and this is a difficult time. Rest assured, the decision has been made by those with far more influence than you. Nod if you understand."

Ella blinked rapidly. Shame colored her face. She nodded.

Not only was Syllenne holding a baby hostage, she held all the cards. Ella hated feeling so helpless.

"May I at least see my sister's accommodations? I understand she was not in Sora very long. Are there any personal items of hers that I can collect?"

Syllenne's mouth creased in a satisfied smile. This was a woman used to getting her way.

"Certainly. Though we live very simply. There may not be

much to find. I will have our novitiate show you to her dormitory."

The High Priestess stood and Ella did the same. "I hope I've alleviated any concerns you may have. Once again, we thank you for your assistance with Kess's birthing. I share your grief over her passing. May she find serenity in the World After."

Ella nodded again, unable to respond. Behind her, the door opened revealing the young girl. On her way out, Ella looked over her shoulder to find Syllenne staring sightlessly into the distance, frowning.

"This is Kess's? No one's used it since she left?"

The narrow bed and footlocker stood in the middle of a row of six on the wall of the dormitory. Six more beds mirrored these on the other side of the room.

The girl mumbled in the affirmative, then stepped aside as Ella approached the footlocker. Only to open it and find it empty. Sister Serra had indicated that Kess had arrived in Sora with nothing more than the clothes on her back, so Ella had hoped to find something here. Some clue as to who her sister had become. Perhaps even a hint as to the father of her child. But there was nothing.

No books or journals. Not the few letters they'd exchanged years earlier, not even so much as a spare robe or ribbon to hold her topknot in place.

"Where are her things?"

"They've been donated to the poor, miss."

Ella turned, incredulous. "Everything? Already?" The girl stayed quiet, eyes darting nervously.

She tried to bring calm to her voice. It wasn't the child's fault. "May I have a few moments alone to remember her?" The young acolyte bobbed her head and curtsied before leaving the room.

Ella sat heavily on the bed's thin little cushion. Why would they get rid of all Kess's things so quickly? Before her body was even cold?

Everything about this entire situation rubbed her the wrong way, from Kess's apparent knowledge of blood magic, to her dying plea, to Serra's warning, the enigmatic conversation with Lalli, and the brief imprisonment at Gizelle's hands.

She sighed and lay down fully, staring up at the cracked ceiling. When she was eight and Kess eighteen, mere weeks before leaving for her world travel adventure, Kess had given Ella her roadster bicycle. She was barely tall enough to ride it, and Kess was not a patient teacher, but even through many falls and scrapes, the bicycle was a hint of freedom. Ella had been able to leave the plantation on her own and ride the country roads for hours. It was the kindest thing her sister had ever done for her.

She turned on her side, sniffing the pillow to see if any of Kess's scent remained, but smelled nothing but lingering detergent. This mattress was untenably uncomfortable. Living simply was one thing, but how were the Sisters expected to serve the poor without at least a decent night's rest? Something hard and lumpy was digging into her thigh.

Ella's palm skated down the mattress. That wasn't just a lump. She rolled out of the bed and crouched down. If she wasn't mistaken, something had been stuffed into the side of the mattress.

She tunneled her hand beneath the sheet to expose the

mattress. The stitching along the side was uniform except for near that one spot where she'd felt something wedged in there. She didn't have a knife with her so she just ripped open the seam and dug into the stuffing until she pulled out a little wooden figurine about the size of her thumb.

It was pale and smooth as porcelain and shaped like a boat with its oars crossed on top. Kess must have put this here. But why had she hidden it? What did it mean?

The door snicked open. Ella bent over as if she was crying. Real tears threatened, but she wouldn't let them fall here. After a few moments, she placed the little carving into her pocket and stood, wiping at her cheeks. The girl in the doorway looked ashamed.

"Ready, miss?" The girl looked over her shoulder nervously as if she'd been instructed to come back in and didn't really want to.

"Yes, thank you. I'm ready to leave."

Syllenne Nidos may rule one of the country's most powerful institutions, and have the ear of princes and aristocrats, she might believe she held the strings and everyone below her were marionettes moving at her direction, but Ella saw behind the curtain. After that first time as a child riding the roadster bicycle, feeling the wind on her face and the prison of others' expectations far behind her, she'd vowed to remain free. She'd escaped the regimented life her parents had prescribed, eluded a dull future, and found love and contentment in a new land. She would not allow the High Priestess, or anyone else, to pull her strings.

CHAPTER TEN

The Mistress of Eagles lived atop the tallest hill in all the land. From there it is said she could hear the voice of the wind more clearly. But when she did not share all the warnings she heard in its whispers, it grew quieter, until one day she could not hear it at all.

—COLLECTED FOLKTALES

"Are you sure you don't want to rest some more?" Jasminda asked. "The storm seems to have lessened a bit, but it will still be a treacherous climb." A trickle of Earthsong zipped through Jack. He did his best to straighten and pretend he did not hurt everywhere.

"No, we don't have any time to waste. And you had better save your magic for the Mantle."

Her lips thinned, but the tingle of power ceased. She

marched over to a wide tree and retrieved a thick branch from beneath it, then presented it to him. He accepted the walking stick gratefully. His shoulder and abdomen were both ablaze with pain; each breath was a struggle.

He fished the little map stone from his pocket and rubbed his thumb across the sleek surface. Then he pulled the knife from his belt—the same one he'd used to kill the soldier. It was clean now, but still he hesitated before pricking his finger and touching it to the stone the old man had given him.

The valley disappeared, the smell of smoke left his nose, and every sound silenced. All of his senses were overtaken by the magical vision stored in the map. He was transported onto the mountain, walking high in its peaks behind a darkly hooded figure. The summer sun shone overhead, and sweat trickled down Jack's brow. His body was whole and healthy. Gravel crunched under his feet and birds trilled nearby.

The most recognizable landmark was up ahead. A peak that was flat on top, making it look like a table sitting high above the earth. The hooded figure's path took him straight for the flattened pinnacle. He approached, but then veered north-northwest, toward a ridge that in summer was coated with a dense layer of green shrubs. It was across this rise they had to travel.

Jack wondered if the person in the hood was the one who had created the Mantle. Such things were lost to history without so much as the whisper of myth to give any clues. The Mantle had always been, at least for the past five centuries. And whoever had created this map had been to the cornerstone before. For now, that was all Jack needed to know.

He struggled to leave the vision—though it had been much

harder the first time he'd tried it, the night the old man had given him the map.

Jack peeled his lids open and found himself staring into the eyes of a scowling Jasminda. She looked from him to the ground where he'd dropped the map after being torn back into the present. "That's an ugly bit of magic," she said, nudging the rock with her toe.

Ugly or not, it was the only way to find the cornerstone, and he needed it. When he bent to retrieve the map, she stopped him and picked it up only after wrapping her hand in her scarf. Grimacing, she dropped it into his palm like a hot coal.

Jack described the flat peak to her and the green ridge. "I know that place," she said. "We can take the path on the north side of the valley."

They set out through the garden rows and trees, Jasminda holding the sack containing the items saved from the house. He protested, but she would not let him carry anything, giving a pointed look to his limping legs when he tried to insist.

"I'm not an invalid."

Her arched eyebrow contradicted him. "Focus on staying upright. I'll do the rest."

He noticed the wince she tried to hide from some injury she wouldn't acknowledge, but overall, she was in far better shape than he. Common sense told him she was right to insist, but his pride stung.

The moon peeked out from the overhead clouds, brightening the way out of the valley and up the trail leading into the mountains. Though the valley was calm, the storm raging ahead worried him. Their path rose, and the temperature fell drastically. Beneath their feet the ground changed from grassy, to dirt covered, to snow covered. Each torturous step brought not only a deepening of the snow but increased pain.

Jasminda led the way, the light from her lantern reflecting off the icy whiteness, now knee-deep. But the surrounding darkness swallowed up the illumination. He trusted that she could find the landmarks at night. The walking stick was a godsend as each step became more difficult than the last. Pausing to catch his breath, a coughing fit struck him, leaving red splatters on the pristine white.

When he straightened, he found Jasminda staring at the blood on the ground. Almost immediately, the warm hum of Earthsong rippled through him.

"Save it," he rasped. "I'm all right."

She scowled. "You are not all right. You are worse than when you arrived. Stop being such a fool." The buzz of Earthsong continued for a few moments before she turned and stomped away.

They battled the storm for hours, their progress arduous. Strong gusts of wind blew against them, sometimes knocking them on their backs and forcing them to stop until the intensity eased. Icy blasts whipped through Jack's coat, freezing his fingers until he could no longer grip the walking stick and had to leave it behind.

"Let's stop here for a moment," Jasminda shouted, pointing to a notch in the rock wall just big enough for two people. Underneath the overhang, the snow stood only ankle high, and the sidewalls protected them from the worst of the wind. They crouched down together, shaking from the cold. She took his hands in hers and rubbed, bringing some feeling back into them. In the flickering lantern light, worry etched a frown on her face.

"Does this storm seem strange to you?"

"Strange how?"

She swiveled her head from side to side. "I don't know. It's almost like it's . . . alive."

Jack's teeth were chattering so hard that he wasn't sure what sort of expression crossed his face, but Jasminda blinked and looked down. "Never mind."

"Is that possible? Can Earthsong do such a thing?" Jack flinched at the thought. A living storm? Could this be the first wave of attack? The True Father had long used environmental means to wage war, but such a storm was unprecedented.

Jasminda brushed away the snow that had accumulated on her lashes. "It would take a great deal of his power, I'd think. An unbelievable amount, but it might be possible." She shivered in a way that didn't seem like it was purely from cold.

"How much farther is it?" he asked.

She motioned with her head, and he craned his neck around. The table-top crest of the next mountain was just ahead of them, glowing in the filtered moonlight reflecting off the snow.

Excitement coursed through his blood, and Jack rallied, drawing whatever inner strength he could into his depleted limbs. He cracked his knuckles and tried to fashion his frozen face into a grin. "We're nearly there."

Jasminda nodded and they stood. Some untapped fount from within propelled him forward. Though snow covered everything, he recognized the change in elevation as the green ridge from his vision.

"Where to now?" she shouted over the vicious wind.

"Just across there."

They had to hold each other up to continue, but pushed forward. He had no feeling in his feet or hands, and not much in his face, either. He could almost believe that the storm did have some evil intent.

The wind battered them as they crossed the narrow ridge single file. Jasminda held the lantern, leading the way across the icy path. Snow crumbled, tumbling down steep inclines, and was swallowed by the darkness.

Jack's foot slipped. He tipped forward, crashing to his hands and knees. Jasminda wrenched him up and they shuffled forward, bitterly slowly, but his legs would not move any faster. The path disappeared over a slight incline in front of them.

"It's j-just . . ." He raised a hand to point. Jasminda looked over her shoulder, her expression grimmer than he'd ever seen it. They crested the rise and Jack blinked snow out of his eyes, wonder growing at the sight before him.

He slipped again and thundered to the ground, sliding down the hill on his back. Jasminda cursed behind him, falling on the ice as well.

When he caught his breath, he lay looking up at a giant pillar of stone rising from the ground. It had to be five stories high. Another stood ten paces away. Jack turned his head to find an entire circle of such irregularly shaped pillars, but the more astonishing sight was that none were touched by snow or ice. Inside the perimeter of rough columns, green grass covered the earth.

Jack crawled forward seeking the warmth. Once he crossed the perimeter, the thrall of the storm no longer touched him.

The stone circle must hold magic that protected it from the elements. Feeling returned to his senseless limbs. Wondering if he was hallucinating, he made his way to his feet. But beside him, Jasminda's slack-jawed face reflected his awe.

"Is this what you saw?" she asked.

"Yes." The first time he'd used the map, he'd seen the hooded figure enter this circle of stones. In the vision, it had been summer. Now, it seemed, no other season existed here.

"What now?" Jasminda's voice held an edge of wariness.

Jack tore his attention from the stark delineation of winter and summer to look to the center of the circle. The space was twenty paces across. But unlike in his vision, the inside of the circle was empty. "It was there. Just there in the middle." He turned to Jasminda.

"A red obelisk rose higher than the outer stone columns. In the vision, I knew it was the cornerstone." He stared at the empty space again. Well, not entirely empty. Where the obelisk once stood now lay a smooth patch of what looked to be dark glass. Somewhat irregularly shaped, the sleek surface held ripples, as if a stone had been tossed in a puddle and then the whole thing had frozen.

Jack moved toward it, studying the area.

"Could it have been moved?" Jasminda asked.

"I don't . . . I don't know." He dropped to his knees, exhaustion catching up with him. Was it his imagination, or did the glass move? Jasminda kneeled beside him, her attention caught as well. Had she seen it?

Like they had practiced the movement, both reached a hand forward at the same time. Only the tips of their fingers brushed the surface, but the glass shattered as if hit with a hammer.

Shards exploded outward, lacerating their hands. He dove for Jasminda, using his body to protect her from the spray of sharp fragments. She landed with an *oomph* beneath him, and Jack struggled to catch his breath. Blood seeped from the many shallow wounds on his hands. It was not so much that it should have made him feel light-headed. He'd had worse wounds only the day before. But still, before he could move off Jasminda, his head dove toward the ground and all went black.

Jasminda's eyelids felt at least three times their normal weight. The last thing she remembered was the breath leaving her lungs as Jack's weight crushed her. Now, the pressure on her chest was gone. She opened her eyes and found Jack two paces away, still out cold. And the world around her had changed.

When they had entered the stone circle, the storm still raged outside its boundaries. But now, she had been transported into a different season altogether. Beyond the pillars, the sun was up, the weather serene. The outside now matched the inside of the circle.

She sat up and looked again at Jack, sprawled beside her. In his open palm lay the map stone. That was odd. She was sure he hadn't been holding it when they entered the circle.

She looked around again and gasped, scrambling backward at the sight of a hooded figure standing across the shattered glass from them. Only now, the glass was whole again, like it hadn't burst apart and sliced her. Her fingers no longer stung from the cuts and there was no blood slicking her palms.

"Who are you?" she called out.

The figure, covered head to toe in a dark cloak, walked

around toward Jasminda. She stood her ground, not wanting to move farther from Jack's vulnerable form.

The cloaked person's arms rose to remove the hood, and Jasminda's chest contracted. Standing before her was a woman, a Lagrimari woman. Her dark hair was pulled back into a thick braid and her eyes, slightly downturned at the corners, gave her a sad look.

She peered in Jasminda's general direction, but the woman was looking through her. Jasminda turned—there was no one else there besides her and Jack.

The sad woman opened her mouth and spoke, shocking Jasminda even more. "You are here for the cornerstone." Her voice had a slight echo to it, a distant quality though the woman stood only a few paces away. "My father built the Mantle. When he died, protecting it fell to me. Father told me that one day there would be seekers. Either to destroy the barrier or to strengthen it. You must prove which you are before the cornerstone may be revealed."

The woman clasped her hands in front of her. "The test is simple. Return the map to the center of the circle."

Confusion furrowed Jasminda's brow. "Return?" She took another look at the odd patch of glass. It was, perhaps, four paces across. But once again, it had changed. Now in the very middle, a chunk was missing. The irregular shape of what was left behind matched that of the map exactly, it was a perfect fit.

"That's all I have to do?" She looked back over her shoulder, but the woman had disappeared.

The test was simple indeed, though a flutter of apprehension sped her heartbeat. Jack still hadn't awoken; concern for him pummeled her, but she knew his priority. With a deep breath, she removed the map stone from his palm, gripping it as gingerly as she would a dead rodent.

To get to the center of the glass, she would have to walk across it—the place where the map fit was too far to reach. But the last time they'd touched it, the glass had shattered.

Jasminda kneeled, feeling on the ground for a pebble or stone. Finding one, she tossed it onto the dark brown glossy surface. It fell with a *thunk,* but the glass held.

She rose and tentatively placed a toe at the very edge of the glass and pressed her weight. It still held, giving no indication of being brittle or delicate at all.

Her heart beating double time, she stepped fully onto the surface. It bore her weight without a groan of complaint and felt just as solid as the ground. When she looked up, her breath caught in her chest.

A different woman stood just in front of her, one she hadn't seen in nearly seven long years. Jasminda's throat thickened. Tears bit her eyes. "Mama?"

Eminette Zinadeel smiled sweetly, but looked off at an angle, staring into the distance. Her auburn hair held streaks of gold. A dusting of freckles lay scattered across her nose. Their pattern was as familiar to Jasminda as her own face.

"Mama!" She reached out to embrace her, but her mother flinched back. Eminette turned to regard her daughter with empty eyes.

"You could have saved me."

"What?" The accusation in her mother's tone was an arrow through Jasminda's flesh.

"How did you not know? The sickness inside me. How did you not sense it?"

Jasminda blinked through freely flowing tears. "I-I'm sorry, Mama. I didn't know. My Song isn't—"

"Your Song is weak. If you were stronger you could have saved me."

A sob yanked itself from Jasminda's chest. In the back of her mind, a thought whispered that Papa hadn't sensed Mama's illness, either, and his Song had been much stronger than hers. But most of her acknowledged that her mother was right. If Jasminda had only been stronger. Had only worked harder at learning Earthsong, then she would have known.

Mama shook her head bitterly and faded away.

"No!" Jasminda fell to her knees; her bones shook from the impact with the glass. She could not catch her breath. Her lungs spasmed fighting for air.

The map stung her fist. She choked down her grief. The center of the circle was so close, just another two steps. Though this simple test might be the end of her.

She closed her eyes and steadied her breath.

"Jasminda?"

She looked up. Her papa stood just in front of her, the twins on either side. She fell back, taking them all in.

"Papa? Roshon? Varten?" Neither the boys nor her father had changed. The twins were identical except for their expressions. Roshon scowled down at her, and Varten shook his head. Her father's heavy eyes echoed the boys' disappointment.

"If you had come with us that day, you could have saved us," Papa said.

Roshon crossed his arms. "You never wanted to go to town, always begging off, afraid of the townsfolk."

Varten pursed his lips, but didn't speak.

Jasminda's stomach lurched, threatening to empty itself. "B-but how could I have saved you?"

"I never thought I'd raised a coward, Jasminda." Papa's voice cut through to her core.

She tried to tell herself this was the magic, the test, none of it was real. But there they stood, and they *looked* so real. Not a hair on their heads had changed. They blurred through her tears.

She tucked her chin to her chest, and crawled forward, pushing through the place where they stood. Their legs faded away into mist and although part of her was relieved, a larger part would have endured anything—would have gladly accepted their blame if only they had been real.

She stretched out her hand for the center of the circle. It was only an arm's length away. It should have been easy to reach but her whole body had turned leaden.

A heavy foot nearly stomped on her wrist. She looked up yet again to find the county constable towering over her. The smell of smoke filled her nostrils.

"That fine young couple has big plans for that cabin. They don't mind rebuilding. Even if the thing hadn't burned, they would have torn it down and started over. Said it was too rustic for them." The red-faced man gave a deep belly laugh before piercing her with his gaze.

"A shame you couldn't hold onto your family's legacy. Now, not only is it up in smoke, not a chicken or goat will remain once these new homesteaders get their way." He shook his head and adjusted his cap. "Ah, well, that's progress, innit?"

Jasminda's head dropped and all the fight went out of her. The farm lost? The cabin torn down instead of being rebuilt?

She shook in agony as the words of her family and the words of the constable rained down on her like an avalanche. Her limbs were too heavy to move. She was locked in place as if she had turned to stone. Perhaps she would become one of the pillars that guarded this place.

Try as she might to take one more step, she couldn't do it.

Her fingers were pried opened and the map was removed from her hand.

She opened her eyes to find Jack, red-eyed and red-faced, but determined, lurch forward on his hands and knees and drop the small stone into place.

As soon as it settled into the spot of its origin, the ground began to vibrate. An invisible force pushed her back onto the grass as the entire interior of the stone circle shimmered and shifted. A giant red obelisk popped into existence where the map stone had lain.

Jack crouched next to her. His eyes slowly rose to meet hers. He scrubbed away the tears tracking his cheeks.

What had he seen? Whatever it was, it seemed no less harrowing than her own test, only Jack had passed.

The cornerstone rose before them, radiating power.

Jack's golden gaze dimmed. His breathing stuttered, and his eyes rolled up into his head. Blood gushed from one of his nostrils.

"Jack?" Jasminda reached for him, but he fell to the side, unconscious. Fear drummed a cadence inside her chest. She could not heal Jack and have any hope of fixing the cornerstone.

Though it tore at her heart, she swallowed and focused her attention on the obelisk. Her breathing had still not returned to normal, so it took several tries before she could successfully connect to Earthsong. The raging river of power felt wild, rough, and choppy.

She filled her Song to its limited capacity and felt for the magic of the cornerstone. A power ancient and unfamiliar met her. The spell was a tangled webbing of complex pieces, far beyond her skill level.

She could sense cracks in the intricate latticework of energy, but trying to fill them would be like mortaring a brick wall with twig and a bit of mud. She was just too weak. She had the absurd desire to laugh.

The voices of her family echoed in her head. She swatted them away but they persisted.

"It's not just me," she muttered aloud as if their apparitions were still before her. "No Singer alive could repair this spell." The magic was hundreds of years old. Papa had told her the ancient Singers must have had godlike powers to create the Mantle. And yet slivers of doubt pierced her.

She poured her Song into the attempt, feeling her way around the spell, trying to patch even one crack. She drained herself with no effect. The old man who'd given Jack the map must have been delusional. Or was she simply the wrong Singer for the job?

She shivered, suddenly cold. No longer able to hold on to Earthsong, she opened her eyes to find swirling eddies of snow had invaded the protection of the pillars. The remaining grass shriveled before her eyes as the storm breached the circle.

What had happened? How had the magic failed? She drew her coat tighter and bent to Jack. He was still breathing, but his injuries had been severe and the climb up the mountain had only worsened them.

She leaned her head to his chest to find his heartbeat slow, his body temperature scarily low. She lay across his body to try and warm him, but it looked more and more like he would die on this mountain. Likely, they both would.

Tears froze on her face. She squeezed her lids shut against the pain of defeat in so many areas.

Pins and needles skittered across her skin, alternating between tiny jabs of pain and numbness. The evil presence lurking in the storm felt even nearer. She stared up at the obelisk as hope fled.

The ground shook—aftershocks of the cornerstone's appearance? But the gentle vibrations increased in intensity. The rattling grew until the snow bounced and the earth groaned in complaint. Violent, shattering shakes rattled the ridge where the circle stood. The stone columns trembled and crumbled as the shaking grew stronger. Large chunks fell away, barely missing where Jasminda lay protecting Jack with her body. Beneath them, cracks appeared in the earth.

She gripped Jack tight, whispering the Promise of the Queen through stammering lips. "While She sleeps this promise keep; That She dream of us while for Her we weep; May She comfort, counsel, guard, and guide; Those whose love will never die; And when Her betrayer pays for his lies; And finally the World After, occupies; May love's true Song with Her remain; And awaken Her that She may rule again."

What was left of the disintegrating columns swayed and tilted. Two of them crashed into the obelisk. They tore through the gleaming red stone. The other pillars followed suit and rocks tumbled down from somewhere above. They all fell, pounding the ancient artifact into powder until no trace remained.

The ground opened up where the columns had once stood.

Jasminda repeated the prayer twice through, her words a mere whisper at the end, when the earth beneath her fell away, leaving her clutching Jack's limp form as they tumbled down the mountain.

CHAPTER ELEVEN

When bonds of friendship would hold him down, Bobcat
cuts his ties to run free.

—COLLECTED FOLKTALES

She lost Jack in the free fall. In the pummeling of rocks and
snow and debris, her curled fists could not hold on, and he
fell away.

Then the rapid descent stopped. The buzz of Earthsong
surrounded her, lifting her until she was weightless. A soft,
glowing light approached, floating upward as if on wings. Rising along with her lantern was an unconscious Jack. She
grabbed his hand and pulled him into her arms as they floated
straight up. Having him back calmed her enough that she
could take a breath and enjoy the healing warmth surrounding
them.

Her nicks and cuts disappeared; even her frayed emotions were soothed—an accomplishment achievable only by a very powerful Singer. She wished she hadn't exhausted her Song. She longed to reach out and sense the intentions of the Earthsinger who'd found them. Though his or her actions so far had been benevolent.

The spell—strong enough to carry two adults in the air—brought them down the mountain and set them gently on a patch of snowy ground. They were protected from the snow and cold by a bubble of insulated air.

Jack stirred. She brushed a hand across his brow and exhaled when he blinked his eyes.

"Welcome back," she whispered.

"Delighted to be here." He looked around, confused. Flexed his arms and legs.

She crawled closer. "What's wrong? Are you hurt?"

A brilliant smile spread across his face. He shook his head. "Not at all."

She wanted to check for herself to be sure, but the relief in his expression told the story. He was well. Thank the Sovereign.

"What happened?"

She shook her head. "Someone saved us. An Earthsinger."

Jack's eyes widened. "And the Mantle?"

Jasminda swallowed her regret. "It didn't work. I couldn't do it. I wasn't strong enough."

The light in his eyes dimmed, and a new fissure formed on her heart. There was nothing she could do to make it better—their chance to stop the war was gone because she had failed.

She longed to ask him what he'd seen in his vision, but the darkness around them moved. Shadows broke away from the rock wall, stepping into the weak circle of light. Two men and two women, all Lagrimari and armed with rifles, came forward. Jasminda scrambled back, her hand diving into her coat pocket where she'd stored her pistol. Jack, too, produced a revolver, holding it at his side.

Perhaps the Singer who'd saved them hadn't been as benevolent as she'd hoped.

The Lagrimari held their weapons at the ready, pointed down. Instead of uniforms they wore clothes made from tough, gritty-looking material similar to burlap. The men and women themselves seemed tough and gritty, as well. Jasminda held her breath as the group regarded them with hard gazes.

Footsteps crunched in the snow behind the Lagrimari. A small head appeared and pushed its way to the center.

"I told you to go back to the cave," one of the women spat as a little boy pulled away from her grasp. The woman's face was badly scarred on one side with jagged lines. The boy was around six or seven with a shock of black hair and round cheeks. He smiled brightly, revealing two missing front teeth.

Jasminda pointed her pistol to the ground, peering at the boy.

"Well, hello there," Jack said in Lagrimari. "Are you the welcome wagon?"

The boy beamed at Jack, who smiled back uncertainly. Jasminda watched the exchange, confused.

"He's an incorrigible child," the scarred woman said.

"He is only trying to counteract your pigheadedness, Rozyl," another voice said from the darkness. An old woman stepped into the light, her face leathered and wrinkled. She was gray-haired and stooped, and wore a ragged coat of matted fur. "It's too cold out here for all this bother. Pssht. Put those away." She waved her hand, and the armed men and women strapped their rifles to their backs and retreated into the shadows. Rozyl was the last to do so—she scowled at Jasminda before she went.

"Come, children. Come inside where it's warm." The old woman placed a hand on the boy's shoulder. "Thank you, Osar. We wouldn't want our guests to feel unwelcome."

"Who . . . who are you?" Jasminda asked.

"I am Gerda ul-Tahlyro. This little one is Osar, always trying to do good deeds." She smiled down at the child, who seemed a bit abashed.

Jasminda could only stare at the boy. "That was *his* spell?"

"Oh yes. He's the strongest of us all."

"They don't need to know that," Rozyl growled from somewhere in the darkness.

"Osar has already said these two are safe. What reason have we not to trust them?"

"I don't trust anyone." Footsteps crunched away. The cave entrance must be there, hidden in the darkness. When the last footsteps disappeared, Jasminda stood, taking Jack's offered hand.

He was peering at Gerda, his brows drawn. Jasminda expected him to say something, but when he didn't, she offered her hands to Gerda, palms out in greeting. "I'm Jasminda ul-Sarifor, and this is Jack . . ." She waited for him to provide his surname, but he remained silent.

Gerda squinted at her outstretched hands. Jasminda blinked rapidly, unsure of her mistake. Though she'd never actually had anyone greet her properly in Elsira, she hadn't thought this Lagrimari woman would shrink from her touch.

"In Lagrimar, they greet one another by bringing a hand to the forehead," Jack said, reaching for Gerda's right hand and bringing it up to touch his head. Jasminda swallowed and dropped her hands, heat rising in her neck and cheeks.

"Sarifor, you say?" Gerda cocked her head to the side. "Any relation to Dansig ol-Sarifor?"

The world fell away for an instant as an image of Papa's disapproving face crossed her vision. She blinked past it and forced herself to breathe. "You knew my father?"

Gerda nodded. "Long ago." She turned and disappeared into the shadows. "Come along now. There's a warm fire inside."

Utterly shaken, Jasminda moved to grab the bag and lantern, but Jack's quick fingers plucked them away first. He chuckled at her exasperation, but his eyes lacked their usual sparkle.

"What do you think?" Her voice was hushed and cautious. Warily, she watched the storm bluster just on the edge of their little invisible wall of protection.

"I'll go first," he said, then grabbed hold of her hand and charged ahead.

She was glad for his hand in hers. The mountain caves and tunnels frightened her. They had been strictly off-limits growing up, and even her intrepid brothers had listened to Papa's words and stayed away. Half a dozen cave openings lined the mountain path her family used on their way to and from town. But they had never ventured in. Something about the gaping openings sent off danger signals. On a primal level, they felt like places to be avoided.

Like the wretched map and Tensyn's speaking stone, a similar crawling unease pervaded the caves. All set her teeth on edge in their own way.

But the others did not shudder the way she did upon entering the cavern. Jack gave no evidence that his skin was crawling with the oppressive atmosphere. With each step, the temperature grew steadily warmer, but cold goose bumps irritated her skin.

A short tunnel opened to a huge chamber many stories high. The interior was wholly unexpected; instead of the rough surface of rock, the walls and floor were glassy and smooth, like the patch of ground surrounding the cornerstone. The entire interior of the mountain looked as if it had been blown in the forge of a glassmaker. She struggled to calm her rioting belly. Her breath pulsed in short gasps.

Jack's expression mirrored her concern.

"Do you feel the *wrongness* of this place?" she asked. "It's like . . ." The lifeless eyes of the soldier she'd killed swam into her vision. The cave stank of pungent earth and stale air, but underneath it all, she smelled blood. She was glad her Song was depleted for the next half day or so. The idea of trying to sing here caused a ripple of nausea to overwhelm her. That same instinct screaming the danger of the caves told her that this was not a place for magic. For the first time ever, the thought of using Earthsong filled her with dread.

He pulled her closer, wrapping an arm around her. "We can just wait here for the storm to end." Jack's warm breath on her ear pulled her back from the edge of panic. She focused on him, the strength in his body now that he was no longer in pain. He was a solid thing to hold onto.

"And then what?" she asked.

"I think these Lagrimari must be Keepers of the Promise. Rebels against the True Father. Perhaps their young Singer could help to bolster the cornerstone—if we're able to find it again."

A sob escaped Jasminda's pressed lips.

"What is it?" Jack's eyes were frantic.

She sucked in a breath and met his gaze. "It's gone." He grew stricken as she told him of the shaking earth. Of how the cornerstone had been destroyed.

"I don't understand." He pulled away from her and dropped his head in his hands. "What happened? How could it just be crushed like that?"

Jasminda drew away. She wanted to offer some comfort, but what words could she say? If she had been stronger could she have prevented the rock slide? The avalanche?

Off to the right, an opening in the cavern wall was lit by a flickering fire. Voices buzzed from within. Jack trudged forward, toward heat and light, his face a desolate landscape. Jasminda followed, her arms wrapped around her, poor protection from the fears and regrets that pummeled her.

They stood outside the cave in silence. Jasminda watched Jack for a clue of how to proceed, but he was lost in his own mind.

"Come," Gerda called, her voice cracked. "No use skulking about in the corridors."

Jasminda peeked inside to find a well-tended fire roaring in the center, sleeping packs spiraling out from it. A handful of careworn women, each huddled with a small child or two, looked up at her. Osar sat with a slightly older girl near the fire. Rozyl and the others from outside stood grouped together in the corner, hovering over Gerda who sat on the ground with two other elders.

With a hand on Jack's shoulder, Jasminda nudged them forward. Two dozen Lagrimari watched their entrance. She had never seen so many people who looked like her in the same place. But each face she peered into held a sort of quiet desperation, a somberness that hinted at a life of struggle. Except for Rozyl. She merely glared.

Oddly enough, the obvious antagonism was comforting for Jasminda. At least she was in familiar territory. She set her jaw and scowled back, refusing to be cowed by this woman who didn't even know her. Rozyl's gaze dropped to her hand on Jack, and Jasminda froze. He was the only Elsiran here.

He shook himself, his eyes sharpening and scanning the room, then shifted into a protective stance, placing his body in front of hers.

"Have a seat," Gerda said.

Jasminda was still wary of the smooth cave interior. However, with no other options, she settled on the ground in front of the elders. Jack positioned himself by her side, but turned slightly, keeping an eye on the entire space. Rozyl and her crew moved a few paces away.

"This is Turwig ol-Matigor and Lyngar ol-Grimor." Gerda pointed to the old men.

"You are Keepers of the Promise?" Jack asked with a side-long glance.

"We are," Gerda said, motioning to the other elders, Rozyl, and the three guards with her. Rozyl groaned. The other women and children were out of earshot.

"Did you know my father, as well?" Jasminda asked the old men. A look passed between them that she couldn't decipher.

"It was many years ago, child. I can hardly recall," said Turwig, whose kind face held a grandfatherly quality.

The one called Lyngar had deep lines etched into his face, his perpetual scowl making her wonder if he was related to Rozyl. "I can. He was a scoundrel. He abandoned his regiment. Unforgivable!"

Jasminda tensed and focused on the unpleasant man. "He was captured in the Sixth Breach. A prisoner of war." She forced the words out through clenched teeth.

"Is that what he told you?" Lyngar snorted. Gerda shot him a murderous glare, and he looked away, not exactly chastened, more like he'd grown bored with the conversation.

"He journeyed to the World After two years ago along with my brothers . . . to join my mother, who was Elsiran." She said the last as a challenge, to see how he would react. Lyngar's head whipped toward her before his gaze shot to Jack.

"So that is why you cavort with them."

Jasminda moved to stand, wishing she could throttle the old man or, at the very least, get away from him. Jack's hand on her arm stilled her, and she sat stewing in rage. The fire was either far too hot or her blood was ablaze.

"Why have you brought these people across the Mantle?" Jack motioned to the women and children in the center of the room.

"It will fall soon," Gerda said simply. "Better to be on this side than the other when that happens."

Turwig spoke up. "How do you know about the Keepers, boy?"

Beside her, Jack swallowed and cleared his throat. "I met one years ago. After the Seventh Breach, I was stationed at the Eastern Base—"

"You're a soldier?" Rozyl asked through gritted teeth.

Jack nodded tersely. "When we transferred the POWs to the settlement, as per the terms of the treaty, I met a young man called Darvyn." More than one person in the cave sucked in a breath. "You know him?"

Gerda silenced everyone with a glance. "Go on."

Wariness crept into Jack's expression. "We used to talk. We became friendly. He let me practice my Lagrimari with him. One day, a few months later, I went to the settlement, and he was gone. Disappeared. I called for a search, thinking something must have happened to him, but we found nothing."

Jasminda listened, impressed that he had even tried to find a missing settler. It was more than most Elsirans would have done.

"Then, just over three weeks ago, he returned and called for me at the base. He wouldn't tell me where he'd been, just that the Mantle was going to be destroyed and Elsira needed to be warned. I contacted the Council and the Prince Regent, but they wouldn't take the word of a Lagrimari settler. But I believed him."

Jack scrubbed a hand down his face, his eyes growing faraway. His voice dropped as he told of the spell Darvyn had cast to make him appear Lagrimari, of hiding within Tensyn's squad and discovering the terrible truth. "Not just cracks, not just a breach—the entire Mantle will fall. Soon. And the True Father will be unleashed on us all. But then, you already knew."

A chill rippled over Jasminda's skin. The faces of the Lagrimari were pensive.

"And Darvyn's spell, just . . . failed?" Turwig asked. The old man had leaned forward, intent on every word of Jack's story.

Jack nodded, his shoulders sagging with weariness.

"He must be dead," Lyngar said matter-of-factly.

"Or so badly injured he could not maintain the spell." Gerda placed a comforting hand on Turwig as the man shuddered.

Jasminda wondered who he was to them. "You know this Darvyn?" she asked.

"Since he was a small child." Turwig's voice faded almost to nothing.

Lyngar's face was perpetually twisted, as if everything smelled bad to him. "You've got your proof now, boy. What will you do with it?"

Jack made a fist so tight his knuckles cracked. "Now that the . . ." He blinked, looking stricken and cleared his throat. ". . . the Mantle is beyond saving, we must prepare for war. I will go back and make them all listen to reason. Organize our troops. Then ready ourselves for a fight to end all others."

Gerda and the old men shared another meaning-laden glance. Rozyl stalked up, towering over the seated group. Her face was taut as she stared at Gerda, pleading silently. Whatever was going on, it was obvious Rozyl did not want Jasminda or Jack to know about it.

Gerda held up a hand to wave Rozyl off. "What if there were another way?"

Jack looked up, his jaw set. "What other way?"

"You Elsirans worship the Queen, do you not?"

"Yes, of course." He looked from face to face. "Do you? I thought religion was not allowed in Lagrimar."

"Oh no," the old woman said. "The only religion allowed is reverence of the True Father. There are the Avinids, of course, but they believe in nothing. However, the Queen Who Sleeps graces the dreams of some, and there are many who believe in secret."

Turwig hummed in agreement. "If She were awoken, it is said Her power is great enough to stop the True Father."

Jasminda gaped. "Do you believe that?"

"Do you doubt it?" Turwig's dark eyes lit from within with wisdom.

She swallowed, turning to Jack. "She has never graced my dreams," he said slowly. "I've prayed to Her many times without response."

"Just because She didn't speak to you directly, doesn't mean She didn't hear you, child," Gerda said. "I believe She hears us all."

"But She has slept for hundreds of years; there's little chance She will awaken now." Jasminda wondered if the others were all crazy for contemplating such a thing.

"Hmm," was Gerda's only response.

Jack's flame-colored eyes danced in the firelight, the desolate look in them banished with this talk of the Queen. Though Jasminda could not even begin to hope for such a miracle as the Sovereign's awakening, she was grateful for anything that erased the blight of defeat from his brow.

For with the cornerstone's destruction, the miracle of the Queen's awakening might be the only thing that could save them.

CHAPTER TWELVE

Bobcat caught a thorn in his paw and could not remove it.
Horse came by and offered to pull the thorn out.
  Ow! cried Bobcat. I thought you were going to help me.
  I removed the thorn, Horse replied.
  But you left two more behind!
  You are welcome, Horse said and trotted off.
  —COLLECTED FOLKTALES

Jack's arms were wrapped around something warm and soft.
He opened his eyes; any hint of drowsiness fled as a spark
tickled behind his ribs. Jasminda lay curled on her side, her
back pressed against his chest. Her head was tucked just under
his chin, her chest rising and falling with gentle breaths.

After their discussion of the Queen the night before, the
elders had insisted it was time to sleep. Jack had no idea how

long it had been since they'd left Jasminda's farm, but even healed, his weary body was ready to shut down.

Jasminda hadn't wanted to stay with the others and Rozyl's hostility had led Jack to agree. So they'd bunked in a smaller cavern a few hundred paces away. Without a fire, this chamber was quite a bit cooler. They'd curled up on the ground next to each other, using her lumpy sack as a pillow.

Jack didn't want to wake Jasminda by moving too quickly. He gave in to the urge to brush her hair back, letting his fingers get caught in its tangled softness. How was it that she smelled so sweet? He allowed himself a few breaths before inching backward, pulling himself away from her softness. Other parts of his body were awake, too, and he didn't wish to scandalize her.

He owed her his life, there could be no doubt of that. So perhaps these feelings that had sprung up inside him could be traced there. All he knew was that he'd slept better on this hard, cold ground with her in his arms than on the most luxurious mattress in Rosira.

Light footsteps echoed outside the cave entrance. Jack removed an arm from around Jasminda and palmed the pistol he'd left within easy reach, keeping it down by his side. Though he had trusted Darvyn, he could not be completely certain that *these* enemies of his enemy were, in fact, his friends. They could prove to be great allies in the fight against the True Father, but they held secrets. There must be more to their reason for braving this journey than they'd shared.

Lantern light brightened the entrance as a curly head appeared—a head much lower than he'd expected. Osar stood gripping the lantern shakily. Jack released his weapon. The boy's huge eyes glittered, and he beckoned Jack forward with one hand.

"Jasminda." He shook her gently. "We have a visitor." He nodded in the child's direction. Jasminda sat up, yawning.

Osar motioned again for them to follow before disappearing down the hall. They gathered what was left of their things and joined the others in the larger cave. The fire had been put out, lanterns had been lit, and most were packed and ready to go. The armed Keepers and elders stood in the center; Gerda's quiet tones carried over Rozyl's hard voice and wild gesticulations. But all grew quiet once he and Jasminda arrived.

"Sit, sit," Turwig enjoined. "Have something to eat." He rooted around in the pouch at his side and passed them a sparing amount of jerky and dried berries.

"Thank you," Jack said, realizing his own hunger. How long had it been since he'd eaten? He must have lost the basket with their food in the avalanche. He would have even settled for Jasminda's bitter herb mash, but though the Lagrimari food was not tasty, it was far more filling than he'd expected.

Jack inhaled the simple breakfast. He looked up to find that Turwig carried another, smaller pouch, this one cradled in his palm like it was precious.

Jasminda, who'd been wrestling with a tough bit of jerky, froze. Her gaze narrowed on the old man's hand. Gerda appeared next to them, leaning in intently. She made Jack a bit uneasy; her gaze seemed to peer directly into the soul.

"Feel that, do you?" Gerda asked Jasminda. "I suspected you might."

"I don't trust her," Rozyl announced from the corner. "Who knows where her loyalties lie? I think this is a mistake."

"Hush," Gerda replied, still staring at Jasminda. Jack looked to her as well. She was obviously uncomfortable, though she'd been somewhat squirmy since they entered the caves. But now she visibly shook and leaned back as Turwig held the pouch out to her. With obvious reverence for the little bundle, he reached for Jasminda's hand and placed it in her grasp.

She gave a soft cry and jumped. "What is this?"

Jack was on alert, hovering over her, wanting to render aid. Gerda halted him with a hand on his arm.

"Open it," Turwig said.

Jasminda shook her head. Her hand trembled. "I can barely stand to hold it. What's in it?"

"Jasminda, get rid of it," Jack said, not liking her reaction. He went to grab it from her, but she shifted out of reach. Gerda's hand tightened on his arm, displaying impressive strength. He didn't want to hurt the old woman, but if that thing was dangerous, he needed to protect Jasminda. That is, if she would accept his aid. She seemed conflicted.

"Open it," Gerda repeated gently.

A hush fell upon the cave. Jack held his breath as Jasminda slowly pulled the tie on the pouch, revealing its contents.

Nestled in the folds of fabric was a deep red stone—the same color as the cornerstone, but small enough to fit in the palm of her hand. It was multifaceted, but smooth, like an oddly shaped gemstone.

Jasminda held it up to her face, inspecting it. Jack was entranced by the stone as well. A surge of longing shot through him. He wanted to touch it, feel its smoothness beneath his skin. But he could not move.

Lyngar brought one of the lamps closer to illuminate the stone better. Embedded within were dark, swirling lines. Was this the fossil of an insect like the ones he'd been intrigued with as a boy? But the curves of the shape trapped inside were no skeleton. Jack recognized the familiar symbol embedded beneath the surface.

"The sigil of the Queen," he whispered.

Jasminda raised her free hand until it hovered over the bloodred stone. She met Jack's eyes—hers sparked with anticipation and fear.

He wanted to tell her not to touch it, but the longing was so strong within himself that he couldn't speak the words. His breath caught in his chest when he tried to voice the warning.

Jasminda's finger traced the surface of the stone. Her eyes closed and long, dark lashes brushed her cheeks. Then, as if she'd instantly fallen asleep, her face slackened, and her whole body pitched backward to tumble to the ground.

We run through the woods laughing. Yllis's fingers are intertwined with mine, and when he looks over, the love in his eyes makes my breath catch. My heart is so full.

Eero is behind us, thundering through the underbrush. I do not have to turn to sense my brother tripping over a root that Yllis and I had jumped over. It would be funny to let him fall, but it is not his fault he has no Song and cannot feel the forest around him the way we do. In the blink of an eye, I sing a spell to lift him back upright and set him on his feet. He stumbles a bit but rights himself, his emotions confused for a moment, before refocusing on the competition.

We clear the tree line, and Eero races ahead, beating us to the water's edge. He dives underneath and swims out a little ways, shouting, berating us for our slowness. Yllis and I splash into the waves, soaking each other, and I think this is the happiest I have ever been. The two people I care most for in this world are here, and it is the most beautiful day I could have dreamed.

Yllis said he would not let it rain on Eero's and my birthday, and he did not. I shall bring the clouds back myself tomorrow to keep things in balance, but for today, watching the smiles on his and Eero's faces as the sun shines down on us is the best present ever.

Later, the fire crackles before us, and I lean back into the strong hold of Yllis's arms around me. Eero sits just across from us, roasting tubers on a stick. His melancholy calls to me and I yearn to soothe it, but long ago he made me promise not to sing away his moods. I endeavor to respect his wishes, though it is difficult to see my twin so sad.

"What ails, Eero?" I say to him.

He continues to stare into the fire, his eyes faraway. I disengage from Yllis and move around to sit beside him. "We celebrate our birth today. Why are you downhearted?"

I nudge his shoulder. His mouth quirks slightly in the beginnings of a smile.

"I do not aim to diminish any happiness of yours. I only wish . . ."

I remain patient as he forms his thoughts. Words are not always easy for him, but they eventually flow. I do not push.

"I wish I could sing, as you do. As Father did."

I reach out to him, placing my hand on his. "And I wish I shared Mother's talent at drawing the way you do. The pictures you create are unequaled. Everyone's talents lie in different directions."

"Yes, but to control the earth and the sky? It is magnificent." Wonder fills his voice. I feel ashamed for taking for granted the Song that swells within me, the feeling of oneness that I have with the life energy of the world.

"We are different," I say. *He looks pointedly at my hand, still on his arm, an example of the difference clearly displayed by the contrasting hues of our skin. Mine like our father and the other Songbearers with our dark hair and dark eyes, his the shade of Mother's and the other Silent, with eyes of vivid golden copper.* *"The blue of the day's sky and the black of the night's are different, but one is not better than the other. We need both. If I could give you part of my Song, I would, so you could feel what it is like. And perhaps you could give me some of your talent so that I could paint the murals that bring such delight to all who see them, and it will equal out."*

He pulls away from my touch and stands, offering me his roasted tuber before turning to look at the water. "We will never be equals, Oola." My name on his lips has never sounded so hopeless.

My twin walks toward the water, and I move back to Yllis's arms.

"He offered for the daughter of the Head Cantor," Yllis says as *I watch Eero's retreating form. "She turned him down for one of the Healers." A fissure forms in my heart.*

"I did not know. He tells me little of his love life. Once upon a time, we were close as heartbeats." I shift to face Yllis. "Do you think there is a way?"

He leans his forehead to mine, his Song dancing at the edge of my perception, offering solace and comfort. I do not reach for it, but I am glad it is there.

"A way for what?" he says.

"To share my Song with him?"

A thoughtful look crosses his face. His studies with the Cantors are progressing; he is learning much about new spells, new ways to funnel and control the massive energy of Earthsong. "If there is a way, we will find it. I promise."

His lips slide to mine; the kiss is not all-consuming, it is simply a reminder that he is here for me and that any problem I face, he faces, as well. My worries flee. I would do anything for my twin, and if it is a Song he desires, I will do all I can to give it to him.

Jasminda winced at the burning sensation in her palm. Her empty palm. When her vision focused, an anxious face filled her view. Fire-lit eyes regarded her, and a familiar scent filled her nostrils. Jack. His face relaxed as she stared up at him, hypnotized by the color of his eyes.

"What happened?" she asked, dazed.

He frowned. "I should ask you that. You collapsed."

Clarity came back quickly. The cave, the storm, the elders, the stone . . . which had disappeared from her hand. She looked over to find Turwig wrapping it up again. Jack helped her to a seated position as the chatter of several voices quieted.

"You saw something, didn't you?" Gerda asked.

Unlike the vision in the circle of stones, when she'd touched this stone she'd been drawn in to someone else's life. She'd actually *been* someone else. Someone deliriously in love. The girl, Oola, was an Earthsinger with skin the color of Jasminda's own, and she had been born a twin to Eero, a Silent—as Oola called him—who resembled an Elsiran, like Jasminda's brothers. This was a world where Singers and Silent wed and apparently lived in peace with their children, normal and accepted. There had been no feeling of isolation in Oola's thoughts, no sense of being always mistrusted or feared for her magic. On the contrary, her brother was jealous of her power.

The vision had been all-encompassing, and it took a moment to adjust to being torn away and inhabiting her own body again. Jasminda related the brief vision and watched the elders' reactions, everything from puzzled to stupefied.

She flexed her arms and legs, bringing feeling back into them. "What is that stone, and why does it cause visions?"

Turwig and Gerda shared one of their meaningful looks. The old man still held the wrapped stone. Jasminda's fingers itched to snatch it from him. She couldn't explain the strange possessive instinct that had arisen within her toward the thing, but she wanted it back.

After a few moments of silence, Rozyl spoke up. "She passed the test, you might as well tell her."

"Test?" Jasminda was not interested in any more tests. Anger fired within her. Jack grew rigid as well.

"Throughout the war," Turwig began, "the Keepers have fought against the True Father's tyranny, searching for a way to overcome his great power in order to awaken *Her*. We have always believed that killing the True Father was the only way to awaken the Queen. But the masked fiend is hard to kill."

"Almost impossible," Gerda said. "And there are those who believe he walks among us in secret, taking on the appearance of our trusted friends and confidantes."

Rozyl crossed her arms and sniffed. Could the woman's paranoia be justified? "It's true that no one has ever seen his face?" Jasminda asked.

"No one has seen any part of him," Turwig replied. "He is always covered from head to toe and wears a jeweled mask to hide his face. The women of his harems are kept blindfolded when they are with him. And aside from the Cantor, only the Songless are allowed in his inner circle."

"The Cantor?" Jasminda frowned. "Who is that?"

"Every few generations, a powerful Earthsinger is spared the tribute and serves as the True Father's Cantor, someone who studies Earthsong, finds new ways to create the breaches. They develop new spells and increase the True Father's power."

Jasminda had never known how the breaches were created. She doubted anyone on this side of the Mantle knew. "And what about those who give tribute? They must be able to get close to him."

Turwig's expression grew grim. "Tribute is given while unconscious. Only the Cantor and the True Father knows how it is done. But we have chipped away, little by little, doing what we could, saving who we could. We've grown a network to hide as many as we can, so they may retain their Songs." He looked to Osar and the other children who were busy on the other side of the cave, far out of earshot.

"Do you all still have your Songs?" Jasminda asked.

"We lost ours long ago," Gerda said, motioning to herself and the elders. "Aside from some of the young ones, only Rozyl and Sevora have their Songs."

Sevora was the other female Keeper. Jasminda hadn't heard the woman utter a word, but her dark eyes were engraved with sorrow. Jasminda shuddered to imagine life without her Song; it was a part of her, weak though it was. Rozyl caught her stare and turned her closely shorn head away from the scrutiny. But for once, there was no spite from the Keeper.

Jasminda faced the elders again. "You all helped the young man who disguised Jack?"

"Yes . . . Darvyn. The poor boy spent his entire life hiding from tribute-camp thugs, being shuffled from place to place. His power . . ." Turwig shook his head at some memory clouding his mind. "His power is blinding. Darvyn was the one who discovered this." He motioned to the stone. "Years ago, when he was a small boy, we were secreting him away one night—there had been some betrayal at his previous residence, as was often the case. The boy was hidden in a wagon of straw pallets, but when we arrived at the checkpoint, he had disappeared.

"We doubled back, searching for him, but it was the middle of the night and the roads in Lagrimar are not somewhere you want to be caught after dark. I tracked him to the ruins of Tanagol, one of the first border cities destroyed early in the war."

Turwig's eyes softened as he became lost in the memory. "Imagine a child of four or five digging through centuries-old rubble, only to come out covered in dirt and muck with this treasure. He had felt the pull of the ancient spell within calling to him. Later, Darvyn began having the Dream of the Queen. She gave him certain instructions that we have been endeavoring to bring to pass for many years."

"She told him to disguise me and send me over the border," Jack said.

Understanding dawned on Jasminda. "She told Darvyn that you all should bring the stone here?" Turwig and Gerda nodded. "And did She say what it was? What it does?" She held her hand out for the stone, and to her surprise, Turwig gave it to her.

"No, She does not have control over the length or frequency of the dreams," he said, "so sometimes information is disjointed. We believe this is a caldera, an object that serves as a container for spells."

"Like the map and the speaking stone," Jack said, leaning forward. "Are these objects common in Lagrimar?"

"Not at all," Turwig answered. "About a hundred years ago, a Keeper managed to get his hands on the journal of the Cantor. Everything we know about calderas comes from that book, and it's not much. They can serve various purposes—Earthsong isn't required to create them, though powerful Singers can use them to hold parts of their Songs. Creation requires . . ."

Jasminda looked up from her inspection of the bundle in her hand. Part of her longed to touch it again, but another part was afraid. "It requires what?"

"A blood sacrifice. And with the strongest ones, a death."

Jasminda froze. "Blood magic?" It didn't exist anymore, at least not according to Papa. But merely saying the words brought to mind the wrongness of these caves, the skin crawling feeling she'd gotten from both Jack's map and the speaking stone. This caldera was different than the other ones, potent certainly, but it didn't feel tainted. And it hadn't required any blood before sharing its vision with her.

"It's magic we've never seen before," Turwig said. "Stronger than any known today, saving the Cantor and the True Father."

"Did you all have the same vision I had then?" Jasminda asked.

"Oh, no, child," Gerda said. "Nothing at all happens when any of us touch the caldera."

Jasminda shuddered. "*No one* else has seen a vision when they touch it? Not even Darvyn?" The Keepers all shook their heads. "You've tried using your blood?"

"We've tried everything," Turwig said.

"So what made you think to test me with it?"

Gerda tilted her head to the side, regarding her. "Intuition."

Jasminda looked at her skeptically.

"And you wear the Queen's sigil around your neck," Lyngar said. "Maybe it was a sign." He didn't sound as though he was happy about that.

"But why does it work for me?" Jasminda's hand flew to her mother's pendant. It wasn't unique, all Sisters wore them.

Turwig shrugged. "Perhaps because you're half Elsiran. Perhaps some other reason. But since it opened itself to you, I believe you must be the one to unlock the mysteries of this stone. None of us are able."

Her failure with the cornerstone—to even pass the test to reveal the cornerstone—gnawed at her. The words of her family echoed in her head. Too weak. Too afraid. Jasminda shook her head in disbelief. "What were the Queen's instructions? What did She say specifically?"

"She is rarely specific," Gerda said. "Her guidance has led us this far, though it has taken twenty years to find a way to get the caldera safely into Elsira. We had to trust that once we made it here, a way would be shown." She leaned forward, her intensity piercing. "You are that way." She placed her hand on top of Jasminda's closed fist, and the caldera pulsed in response.

The trust these people were placing in her was staggering. And very much undeserved. "Who else knows about it?" Her voice was small.

The elders shared a glance, looks of resignation appearing on their faces. Rozyl sighed. "The Cantor knows, so we must assume she's told the True Father—"

"The Cantor is a woman?" Somehow Jasminda had assumed the powerful Earthsinger must be a man.

"Yes." Rozyl spat. "Her name is Ydaris, and she is menace personified."

Jasminda shared a look with Jack. His eyes lit. Could he be thinking what she was? Could this Ydaris be the mystery woman giving orders to Tensyn?

"Anyway, we believe the king is searching for the caldera. All along we had planned to use decoys to sneak it out." Rozyl waved her hand toward the women and children at the far end of the cave. "Word spread more quickly than we'd planned and many have heeded the call to leave Lagrimar."

"There are more refugees?" Jack asked.

"Yes, being led by groups of Keepers through known cracks in the Mantle. And more will follow them."

Jasminda's heart drummed, ready to beat out of her chest. "Can you stop them? Send word somehow?"

"Why?" Gerda asked. "Why should they not seek better lives for themselves?"

"Better lives like those in the settlements?" Jasminda scoffed. "There are no better lives for those who look like us here. Those who can sing. There will be no welcoming party for you. In fact, I would be surprised if they don't send you right back the way you came."

"They would not do that." Jack's voice was grim. "It is the Prince Regent's duty to protect all within the borders of Elsira. He is honor bound."

Jack had not suffered the stares and cutting remarks. The bad trades and cheating merchants. The insult "*grol* witch" uttered over and over.

Jasminda reached out for Gerda's gnarled hand. "I do not

think it will be a good place for the children. I do not think they will be safe there." From the corner of her eye, she saw Jack's jaw tighten, but he stayed quiet.

"You have never been to Lagrimar, have you, girl?" Gerda said.

Jasminda shook her head.

"Of course not, for you seem to believe they were safe back there." Her voice was kind but stern. Admonishing her ignorance. Jasminda looked again at the gaunt and hollow expressions of the mothers, the wordless appeals in the eyes of the children. They clung to each other like lifelines in a raging storm.

Rozyl's voice broke the silence. "Do you know what awaits these children? Slavery. For most it's either the mines, the labor camps, the harems, or the army." She ticked the list off with her fingers. "In the mines, at least you get to keep your Song. Though you exhaust it every day chipping away at bits of rock, pulling precious jewels from the mountain, and filling your lungs with dust. And after fifty years of service, you are released to die in poverty. The camps are for the boys to have their Songs sucked away, then be sentenced to hard labor for the rest of their lives. Girls go to the harems to 'bless' the Father with sons for his army."

"The suffering is immense," Gerda added.

Jasminda brought her hands to cover her face, not wanting these people to see her cry, especially not after what they had all been through. She'd had no idea how terrible Lagrimar actually was. Life in Elsira would not be easy, with little opportunity and even less dignity, but it was not slavery.

"More are coming," Rozyl said, "and the caldera is the last hope for all of us. If it falls into the True Father's hands, then all is lost. If he breaks out of Lagrimar, not only Elsira will fall but other lands will follow. The world could be his to control. We've got to end this."

Jack turned to face her. "She's right. This caldera is the best option for winning the war. You must have been chosen for a reason, Jasminda. Maybe everything that's happened was supposed to."

Jasminda snorted. If Jack's suffering, the soldiers invading her cabin, the fire—if all of those things were the Queen's plan and if Jasminda was truly chosen, then the Queen had quite the sense of humor.

The weight of the expectant eyes peering at her sealed her mouth shut, silencing the doubts she longed to raise. She'd started this journey with one impossible goal, to help Jack so that he would help her get to Rosira to save her land. Now an even more unattainable task was being set before her.

"So what do I do?"

Uncertainty crossed more than one face. "We'd planned to bring the caldera to Rosira, to be near the Queen's resting place in the palace," Turwig said. "After that, simply rely on Her guidance." The old Keeper smiled at Jasminda. "For now, follow the visions. Learn what the caldera wants to show you. It must lead to a way to awaken Her."

Anxiety lay heavy on her shoulders. Perhaps the Queen would lead them to another, someone truly able to solve the mystery of awakening Her. For now, Jasminda had little choice but to accept the duty and pray the person they really needed would reveal themselves.

Jack squeezed her arm, lending her strength. She would need all of it to face disappointing those who'd placed their faith in her.

CHAPTER THIRTEEN

Eagle and Shark were once as close as petals closed for eve-
ning. Not even a strong wind could tear them apart. But
harmony both wilts and thrives via the same forces. Sunshine
and rain can sustain or doom, depending on the intensity.

—COLLECTED FOLKTALES

The Sora temple loomed overhead, glistering in the sun.
Though Benn had been raised as a devout follower of the
Queen, his family had never had much time for temples. He
shivered entering through the wide double doors. As always,
the cold interior made him wonder how anyone could sleep
here. He would have loved to receive the Dream of the Queen,
but at home in his own bed, not sleeping head to foot with
hundreds of others.

He was here on official business, and yet his head remained

on a swivel, looking at every passing form, longing for a glimpse of his Ella. He hadn't heard from her since her arrival in Sora. Whatever Kess's emergency was, he hoped it would not keep him from his wife for long.

"Lt. Ravel." Sister Amelynne's dimpled face greeted him from an alcove at the side of the sanctuary. She'd always put him in mind of a grandmother. Not his grandmother, who was hard as nails and had worked alongside her husband on the docks, but someone else's grandmother. "It's a pleasure to see you again."

"And you as well, Priestess."

She led him down a short hallway and into her office. Unlike her predecessor, whose tastes had been showier, Sister Amelynne's office was sparse and austere—still comfortable, but there were no gilded mirrors or heavy tapestries on display. Just white walls and simple, comfortable furniture.

Work first, he reminded himself, even as his thoughts strayed to Ella. He'd been out dealing with the influx of refugees the entire day before, trying to coordinate with the Council in Rosira on what to do with them—where to house and how to feed them. The Council had pointed him toward the Sisterhood, not understanding how, or maybe not caring, to do more than pawn them off as charity recipients. Since he was a lowly Staff Lieutenant, he couldn't push back. General Verados, unlike the High Commander, was not inclined to do much of anything, hence the reason for Benn's visit.

"How many have crossed so far?" Amelynne asked, worry creasing her forehead.

"We have scouts searching up and down the border. At last count, we'd found close to forty refugees, but more are coming all the time and some are hiding in the foothills. I'm afraid not all of our soldiers and countrymen have been welcoming."

Amelynne's frown deepened. "Yes, I heard a tale of some farmers to the south tying up a pair of small boys they found on their property."

Benn shook his head. "We've retrieved them and reunited them with their mother. It'll be rough going. Only the settlers speak the language, though many of them have been helpful in translating. Is there a plan, Priestess?"

"I'm in contact with the other priestesses, we're combining our resources. We are creating a camp where we can take care of them all in one place." She leaned forward. "We've been working to squash rumors left and right. Can you tell me how this is happening? Is the Mantle . . ." She trailed off as if afraid to finish the sentence.

"I wish I knew." Benn sighed. "All the refugees have said is that there are cracks in the Mantle. None are privy to the True Father's plans or to what this might mean. But we all need to be on alert."

"I fear what this means for our country. Another war, so soon after the last one?" She pursed her lips and looked off to the side.

"We should expect many more refugees," Benn said.

"How many?"

"Impossible to know. The flow is steady and seems to be increasing."

She nodded, and gathered some papers on her desk. They spent the next few minutes coordinating the plans for the refugee camp and detailing what army resources Benn thought he could wrangle on his own without having to rely on his higher-ups.

Finally, his business was completed, leaving his body feeling like it was lit at the end of a live wire.

"Thank you, Lieutenant. I can't tell you how wonderful it is to have you working on this."

"It's my pleasure. On a more personal matter, I believe my wife is here. Ella Farmafield?"

Sister Amelynne's warm gaze cooled quickly. She dropped her eyes to her desk. "I'm sorry. I didn't realize she was related to you."

Benn swallowed, unnerved by her sudden change in demeanor.

"She left yesterday on the cross-country bus. I'm sure she's back in Rosira by now."

His mouth hung open. Shock and disappointment sliced at his chest. It took a moment to regain his voice. "And her sister, Kess?"

Amelynne's eyes filled with tears. "Sister Kess has passed to the World After, I'm afraid. I am so sorry, I wish I'd known she was . . . They were . . ." She shook her head.

"W-what happened?"

The priestess began fidgeting with the few items on her desk. "I'm . . . not at liberty to say. I'm afraid it's Sisterhood business."

Her evasion put him on alert. "I have a hard time believing that my wife would cross the country and then leave again without even contacting me. I'm stationed less than a half hour away. And so soon after losing her sister? Can you explain why she left so quickly?"

Amelynne continued to stare at the papers on her desk. "I'm afraid I can't. All I know is that she left."

Benn's finger tapped rapidly on the chair's arm. "What aren't you telling me?"

Finally she met his gaze. Hers was unsteady but resolved. "I've told you all I can. I'm sorry your wife was disturbed in the first place. There will be reprimands regarding that." She shivered. He got the feeling that the one being reprimanded was her. But by whom? Amelynne was the priestess of this temple. The only one with more authority than her was the High Priestess back in Rosira.

"I'm afraid this comes from on high, as it were," she said, confirming his thoughts.

His jaw tensed, bringing with it a tension headache. Something was very wrong here, but Amelynne's jittering hands and rabbit-in-the-sights expression made it clear that he'd get no further answers from her.

"Yes, I understand. Orders."

She visibly deflated. "Quite so," she said, hurriedly. "Quite so. And now I must continue our preparations. I thank you for your assistance with all of this. I will keep in close contact as plans progress."

They stood and she showed him to the door. He walked out of the temple, head still full of questions and self-recrimination for having missed Ella. His fists tightened and he struggled to control his anger, which burned bright with nowhere to go. What wasn't Amelynne saying? Why hadn't Ella contacted him? He couldn't blame the poor refugees for interrupting his plans to see her. They were escaping unknown horrors in Lagrimar. Verados was partially at fault—if the general were at all competent, Benn wouldn't have to run everything.

He stopped outside, just at the gate to the temple's garden, looking without seeing the lush greenery. The strong floral perfume focused him. Perhaps he could arrange to have flowers sent to Ella as an apology. She must be as angry with him as he was with himself. He could contact a florist in Portside and have them delivered. His resolve now strengthened, he spun around swiftly and bumped into a woman carrying a pair of trimming shears coming out of the garden gate.

"Excuse me."

"Never worry, Lieutenant," she responded in a broad Borderlander accent.

He smiled in recognition. "Mistress Lalli, how does your garden grow?"

"Same as yesterday, I reckon." The woman grinned, uncharacteristically. Benn tipped an imaginary hat. He'd known Lalli since he was first deployed to the Eastern Base as a teen. At the time, she'd been employed there as a cleaner. Her curt manner and prickly disposition reminded him of his mother and made him think of home.

"Maybe you can help me. What flowers do you recommend to say 'I'm sorry'?"

She raised an eyebrow. "Done wrong, have you?"

Guilt sank talons into his heart. "My wife traveled all the way out here and I missed her. Now she's gone again."

"Chatty woman, strange eyes?"

Benn grinned. "Yes, they're the color of chocolate. You saw her?"

Lalli tilted her head. "I reckon she may be in for a mite of trouble."

"What?" All the warmth fled from his body. "What do you mean?"

"She caught the attention of those it's best not to. Stepped into something she's not quite ready for." Lalli moved toward the bushes bordering the garden fence.

"Who? What is it?"

But a trio of Sisters exited the main doors and headed down the steps toward them. Lalli made her way to her knees and began to trim the lower branches of the fat bush. Benn turned her words over in his mind. Foot traffic had picked up outside the temple and it was fairly clear she wouldn't say more.

Still dazed, he turned to go.

"Floralily. That's the flower to send. To apologize for being a dunderhead."

"Floralily," he repeated. "Right."

"Nice of you to turn up today." Doreen's snide voice greeted Ella as she entered the salon. It was midmorning and Ella was late. She set her bag down at her station then slumped into her chair.

"You look terrible."

"Thank you, Doreen. How very helpful of you." Ella reflexively looked into the mirror, unsurprised at the deep circles under her eyes and washed out complexion. Doreen hadn't been wrong. But that's what happened when you went without sleep for two nights in a row.

After her meeting with Syllene, Ella had returned home, her mind tangled with grief and confusion. She'd lain awake replaying everything that happened. The sunlight pouring through the windows in the tiny apartment had been jarring. She might have caught a wink or two, but nothing restful.

So she'd dragged herself to work—missing a day and a half was a serious hit to her income. The booth rental fee had to be paid regardless of how many hours she'd worked. And while Benn's paycheck covered the necessities—rent, food, and heat—a large chunk of it went to the ongoing fees to keep her place in the queue for citizenship. Miss a payment and you were shucked back to the end of the line. She sighed and lay her head back in the cushioned chair.

"What's bothering you, Miss Ella?" a soft voice asked. She looked up to find Rona, one of the wash girls, hovering over her. She was a twiggy creature of about thirteen with mouse-brown hair and eyes. Yalyish as well, with a faint accent.

"I had a long trip with a sad outcome, that's all." She didn't want to burden anyone in the shop with news of her sister's death. She wasn't really close enough with any of them to discuss personal matters. Other than Doreen, the women were mostly friendly. But she was always conscious of being the newest girl and the only foreign hairdresser. And she couldn't share this trouble she'd fallen into with the Sisterhood.

"While you were gone, I used your hot iron," Rona whispered, bashful. She shook her shoulder-length locks, gently curled at the ends. "I want to be a hairdresser, too."

Doreen snorted. The woman must have bat ears to have heard the girl's soft voice.

"Very nice work," Ella said. "Have you talked with Mistress Soreel about studying with her? She trained most of the girls here."

"Train is a strong word," Doreen muttered. They both ignored her.

Rona dimmed. "She says I have to wait until I'm fifteen."

"I know that feels far away, but it isn't."

Hopeful eyes looked up at her from beneath a thick fringe of lashes. "How did you learn?"

"I went to school in Fremia—boarding school at first and then university. I studied a lot of things."

"Like what?"

"Oh, animal husbandry, architecture, printmaking, electrics, welding." She ticked them off on her fingers. "I took most of the coursework to be certified as a pastry chef, but not the final project. When I first moved to Elsira, I was a cobbler's apprentice. I thought the job was for helping to bake cobblers, not mend shoes." Rona giggled, as Ella had intended.

"Have you had a lot of jobs?"

Ella nodded gravely. "Quite a few."

"Why?"

"Because I'm trying to find out what I really want to do with my life."

"Do you think it's hairdressing?"

Ella smiled. She had thought so. Then again, she'd thought the same thing when she'd driven a taxi and sold hats and run a lithography machine. Perhaps she wouldn't ever find it. She'd imagined herself with a child or two by now, kept busy by the demands of motherhood. But that hadn't been St. Siruna's plan.

Almost unconsciously, she fished the little figurine out of her pocket. "I think that life is long and you don't need to be in an any rush to find out."

Had Kess been happy with her path? If she'd lived, would she have raised her child in the Sisterhood or left, perhaps to be with the father? She wished she knew why Kess had shut her out for so long and then called for her help just at the end.

"What's that, miss?" Rona asked. "St. Maasael's symbol?"

He was the champion of horses, travelers, and sailors. His symbol was a pair of crossed oars, but usually paired with a starfish or horseshoe.

Ella placed the figurine on the counter in front of her. "Are you from Maasaelea originally?"

"Yes. St. Maasael brought my parents and I to Elsira safely." She made the sign of the saints over her heart and kissed her fingers.

"I've never seen his symbol with a boat included, have you?"

The girl leaned closer. "No. I suppose you're right. And the oars aren't crossed quite right."

Doreen wandered over, twirling a brush on the end of her finger. "I've seen that. My brother's got one of those on a little wooden medallion. Wears it round his neck like some kind of badge of honor." She shuddered. "Whole lot of foolishness, I think it is. You're not caught up with that lot, are you?"

"No, I-I just found this. I thought it was interesting. What is it?" Ella asked.

"I don't know. But I don't hold with those new friends of his. He was a good boy, a fisherman like our father. Upstanding Elsiran, temple once a month like he should. Now he's gathering with these new lads in some sort of club by the pier, spouting nonsense about how the Queen shouldn't run our lives. Giving my mother the apoplexy, you know?"

"That's—that's a real shame," Ella said. "I'm sorry to hear it."

Doreen shrugged. "Dad thinks it's a phase. But when they start getting tokens and hanging on to them like they're precious jewels and not just a bit of wood . . ." She shook her head. "Might be something to worry about, I think." Her gaze looked a bit haunted.

"What's the group called?"

"Dominants or Dominations or some such."

Rona sucked in a breath. "Dominionists?"

"Yes, that's it." The front door swung open and one of Doreen's regulars entered. Doreen moved back to her chair to deal with her client.

Rona tugged at Ella's sleeve, pulling her further away. "You've heard of them, right?"

Ella shook her head. "Not really. I've heard the name, but I'm not really sure what they're about."

"They're mostly in the larger commonwealths in Yaly: Melbain and Gilmeria. Our sermoneer likened them to a plague. They don't believe in the saints or any sort of divinity. They like to hold protests on the holy days."

"Protesting what?"

She shrugged. "Anything beyond what they can make with their own two hands. There was a brawl in Gilmeria last year at winter solstice." She looked back at the little carving suspiciously. "Best throw that away. You don't want anything to do with those people, miss."

"Rona!" Doreen barked, making the girl jump. "I need a wash."

Rona scurried away to get back to work.

What was Kess doing with the symbol of some group of Yalyish hooligans hidden in her mattress? What did it mean?

Ella stood, languidly straightening her bottles and sprays. Next to her, Doreen was inspecting her curlers and sticking them into the heating unit.

"So, these meetings—the ones the Dominionists have. Where are they again?"

Doreen narrowed her eyes. "Why do you want to know?"

Ella sighed and dropped her head. "Been slow the past few weeks, hasn't it?"

"A bit."

"How many appointments do you have today?"

"Just three." Doreen frowned. "Why?"

"I'll give you two of my walk-ins if you tell me where those meetings are." Ella had no regulars yet, so she got first shot at the walk-ins.

Doreen snapped to attention, suspicion replaced, no doubt, by the thought of the extra money. "All right," she said slowly. "Billiard hall, pier seventeen. Sometime after second dock shift ends."

"Thank you," Ella said smiling tightly.

She'd definitely be dipping into her savings this month.

CHAPTER FOURTEEN

The Mistress of Horses never met a field she could not coax to grow just a little brighter. Her voice can still be heard in the whisper of the leaves that shoot from the ground.

—COLLECTED FOLKTALES

"Are you going to try again?" Jack's voice hummed in Jasminda's ear.

The others completed their preparations to leave the caves, but Jack's gaze never left her. She felt it like a physical touch. "I should, shouldn't I?"

"But you don't want to? What's stopping you?"

She opened her mouth to admit to him her failures—if she could not save those closest to her, how could she do something so big? Thankfully, Rozyl's raised voice kept her from answering.

"We have little choice. It makes no sense to travel down a tunnel we can't feel or see the ending of."

Jack rose and moved to where Rozyl and the elders stood. Jasminda followed. "What's the problem?" he asked.

To Jasminda's surprise, Rozyl answered. "We can't connect to Earthsong in the caves. Somehow, the mountain is blocking us. Without singing, we'll never find our way through this maze of tunnels."

"Has the storm not stopped?" Jack asked.

Rozyl was grim. "It's getting worse."

"Worse?" Jasminda cried out. "No storm has ever lasted this long."

"Not a normal storm, is it?" Lyngar raised an eyebrow.

Dread snaked its way across Jasminda's skin. "So what do we do?"

"I bloody well don't know," Rozyl said, exasperated. "What *can* we do? Wait until we can cross above the mountain."

"That storm won't die a natural death, I promise you that," Lyngar said ominously.

"What happens when you try to sing?" Jasminda asked. For the first time, she realized that her Song, which should have been fully restored by now, was not at full capacity. It had been hours since she'd used the last of her power on the cornerstone. Had the caldera sapped her?

Turwig spoke up. "The children say their Song calls out but nothing's there to answer it. Like the world has disappeared. Try it yourself if you like, child."

Jasminda drew in a shaky breath, then closed her eyes. Part of her was afraid to try—the foreboding she'd felt when first entering the cave had not dimmed. That sense that her magic had no place here was as strong as ever, but curiosity won out over the fear.

With a deep breath, she reached out to Earthsong. The first moments of opening herself to that infinite sea of life energy felt like drowning. Flowing through her was just a small trickle of the combined life force of every living thing. It was overwhelming. The energy made her sensitive to the raging emotions around her, fear and longing, anger and hope. The normally strong pull of the power was nearly overwhelming; the tide tried to pull her under, harder than ever before. "I feel untethered. I can barely hold on."

"But you can draw upon Earthsong?" Rozyl asked.

Jasminda nodded, eyes still closed. She was connected to every living thing, but also more. Nature itself thrummed with life energy. Somehow Earthsong intertwined with all natural forces: earth, air, water, and fire. Plants and animals, the weather, the soul of the world. The chorus of all beings comprised the infinite energy that filled her, allowing her to channel and manipulate it.

Her attention was on her awareness of the cave, the tunnels beyond, and the mountain surrounding them. Ghosts of the ancient inhabitants brushed the edge of her senses—but how could that be? Their energy was long dead. She thought briefly of the legends of the Cavefolk, the race of people who had lived within these mountains generations ago and then disappeared. There was a kind of primeval power here, locked in the fabric of the rock, but it thrummed with a different pattern than Earthsong.

Still, a thread of life wove through this place. Crawling things and creatures too small to see, and moss-like vegetation that needed no light. She pulled the energy inside her; it formed a path, though faint, that led through to the other side of the mountain.

She let the power slide away and opened her eyes, taking a shaky breath.

"What does it mean, they can't connect to Earthsong?" Jack asked.

Jasminda thought back to how Papa had explained the power to her. "Imagine a spark inside every living thing in the world—people, trees, birds, insects. We all have a life force, an energy that keeps us alive. The combined force of all that energy is Earthsong. When a Singer connects, it's like opening a tap and pouring some of that into us so we can use it. Different Singers have different capacities, some Songs are large and some are small, just like cups full of water. The caves have shut off the tap for the rest of them."

"But not you?"

She shook her head. "I can sense the route, but it's long. I'm not sure I'll be able to stay connected and sing for the whole journey. Using the caldera sapped my Song." She looked down. "My cup is small."

"Why in pip's name must it always be her?" Rozyl grumbled. "She's not even full Lagrimari."

Jack's breathing turned heavy as he glared. His reaction lit a spark of satisfaction within Jasminda.

"Perhaps she can link with someone," Turwig suggested.

Rozyl gave him a look that could shear the shell off a beetle. "Why can she sing and no one else? Why does the caldera respond to her only? Her magic must be different. I'm not linking with her." Jasminda flinched internally at the bite in the woman's voice, though she had no desire to link with Rozyl, either.

"What is linking?" Jack asked, looking from Rozyl to Jasminda.

Gerda patiently began to explain. "It's when two Earthsingers share their connection. They—"

"It's when one Singer gives control of their entire Song to another to do with as they please," Rozyl interjected. "And *that* is not going to happen."

"It's a sharing of power," Gerda continued, "but only one Singer can be in control. It must be done voluntarily, of the giver's free will. If we still had our Songs, we would do it."

"Speak for yourself," Lyngar hissed. Jasminda had linked with Papa when she was young and still learning. He'd shown her how to control her power through the link, but she could not imagine linking with a stranger. To do so was to become extremely vulnerable to another. It was like letting someone into her soul.

The elders and Rozyl bickered over what to do. Neither Rozyl nor Sevora would link with Jasminda.

A small hand slipped into her own. Osar's round face beamed up at her. She squeezed his hand, and he leaned in, resting his head against her leg.

"You would link with me, wouldn't you?" she asked, smoothing down his hair. "You're not afraid?" He shook his head, then offered her his other hand, which was closed in a fist.

"What do you have there?"

He unfurled tiny fingers to reveal a shoot of green with delicate white petals sparking out of it.

"Where did you get this?" she asked, incredulous, picking up the tiny flower. It could not have grown in the cave, and with the snow outside it was doubtful he'd brought it in with him. Yet here it was. Something beautiful and impossible amid the bleakness. "Thank you."

Silence descended. Jasminda looked up to find the others staring at her and the blossom in her hand. She straightened her shoulders, looking at Rozyl and Lyngar as she spoke. "Osar will link with me."

Rozyl narrowed her eyes. Lyngar merely turned toward the exit, speaking over his shoulder. "Fine. Let's get going. We've wasted far too much time as it is."

Ella pushed her way through the crowded Portside streets, the smooth wooden carving warm in her palm. The noise and signs of life that she usually adored grated on her today. Fishermen pushing carts overflowing with reeking fish, horses drawing wagons leaving their droppings in the street, exhaust from trucks clogging the air. She passed one of the gates dividing Portside from the rest of the city and sneered.

The billiard hall Doreen had directed her to was a clean establishment. Not as run-down as most businesses in the neighborhood. It was Elsiran-run with a mostly Elsiran clientele, from what she could see through the front window. One of those places in Portside that liked to pretend they were on the other side of the gate, and turned up their noses at foreigners.

Ella hadn't wanted to use permanent dye on her hair, so her natural color was already starting to show through; she hoped that wouldn't turn into a problem here. Inside, billiard tables stood in neat rows, wood shined to a polish. There were only a smattering of people playing, mostly retirees.

She stood in the entry, apparently looking confused. "You lost?" the gnarled man behind the bar asked.

"No, I just . . ." She looked around again, wondering if she was in the right place.

"Meeting's through there." He motioned to the curtain leading to a back room. She thanked him and headed in the direction he'd indicated.

If this truly was a Dominionist meeting, and the group had its roots in Yaly, why did she feel such a strong sense of foreboding about this? She could only hope that she wasn't really walking into some sort of anti-foreigner gathering. Just in case, she reached into her bag and palmed the leather-wrapped handle of her shael. The short, weighted club was used for close-combat by the Summ-Yalyish, her grandfather's ethnic group. This had been his, taken from home before she'd been sent off kicking and screaming to boarding school. Living in Rosira, she'd had to brandish it more than once, but so far had never used the weapon.

Cautiously, she stepped through the curtain.

The small dining room was full of Elsiran men sitting at square tables. Only a few women were among their number. Ella lingered near the doorway, hoping to remain inconspicuous. Everyone's attention was on the rather nondescript fellow standing before the hall's front windows. He wasn't especially short or tall. His face wasn't one you'd remember after looking away. A closely shorn head showed more scalp than hair, and yet, the room hung on his every word.

"The common man is bending under the weight of these so-called mystics. The fishmonger, the builder, the mechanic, the boatswain—we worship every day at the altar of our sweat. It's our blood and hard work that have built this land. We can't dream our lives away, waiting on some sleeping woman to whisper riddles in our ears. Who would feed our families if we napped all day long?"

Laughter peppered the small audience. "Would the Followers of the Queen, the Sisters and their ilk pay our rents and buy our heating oil? Would they?"

"No!" The response was vociferous.

"Who labors and toils for the crusts of bread we earn?"

"We do!"

"So what do they give us then? Pretty stories. Ancient platitudes. But *The Book of Dominion* gives us more." The man held up a small, leather-bound book. "Wisdom that's useful. A book for hardworking men with no time to chase mist or bow and scrape to invisible leaders."

"But Zann," a man called out from near the front. "My grandmother had the Dream of the Queen. She said it changed her life forever."

The apparent leader, Zann, nodded. "It may well have. But who have you known since then that's had this dream? If only a chosen few can benefit from it, what's the use? To my mind, that makes the Queen no better than any of the other aristocrats who live on high, looking down their noses at us."

The questioner sat back, apparently satisfied.

Zann held up the book again. "I don't want to take up too much of your time. I know you have jobs and lives to return to. Just think about what I've said. Think about what *The Book of Dominion* has to offer. And let me know if you'd like a copy. Free of charge. All men deserve comforting, not just a chosen few."

Chairs scraped against the scarred floor as the audience began to rise. Some headed for the door, forcing Ella to push in further toward the corner. A substantial number approached the speaker, taking him up on his offer of the free book.

Ella studied the crowd of about two dozen. They all seemed to be working men, unsurprising here in Portside. One of the few women, sturdy-limbed with bright copper hair, looked over at her curiously, but otherwise no one paid her any undue notice.

Ella joined the group at the front, thinking at least she would get one of the books and see if the boat and oars symbol appeared within. Waiting for her turn, she noticed the copper-haired woman had hung back to tidy the room.

"A new face." Ella turned forward to find Zann addressing her. "What did you think of the talk, Mistress . . ."

"Ravel," she said, relying on her husband's working class Elsiran name to grease her way. "Ella Ravel."

"Zann Biddel," he said, holding out his hands politely.

She met him palm to palm. "I found much of what you said fascinating, Master Biddel. I've long thought the Sisterhood overreached their bounds in terms of influence."

Zann nodded, eyes alight. "Indeed. We must master our own destinies. I'm sure those women mean well, but I've always found wakefulness more profitable than dreaming." He chuckled. Unremarkable appearance aside, Zann Biddel was a charismatic speaker who knew how to capture the attention of his audience. He focused on Ella with a gentle intensity that made her feel seen and heard. It would be easy to be swayed by him.

She was conscious that only a few people lingered in the room—the woman still straightening tables and chairs, along with two other stragglers in conversation by the doorway. Putting off her query made no sense.

"How did you find out about our little gathering, I wonder?" Biddel asked, giving her the opening she needed.

"My sister gave me this," she said pulling the carving out of her pocket. "It's your symbol isn't it?"

He blinked, looking at the figure in her hands. Was it her imagination or had he paled just a fraction? "Yes, yes it is. The oars represent steering toward your path and the boat is the vessel that brings you to truth." He stared a bit longer. "You say your sister *gave* that to you?"

"Left it for me, is more accurate. Her name was Kess."

His gazed jumped to meet hers. "Was?"

"Sadly she passed away a few days ago."

His eyes widened. "Did she? I'm—I'm sorry to hear it." His eyes lost focus for a moment. "May she find serenity in the World After," he whispered.

"I thank you. Did you know her? Do you happen to know who might have given this to her?"

With a little shake, he seemed to gather his wits. "We get many newcomers drawn to our gatherings. Sadly, I don't have the chance to greet them all."

A clever evasion. Ella closed her fist over the figurine, breaking his eye contact with it. "Do all newcomers receive these, then? It's so beautifully made. It seems . . . special."

Biddel took a step back. "They're common enough. Those who accept the path of dominion and self-determination receive them."

"And you are the only one in Portside showing people that path, is that right? I'd heard your group began in Yaly."

All the color had drained from his face. He looked around

as if trying to find an escape from this conversation. "Dominionism is spreading quickly. The truth tends to. I was lucky to find it and felt called to help my brothers and sisters along."

Ella bit her lip. "I see." His reaction was so odd, she could feel the stares of the others on her. It was obvious that Biddel had known Kess, though why was he unwilling to admit it?

"I don't want to take up any more of your time. I had hoped to find some answers to one day pass them on to Kess's child, you see."

"Her . . . child?"

"My sister died in childbirth."

He visibly shuddered.

Ella tilted her head. "Are you sure you don't recall a pregnant woman attending one of your meetings?"

He stared off into space as if very shocked indeed. "People come and go. Perhaps she stopped attending before it became visible that she was pregnant."

"Perhaps. She and I weren't very close. I'm only learning about her life now, after she's gone. It's a shame really."

"Yes, quite a shame." He pulled himself together, cleared his throat, and looked around again. "I hope you find the answers you seek. You are welcome to come back at any time, Mistress Ravel."

He nodded and then turned away to hustle out of the room.

CHAPTER FIFTEEN

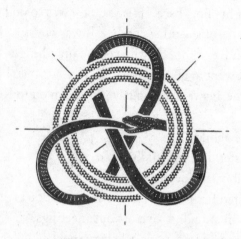

What of peace? Asked a soldier to the Mistress of Serpents.
A warrior who fights for peace is like a man leaving the
shore to climb a hill so he may better view the ocean.

—COLLECTED FOLKTALES

Jack kept to the rear of the party as they made their way
through the tunnels. He did not like to be so far from Jasminda, who led the group with Osar at her side, but he also
did not want Rozyl or the other armed Keepers at his back.
They seemed to feel the same about him, which left him walking side by side with Sevora, the tall Lagrimari woman who
never said a word to him.

On the whole, the refugees were not a talkative bunch. The
only sounds were footsteps that echoed against the oddly
smooth cave walls and the soft babbling of the youngest

children. The group did not dawdle, either, deftly navigating the twisting path, which edged steeply downward, leveled off, then dipped low again.

They took no breaks, and not even the smaller children walking on their own complained. Nor did the elders, who were remarkably spry for their ages. Hours passed like this, the silence companionable but complete.

Slowly, the air began to change. A thick humidity replaced the cool, earthy scent of the mountain. They extinguished their lanterns when light glowed softly up ahead. Over the thump of their footsteps, water trickled, insects whirred, birds called.

Home.

The tunnel ended abruptly, leaving them at the edge of a huge cavern, much like the one they'd entered on the other side with some key differences. This cave was filled with trees and vines and greenery. Rain poured down through openings in the rock far overhead. A narrow and somewhat hidden path led down to the forest floor. Just beyond it, a stream of water flowed gently down, vanishing below. The view stole Jack's breath.

The group formed a queue as the path was only wide enough for one. Jasminda disappeared from sight first. Not being able to see her made his palms itch. He was returning to civilization and, with it, all his duties and responsibilities. Not the least of which was Jasminda.

She had stolen into his life—his very complicated life— and he was in no hurry for her to leave. But the war on the horizon would make everything immeasurably harder. Anti-Lagrimari sentiments would kick into effect once again, and her Elsiran blood would not protect her from the ire of the people who saw only her skin. He could tell from the way she spoke, the haunted look in her eye when the refugees discussed Elsira, that it never had.

The path ended in a wide cave mouth overlooking the Elsiran Borderlands. A steady rain fell from the overcast sky. Jack had little sense of the time of day but was very glad to be once again on Elsiran soil.

Still in the shadow of the mountain, the group wound their way through a thick copse of trees; Jack struggled to get his bearings. How far had their trip through the mountain taken them? How close was his army base?

A gathering of flimsy structures became visible a few thousand paces ahead. This was a place he recognized; the community was called Baalingrove, one of the settlements of former Lagrimari prisoners of war. It was here he had first met Darvyn years ago.

As always, Jack was struck by the living conditions of the settlers: makeshift wooden shacks with leaky tin roofs, tiny patches of garden, no running water, no electricity—though the last wasn't uncommon in the Borderlands. The men gardened and hunted in the foothills, but survived in large part due to the kindness of the Sisterhood, who provided food and supplies. Neither the Prince Regent nor the Council saw fit to do any more, and the Elsirans preferred to pretend the settlers didn't exist.

The refugees walked through what amounted to the main road of the settlement, an unpaved path that was slowly becoming a river of mud in the insistent precipitation.

Unease prickled his spine. No one emerged from any of the shacks to peer at the group of newcomers. So far they hadn't seen a single soul in a place that housed nearly one hundred men.

Jack approached Gerda and pulled her to the side. "Why don't you and the civilians stay here? I think something may be wrong."

"We go together." Gerda's response was maddening.

"There might be danger." Jack's plea fell on deaf ears.

Turwig patted his arm. "There is danger everywhere, son. Who's to say it won't find us here, as well?"

Jack muttered under his breath and moved to the front, but stopped when angry voices rent the air, shouting in Elsiran. He couldn't make out the words through the clatter of rain on metal but recognized the heavy Borderlander accent. Gunshots rang out.

"For Sovereign's sake, get the children back!" he shouted.

He shared a frenzied glance with Rozyl, who pursed her lips and made a hand signal to her crew. One of the men peeled off and helped direct the mothers and children to squat behind the nearest shacks.

Jack and the four armed Keepers remained on the main path, along with Jasminda and the elders.

"Go with them," he told Jasminda. She merely rolled her eyes and cocked her pistol.

The voices came from the edge of the settlement. As they approached, gunfire continued to pop, and the shouting grew louder. Movement flickered in the corner of his eye; a Lagrimari woman sat huddled with two children behind another shack under the limited protection of the roof's overhang. She had not been part of his group. Her eyes widened when she saw him, confusion crossing her features as she took in his companions.

Rozyl rushed over to speak with her. "What happened here?"

"There was some trouble in the town, I think. A girl went missing. Seems her father got it in his head that one of the settlers took her, and a mob of farmers came here to search." The woman's eyes kept darting to Jack. He took a few steps back, aware that, to her, he must look like one of the men in the mob.

"Are you injured?" Rozyl's voice was softer and kinder than he'd heard it before.

"No, but my boy's up there. He wanted to fight with the men. I can't leave him." She pointed toward where the noise of battle was audible.

"Not even for the safety of these little ones?" Jasminda said. The solemn, dripping faces of two boys, each under five, stared up at them.

"We made it out together. I won't lose one of them now."

Jack's heart stung for the woman. "Are you a refugee?" he asked. She shrank back at his voice, her face twisted in fear. Her gaze, full of questions, shot to Rozyl.

"He's"—Rozyl looked back at Jack and shrugged—"with us."

The mother's expression was still rigid with suspicion. "We crossed with ten others two days ago, but I don't know what became of them once the fighting started."

Jack broke away to investigate, only dimly aware of the others trailing behind him. A turn in the road revealed a makeshift barricade made from an overturned wagon. It offered only meager protection but blocked the mouth of the narrow, dirt road.

A half-dozen Lagrimari crouched in the sodden muck behind the barrier. Around twenty more were gathered nearby, seeking cover behind the dilapidated structures on the edge of the settlement. Several were armed with hunting rifles, the others with pitchforks, machetes, and one man even held a sword. A boy of about twelve was among their number. He must have been the woman's son.

In the road and scattered among the living, were the bodies of more settlers. Some had been shot where they stood but many had wounds in their backs. They'd been cut down while trying to flee the violence.

The insistent rain created a river of blood that streamed down the road. The carnage here was senseless; Jack vibrated with anger.

On the other side of the overturned wagon, a small band of Elsiran farmers, only a dozen strong, clustered together at the base of a tree. They were all armed, but most clutched their rifles like bats, striking at the icicles and dirt clods being flung at them. Every so often, one would get a shot off in the direction of the settlers.

The way the boy knelt among the older men, looking slightly off to the side, his body alert but unmoving, made Jack believe it was he who was singing the spell to attack the farmers.

The Elsirans were penned in a tight group. Anytime one of them tried to break out of it toward the settlers, a chunk of mud or an icicle would hit him in the face or body, knocking him back. Two of them did manage to peel off and run away, back down the road toward the town.

The settlers cheered, and one man finally noticed Rozyl and her group advancing on the barricade with their rifles drawn. The Keepers took up positions and began firing on the farmers. The ice-and-mud attack stopped as the boy looked up, startled. This gave the farmers a chance to dive for cover among the nearby trees and shrubbery. Then the Elsirans returned fire.

The armed settlers must have been out of ammunition, for they didn't shoot, but Rozyl and her team were methodical, efficiently finding their targets and hitting them as man after man fell.

Jack felt no sympathy for the farmers, though they were his countrymen. There had been incidents such as these over the years, when tensions between citizens and settlers had bubbled over, but this would go down as the worst yet.

Jasminda crouched at his side. "I convinced the woman and her children to wait with the others."

The woman's son was staring up in awe as the Keepers made short work of the remaining farmers. Those who hadn't been shot were now beating a quick retreat.

"I knew many of the men who lived here." Jack's voice sounded hollow in his own ears. He was soaked to the skin, but the numbness in his limbs had nothing to do with the weather.

A dead settler lay only a dozen paces away, eyes open and sightless. Jack stayed low as he moved to the man's side to close his eyes. "May you find serenity in the World After."

The gunshots stopped and now the sound of engines took its place. Through the gaps in the trees lining the road ahead, thick wheels churned through the mud.

Jack's tension flared, then quickly fled. An open-topped four-wheeler drove up, bearing four Elsiran soldiers. On its heels were two transports, a dozen men to each if they were following protocol. Sure enough, twenty-four men hopped out of the trucks and dispersed strategically, forming a perimeter around the settlement. The soldiers in the four-wheeler exited, guns drawn, and advanced on the barrier.

Jack stood ready to greet his men. Before he'd taken more than two steps, the soldiers opened fire. They gave no warning, no orders or instructions, just began shooting. Those at the barrier dove for cover, and Jack stood, dumbfounded, until Jasminda pulled him down again.

What in Sovereign's name?

"Can you do the thing with the ice and mud?" The idea of firing upon his own men was something he could not fathom at the moment, and he didn't want the other Lagrimari to do so, either. He needed a distraction.

"I think so." Jasminda drew in a breath and closed her eyes.

The firing stopped as the ooze on the ground rose into a wall of mud to block the view of the soldiers. Jack ran to the barricade, passing the shocked Lagrimari gathered there, and hurdled across.

"All right, Jasminda," he called, pulling out his weapon. When the mud once again fell to the earth, Jack stood face-to-face, pistol drawn on the lead officer, a captain he recognized, but had never personally spoken to before. From the corner of his eye, he saw the soldiers nearby train their weapons on him.

"Hold your fire!" the captain shouted, a dazed look coming over him.

"Do you know who I am?" Jack said through clenched teeth.

"Y-yes, sir."

"Who am I then?" he pressed.

"High Commander Alliaseen."

Soldiers nearby gasped in shock.

"I-I have to ask for your identification code, sir."

"Ylisum two five three zero nine." Jack squeezed his hand around the butt of the pistol still pointed at the captain's head, anger vibrating through his every fiber. "Verified?"

"Verified." A moment was all it took for the demeanor of the other soldiers to change radically. Guns were put away swiftly, and the men all stood at attention. Jack lowered his weapon as well, and tried to control his breathing.

"Commander, I am Captain Daveen Pillos. We didn't realize you'd returned."

"Clearly, I have, Captain." Jack took in another steadying breath and unclamped his jaw by sheer will. "On whose order were you firing upon these settlers?"

Pillos's gaze darted to the barricade and back. "No one's order, sir. We were engaging combatants."

"When you engaged these combatants, were they firing upon you?"

A tic jumped in the captain's jaw. "No, sir. But reports said they had attacked some civilians."

"Under the rules of engagement, under what conditions is it permissible to fire upon residents of your own country when you are not under immediate threat of harm?"

Pillos blinked rapidly as if trying to recall.

Jack exhaled in exasperation. "Has martial law been declared, Captain?"

"No, sir."

"Then am I correct in stating there are no conditions under which it is permissible to fire upon residents of your own country when you are not under immediate threat of harm?"

"Y-yes, sir. But, sir . . . they are settlers."

Jack took a step back and raised his voice so that all present could hear. "Yes, Captain. These are settlers. And as of the Treaty of the Seventh Breach, they have non-enemy status in Elsira. Unless they directly provoke you and are not, as in this case, merely defending themselves against attack, it is our sworn duty as defenders of Elsira to protect them, as well. Is it not?"

"Yes, sir."

Jack took a deep breath, exhausted from the display of leadership. Pillos was doubtless no different than most of his men, than most of Elsira, if he could stand to believe such a thing.

"See if anyone needs medical attention and gather their weapons. But for Sovereign's sake, don't shoot anyone."

Pillos gave the commands, his eyes darting back to Jack every few seconds. "What are we to do with them all, sir?"

Jack scrubbed a hand down his face. "Call in transportation and take them to the Eastern Base for now. And contact the Sisterhood. More refugees will be arriving."

Jack recalled Jasminda's words in the cave. The Lagrimari were coming here searching for a better life, but if this is what they'd find when they arrived, maybe they were better off in Lagrimar.

Jasminda's gaze followed Jack as he dealt with the soldiers. After the initial incident, the men's sudden change in attitude and obvious deference toward him piqued her curiosity. He only had to say a few words and they would take off like a startled horse.

Several soldiers came over to ask, somewhat hesitantly, for

the weapons of the Lagrimari. The settlers understood the commands and translated for the others. Rozyl scowled but added her rifle to the pile.

Once the guns had all been put away, the other refugees were brought out from their hiding places, including nearly two dozen people Jasminda hadn't seen before who'd hidden in the trees just beyond the settlement. They all gathered, seated behind the remains of the makeshift barrier, still wanting some distance between themselves and the Elsirans.

Gerda sat next to Jasminda as she observed Jack giving commands and instructing his men.

"You watch him very closely," Gerda said. "Do you think he will disappear?"

Jasminda pulled her gaze away. "I'd almost forgotten he was one of them." Her heart tied itself in a knot. He'd been so different, so kind, but now, standing in a huddle of other Elsirans, it was difficult to pick him out from the group. The idea of finding warmth and comfort from his presence seemed foreign.

What had she expected? She knew that he was on a mission. He'd risked his life to gain information to save his country. With the cornerstone gone, her only use to him was in unlocking the mystery of the caldera. Just because she'd grown to think of him as a possibility, perhaps even as a friend, did not mean he felt the same. She was an ally; she must do her part and he do his.

With a sigh, she pulled out the pouch that held the caldera.

"Watch over me while I try this again?" she asked Gerda. Jasminda had been insensible to the world during the last vision.

Gerda patted her shoulder. "Of course."

Jasminda inhaled deeply, unwrapped the caldera, and lowered her palm.

In the distance, the clouds have not yet begun to form, but I feel them coming. A raw wind races across the mountain ridge, but I do nothing to block its bite. The sensation of the air whipping against my skin grounds me.

Above my head, Eero turns circles in the air, riding on the wind. I briefly wonder who taught him the trick, but no one needed to. He has been a quick study. He swoops before me, hovering just out of reach. I grab for him anyway, knowing it will make him smile, and he races away.

"You will burn yourself out," I call up to him, making sure my voice carries as his form becomes smaller and smaller. Within minutes, I sense him weakening. He has just enough Song left to land gracefully by my side, laughing, his face full of joy.

"A little more, please," he says, holding out his hand.

"More? So you can waste it flying through the air like a deranged bird? There is a reason you do not see any other Songbearers tearing through the skies disturbing the clouds."

He snorts. "Because you are stodgy curmudgeons with no sense of adventure."

I roll my eyes. "No, because we respect the energy and do not squander it on frivolity. If you needed to fly to escape danger or forestall some terrible event, that would be one thing."

His resonant chuckle echoes off the mountain peaks behind us. "If you give me a little more, I will endeavor to seek out some poor soul in peril and give aid straightaway."

I turn away from him and cross my arms.

"My dearest, most beautiful and talented sister." He leans into me and makes his most pitiful face to engage my sympathy.

"Your only sister."

"Yes, and a more wonderful sister there could never be. I promise not to squander it. I shall give the Song the respect it deserves. Please?"

I want to hold my ground against him. But in the weeks since Yllis discovered the spell that allows gifting a portion of a Song from one to another, Eero has been happier than I have seen him since the loss of our parents. Perhaps happier than I have ever seen him.

We thought it best not to make the spell widely known, and so are all sworn to secrecy. At first, Eero and I would go up into the mountains above town to let him practice so as not to be spotted. But this week we are on assignment in the east, checking in on the colony that has sprung up here in the shadow of the eastern mountains.

It is a quiet place, so far from home. A bleak and dry environment where nothing grows, but the colonists are working to transform it into lush farmland, as our parents and grandparents did long ago in the west. We could not have found a better place for Eero to practice away from prying eyes.

I relent, and take his hand for the spell. The power is always there, humming inside me, a leashed beast waiting for release. I set a trickle free and sing it into my twin, deep into the core of him where it would last him quite a while if he did not waste it.

I give just a little, but he has been using it up faster and faster, asking for more and more. Some part of me advises caution—having been born Silent, there is no telling how the power will affect him—but it brings him such joy.

"No more until tomorrow," I admonish. His eyes shine as he nods his understanding.

With a flick of his wrist, he pulls the moisture from the air until it forms a tiny dense cloud hovering above his palm.

"What are you going to do with that?" I hold back a laugh.

His grin is mischievous. He winks at me. "My tongue is a bit parched. The terraforming is moving at a snail's pace, and the water rations here barely slake my thirst." He opens his mouth and the little cloud becomes a stream of water that arcs, landing on his tongue.

I shake my head and turn back toward the imposing mountain range. "The storm will be here in a few hours," I say. "We had better head back so I can help the Songbearers with today's work. That way they will not fall too far behind because of the weather."

The Songbearers work together to sing the barren ground to fertility. One day, farms will grow where this desert stands. That is the true power of Earthsong.

My brother squints into the distance unable to see what I see. "Would it not be better to halt the tempest and leave more time for the work?"

I shrug. "If we stopped every storm, nothing would ever grow." A greater unease pushes at me, but I brush it away. One storm at a time is all I can deal with.

Jasminda stared ahead blindly, replaying the last vision in her mind. Changing desert into farmland—she was awestruck by the power of these ancient Singers.

To the west of the settlement of Baalingrove were green fields and rolling hills. Clusters of trees sprung up here and there, and according to the settlers, the nearest farming village was about two kilometers away. But the settlement stood in the shade of the bordering mountains. She recognized the profile from the vision. Baalingrove was very close to where this colony of Earthsingers had been. All of this beauty and green-ery had been transformed from desert wasteland long ago.

She stood, wincing at the way her sodden clothes stuck to her, and turned to the distinctive peaks. In her mind, she tried to triangulate the location of the colony. How long ago had it been since the Singers had done their work here? Was this vision a clue of some kind? Could the colony's location offer some insight into how to awaken the Queen?

"They wish the refugees to sleep at the Eastern Base to-night," one of the settlers told the others. The men sat together, appearing impervious to the rain that poured down. "The Sis-terhood is setting up a camp for them near Rosira. The plan is to travel there tomorrow."

This elicited a chorus of grumbles from the other men. "I reckon we should go with them," another grizzled man said.

"And leave our homes? Who are they to us?" Voices mur-mured in agreement.

The first man stiffened. "Those who need protecting." Protests rose, but he leaned forward. "Most of us were born in the harems and grew up in the army. No family and no choices. We've been cast off here going on twenty years, but these women and children coming across need our help. They don't know the language nor do they know what to expect from these flame-haired bastards—though after today, I'm sure they can guess."

The others quieted, and he continued. "I can't make none of you go. All I know is a man protects those weaker than himself. And no matter what they think, we're still men."

Jasminda blinked back tears. Had Papa not met Mama, he would be one of these men. The settlers remained silent, but she saw renewed purpose in the set of their jaws. They would go to protect the others.

And she would go as well—it's where she'd intended to end up all along. Appeal to the Tax Bureau, save her land. And discover a way to awaken the sleeping Queen. No, not difficult at all.

But first, she needed to visit the site of the colony. If the way to awaken the Queen was truly tied to these visions, then she couldn't ignore any possibilities.

She looked for Jack, but didn't want to ask any of the Elsirans. Finally, she spotted him near one of the vehicles talking with some of the soldiers. She called to him, waving to get his attention. Their eyes met, and a chill raced through her. She told herself it was just the unyielding rain. Jack broke away from the group; the other Elsirans looked her way, confusion evident on their faces.

He approached wearily. He looked so tired and burdened. Perhaps that was her imagination; however, his demeanor *had* changed. Gone were even the hints of the man she'd once confused for an artist. He was all warrior now.

His presence beside her dried her throat. Whatever she had been planning to say flew out of her head.

"You are in charge of these men?" The question had been weighing on her since the soldiers lowered the weapons pointed at him and showed him such deference. She didn't know much about military ranks, but High Commander sounded awfully important.

"Yes," he said simply.

Her heart grew heavy. Though he stood next to her, suddenly he seemed very far away. "You are very young."

"I started early. Practically at birth. And my family is very . . . well-connected." There was no pride in his voice.

"The men respect you. It isn't false regard in their eyes. You must be quite good."

He shrugged and looked away as though uncomfortable with this topic of conversation. She changed the subject.

"You're taking us all to the base?"

"Yes, all the refugees and any of the settlers who want to come. Tomorrow, we'll head for Rosira."

And what would happen after that? Would she ever see him again? She pushed the question back. It would probably be for the best. Before she got any more attached.

She cleared her throat. "I saw something with the stone."

Jack's brows raised; he stepped closer. "What?"

She briefly relayed the last vision. "The twins were near here. I recognize the formations." She pointed to the mountain. "Perhaps a few kilometers north. I thought maybe we could go there and look around. There could be something we're meant to find."

"Do you think the caldera is like the map?" he asked, following her line of thought.

"We know so little. There might be nothing there, but since we're so close, I thought we should check."

He looked off into the distance. "The only thing I can think of up there are the ruins of the Citadel. Do you think that's where this colony was?"

"Could be."

Jack nodded, decision etched on his face. "Then we'll go. It's very near the base, so we can stop at the ruins on our way." He moved to walk away then stopped and turned back to grab her hands. "Thank you."

The action was one of gratitude only, he wasn't holding her hands, not really. "Don't thank me yet. I still don't know how any of this will help awaken the Queen."

He grinned at her. "Still. Oh, and I don't think we should mention the caldera or the plan to wake the Queen to anyone else. Getting anyone in the government involved could be . . . complicated."

"All right." Jasminda agreed. "I don't have anyone to tell anyway."

He squeezed her hands then marched away, barking out orders. Jasminda clenched her fists, trying to stop the racing of her ridiculous heart. She reminded herself of her mission: save her land, awaken the Queen, go back home. Alone.

There were only so many impossible things she could handle.

CHAPTER SIXTEEN

The Mistress of Frogs was called to the bedside of an old woman who wanted to be assured of peace in the World After.

She said, Peace can be found only in memory. To seek it in the future is folly.

—COLLECTED FOLKTALES

As the transports carrying the refugees and settlers rumbled away, another vehicle approached. Jack grinned to see his assistant Benn at the wheel. A mountain's worth of tension rolled off Jack's shoulders. He'd never been more grateful to see someone.

When Jack had assumed his position as High Commander five years before, and the pressure of the job had nearly crushed him, the staff assistant assigned to him had stepped up to lighten the load with impeccable organization, efficiency, and friendship. Benn was the most competent person he'd ever met and the only man in the army Jack truly trusted.

When he walked up and saluted him, Jack grabbed his old friend in a bear hug.

"I'm happy to see you, too, sir," Benn said, clapping him on the back. They separated and Benn looked him over. "No worse for the wear, I see. Though you are rather late."

Jack grimaced. The official story was that he'd gone on a high-level, two-week training mission out of the country. Only a few key people knew that country was Lagrimar. In order to protect Benn, Jack had kept him out of the loop. He'd felt guilty rescinding the man's leave and not giving him the full story, but if Jack hadn't returned and it was discovered Benn knew the details of the dangerous mission, it would have put him in the crosshairs of people the young lieutenant was unequipped to battle.

"Yes, well, I'll tell you the story on the way."

Benn's eyes narrowed. "Why do I think we're not headed back to base?"

"Because you're a smart man." Jack turned to Jasminda standing several steps away. "Jasminda ul-Sarifor, Lt. Benn Ravel."

"Miss," Benn said, holding his hands out to greet her. Jasminda's mouth opened in surprise, but she quickly stepped up to press her palms to his.

"Jasminda here saved my life. She's Elsiran," Jack said emphatically.

The few soldiers still lingering around the entrance to the settlement sent questioning looks toward them as Jack helped Jasminda into the vehicle. Jack didn't have to explain himself to his men, but irritation and anger rose within him nonetheless on Jasminda's behalf.

"Where to?" Benn asked settling into the driver's seat.

"The Citadel. We need to take a look at the ruins."

As they drove, Jack gave him the broad strokes of his mission, glossing over his capture and injury and much of the ordeal at Jasminda's cabin. Benn's jaw tightened—he knew Jack well enough to fill in the gaps in the telling, but didn't interrupt.

"I'm sorry I didn't tell you."

Benn's finger tapped the steering wheel. He sighed. "I'm sorry, too, sir."

The rest of the drive was quiet, with only the movement of wheels through the muddy roads to disturb the silence. Before long, their destination loomed ahead.

The Citadel had been built after the First Breach just a few decades after the Mantle's erection. The invading Lagrimari had taken over much of the eastern farmland. They built a wall to keep the Elsirans out and used their considerable power in the form of earthquakes, fires, storms, and floods to do battle.

Elsiran engineers responded by constructing a mighty battle ram that eventually tore down the wall. Their superior numbers pushed the Lagrimari back, and the tear in the Mantle closed again, without the Elsirans quite knowing how.

That's when the Citadel was built—a walled city that could withstand a year-long siege. The Elsirans bolstered their army, making the city its headquarters. That long-ago Prince Regent knew it was just a matter of time before the True Father attacked again.

Their four-wheeler came to a stop at the edge of the ruins. A vast sea of tumbled rock and stone stretched out before them. Tough grasses and shrubbery pushed its way through gaps in the stones. Here or there an archway remained mostly intact. The foundations and first stories of many of the buildings had also lasted. Though the formerly cobbled streets were just greenery now.

"Why was it never rebuilt, I wonder?" Benn asked.

"I don't think we had the heart. A city of stone is no match for men who can cause it to crumble with a thought." The Elsirans had underestimated the Earthsingers, and they had suffered for it. Jack exited the vehicle, wading through the somber atmosphere that had settled over them.

"But this city stood for hundreds of years," Jasminda said, coming to his side.

"Because the True Father wanted to use it." Jack snorted. "After all the work it took to build, the Lagrimari tunneled in during the Second Breach and took over. It changed hands throughout the years more than once."

The rain had subsided for the moment, though the gray sky promised more. Jasminda turned in a circle taking it all in. She shivered, wrapping her arms around her middle.

"Are you cold?"

Jack still wore her brother's pants, but had changed his wet shirt for a dry one and donned a brown army jacket back at Baalingrove. The refugees had been issued blankets while waiting for transport, but Jasminda must have left hers behind.

He took off his jacket and handed it to her. She smiled, almost shyly, before accepting it.

"Thank you," she whispered. It engulfed her, and she had to roll up the sleeves. Jack looked away. The jacket wasn't even really his, but it sparked something possessive in him that was wholly inappropriate.

The Citadel sat slightly to the northwest of the only gap in the mountain range. This stretch of land was a few thousand paces wide, and was the sole location from which you could see the country of Lagrimar.

"That's it, isn't it?" Jasminda asked. "Breach Valley? I've never . . ." She looked visibly shaken.

The Mantle was invisible to the eye, but try to cross the gap and you would hit an impenetrable force. Well, mostly impenetrable.

Every breach had occurred right here. Every breach save for the current one.

"What does he want?" Jasminda asked. "Why invade this place again and again?"

"Farmland, food for his people. I suspect everyone is easier to control when they're well-fed." Elsirans certainly were. The most unrest always happened in times of strife.

"But he has magic."

Jack turned away from the valley, back to the ruins. "They say he hates to use it. Darvyn told me that the True Father's power is tainted, so he himself cannot transform the land from desert to fertile. Apparently, he tried at the beginning and it only made the land worse. But he had already stolen the power from the strongest Earthsingers so there were few left to terraform. So he sets his sights on this side of the mountain."

After the Citadel's destruction, the Eastern Base became the hub of army operations. It was to the west of Breach Valley, just out of sight of the constant reminder of failure the destroyed city held.

Benn walked on a bit farther out of earshot. "Do you recognize anything?" Jack asked Jasminda.

"This does seem to be the location of the colony I saw. But

I don't know." She headed down an overgrown path that was once, no doubt, a vibrant city street. Every so often she would stop and squint. He wondered if she were using her Song to search for clues, but didn't pierce the quiet to ask.

The low hum of voices rose nearby. Jack grabbed his side-arm and moved in front of Jasminda, scanning the area.

His skin tightened with apprehension until a bugle trilled out. They turned a corner and found three dozen old men gathered before the remains of the clock tower. Though not much of the structure was left, it was still the tallest thing standing in the city.

Some of the old-timers were in military dress uniforms, some in suits and ties with sashes of honor covering their chests. They all stood at attention while a lone bugler played a plaintive melody. Two at the front of the group folded the Elsiran flag, its blue and gold symbols of the country's crest disappearing into the folds.

Jack came to attention and saluted. When the bugle died, the men's voices rose singing the Elsiran national anthem.

"From sandy shores near oceans deep,
To mountains near and far,
Her memory, alive we keep
Elsira's in our hearts
Shining brightly, coast to hill
Her beauty waning never,
Elsira lives on by our will
Elsira is forever."

Quiet replaced the voices and then the ceremony was done. The skies picked that point to open, dousing them in a cold drizzle.

Some of the men looked up, noticing Jasminda and Jack

for the first time. Jack wore only the plain brown shirt; none of his stripes were visible to indicate his rank, yet one of the men recognized him. The old-timer snapped to attention and saluted.

"High Commander Alliaseen. It's a pleasure, sir." The other men followed his lead.

Jack reciprocated, conscious of his intrusion upon them. "As you were," he ordered.

By the age of the men present, he gathered they must be Fifth Breach veterans. Some tough old bastards. What he'd heard about those fights made his stomach sour.

"Jasminda?" one of the men called out, stepping forward. She grew rigid beside him before her expression morphed into a smile.

"Bindeen?" A graying figure approached and bowed slightly as she beamed. "What in Sovereign's name are you doing here?"

"I might ask you the same. Those what are left from our regiment get together this time every year to pay our respects. It's the anniversary of our last stand here."

"This is Master Bindeen, the blacksmith in town," Jasminda said by way of introduction. Jack liked that she smiled at the old man fondly. He sensed there were not many who could claim her friendship.

Bindeen nodded at him. "Sir."

Jack looked more closely at the uniforms of the men. "You say you shared a regiment?" Bindeen wore the patch of the 23rd Infantry, the Black Skulls. While the two who'd folded the flag were both from the 18th, the Stormwalkers. And over there was a fellow from the 49th.

Bindeen eyed the others with a sidelong glance, then

grinned. "We share a regiment that no patch was ever made for, sir." The old man peered at him meaningfully.

"The Phantoms?" Jack was incredulous.

"Aye."

Jack viewed the man with renewed admiration. He bowed slightly. "It is an honor."

Bindeen scoffed, his face reddening. "It was Qerwall over there who brought me in and watched our backs every day of that mission." He motioned to a wiry man with a full head of gray hair still tinged with the red of his youth.

Jasminda looked back and forth between them. "What are the Phantoms?"

Bindeen's mouth clamped shut, a guilty look crossing his face, but Jack grinned. "I think fifty years of being classified is long enough. What do you think, Sergeant?"

The man smiled. "Why don't you step into our office? I'll tell you all about it."

Jack followed the others into a large tent erected just outside the ruins. Tankards of ale poured from fat barrels were shared liberally. The rain pattering against the tent's fabric lent a steady soundtrack to the tale the old men spun.

Benn, Bindeen, and Qerwall sat together with Jack and Jasminda on folding camp chairs. The other soldiers sat in small groups nearby, sharing memories and catching up.

"We're honored to have you here, Commander," Qerwall said. His steely eyes were so light they almost seemed leached of all color. Different from the amber shade of most Elsirans.

"I'm honored to be here. Will you tell us about the Phantoms?"

Qerwall eyed Jasminda with more curiosity than suspicion and launched into his story. "I had the dream of the Queen once when I was a lad, no more than three or four years old. I didn't rightly know what I'd seen, but when I told my mama, she nearly fainted dead away. Got a lot of attention from that, I did, in our village. A group of Sisters came and questioned me for the Dream Record. But wasn't until years later, when we deployed during the Fifth, that I had another one."

He rested his elbows on his knees and spread his gnarled fingers apart. "The Breach had been open going on sixty years, and at that point we were in a long standoff. They'd send a storm and then we'd bomb the living daylights out of them, and on and on. But when I got to the front line, things had just started turning ugly.

"The day before had been the first time we'd been hit with those bloody apple bombs they conjured." He snorted at Jasminda's questioning expression. "They didn't whistle or hiss like normal shells. But if you smelled apples, you were in for it. Those blasted things eventually destroyed the Citadel."

"Haven't been able to eat an apple since," Bindeen added.

Qerwall grunted in agreement. "But that first night I had the dream. I was transported to this dark place where I couldn't see anything, not even myself. I heard *Her* voice. It flowed through me like lava in my veins. Never heard a sound like it before or since.

"She told me that there were others I had to find. Men I could trust, plus a few names She gave. Also, there were Lagrimari working against the True Father and we had to meet up with them. Said they'd found a weakness in the True Father's plan and we had to be ready."

"See there's this fella called a Cantor," Bindeen broke in.

"The True Father's second in command. I suppose they don't last long, that madman kills people close to him after a while, but this one's name was Morryn. He's the one what made the apples. This Morryn had a son in secret. The True Father didn't know about him, and Morryn wanted to keep it that way."

"That was the weakness, see," Qerwall continued smoothly. "These Lagrimari rebels had found it out and taken the son captive. They brought him to us and we hid him in Elsira. Then got word to Morryn that we had his boy and if he didn't stop shelling us with them apples, we couldn't guarantee his son's safety."

"That's when the tide turned in our favor," Bindeen said. "We couldn't do much against those bloody bombs, but once Morryn stopped creating them, we were able to mount an offensive."

"That's how we won the Fifth Breach." Qerwall nodded and sat back, taking a long drink of his ale.

Jack took in Jasminda's stunned expression. He had studied military history, and while there were no public records of the classified mission, when he'd taken over as Army High Commander, he'd been briefed using the broad strokes. But had never actually met any of the men involved.

"What happened to Morryn and his son?" Jasminda asked.

Bindeen sobered. "The father wanted to defect. We had a plan to get him and the boy out of the country and on a ship headed for Raun. But . . ." He shook his head.

"The True Father found out. Killed the son. Drained the father's Song." Qerwall stared into his mug.

"But left Morryn alive?" she asked.

"For a time." Qerwall nodded. "We got word from one of

our contacts that the man escaped after his tribute. Don't know what happened to him. Can't imagine the True Father didn't hunt him down and have him killed. After the breach closed we were cut off from the rebels and heard nothing else about him."

"It wouldn't have been easy for him to hide with that hair of his," Bindeen mused. "When we had him, we shaved his head so he wouldn't stand out so much, but you could still see that mark he had."

Jack looked up sharply from his ale. "What mark?"

"Birthmark. Shape of an *S* running from the front of his head to the back. A streak of white in his dark hair. All the way down to his scalp."

A vise gripped Jack's chest, making his breath short. "Describe him to me. How tall was he? How old then?"

Bindeen scratched his chin. "Average height for a Lagrimari. Thick build. Would have been in his fifties back then, I reckon. Why?"

Jack looked at Jasminda. "The old man I met, the one who gave me the map. He had a white streak in his hair just like that. The rest had turned a dark gray, but that streak was pure white."

Jasminda stared at him, her eyes reflecting the foreboding he felt.

"But he would have to be going on one hundred years old now," Bindeen said.

"You think it could have been this Morryn who gave you the map?" Jasminda's voice was hushed. The conversation in the tent stayed at a low hum, but to Jack's ears it was deafening.

He sat back in his seat, hands shaking. He pushed away the vision he'd seen during the quest to find the cornerstone.

That had broken his heart, but this suspicion rising within him threatened to break his spirit.

"What if Morryn is still working for the True Father?" Jack said. "What if giving me the map was a trick, a plot to find a way to destroy the cornerstone and keep their plans in motion?"

A growing dread unfolded as his thoughts continued. "You said the storm was magical, and after we revealed the cornerstone, the storm demolished it." He met Jasminda's gaze. "The current Cantor. She must have ordered Tensyn to let us go. Because she *knew* what I was going to do."

Jasminda shook her head. "But you can't know. We don't . . ." She frowned, staring at the ground. "The fire at the cabin? The stone caused it. They were . . . manipulating us. Forcing us to leave."

It was harder and harder to deny. The bottom dropped out of Jack's stomach. "This is my fault. I believed Morryn. I didn't ask enough questions, and I walked right into a trap."

He recalled the first time he'd touched his blood to the stone and been taken into the map's vision. Seeing the cornerstone and knowing that he had a chance to avoid the war. It had consumed him, made him foolish.

"They knew who I was and they used me to further weaken the Mantle." He massaged his head as the truth struck him. "By pursuing the cornerstone, I brought about its destruction."

"If this is true, the True Father destroyed the cornerstone, Jack. Not you." Jasminda placed a hand on his forearm and squeezed gently.

"But remember the hooded woman in the vision? No one the True Father sent would have passed the test and even found the cornerstone. He needed someone to lead him to it."

A pained expression crossed her face. "You said you felt like the storm was watching you. What if it was? I should have listened to you. It *was* bad magic."

A crackle of static interrupted whatever she'd been about to say.

Benn sat up and grabbed the portable radio at his waist. He stepped outside to hear the caller, but ran back in almost immediately.

"Urgent call for you from the capital, sir."

Jack stood, his whole body heavy as he walked out of the tent to take the call.

"Jack? Is that you?" a familiar voice warbled down the line.

"Usher? What's wrong?"

"Oh, Jack." The man exhaled in relief. "Thank the Queen you're alive!"

"What's happened?"

"It's Alariq." The old man's voice cracked, weighed down with misery. "Your brother is dead."

CHAPTER SEVENTEEN

*The Master of Monkeys came across a hunter caught in his
own trap in the forest.*

Will you free me? the hunter cried.

*Nay, answered Monkey. However, in leaving you en-
snared, I free your prey from your pursuit.*

—COLLECTED FOLKTALES

"Do you think this will work?" Ella asked, grabbing the small
square of paper Milner held out to her.

"If they don't inspect it too carefully, it will. You know I'm
the best in Portside, but citizenship documents are hard to
counterfeit."

Her former boss was a master printmaker from Fremia
who had worked all over the world, eventually landing in
Elsira. She'd enjoyed her time working in his printshop.

She might even have stayed longer if he hadn't decided to retire.

Her hand shook as she looked over the fake papers. To her untrained eye they looked legitimate, but she had never scrutinized the real thing before.

"Use the Bishop Street Gate. It's the most crowded one. Gives the guards more to pay attention to. Less time to observe the inconsistencies."

Nerves fluttered in her belly. "Thank you for this." She'd long suspected that Milner dabbled in counterfeiting, but hadn't really wanted to know any more until she'd come up with this plan to try and locate her nephew.

"You sure you want to do this?" Milner asked, his bushy eyebrows lowered. "From what you told me, it doesn't seem likely those Sisters would give your little nephew over to an orphanage."

She'd confided in him mostly just to have someone to tell. She'd wanted to call Benn and tell him everything that had happened but was out of money and a bit paranoid about speaking of such things on the open phone lines. What if the operator was listening in and was a devout follower of the Queen? Milner had been a good listener. He'd always reminded her of PawPaw, with a gentle manner that belied a spine of steel.

Ella tucked a strand of her hair away. "I don't think most Sisters have experience caring for a newborn. If it proved too much for them they just might have handed him off to someone else. I still don't know why they'd keep him in the first place, and I have to do something."

While the carved figurine hadn't exactly led to a dead end—she was certain Zann Biddel knew more about Kess than he was saying—she had run out of road in her search for the baby. She'd already searched the orphanages in Portside with no luck, but there were several in Rosira, not far from the Southern temple.

On the kitchen table, a bouquet of fragrant floralilies sat in a glass vase. Benn had sent them. She hadn't written him in days. Setting everything that had happened to paper also felt like a risk. Paranoia had taken over. Could the Sisterhood be checking the post? Unlikely. Besides, what was the point of unloading her troubles on him? It would only make him worry and feel helpless and she didn't want that. He was practically in charge of an entire army base, for saint's sake. If he'd been home, that would be a different story, but he was off pursuing his dreams. The dream she wanted for him as well, since it was so important to him.

If she got into real trouble, he'd be there for her. Right now, she was just sad and determined.

The fact that he hadn't called her, either—she'd received no messages from the bodega's telephone—just reinforced how busy he must be. She closed a door on the aching in her chest and placed her fake citizenship papers into her purse.

Milner patted her shoulder in the same way PawPaw used to. "I don't know if you're foolish or brave, sweetheart. But you certainly are something."

Ella chuckled and tugged on her old cloche hat. Though the papers marked her as a Yalyish immigrant, she would still stand out less in Rosira without her hair drawing attention to her. She thanked Milner again on their way out the door, then headed off.

She made her way south, crossing streets still wet from last night's storm, toward the Bishop Street Gate, one of three which led in and out of Portside. Barricades blocked the other east-west running streets, cutting off access to the rest of Rosira. When she arrived, the line of pedestrians was quite long. Alongside them, carts, carriages, and vehicles waited their turn as well. This gate was the closest to downtown Rosira and most of those in line were Elsirans from what she could tell. Having never passed through one before, except for her bus trip, Ella watched the exchanges carefully as she approached.

One of the city guard, clad in a navy blue uniform, would hold out a hand, requesting papers. He gave them a quick scan and then waved the person on his or her way. It was simple, and just as Milner had said, the guard never spent too much time examining the documents.

A cool breeze blew in off the ocean. Ella was shaking; she tried to convince herself it was from the sudden bite in the air and not the fear that enveloped her. If she didn't get herself together, she was sure to be called out for acting suspiciously.

The Elsiran man in front of her grumbled under his breath with impatience. When his turn came, he flashed his papers and was admitted through. Then it was her turn.

"Papers?" the guard said, holding out his hand. Was that boredom on his face or suspicion?

Ella placed the folded square in his upturned palm and held her breath. He frowned, the lines grooved into the corners of his mouth, as his gaze roamed the paper.

Ella's heartbeat sped. She glanced around, cursing herself for not planning an escape route.

Then he handed the document back to her and waved her through. She took a ragged breath and walked quickly, holding herself back from breaking into a run as she passed the threshold of the imposing iron gate.

Already the air seemed clearer and sweeter; the streets were definitely cleaner on this side. Appetizing aromas from a nearby bakery made her mouth water. Far more automobiles than horses filled the streets and the steps of people on the sidewalks seemed lighter, more carefree. Or maybe it was just her imagination.

She shook the foolish thoughts from her head. None of that mattered. She just needed to find the orphanage.

A streetcar whizzed by, its bell ringing, but Ella walked. A full day's work had still eluded her since receiving Kess's fateful telegram and she had no coins to spare. There were two orphanages she wanted to visit, both relatively close to the Southern temple. If the Sisters had stashed the baby somewhere, perhaps it would have been nearby, so Syllenne could keep an eye on him.

Of course, they could have sent him far away, to a place Ella would never find him. But she couldn't think like that. She had to believe that she could carry out Kess's final wish.

A constable strolled down the other side of the street. Ella tilted her head down and walked with purpose, hoping she blended into the crowd.

Her feet had begun to ache by the time the aging building came into view. The painted sign attached to the fence read "Night Blossoms Home for Orphans." The stucco had been painted a pale yellow, perhaps in an effort to be cheery, but the exterior walls were crumbling and water stained, in need of serious repair.

The front garden was unwieldy, and the gravel walkway

held more weeds than path. She approached a splintery main door and knocked using the large, corroded knocker. After a short wait, an elderly woman answered.

"Yes?"

"Pleasant afternoon to you, mistress. I-I'm interested in adopting. I'd like to see about a child."

"Well, we have plenty of those." The tiny woman's head barely reached Ella's shoulder. A lace cap covered her white hair. She shuffled backward to let Ella through.

"Any particular sort of child you're interested in?" The woman set a slow pace that Ella matched as they walked through hallways that smelled of cleaning solution.

"A baby. Do you have any newborns?"

The woman looked up at her with rheumy eyes. "Lot of work, newborns are. Let's see what they have in the nursery."

Ella kept her shock to herself. It seemed they treated the process of adopting a child the same as choosing a ripe melon at the market.

The muffled sounds of children's voices reached her as they moved through the dingy hallways. The floor tile was cracked everywhere and the walls could use a good washing. Her heart broke to think of the many children housed here who needed homes.

As the years went by, she'd begun to think of adopting. Was she selfish to not have considered it earlier? Perhaps there was some flaw within her. Maybe St. Siruna had abandoned her for being overly self-interested, unfit for motherhood in some fundamental way.

She swallowed the lump in her throat and followed the matron up a set of stairs to a large room with enormous windows.

"This is the nursery," the old woman stated, waving an arm around at the dozen bassinets scattered around. "Nurse Neena here will show you around." A rosy cheeked woman of about Ella's age approached from her seat in the corner.

In the distance, a phone rang. "I'd better get that," the old woman said, then shuffled away.

"Looking to adopt?" Nurse Neena asked, a warm smile brightening her face.

Ella immediately felt more comfortable. "Yes. Are all these cribs occupied?"

Neena nodded. "Come, have a look." She led her to the nearest crib where a very round baby blinked up at them with golden eyes. This child was close to six months old, but Ella reached for his hand and gave a soft exclamation when he gripped her finger.

"He's a strong one," Neena said, laughter in her voice. Across the room, a cry sounded.

"I'd better see to that." And she was off.

Ella made a circuit of the room, peering into each bassinet. Most of the babies were several months old and hairless. Chubby little cherubs gurgling in their sleep or kicking their arms and legs out, staring up at her with wide, round eyes. A few had a bit of ginger fuzz grazing their heads, but none had that curious shock of white-blond hair. And none were under one week old.

Nurse Neena confirmed that there had been no newborns left at the orphanage for several months. Ella had known it was a long shot, but disappointment still pressed against her chest. She turned to go, giving a last, lingering look at the bassinets.

Just outside the door to the nursery she stopped short at

the sight of two constables striding up the stairs, the old matron several steps behind them.

"That's her," she said, pointing to Ella, who took an instinctive step back and bumped into the door.

"Papers, miss?" the first constable said.

Her stomach plummeted. "Excuse me? W-what is this about?"

"We need to see your papers." Both men were tall and stocky. One had a ginger mustache; the other was clean shaven.

"I-I don't understand why you need to see them."

The clean shaven one shrugged. "We have the right to ask for them at any time." He held out his hand, eyes cold.

Ella took a deep breath and reached into her purse for the square card that had gotten her through the gate. She dropped it into the waiting palm and held herself rigid.

The constable looked at it, then scratched at the ink with his thumbnail. Ella's pulse thrummed.

"Sorry, miss. This won't do. The seal is off. Doesn't have the proper watermark. I'm going to have to place you under arrest."

"Arrest? You can't be serious." She looked back and forth between them, then to the unsmiling old woman whose gaze was hard.

The mustached constable took a menacing step forward and Ella shrank back, but had nowhere to go. Silver handcuffs gleamed in his hand.

"Holding counterfeit papers is a serious offense. As is illegal entry."

Tears welled in her eyes as the officer wrenched her arms around and slapped the icy cold cuffs on her wrists. They closed with a terrifying *clink* that caused her spine to shrink.

CHAPTER EIGHTEEN

And what of evil? said the town's mayor to the Master of Bobcats.

Evil is a powerful man's greatest friend. It will either fill his heart or line his pockets.

—COLLECTED FOLKTALES

Jasminda pulled Jack's coat around her tighter. The thick, wet fabric did relatively little to keep out the driving chill of the rain. He hadn't worn it long enough for his scent to permeate— and the dampness would have washed it away in any case— yet since she could not hold him, she settled for the jacket.

Dusk had fallen and the murky haze was penetrated only slightly by the vehicle's headlamps. Benn navigated the four-wheeler with ease despite the sodden roads.

Jack's pensive mood was so present, it could have taken up

an entire seat. He was eating himself up with blame for the cornerstone's destruction. Jasminda wished she could soothe him. If he hadn't taken Morryn's map and tried to use it, the True Father would have just found another. And that person might not have been so lucky as to have been saved by someone like Osar.

But guilt was guilt, and Jack continued to stew in his. The unvoiced question was this: had the cornerstone's ruin hastened the fall of the Mantle?

Nothing catastrophic had happened in the days since the avalanche, but maybe the worst was yet to come. A headache formed at the base of her skull. They could only move forward, not back. What was done was past.

The four-wheeler approached a grouping of low, gray structures hugging the earth. The Eastern Army Base was all bland concrete, straight lines, and harsh corners, made drearier by the persistent rain.

Benn pulled to a stop beside a row of other vehicles, and Jack faced her, his expression grim. "I need to check on some things. Benn will have sleeping quarters located for you."

"I won't be with the others?"

Jack shook his head emphatically. "You are an Elsiran citizen, not a refugee. That must be made clear."

He leaned in to speak a few words to Benn and then was off, disappearing into one of the nondescript buildings.

"Miss Jasminda, if you'll follow me."

Benn led her into the largest building on the base. Concrete floors and cinder block walls did not make the hallway inviting. Harsh overhead light gave everything a pallid sheen. They passed a number of doors with square glass embedded within. Beyond was a large space, a gymnasium perhaps, holding rows and rows of cots. Lagrimari huddled together as Elsiran soldiers finished setting up the pallets.

Jasminda shivered, glad she would not have to spend the night among so many strangers.

Benn led her down another hallway and motioned her to a small row of metal chairs. "Would you like something hot to drink? Coffee or tea?"

She sank into a seat. "Coffee would be nice." He nodded and disappeared into one of the many rooms. Though she sat alone, the building buzzed with energy. She reached for Earthsong to sense the people around her, hidden behind walls and doors. Wariness and anxiety pervaded.

The Elsiran soldiers were now tasked with housing those whom they'd only ever seen as the enemy. The atmosphere was taut with tension.

Two soldiers tramped down the hall. Their conversation halted when they caught sight of her. Jasminda averted her eyes, but couldn't avoid the hostility rolling off them.

The men continued on, but their voices reached her. "Looks like the commander has himself a new pet."

A snort. "A *grol* bitch to fetch the paper and eat the table scraps." Laughter.

Jasminda hunched over, ducking her head. But her shame was quickly replaced by anger, which raced like a streak of lightning sizzling through her veins. The sensation of pins and needles pricked her skin. The hair on her arms stood up.

"Wonder what he's thinking, keeping them all here. Could be the lot of them are spies seeking intel."

One man chuckled derisively. "Fat lot of intel available in the mess hall."

"That's not the point. We should gut every *grol* we come

across. That's less of them to fight when the next breach comes."

A third voice spoke up. "I don't know. There's a couple of fit birds out there I wouldn't mind tussling with." More laughter.

Jasminda clenched her fists until her knuckles hurt. Though the area around her was empty, she was aware of another presence nearby. At first she thought her Song sensed someone in an adjoining room, but this was closer than that. As close as frost coating her skin. An unseen entity stoking her anger like bellows to a fire.

Untethered emotions swirled inside her. Her Song pulsed, drawing in more Earthsong until she was pregnant with power.

"The one the commander picked out is the fittest, though. Maybe once he's done with her, he'll give us a turn."

She couldn't hold on anymore. Her rage exploded, funneling itself through her Song.

Her chair vibrated. The floor shook in gentle waves, then more forcefully. A violent wind blasted down the hallway. Doors slammed wildly. Furniture rattled.

Frantic soldiers rushed into the hall. Jasminda kept her head down trying to control herself. In moments, the flare-up was over. Her Song was simply too weak to sustain that much energy. She was burned out and moreover, horrified at what had just happened.

The foreign presence had disappeared, and the building was in chaos. Men with guns drawn raced past her and around the corner.

What in Sovereign's name had she done? She stood on

wobbly legs and followed them into the mess hall. The refugees were crushed together in the center with weapons trained
on them by wild-eyed soldiers.

Jasminda covered her mouth, stifling a gasp. She caught
Gerda's terrified gaze and wanted to melt into a puddle of
shame. Jack appeared, calling for calm. Despite his words, the
tension in the room was oppressive.

"What happened?" he asked, looking around. "Who was
responsible for that?" He repeated it in Lagrimari.

Jasminda swallowed her fear and took a deep breath, preparing to step forward.

"The children are frightened, sir. They acted without
thought." Gerda's voice was calm and even. She stood beside
Osar, an arm around him.

Jasminda's breath staggered. She couldn't let the old woman
shift the blame to the poor children. When she moved forward, Gerda held out a hand surreptitiously to stop her. "We
will make sure it doesn't happen again," the gray-haired woman
said.

Jack expelled a breath and rubbed his face. His shoulders
sagged. He stepped closer to Gerda. "Tensions are high, as
I'm sure you know. If my men feel threatened they will react,
and I may not be here to stop them. Many of these soldiers
were in the Seventh Breach. Any display of Earthsong will
enflame them."

"I understand." Gerda's gaze seemed to cut through Jack
straight to Jasminda, who stood several dozen paces behind
him, hovering near the wall. "We will stay watchful and calm."

"I would appreciate it." Jack turned and spoke to his
men, but his words blended together in Jasminda's ears. As

soldiers left to go back to wherever they'd come from, Gerda approached.

"You must beware, child. We are not the only ones slipping through the Mantle's cracks."

"What do you mean?" Jasminda's voice shook.

"You felt something, did you not, in the wind and rain and snow?"

Jasminda's eyes widened. "How did you know? I sensed . . . someone. Something. And just now it happened again. Only this time it set upon me, made me lose control of my Song."

Gerda nodded. "The storm, it is tainted. The True Father is breaking free of his chains. And you are a target now because of the caldera."

"He knows I have it?"

"Not exactly." Gerda tilted her head to the side. "While the Mantle stands he is limited. But his spell is drawn to the stone like a tracking dog. This storm will seek you out, looking for weakness to exploit. Feeding on your anger. You must be stronger than it. Protect your mind." She tapped a wrinkled finger against the side of her head.

Jasminda tightened her arms around her waist. "Why didn't you warn me before?"

Gerda shrugged. "We weren't sure it would affect you. I was hoping you would be immune."

"Well, I'm not." Jasminda stepped back. At least her Song was depleted until tomorrow. She could do no further damage.

Benn appeared, bearing a perplexed expression and a mug of coffee.

"I have to go," Jasminda said, sullen. Gerda smiled and shuffled away.

Jasminda accepted the coffee gratefully, allowing the liquid to scald her tongue. The discomfort grounded her. The invasive vileness of the True Father's magic was nothing she would soon forget. She only hoped she could somehow steel herself against it.

Jack left the Administrative building well after midnight and trudged out into the soggy night. The rain had tapered to a light mist, matching his downcast mood. He wound his way through the narrow lanes of the base until he reached the supply building where Jasminda was staying.

There was no place in the barracks secure enough for a single woman, and Jack wanted to make sure Jasminda was protected. Sleeping space was at a premium, so a cot had been set up for her in this small warehouse.

He opened the door; a tall stack of boxes cluttered the entryway, blocking his view.

"Jasminda. It's me," he called out, rounding the mountain of crates to find her crouched on her cot, a knife in hand. Her skirt had rucked up, revealing the garter housing the blade.

Warmth shot through him. With a shy look, she set her skirt to rights. He swallowed and forced his gaze up to her face. She was looking anywhere but at him, so he pulled up a box and sat beside her. "How do you like the accommodations?"

"It's no cave floor, but it will serve." Her eyes finally rose to meet his, and he relaxed a notch. Seeing her after this endless, excruciating day was what he'd needed. He reached for her hand and threaded his fingers with hers, hoping she would not pull away.

"Are you all right?" she whispered, squeezing him gently.

"I've been worse." He tried to inject lightness into his voice, but failed. Guilt had nearly paralyzed him and now grief threatened to finish the job.

"And you've been better?" She dipped her chin to meet his lowered gaze.

"Haven't we all?" He stood on a tightrope with doom on one side and failure on the other, but in only a handful of days Jasminda had become the bar he gripped to balance himself. How had she managed such a thing? Under his fingertips, her velvet skin soothed him. "How is your skin so soft?"

"It's the balm." She shrugged off his question, but he could not recall even the hands of the gently bred young ladies often trotted out before him being so smooth. How was it that a girl who worked a farm could have skin like this?

Her eyes narrowed, as if seeing inside him. "Something happened. Before we left the Citadel." Her soft voice clung to him in places unused to such tenderness.

"You mean besides discovering that I've nearly singlehandedly brought down the Mantle myself?"

She squeezed his hand. "Unless you've developed a Song in the past day, you did not."

"I led him to it. It's the same thing."

"It's not. And that's not why we left the tent so quickly."

He swallowed, closing his eyes. "My brother . . . is dead." Saying the words aloud made them all the more real. Alariq was gone, and with him, Jack's chance at a normal life.

"I-I'm sorry. I'm so sorry, Jack."

Her emotions showed on her face, but his were buried. He was not supposed to tell anyone yet, but found himself opening up to Jasminda. "He was piloting his airship and ran into a thunderstorm. The craft crashed. He was thrown through the window."

Imagining his elder brother broken in such a way was simply too much. He pushed the vivid images out of his mind. Jasminda stared, sorrow and pity in her eyes. He took a deep breath. "I haven't told you all you need to know about me."

His mouth opened but no more words would come. Pain clawed at his heart.

"Will you tell me?" she asked.

He would have to. It would soon become unavoidable, but this day had already gone on for too long. "I want to, but let us wait until tomorrow, if that is all right. It is not something I want to think about now. Worries on top of worries."

"Of course." She smiled, but it didn't reach her eyes. He had no wish to make her unhappy; however, his heart was too heavy for much more. "Was he your only family?"

The sole relative he still spoke to, if only occasionally. He shook his head. "My mother lives in Fremia now." He didn't mention her abandonment. He supposed Jasminda would find that out soon enough.

"Has she been told?"

"She's in seclusion. But we are half brothers. Were . . . His mother is long passed. He and I were never close. We didn't see eye to eye, but . . ."

"But he was kin."

Jack nodded. "Kin. And now it falls to me." He stroked each of her knuckles and massaged the delicate skin between her fingers.

"What falls to you?"

"I . . ." He dropped his head. Shook it. "It is late. You should rest."

"Tomorrow then." Her hand slipped out of his. He wanted to grab it again, but he wasn't being completely honest and perhaps didn't deserve her touch.

He should leave, and yet sat firmly rooted in place. Was it only last night she had slept in his arms? Could he admit to her that he wanted to do so again?

Her voice shook when she spoke up. "Jack, what do you see when you look at me?"

He was tongue-tied. Beauty. Bravery. An intensity that took him by surprise, even when it shouldn't. He wasn't sure what to say.

"Your men . . . they see me as the enemy. How is it you don't?"

His back straightened. A haze of anger colored his vision. "You're not the enemy. Did someone say something to you?" She grabbed his arm when he went to stand. He didn't know what he was going to do, but it involved finding whomever had caused her pain and inflicting some of his own.

"No, no. Just . . . they think it."

He froze. "Does Earthsong tell you that?"

She shook her head. "I can just tell."

"You're safe here, I promise." He was responsible for this base and these men. He'd reiterated to them that if something happened to one of the refugees, it better be because one of the Lagrimari had caused some bodily harm, else a court-martial was in store. But he would protect Jasminda himself.

She smiled weakly and lay down on her cot, looking over at him. Without consciously thinking about it, he slid onto the ground, stretching out beside her.

Jasminda shot up like a catapult. "You're not going to sleep here, are you?"

"I made you a promise, and I plan to keep it." He settled back, propping his head on his hands behind him. This was better. His muscles had balked at the idea of leaving her, but lying beside her on the unforgiving concrete floor was almost soothing.

"You don't need to do that. You can't sleep on the ground!"

"I've been doing it for the past few weeks. Another night won't hurt anything."

"But you have a whole set of rooms here. With comfortable beds, I'm sure."

He held her gaze, willing her to feel his truth. "I won't let anything happen to you. Besides, this is better than sleeping standing up, which I've done a time or two. I wouldn't recommend it." He grinned, but the worry in her eyes didn't fade.

She lay back down then shifted to her side, watching him. Though he could stare at her all night, he forced his eyes to close. There she was behind his eyelids; at least she wouldn't feel uncomfortable with him gaping at her openly.

Her steady breaths lulled him to the edge of sleep. Then she spoke. "You could probably fit on the cot."

His eyes flew open. He waited half a moment to be sure she wasn't joking. When she made no move to rescind the offer, he shot up so quickly she gasped in surprise. In a heartbeat, he was squeezed in behind her on the narrow cot. It was not much more pliant than the concrete had been, and yet the tension of the day flowed away completely as they lay on their sides, his body spooning hers. She shifted her hair out of the way, baring her neck to his gaze.

Her back sank into his chest. He squeezed her waist and exhaled, feeling content for the first time in many hours.

Suddenly, she stiffened. "What's wrong?" he whispered.

"Nothing. Nothing's wrong." She pulled his arm tighter against her abdomen. His shoulders dropped; he splayed his hand out, feeling the rise and fall of her breath.

Her neck was so inviting, smooth, and fragrant, with her unique scent filling his nostrils. He couldn't resist, his lips met her skin almost of their own accord. Jasminda shivered and pressed even closer to him, so he did it again, whispering his lips across her skin.

"Jack." Her voice held a plea that zipped through him, heightening his attraction.

He kissed her again at the spot where her neck met her shoulder.

"I haven't ever . . . I mean, I want . . ." She was breathless and trembling.

"What do you want, Jasminda?" he said, speaking against her neck. He had wanted to do this for so long, and she was soft and pliant in his arms.

He took a chance and nudged the fabric of her dress aside to press a kiss to her shoulder. "Tell me. I'll give you anything I can."

When his lips touched her, she gave a little moan, which made him never want to stop. But then she turned in his arms to face him. Her tears threatened to overflow, halting him.

"Some things are not for me." She raised her gaze to meet his, sorrow evident, but no regret, to his relief. Her fingers hovered above his lips. He held his breath until they descended in a feather-light touch, tracing his mouth. "*You* aren't for me."

"So why is it that I can't stop thinking about you?"

She leaned even closer, until she was only a breath away, and then she kissed him.

Jack was drenched in sunshine and light, the gray day and

dreary night burned away as he sank into her kiss. He threaded his fingers through her hair, holding her to him. When he prodded her gently with his tongue, she opened, giving him entry.

He lost himself inside her mouth, her lips, the occasional, sensual clash of teeth. When they broke apart, both breathing heavily, he captured her hand in his and pressed a kiss to her palm. He wanted to kiss her everywhere.

Their foreheads met. He stroked her cheek and slid an arm beneath her before rolling them so he was on his back with her on top of him. His hands rested on her lower back as he captured her lips again.

She wiggled on top of him and a pulse shot through him. He turned his head to the side to exhale the deep longing. "Please don't move," he begged, willing his blood to slow.

She rubbed her thigh against the hard length between his legs. Any more of that and he could not guarantee his sanity would stay intact much longer. He flipped them over to hover atop her on shaky arms.

There was no shyness in her expression. She leaned up and kissed him, stroked from his jaw down his neck, to his chest. Her hand came to a stop at his belt. Jack swallowed.

When she moved lower, he grabbed her hand and placed it next to her head. Before she could tempt him with her other hand, he grabbed that as well. She was well and truly trapped now. He claimed another kiss before rising from the cot. He adjusted himself, though there would be no relief in that quarter tonight, and settled on the ground again.

Jasminda peered down at him, pouting. "You can come back. I'll be good. I promise."

"I don't want to make you an oath-breaker. And I will

make no such promises." He took deep, calming breaths, trying his best to ignore the pull of desire that would have him once again on top of her and far more. "Tonight, we should sleep. I do not want to do something that you will regret."

"Would *you* regret it?"

He wanted to laugh but instead reached for her hand and drew it to his lips. "No. But it is not my virtue we are speaking of." He kept her hand in his as he stretched out on the ground.

Jasminda was an innocent, of that he was certain. And though he wanted her beyond reason, it would not be right. Not here, not now. With so much about to change, the last thing he wanted to do was hurt her. Not in any way.

He gripped her, enjoying the play of soft skin against his rougher hands. Sleeping on the ground was no hardship when he was near her.

CHAPTER NINETEEN

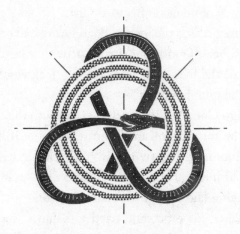

*Can man's judgement ever be righteous? asked a prisoner to
the Mistress of Serpents.*

*Serpent replied, Righteous judgement is a fertile field,
providing a bountiful harvest for those who sowed the seeds.*

*But what of blight, then? a farmer asked. Is it just the
way of things?*

*The way is a path whose end cannot be seen, Serpent said.
You walk the way, believing you know where you're going,
but who has come back from the destination to tell you? In
times of plenty and in want, righteousness lies around every
bend in the path.*

—COLLECTED FOLKTALES

A low, dull ache had formed in Benn's lower back. He couldn't
ignore it—not if he didn't want it to morph into something

much worse. But he didn't have time to run back to his quarters and do the stretching exercises that would alleviate the pain. The stack of folders in his arms represented just a few of the multitude of items on his to-do list.

The farm girl who the mob at Baalingrove had been searching for had been found. She'd run off with a beau. All that mayhem, all the lives lost—for nothing. Jack would be furious when he found out.

The High Commander's arrival along with the continuing plight of the refugees meant Benn wasn't sure if he'd get to sleep at all tonight. The twinge in his back radiated outward from his old injury. He'd have to make time to address it or he'd risk being laid up in bed, unable to work.

He reached his office and tried to balance the folders to gain a free hand and grab the door handle. But the door opened inward revealing Zaura's feverish face. Benn closed his eyes for a moment, sending up a quick prayer for strength, and then stepped inside.

"There you are," Zaura said, waving a notebook in his face. "Someone came by looking for you. A barely out of the womb private from the Communications office." She pulled a stack of message slips from her notebook and thunked them down on his desk, before sitting, vibrating with pent-up energy.

Benn set his folders down then bent to touch his toes, alleviating the ache in his muscles. His usually neatly organized desk looked like a hurricane had passed over it.

"The lack of available Lagrimari translators is proving a hindrance to my research," Zaura complained.

"I thought you were here to research Elsiran folktales?" Benn squatted down, holding his arms out in front of him ready to weep with relief as the pain began to shrink.

"Yes, I'm compiling them for a book. *Collected Folktales* will be the definitive publication of the oral traditions of your people. What few books you have are woefully incomplete. It's a travesty, really. You close yourself off from the rest of the world and live like modern innovations were never invented. A country with no railroads? Really, I just—"

"I think you were talking about the Lagrimari?" If Benn didn't get her back on track she'd complain to him about the so-called "backwoods" ways of the Elsirans for the next hour.

"Ah, yes. Well, it's such an opportunity. Researchers would give up their firstborn for the chance to learn more about a people separated from the world not by choice, but by geography and magic."

She opened her notebook and began flipping through the pages. "And the language is so unique. From what I can tell, it isn't descended in any way from the progenitor of the other languages in the region. It's something completely new." Her eyes glowed with excitement.

"That's all very interesting, Zaura—" He was bent over his desk in a satisfying twist when he noticed the name scrawled on the message slip on top of the stack. Lem Orro. He hadn't heard from Lem in a couple of years. They'd received their commissions and gone through training together. Lem had served a few years then gotten out to join the city constabulary.

Benn straightened and flipped through the messages. Lem had called several times. Stones sank in his gut. He sat down in his chair, hands suddenly cold.

"What is it?" Zaura asked.

He swallowed. "Not sure. But it can't be good." Lem wouldn't call this many times to shoot the breeze.

Benn grabbed the phone. It took two tries to grip the handset properly. Years passed while the switchboard operator connected the call.

"Bitter Street Constabulary."

"I'm looking for Lem Orro."

"Wait just a tick."

A hole opened inside him.

"This is Orro."

"Orro, Benn Ravel."

"Benn, thank the Sovereign." The relief in his voice on made Benn's heart hammer against his sternum.

"What's wrong?"

"It's Ella. She's been arrested."

His vision whited out. He thought he might have passed out for a fraction of a second. "What . . . what happened?"

"Not quite sure. There's no paperwork. I saw her being brought in, but I think she's being black-holed. No arrest report. Nothing posted on the board. The guys that brought her in aren't, ah . . ." He lowered his voice. "They don't exactly uphold the ideals of the force, you know?"

"You mean they're for sale?"

"Something like that."

Benn scrubbed a hand over his head. "I haven't talked to her since Seconday. I don't even know . . . Shite. Is she in danger?"

"She's being held in the woman's ward. Not in solitary or anything like that where mysterious accidents can happen. She should be okay for now. I've been keeping an eye on her."

"Thank you." The moment of relief was short-lived. "What happens to people who are black-holed?"

"That's just it. There's no way to know. I think—I think

with foreigners they're fast-tracked for deportation. No hearing, no appeal."

"Sovereign save us," Benn said, his head falling into his hand. He was at fault for this. An image of the smiling girl he'd met on the beach filled his vision. A group from his squad had rented a cottage for a week—his first leave spent away from home. He'd been walking the sand when he came upon the prettiest girl he'd ever seen lounging on a towel, reading. Her golden brown hair was so unusual and her chocolate eyes drew him in. She'd laughed when he gaped at her. Accused him of blocking out the sun by standing over her. He'd been dripping wet, just out from the ocean.

At his stammered apology, she'd merely grinned. "I didn't realize they made Elsirans quite so large." Her gaze had roamed his wide shoulders and tracked down to his scarred legs. He had the twin urges to back up, removing himself from her perusal, and preen under her appreciative expression. "Are you sure you're a person and not some creature spat out by the sea?"

He crouched down, drawn to her, needing to see the exact shade of her eyes. "I'm honestly not sure anymore."

Her laugh filled him up with something he hadn't known in a long while. Joy.

"Well, seamonster. I'm Ella." She stuck her right hand out in what he'd learned was the Yalyish way of greeting. His hand engulfed hers and he knew right then he would never want another. Two months later, they were married.

She had agreed to move to Elsira and give up school. He'd protested, but she said the degree was something her parents had wanted for her. She'd simply been marking time, changing majors as often as she'd changed her hair. He should have fought harder, insisted she complete her studies, not allowed her to upend her life just to live in Portside in a tiny apartment above a bodega.

A hand clapped down on his shoulder. Zaura stood there, a frown creasing her lined face. She could probably hear the conversation through the handset's speaker. Benn shut out everything else and racked his brain for something, anything, that would help.

"Will you let me know if they move her?" he asked.

"I'll do my best. But something like this . . . it means someone important is calling the shots. Somebody pretty high up the ladder, you know?"

Benn thought of Lalli's warning. That Ella had gotten caught up in something she wasn't prepared for. He cursed himself for not pressing her for more details. "Yeah, I know. Thank you, mate."

"No problem, I know you'd do the same for me."

They clicked off the line and Benn stared at the shiny plastic of the telephone. Something was wrong with his chest. He couldn't feel it anymore.

"You need a solicitor," Zaura announced.

"I'm not sure that would help. I don't think we can afford the kind of solicitor who could break through something as nefarious sounding as being black-holed." Jack could help. But could Benn track down the High Commander and pull him away from the life and death issues of the refugees and the impending war in order to untangle his personal knot hundreds of kilometers away?

"Not always about money, boy. It's about know-how." She tapped her forehead. "Let me have that phone. I happen to know a master attorney in Rosira. She retired some years ago, but she owes me a favor."

Benn slid away from the desk to let Zaura have the phone. There was no point in refusing her. Once she got it in her head to do something, she couldn't be stopped. In that way, she was like his wife.

But he had no illusions about what her attorney friend could achieve. Corruption eventually corroded the heart of all institutions. He'd certainly seen it in the army—the constables were no different. One of the reasons that Benn worked so hard, was so determined to advance, was to try and tackle the plague that infected the army and fix it from the inside out. Jack had been working hard to do the same.

In a moment, he'd have to get up and locate his boss. Beg him to intervene. And hope that whoever was responsible for arresting Ella and hiding it couldn't also hide her from Jack, or put up roadblocks in his ability to do anything. What if they just lied to him and said Ella wasn't being held at all? How long would it take to sort out, and did his wife have that kind of time? The various possibilities for what "black-holing" could really mean chilled him.

Vaguely, he heard Zaura chatting away in a language he assumed was Fremian. He made his way to his feet. Jack could be anywhere on base right now, tracking him down might not be easy.

"What's your wife's name again, child?" Zaura squinted up at him.

"Ella. Ella Farmafield."

"She cuts hair or something like that?"

He frowned. "Yes. What's that have to do with it?"

Zaura spoke again in Fremian and then smiled broadly. She turned back to him. "She'll do it. She's heading over to the constabulary now. The one on Bitter Street, right?"

Benn backed up in shock. "Really?"

"Oh, yes, there's no time to lose when justice is at stake."

Traces of feeling came back into his numb limbs, but he still just stood there, mouth hanging open.

"She'll give us a call once she's got the situation in hand," Zaura said.

Benn simply stared.

"Sit down boy, you look like you're going to pass out."

A bitter taste coated Ella's tongue. Added to the fetid stink of the jail cell, it made her somewhat nauseous.

She stretched her neck, listening to the satisfying *pop* as her joints cracked. Nothing would help her poor, numb tushy. Those muscles had long ago lost feeling from the hard bench on which she sat. She tucked herself into a ball, arms curled around her legs and rested her head on her knees.

She'd never been inside a jail before. It was just as unpleasant as she'd imagined. Four other women shared the cell with her, three on benches and one standing at the front, gripping the iron bars.

The apple-cheeked older woman next to her sighed deeply. She smelled like cookies and Ella wondered what she'd done to land her here. Laying prone on the bench across the way, a woman wrapped in a long, felt coat was sleeping. The other two sharing the cell appeared to be ladies of the evening.

None were in the mood to chat, which, for maybe the first

time ever, was just fine with Ella. The memory of being man-handled into the constable's wagon, brought in through the alley behind the station, and then dragged into this cell assaulted her. And the words of her one and only visitor, whispered and venomous, reverberated in her head.

"You are nothing. You are no one. Do you think you matter to anyone of consequence?"

She shivered, squeezing her legs tighter.

A commotion in the hallway outside the cell block broke the silence. Voices rose and doors slammed, echoing off the stone wall.

The sleeping woman stopped her snoring, briefly, to look up. Tension thickened the air. Ella dropped her feet to the floor, readying herself for something even if she didn't know what it was.

The outer door swung open revealing a trio of grim-faced constables. Thankfully, none of them were the rough men who had brought her in. Right behind them was a thin woman, dressed in an old-fashioned navy suit and hat. Her clothes were finely cut, expensive looking, if out of style by a decade or two.

"Ella? Ella Farmafield," she called out. Ella stood peering at the silver-haired lady as she approached.

"Anneli?" She barely recognized the woman who'd sat in her chair at the beauty parlor days earlier.

Anneli grinned. But her expression changed to one of fury the instant she turned to the officer. "My client is to be released at once."

The officer jerked into action, dropping his keys once in his haste. Finally, he managed to unlock the cell door and pull it open. Ella walked out, sparing a glance behind her at the other women. Her bench mate gave a jaunty wave. No one else paid her much attention.

Ella stared at the woman. "Anneli, what are you doing here?"

"Come along now dear, let's get you out of here."

"How did you even know—" But she was cut off by Anneli's rising voice as she addressed the constables escorting them down the hall.

"This isn't some gulag in the east of nowhere. This is a country of laws and human rights. Don't think that I won't be taking this up with the Chief of Constables and the Council."

The constable next to them paled. "It was a simple paperwork error, mistress. Human error."

Anneli rolled her eyes. "Human error, my arsehole. I learned more about intimidation techniques before you were born, young man, than you'll ever know. And I know how things in this country work." She snorted.

They'd reached the lobby of the station and attracted quite a few stares. Anneli wrapped a surprisingly strong hand around Ella's forearm and pulled her toward the door.

"Let's get out of here, dear, before word gets back to whomever it was you ticked off."

Outside, the moon shone brightly. Ella had no idea of the time; she'd left Benn's watch at home and was now grateful of it. She stood, mind still reeling, while Anneli flagged down a horse-drawn taxi. The driver seemed none too happy to be heading to Portside, but Anneli browbeat him into it.

"You're an attorney?" Ella finally said, once they were secured inside the carriage.

"Practiced in Fremia for forty years and then came here to teach law until my Henrik got sick. After that, I mostly kept to myself." That was putting it mildly, Ella thought.

Anneli swallowed, then cleared her throat. "At any rate. Got a call from an old school friend who knows your husband. Said you were in a bind."

Ella's eyes welled with tears. "How did he even know? I-I don't know how to thank you."

Anneli waved her off. "Don't thank me, thank your husband. Good lad you've got."

Warmth spread through Ella's chest. It had been a mistake not to contact Benn. She needed to tell him everything as soon as possible. He was probably sick with worry.

"So what all did you get yourself into?" Anneli raised an eyebrow.

Ella cringed. "Well . . ."

On their way back to Portside, she told the whole story. Of Kess and the baby, Syllenne and Zann Biddel. Her fateful trip to the orphanage and arrest. The visitor who arrived shortly after she was brought into the station.

The taxi stopped and Ella looked up, not recognizing the street. "Thought it best for you to stay with me tonight," Anneli said. "Go back to your flat in the morning, make sure no one's watching you."

"Oh, thank you. I never would have thought of that."

Anneli lived in a narrow, four-story townhouse in one of the nicest sections of Portside. The interior was cluttered, but not filthy. Stacks of books, newspapers, folders, and loose papers were piled up waist-high in the hallways. Surfaces were covered in knickknacks, framed photographs and sketches, and more books.

Most of the rooms they passed had sheets covering the furniture—she couldn't help peering into the dining room where rumors whispered Anneli kept her mummified husband, to find only a covered table and chairs. The kitchen in the back was warm and lively, with two plush armchairs in the corner by the fireplace. The appliances and decor were from the last century, but amazingly enough, Anneli had her own telephone.

"Would you mind if I called my husband?"

"Of course not, dear. He's waiting for your call. I'll brew some tea."

Ella settled into one of the armchairs, cradling the phone in her arm. Her nerves rattled as she waited for the call to connect. It was so late; would he still be in his office?

"Ravel."

"Oh, Benn." Whatever composure she'd managed to gather fell apart at the sound of his voice.

"Thank the Sovereign you're all right."

"Yes, I'm fine." She sniffed.

"Where are you?"

"At Anneli's house. The attorney. My client." She took a breath. "So much has happened." The story gushed out of her in detail for the second time that night. At some point, Anneli pushed a mug of steaming tea into her hands.

Benn listened patiently without comment.

"I was so scared," she said, "but I think . . . I think I'm getting closer now."

"Closer to what? Being deported? I'd say so." The connection was so clear, she heard the familiar exasperation in his voice, but she also heard the love.

"Well, yes, that, too. But right after I was brought in, I

received a visitor. Sister Gizelle, she's the lackey of the High Priestess, the one who was there at the birth, she came to the station. Apparently it's not unusual for Sisters to go and minister to the prisoners, but I'm pretty sure that's not her main duty. Plus, I hadn't been there ten minutes before she showed up. She was waiting for me. Syllenne must have had me followed to the orphanage."

"Why do you sound so excited?"

"Because, this means that I'm getting under Syllenne's skin. I must be getting close to something, to finding Kess's baby. They wouldn't be threatening me with deportation if—"

"Wait, what did this Sister say to you?"

"At first she said all the usual nonsense about praying for the Queen's guidance. Then once we were alone, she was practically gloating about forcing me out of the country. She told me to never think I could cross the Sisterhood. They *were* Elsira."

Benn sighed.

"But don't you see?" she asked, voice rising.

"See what, seashell?"

"The baby has got to be nearby, otherwise why would the Sisterhood view me as such a threat? Why go to the trouble to silence me if I wasn't making progress?"

She could practically see Benn rubbing the bridge of his nose.

"I'm sorry," she whispered. She knew he had a lot on his mind.

"No. No, I'm sorry. I wish I could . . ." His breathing deepened. "Jack is back. He's headed to Rosira in the morning, but I've been ordered to stay here. I thought I'd be able to go with him, but we're in a state of emergency. War is coming,

El. The Mantle is going to fall and . . . Things are going to change."

"What things?"

"Everything." He was quiet for a while. "I need you to be safe. Maybe leaving the country isn't a bad idea."

"What?" she screeched.

"Trust me, I don't want you any further away than you are already. It's just that we're teetering on the edge of a cliff right now. And there's nowhere to go but down. Between the Mantle and the war, you going up against the Sisterhood is just . . . Syllenne Nidos is a bad enemy to have, seashell."

"So am I, Benn. So am I."

CHAPTER TWENTY

The Master of Jackals walked into the desert bearing only one skin of water.

Are you not afraid? a boy cried, as Jackal disappeared into the sands.

I will return or I will not, he said. My fear has no bearing on the outcome.

—COLLECTED FOLKTALES

Yllis careens around the corner nearly crashing into a servant. His dark eyes are stormy.

"Did you find him?" I ask, breathless.

He shakes his head. "What exactly did he say to you, Oola?"

I twist my fingers in frustration, recalling my brother's words. "He wanted more, begged me for a little more power. When I refused, he got upset. Yllis, I've never seen him like this before. He was . . ."

Eero's eyes had bugged out of his head. The veins in his fore-head and neck had been so prominent, I thought he might burst.

His frustration and jealousy and anger ripped at me. Clawed me open. I knew then that his gift had been a terrible mistake. I could never give him any more of my Song.

My voice is a quiet hush. "He said that he would find a way to get more. That I could not stop him."

Yllis wraps strong arms around me. I sob into his chest, feeling the weight of my failure drag me down. He calms me with tender, wordless sounds and his solid presence, but I feel selfish for relying upon him.

"You have not told anyone, have you?" I say into his chest.

"No, of course not. And none of the other Cantors know the spell nor have an interest in it."

That, at least, is something. "But still, someone could discover it. Or craft a similar spell. Eero has a way of getting what he wants." Or maybe that was just with me.

"I think we have created a monster," Yllis says. He pulls back to look into my eyes. I can only agree.

Whatever happens next will be my fault. I crumple inside to consider it.

The vision was interrupted by the bleating of a horn as the base residents were called to the mess hall for breakfast. Jasminda tucked away the caldera, and followed the blaring noise to the morning meal.

She hoped to see Jack again—he'd woken her with a kiss before disappearing back to his work—but as soon as the plates

were cleared away, a line of soldiers led the refugees to a caravan of buses for the trip to Rosira.

Benn appeared and directed her to a special vehicle, a boxy,
close-topped four-wheeler. He explained that for security purposes, Jack rode in an armored vehicle, which couldn't legally
transport civilians. Jasminda had wanted to share the long
journey with him from the eastern border of Elsira to the capital city on the western coast, but it wasn't to be. Instead she
had to put up with a lonely trip, complete with a driver whose
eyes would flick to the rearview mirror, shooting cold, suspicious glances at her. She didn't waver, meeting his gaze each
time until he looked away. He was no doubt wondering why
he was chauffeuring around a Lagrimari-looking Elsiran girl.

The rain stopped as they drove west, and a tension she
hadn't realized she was holding released. She admired the
rolling hills and dense forests of Elsira's picture-perfect countryside. Night fell, and dusty, unpaved roads eventually gave
way to wider, paved highways, illuminated by electric lights
and full of vehicles of all shapes and sizes.

Jasminda sucked in a breath when she got her first glimpse
of Rosira from the crest of a hill. The city swept up and away
from the ocean like a gentle wave. Lights sparkled from thousands of houses, which from this distance gave the impres-
sion of being stacked on top of one another, but as they drew
closer, were really etched in layers going up the steep hillside.

There were no skyscrapers or especially tall buildings like
in the pictures she'd seen of the megacities of Yaly. The main
industry here was commerce, and docks stretched the entire
length of the coastline with an assortment of vessels anchored
there like great beasts asleep in their pens.

She tested her connection to Earthsong, then dropped it,

immediately overwhelmed by the dense press of so many energies. How could anyone use magic in a place so heavily populated? Did Lagrimar have cities, and if so, how were the residents able to cope?

Her vehicle traveled a serpentine path through the city. Jack had assured her he would find lodging for her, though he hadn't mentioned where. She suspected the Sisterhood had a dormitory of some kind where she could stay. Surely women whose mission was to feed and care for the settlers would not view her as terribly as the soldiers had. She could only hope.

The steep road through the densely packed buildings turned back on itself several times, dizzying her. After half a dozen twists and turns, the truck approached a gilded gate guarded by soldiers wearing black uniforms with gold trim and fringed epaulets. The gates swung open revealing a brightly lit, curving drive that ascended even higher.

The Royal Palace of Elsira loomed in front of them, white stones gleaming under the illumination of a shocking quantity of electric lights. The pictures in her textbooks did not do it justice. Columned porches ran along the first floor with a seemingly endless number of arched windows just beyond. Carved into the stone above each window were images of the Founders, the magical Lord and Lady in various poses showing how they'd transformed Elsira.

Somewhere within this building lay the sleeping body of their descendent, the Queen Herself, protected by the Prince Regent who ruled in Her stead until She awoke and returned to power. Seeing it in person, Jasminda was transfixed. Though there was no longer any magic in Elsira, the palace seemed to give off its own energy and spoke to her in an unfamiliar way.

The driver exited the vehicle and Jasminda remained, hoping that whatever business Jack had here would be quick. The trip had been exhausting, and she wanted nothing more than to fall into whatever bed she was assigned. The door she leaned against jerked open and there stood Jack, holding out his hand.

She stared at it uncomprehendingly. "Can I not wait here for you?"

"You would prefer to sleep in the truck?" The corner of his mouth quirked, shattering his grim expression.

She looked from him to the palace and back again. A knowing smile crept up Jack's face.

"When you said you'd find lodging for me, I didn't think . . . Jack, I can't sleep in the *palace*."

"Why ever not?" He crossed his arms and leaned against the truck.

"Because I'm a goat farmer. Palaces are for royalty. The Prince Regent cannot possibly allow someone like me here."

"Trust me, it's all right. Many officials and dignitaries live in the palace. A whole wing is devoted to ranking officers and their families. Honestly, it's more like an inn than a proper palace these days."

"But—"

"I'm well acquainted with whom the Prince Regent allows under his roof." A flicker of pain crossed his face, and he took a deep breath. "Jasminda—"

"Commander!" an insistent voice bellowed from across the driveway.

"One moment, General," Jack responded while his eyes pleaded with her. She accepted his offered palm, gripping it as she stepped from the vehicle and approached the palace.

A battalion of servants greeted them inside the entry. Jack announced her as an honored guest and conferred with a matronly woman who must have been in charge of things. Two maids whisked her away before she could even thank Jack or say good night, let alone find out what he had wanted to tell her. Hopefully it was whatever he'd said she needed to know about him. Her heart burned to know his secrets, even as part of her was glad she didn't.

She barely registered the dazzling hallways of the palace, the opulent room she was led to, the plush carpeting, detailed tapestries, or hand-carved furniture. She saw only the bed, canopied and enormous, and then the backs of her eyelids as she sank into the extravagant mattress.

A knock at the door brought Jasminda fully awake. She garbled a greeting and a tiny maid, not yet out of her teens, appeared with reams of fabric in her arms.

"Have a nice rest, miss?" the girl said in a crisp city accent. Jasminda tried to prop herself on her elbows but gave up after a few moments and collapsed back down.

"I've never slept better," she said, mostly to the pillow.

The girl chuckled, then flitted around the room, opening the curtains. Late-afternoon sunshine filtered in.

"It's time to bathe and change, miss. The Prince Regent has requested you for dinner."

She startled into wakefulness. Was she to be the main course? Neither the servants last night nor this girl reacted to her appearance, but Jasminda remained on her guard. Why could the prince want to dine with her? Jack must have set it up, though after enduring the suspicious glares and harsh words of the soldiers, she could not imagine the prince would be more welcoming to her than they had been. However, it stood to reason that Jack would be in attendance, as well; he was the reason she was staying there, after all. Her excitement at being near him again grew as she followed the maid into the gold-trimmed bathroom.

Marble floors and walls greeted her. She gaped at the ivory-handled sinks with hot water flowing from the taps and marveled at the modern efficiency of a water closet with a seat that warmed her bottom. Papa had devised a plan for plumbing in the cabin, using some spell she suspected, but water still needed to be heated on the stove.

The bathtub, however, proved to be a stumbling block. The little maid was adamant about bathing her. Jasminda protested that she could very well bathe herself—she wasn't a child—but finally gave in to the girl's steely determination.

At least a bucketful of dirt disappeared down the drain. Her hair was washed and doused with a sweet-smelling concoction. Nadal—for if another woman was to see her naked, Jasminda should at least know her name—carefully combed Jasminda's thick, tightly coiled locks free of snags in front of the fire, drying it as much as possible. Then she helped her into a complicated dress she wasn't sure she'd be able to get out of again. At a gentle tap on the shoulder, Jasminda turned to face the full-length mirror in the dressing room.

She gasped at the vision in front of her. Shiny, golden fabric flowed around her body, hugging her curves and making her appear, for the first time, like she was worthy of staying in the palace. Her hair was even tamed into a cascade of thick waves.

"You are a miracle worker," she praised Nadal, who blushed.

Nadal searched the pocket of her apron and pulled out a tiny oval mirror on a gold chain. "Where would you like it, miss?"

Jasminda gaped. "Who is it for?" Mourning mirrors like the one Nadal held were worn after the death of a loved one. It was said those in the World After could peer through the mirrors and say their final good-byes to the living. After her mother died, she'd worn one around her neck for a year. When her father and brothers died, she hadn't had the heart.

"You haven't heard?" Nadal's hushed voice filled with wonder. "I'd thought since you arrived with . . . Miss, the Prince Regent has gone to the World After."

Jasminda took the mirror from the girl, gripping it lightly, and shook her head. "When did this happen? And how could he have invited me for dinner?"

"They made the announcement this morning, but he could have been dead for days. They never proclaim the death of a royal until his heir has been sworn in. Fear of attack during the changeover or some such. I heard from a girl who works in the prince's wing that she'd seen His Grace last week, Thirday. But she's just a duster, and she didn't see him that often." The torrent of words seemed to take something out of the girl, and she dropped her chin, staring at the floor as if embarrassed to have spoken at all.

"So the new prince invited me?" Her skin went clammy. The air in the room suddenly grew thin, as if Jasminda stood at the peak of a mountain. Jack had wanted to tell her something that night at the base, and again before they'd entered the palace . . .

She shook her head, unwilling to believe such a thing. He was a warrior, and perhaps a poet. He was almost certainly not a . . . She couldn't even attach the word to him. An image of his face slightly twisted in one of his grim smiles filled her vision. He would have told her something so monumental.

"Is this dinner special in some way? Is it in honor of the prince?"

Nadal shook her head. "It is just dinner. The changeover is seamless. Outside, the people will mourn and most here will wear the mirrors for a week or so, but the business of the palace never stops, not even for death."

Jasminda sucked in a breath and fastened the gold chain around her neck. It fit snugly at the base of her throat. Not quite tight enough to choke her.

"It's time, miss," Nadal said.

Jasminda steeled her nerves and ignored the questions battling for dominance in her mind. They exited the rooms, and Nadal led her to the top of a grand staircase where a black-clad butler ushered her down and through a maze of hallways to a grand dining room. The grandeur of the palace was a blur, the empty feeling in her bones stealing most of her attention.

"Jasminda ul-Sarifor." A hush descended over the vast room as her name was announced by a silver-haired attendant. Every head swiveled in her direction, and she froze under the weight of expectation in the air. The sense of foreboding remained, but she tilted her chin a few notches higher and stepped farther into the hall. Yet another butler appeared at her elbow, a kindly faced man who, despite his Elsiran appearance, reminded her of Papa.

"Miss Jasminda, this way, please," he said, and led her deeper into the dining room. She followed his straight back, walking carefully in her delicate gold slippers. A four-piece string ensemble sat in the corner playing muted orchestral music. Three enormous U-shaped tables took up the majority of the room, with seating around the sides and a wide space for the servants to come and go in the middle. The end of the center table faced a slightly raised dais on which stood a smaller table. She surmised that must be where the Prince Regent sat. The space was magnificent—more carvings of the Lord and Lady adorned the tops of each window and the ceiling was a grid of carved stone. Around each table sat several dozen people, all watching her. Conversations restarted, but their stares drilled into her as the butler led her to a setting only a half-dozen paces away from the dais.

She was seated next to a posh woman in an elaborate, feathered hat, her snakelike figure poured into a silken black sheath dress. Directly across from Jasminda, an old man with a hearing cone pressed to one ear and thick spectacles leaned toward the man to his right, complaining loudly of the noise. Each wore a mourning mirror. The most ostentatious display was from an older gentleman farther down the table whose mirror was affixed to his eye patch.

Jasminda fought the urge to squirm as the gazes of so many in the room raked over her, not bothering to hide their inquisitiveness. Her glass was filled by a passing waiter, and she grabbed at it, gulping greedily to soothe the sudden ache in her throat. The hall quieted again, and Jasminda turned to see what had captured everyone's attention this time.

A hidden door built into the wall behind the dais had opened. A group of guards in the fancy black uniforms emerged, then flanked the door. Chairs groaned across the floor as everyone at the tables stood, almost as one. Jasminda raced to catch up.

The same man who announced her stepped forward and cleared his throat. "Jaqros Edvard Alliaseen, High Commander of the Royal Army, First Duke of Cavill, and Prince Regent of Elsira."

The servant slid away, and Jasminda's heart dissolved into a pool of liquid at her feet. Directly in front of her, in full regalia, stood Jack.

CHAPTER TWENTY-ONE

The Mistress of Frogs held a banquet for her closest friends.
Friendship is like a mirage in the desert, she said. It gives
you great hope and encouragement when you need it the most.

—COLLECTED FOLKTALES

She had thought him beautiful in dirty fatigues and covered in bruises and blood, but in his royal uniform and freshly trimmed hair, he was nothing short of divine. The spark of hope she'd held inside, the one she'd foolishly allowed to grow into a tiny flame, flickered then snuffed itself out completely.

Jack—*Prince* Jack—sat stiffly at the raised table mere steps away from her. His face was a rigid mask. He looked straight ahead, acknowledging no one.

The head butler was speaking again, making announcements about the dinner, the soup, the ingredients, but Jasminda's attention was wholly focused on the man in front of her.

Gone was the ragged creature she'd discovered on the mountain and thought mad, the bruised and bloodied soldier who had sacrificed himself to protect a woman he didn't know. A woman who could have been his enemy. When did he become this statue sitting before her, neither warrior nor poet, but prince?

The coronation must have happened as soon as he'd arrived in the palace, but even more than the shock at his new position, she couldn't believe how his whole nature seemed to have transformed. The light in his eyes that had withstood capture, gunshot, and beatings was now dimmed.

The kindly butler approached and cleared his throat politely, placing his hands on her chair. She pulled her attention away from Jack to find that she was the only one still standing. As every eye in the room, except Jack's, bored into her, she took her seat as gracefully as possible, smoothing her dress and thanking the butler in a trembling voice as he slid in her chair.

Her hands shook. She flattened them on the table, imprinting the grooves of the wood onto her palms. Anger flared hot for a moment, then melted just as suddenly into despair. Neither emotion would help her. She was lost in an unforgiving sea. There was no way to escape the glares from around the room, and the one person who had given her comfort during these past days of upheaval was now a stranger to her.

Tears stabbed the backs of her eyes. She used every trick she could to hold them back, resorting to digging her nails into the inside of her elbow until she could focus on the external pain a little more than the internal.

The first course began, and chatter resumed around the room. The soup set before her was completely foreign. The stunning silverware of her place setting offered four spoons. Jasminda took a deep breath and clasped her hands together, darting glances around the table. The woman next to her had already chosen a spoon, and Jasminda couldn't see from her position which one it had been.

She didn't want to make a misstep. Jack had invited her here, whatever his reasons were, whoever he was now, and she was determined to get through this meal with as much dignity as she could muster. She buried her shock and dismay, replacing it with determination. If she was the only *grol* these snooty city folk ever encountered, she wasn't going to give them any more fuel for their fire of scorn.

Jack filled her peripheral vision, but she refused to look at him again. He cleared his throat, then did so again a few moments later. A waiter hurried to tend to his water glass, but he brushed the man aside. The third time he cleared his throat she snapped her head toward him, narrowing her eyes and clenching her jaw against the swarm of emotion rising inside her.

He slowly drew his hand down and selected the second spoon from the left, all the time staring down at his bowl. At her place setting, she chose the same spoon. The woman next to her tilted her bowl toward her body, then shoveled the spoon in the opposite direction before bringing it to her mouth.

Jasminda glanced back at Jack as he slowly, slowly ate his soup in the same way. She copied his movements, happy to get something in her stomach. She had slept all day and hadn't eaten anything since the day before. Dinner went on like this, course after course. She would be presented with some new obstacle—bread, salad, three entrées—and Jack would model the behavior for her.

The Prince Regent—she vowed to stop being so familiar with him, even in her head—did not speak to anyone during dinner, and this appeared to be taken as normal by those present. It made her feel better that she would not have to talk to him. Just hearing his voice would make it that much harder to mend the gaping hole inside her.

Blessedly, after what felt like hours, dinner finally ended. The last dessert dishes were cleared away by the staff, and the various characters at the table patted their bellies obnoxiously. Jasminda had never eaten so much food at one time in her life. Guiltily, she thought of the refugees. What rations had they been provided? Her meal sank like lead in her stomach.

The company rose from the table and, just when she thought there would be a reprieve from the unrelenting pressure of the evening, the butlers ushered everyone into a huge adjoining sitting room. Small groups split off and clustered around settees or card tables, chatting amiably. Jack was nowhere to be seen. Jasminda stood alone next to the massive fireplace, enduring the uncomfortable heat.

Glances sent her way ranged from mere curiosity to outright contempt. Her back remained straight and head high, but inside, she was wilting.

A girl about her age approached the other end of the fireplace, setting a glass on the mantel. She stood for a moment peering at the flames before approaching Jasminda. Slender and beautiful, she wore a peach-and-gold dress that made her skin appear to glow. Amber eyes the color of her hair appraised Jasminda, not unkindly.

"These things are positively awful."

Jasminda stared at her, unsure of the girl's intentions.

"I'm Lizvette." She held out her hands.

"Jasminda." She placed her palms to Lizvette's and pressed gently.

"Welcome. I'm told you're responsible for saving the life of our new prince." Lizvette's friendly smile seemed genuine, but Jasminda did not dare attempt a connection to Earthsong to determine her true intentions. She scanned the room to find they had attracted a great deal of attention.

"I did save him once, or perhaps twice. But I cannot take credit for the last time."

"Our Jack, always getting into trouble." Lizvette smiled, but her eyes were lakes of sadness.

"You are . . . friends with the Prince Regent?"

Her smile changed, though Jasminda could not determine precisely what was different about it. It was bleaker, perhaps. "I was betrothed to his brother."

"May he find serenity in the World After," Jasminda responded, bowing her head. Lizvette repeated the blessing. Jasminda considered the young woman's dress more closely. What she'd initially thought was shiny gold beading were actually dozens of mirrors embroidered into the material. A conspicuous show of grief that seemed at odds with Lizvette's unassuming manner.

There were not enough mirrors in the world to adequately represent everything Jasminda mourned. So many lives gone, so many failures. She'd thought for a moment as she lay beside Jack that perhaps . . . But now that was gone, too. Perhaps it was for the best. She did not want to imagine the look in his eye when she failed him, too.

An exceptionally tall man stalked toward them, his face

contorted in indignation. She could read his intention quite clearly without Earthsong and took a step backward. Lizvette followed Jasminda's gaze and turned to face him. He took hold of Lizvette's elbow and leaned down to whisper loudly in her ear.

"What do you think you're doing?"

"I'm greeting our visitor, Zavros. She is the Prince Regent's guest. Jasminda, this is my cousin—"

"It's time to go, Lizvette. You're keeping your father waiting."

She smiled apologetically at Jasminda. "It was lovely meeting you. I'm sure we'll be seeing each other again soon. May She bless your dreams."

Jasminda repeated the farewell and stood rigidly as Lizvette was towed away to a card table in the back. The blazing fire had grown unbearable, and the perimeter around her was a quarantine zone. What a surprise not to be the belle of the ball. With a final glance about the room, in which she refused to admit she was searching for Jack, she slipped out the door.

Thick silence draped the empty hallway; each direction stretched on identically. She had absolutely no idea how to get back to her rooms. With no orientation or memory of the route she'd taken to get to the dining room, she took a few tentative steps to the left before a voice halted her progress.

"Leaving?"

She turned to find Jack standing behind her, regal and gorgeous. He was so close, but now untouchable. She hardened her features, not looking directly at him, not wanting to give away the storm of emotions fighting for dominance within her. Her fists clenched and opened as her body stiffened with tension. Traitorous tears welled; she blinked them back.

"I'm not sure if I should bow or curtsy or what," she said, gripping her hands in front of her to stop their movement.

"I am sorry I didn't tell you," he said, voice pitched low. "I wanted to. I should have. It's inexcusable, I just . . ."

She longed to hear an excuse that would satisfy her and return things to the way they were. No words came. He shook his head and rubbed at his chest, just below his collarbone where his bullet wound had been.

"Jasminda." He stepped closer, and she took a step back.

"That wound was healed. Does it still bother you?"

He dropped his hand to his side and drew even closer, backing her against the wall. She stared at the carpet, but he tilted her face up with a finger on her chin. Wanting to numb herself to the feeling of his skin on hers, she refused to meet his eyes and focused instead on his chest, covered in rich-looking fabric with brightly colored insignias on his uniform. He released her chin, but she stubbornly continued avoiding his face.

"Jasminda," he repeated. Her name on his lips was more than she could bear. "If I could change who I am, I'd do it in a heartbeat. You deserved the truth. I owed you that much."

"You can have no debt to me. I helped a captive soldier, not a prince." As much as she tried to avoid it, she was drawn to him. Perhaps this was the last time she'd be this close to him. The tears escaped; she could not stop them. "Now if you'll excuse me, Your Grace, I have urgent business in my room that needs attending to. Pleasant evening."

She slid out of the cage of his body and gave a wobbly curtsy before picking up her beautiful skirt and running. When one hallway ended, she picked another at random. She had no idea where she was going, but she'd rather be lost in the palace for a thousand years than see Prince Jack again.

Blinded by her tears, she finally stopped in a blue hallway full of mirrors. She leaned against a little table but refused to look at her face, ashamed of her reaction to him. He could no longer be Jack. He could no longer be her hope. He could be nothing to her at all.

"One of the maids escorted her to her chambers," Usher said, entering the dimly lit space. Jack paused midstep from where he'd been pacing the floor of his sitting room, only half listening to the evening news.

"Thank you, Usher. Make sure she has a servant assigned to her at all times so she doesn't become lost again."

The old man nodded.

"But don't let her know that I ordered it. I don't think she would like that."

To his credit, Usher didn't even raise an eyebrow. The valet had been with Jack's family since before he was born. The old man's kindly face was a warmer, more familiar sight than his own father's had been. Jack switched off the radiophonic, silencing the newsreader midsentence, then fell into an armchair in front of the fireplace. He could not begrudge Jasminda her anger and pain. It had been unacceptable for him to keep the truth from her.

But each chance he'd had to tell her—that night at the base, or the morning before they'd left for Rosira when he could have found a quiet place to explain—he'd avoided it. Reality was coming faster than he had wanted, and he'd been certain he could outpace it.

His return had been chaotic, with the secret coronation last night and then a flurry of briefings. He'd ordered the bulk of the armed forces to the eastern border in preparation for the breach, and logistics had taken up much of his time.

Aside from the pending disaster with Lagrimar, he'd had calls with the leaders of their allies Fremia and Yaly, letters to read and sign, introductions to staff and security personnel to make. He'd hardly looked up when he was being called for dinner, and then it was too late.

He'd been a fool, and worse, a cowardly one. His desire to put off any change to the way she saw him had won out over his good sense, and Jasminda had suffered. The weight of the crown threatened to press him down into the earth.

But her expression as she'd stood in the dining hall, the devastation marring her lovely face, made him feel like a villain. It gutted him. The guilt and shame were heavier than the crown.

Somehow, he could not keep the women in his life from hating him.

"Has word been sent to my mother?"

"Yes, sir. But it may be some time before she receives the message."

The last he'd heard, his mother was cloistered in a jungle sanctuary, hours from the nearest Fremian city. "She finally has her wish—her son is the Prince Regent. Too late to do her any good."

The little he'd heard of the news report had confirmed his fears that his coronation was being met with more than a few misgivings. His mother's defection to Fremia, Elsira's southern neighbor, twelve years earlier had cast a long shadow, especially on her only son.

"I only hope she's found peace," Usher said.

Jack hoped so, as well. He stared at the crackling fire until the flames burned themselves into his vision. His fingers picked at the fringe on his jacket, unraveling one of the threads, and he tapped an impatient rhythm on his knee.

"Say what you must," he said, after the silence had grown more oppressive than companionable.

Usher's bushy gray eyebrows rose. "What makes you think I have something to say?"

"Twenty-two years of knowing you, old man. And I suspect I won't like whatever it is, so spit it out."

"I believe I said everything I had to say before you left on your foolhardy mission." Usher and Jack's brother, Alariq, had been the only two who'd known about Jack's trip to Lagrimar.

He raked a hand through his hair. "Protecting Elsira is my only mission, and I would do anything, even sacrifice myself, to see that happen. The opportunity was once in a lifetime, too great to miss."

"The opportunity for the army's High Commander to go undercover in enemy territory? It is unheard of."

"I was the only one for it. The only Elsiran to speak their bloody language well enough to blend in with them. If I hadn't gone and verified what they were planning, the Council would never release funds for the preparation we need. We would have been blindsided by the breach." Although if he'd acted with more circumspection, the cornerstone might still be intact, but he could not say those words out loud.

"You paid a heavy cost for that information, young sir."

Jack absently rubbed the place on his chest where the bullet had pierced his flesh. The pain had been gone for days but now there was a phantom ache. He must have been imagining it. "I don't regret accepting the mission."

"And being captured?" Usher's voice was soft, without a hint of censure, but a pinprick of guilt stabbed at Jack.

The fire crackled and jumped, flames leaping upward. The vibrancy of the fire reminded him of her, on the porch with her shotgun, of the blade she kept strapped to her leg. Fearsome beauty. The pain in his chest shifted and grew. It lay mere inches from his heart.

"Being captured nearly killed me. But it also brought me a wonderful gift."

He slumped down in his chair. When had he come to care so much for her? She had been a bright light at the end of a tunnel of pain and desperation, but what Jack felt was not merely due to the debt he owed her for saving him, not just for her kindness toward him. She was strong, with a sharp mind, passionate, and brave. So unlike the giggling, gossiping society girls who had vied for his affection for so many years. Jasminda slit a man's throat and kept her wits about her, for Sovereign's sake; she had a warrior's heart.

Usher steepled his fingers below his chin. "This gift you speak of, is it the kind worth keeping?"

Jack looked up sharply.

"Is it the kind that you would regret allowing to slip through your fingers?" the old man said.

"She is angry and hurt. I was, if not dishonest, at least not forthcoming. She has every right—"

"You do not balk at walking across enemy lines and pretending to be one of them, at great peril, I might add, yet you quiver with fear at one young woman."

"I'm not quivering with fear," Jack scoffed.

"I believe I see a quiver, young sir. Just there." Usher extended his finger, waggling it about, pointing at most of Jack's body.

A smile edged its way across Jack's face. "The Queen Who Sleeps must have a sense of humor to send you to look after me."

"That She must," Usher said.

Jack regarded the fire for another moment before jumping from his seat, what he must do now suddenly clear. "And I thank Her every day for that," he said, kissing Usher on the forehead.

He raced out of the room and down the corridor, flying up the stairs to the great alarm of several passing servants. Jasminda's rooms in the guest wing were on the other side of the palace. He wished she were closer, though visiting her rooms, wherever they were and especially at this hour, was unseemly and could put her reputation in jeopardy. Based on the chilly reception she'd received from the gathered aristocracy at dinner, however, her current reputation was no great asset.

Jack had been caught in the dining hall after dinner by Minister Stevenot, who had profusely dispatched his condolences. Over his shoulder, through the cracked door to the adjoining parlor, he'd watched, heartsick, as Jasminda stood alone, an island in an unfriendly sea. He'd been on his way to her when Lizvette approached Jasminda, and her kindness filled him with gratitude.

As if conjured by his thoughts, Lizvette now appeared on the staircase above him in the grand hall.

"Your Grace," she said, curtseying, an amused smile playing upon her lips.

He climbed up to the landing to stand beside her. "You know, you must try to keep a straight face when you say that."

She nodded, her eyes alight. "I shall keep that in mind." Her expression sobered, and she laid a hand on his arm. "I haven't gotten a chance to tell you how sorry I am for the loss of your brother."

"No, I'm sorry I haven't been to see you. And for your loss. Not only a husband gone, but you were to be the princess."

Her lips pressed to a thin line. "Yes, well, Mother and Father are inconsolable." Her voice was light, but shadows danced in her eyes.

He and Lizvette had raced around the palace as children, under the disapproving eyes of their parents. Her father had been a close friend and advisor to his, and still retained a place on the Council. She and his brother had been engaged for two years and were to be married in just a few weeks.

"And you?" Jack asked, craning his neck down to look her in the eye.

"It happened so fast." She dipped her head and ran her fingers across the mirrors embedded in her gown, avoiding his gaze. "Alariq did love his gadgets, though. He would probably have lived in that airship if he could have." She managed a weak smile. "I can't imagine what was going through his mind, piloting through that kind of storm."

"Nor I. He was always so reasonable. I just hope I'm up to the task of filling his shoes."

"You are. Of course you are. You will be a wonderful prince." She finally met his eyes, beaming up at him, though her smile overflowed with sadness. She took hold of his hand and squeezed. He hoped she was holding up well, despite appearing so tired. Dark circles under her eyes were starting to show through her makeup.

"I don't want to keep you," he said, pulling away. She held on a moment longer before releasing him.

"Whatever are you doing on this end of the palace?"

He shifted on his feet, his gaze involuntarily drawn toward the hall leading to Jasminda's room.

Lizvette looked, then frowned slightly. She sighed. "Are you . . . *with* her?"

"I owe her an apology. One that is overdue."

Lizvette took a step back. "The whole palace is talking. They're watching her. Wondering."

"I don't have time for Rosiran busybodies." Indignation shaded his voice.

"Jack, she will be trouble for you."

His protective instincts kicked in. Jasminda was not anyone else's concern. She belonged here, had more right than most who called the palace home.

The worry in Lizvette's face cut through his rising ire. His anger was not for her. "May She bless your dreams, Vette."

"And yours as well, Your Grace."

He walked away, his skin prickling with the sensation of being watched until he turned the corner.

CHAPTER TWENTY-TWO

The Mistress of Horses oft traversed the countryside at night singing the moon's song. Her voice was coarse soil in which no melody could take root and yet she brought joy to all who heard her.

—COLLECTED FOLKTALES

The marketplace teemed with shoppers shouting over each other, haggling for the best price. Ella stood before her favorite fruit-monger, bartering over the exorbitant cost of cherries. She'd wanted to bake a pie, but for what the woman was charging, she may as well buy a steak.

"I've got children to feed," the merchant stated, spreading her arms.

Ella gritted her teeth and forced a smile. "Well then, you should feed them the cherries."

She walked away, a twinge of guilt compressing her chest. She'd been out of sorts for two days, perhaps being arrested did that to a person.

After staying the night in Anneli's spacious but cluttered guest room, she'd gone back to her apartment yesterday morning. She'd promised the teenaged son of the bodega owner downstairs a tenthpiece if he'd go up with her, just in case someone was there waiting. Of course, no one had been.

And then she'd gone to work because she could scarcely spare the coin she'd given the boy. Working yesterday and today had given her enough money to visit the evening market, but her nerves were raw. It didn't help that now that she knew she was being followed; she felt eyes on her wherever she went.

She scanned the crowded marketplace, hoping to catch a glimpse of whoever was reporting her movements to Syllenne.

A woman near the bake shop caught her eye. Ella knew everyone in the neighborhood by sight, and while this woman looked familiar, it wasn't because she lived nearby. Her golden gaze marked her as Elsiran. She was dressed simply, with the long apron of a washerwoman. Her copper-colored hair was pulled back in a braid. Ella racked her brain for where she'd seen the woman before.

She turned onto a quiet side street, heading away from the market and stopped, gazing in the window of a seamstress's shop. Footsteps behind her slowed, and Ella tensed, her heart rising to her throat. She reached inside her bag for her shael before turning around.

The woman she'd noticed moments ago approached her boldly. She was perhaps a few years older than Ella, though it was hard to tell. She had the look of someone prematurely weathered by a hard life—the way the street urchins who scampered underfoot might if they managed to grow up.

"Can I help you?" Ella asked.

"Name's Mayzi. Mayzi Biddel."

It came back to her then, the woman straightening up at the billiard hall after the Dominionist meeting. "I'm Zann's wife. Can I talk to you? Buy you a pint?"

Ella scrutinized the woman's work-roughened hands and fiery hair. She had a wariness about her mixed with a helping of melancholy, but an underlying warmth put Ella somewhat at ease. Still, she felt the need to stay alert. And after the past few days, one pint could easily turn into far too many. "How about tea?"

Mayzi shrugged and Ella led the way to the tea shop on the corner. They settled into a quiet table in the back.

Steam rose from the kettle between them. Mayzi studied Ella, then seemed to come to a decision. "You should know that Zann and I been married going on ten years. No babies. Wasn't sure who the fault lay with but now . . ." She looked out the window toward the docks, tears misting her eyes. "Wanted to know more about the baby I heard you all talking about."

Ella straightened. "You think the baby is his?"

"Wouldn't surprise me none. I know he's stepped out on me before. Always been discreet about it. But this last one, the lady you mentioned, Kess." Mayzi shook her head. "I was a little scared of her."

"Why?"

"She was so self-possessed. Focused on him so much. Not like the little nymphs running around that he snares in his web. She was older, wiser. Went after him like it was her job."

Ella sat back, stirring her tea. "I'd never taken my sister as one to go after another woman's husband. I didn't know her very well, but . . ." She sighed. She hadn't known grown-up Kess at all. "As for the baby, he's missing. I'm trying to find him."

"Missing?"

"It's a long story. Probably best you don't know too much about it."

Mayzi frowned, but seemed to accept this without further comment. "What did he look like?" The wistful tone in her voice resonated; the two women were much in the same position. Married for years with the hope of children fading more and more every month.

"Tiny little thing. Strong lungs. Face like a wet sack of potatoes, but adorable in his own way. I only held him for a few minutes." The memory of the baby in her arms made her shiver. "Strange white-blond hair, though. Makes me wonder if he really could be your husband's. That hair didn't come from Kess."

Mayzi stiffened. "Zann's mother was an Udlander."

Ella's eyes widened.

"I know. Very few Udlander women ever leave their homes. The men wander a bit from time to time, but they tend to keep the women close. I met one once, pale as a ghost from head to toe. Hair that same shade, like white gold. Zann's father was a fisherman and claimed to have fished the woman out of the sea. She stayed long enough to give him a son and then disappeared again. Back where she came from, most likely."

"So maybe the trait is recessive," Ella murmured.

"Zann takes after his father. But his hair has a strange sheen to it when he grows it out. It's why he keeps it so short."

Mayzi looked up, eyes haunted. "He don't want no one to know he's not full Elsiran, though. You can't tell anyone."

Ella held a hand up. "I won't say anything."

"Folk find out he's half Iceman . . ." She shuddered. "Seen him hurt a man before to keep the secret." The shadows in the contours of her face seemed to deepen. "Zann's got a temper on him. If you find that baby, you keep him away, you hear?"

Ella nodded, rendered mute by the implication.

"Time was, I was real low about not having any children. Now I think the Queen willed it." Mayzi sniffed and dabbed at her eyes with the heel of her hand.

Ella had felt much the same about St. Siruna. "I take it you don't agree with your husband's Dominionist beliefs?"

"The Queen's never done wrong by me. I mean, much of what Zann preaches is good common sense, but there's something about that little book of his that don't feel right. Can't say exactly what."

"And my sister, you're sure she was with your husband?"

Mayzi nodded. "She'd really turned his head. Had a way about her. Confidence, I suppose you'd say. Different to most women. But I stayed away from her. Hurt too much to see them together."

Ella nodded. They sat in silence for a while, the tea growing colder.

A young girl entered the shop, face and dress streaked with dirt. The only other customers were a couple of old women near the front. The girl approached them, asking for money it looked like, and the women shooed her away.

The girl turned toward Ella's table, big eyes filled with

hope. Ella sighed and rooted in her purse for a couple of hun-nies, all she could really spare.

"Here you go," she said, dropping them into the girl's palm.

The child grinned. Mayzi passed her a coin as well. Then the shopkeeper emerged and shouted for the girl to leave. "No soliciting in my shop! Dirty little street urchins."

Ella watched the girl scamper away. When she turned back to Mayzi, the woman was eyeing her carefully.

"What?"

"Most folk would send a child like that on their way with a kick and a shout."

Ella lifted a shoulder. "Kindness is cheaper than you think. Or at least that's what my grandfather used to say."

Mayzi hummed in response. "You're Yalyish, right?"

"Yes, I am. Why?"

"Asked around about you before I came to find you. Folk seem to like you. Say you're good people."

"I try to help." Ella gave a weak smile, then stared at Mayzi for a beat. "Do you need help?"

Mayzi fished something out of her pocket. "You have your letters? You can read this? Think it's in your language." She passed over a scrap of paper with slanted lines handwritten in Summ-Yalyish. While there was a common language and sys-tem of writing in Yaly, each ethnic group maintained their own spoken dialect as well as unique written symbols com-prising a separate alphabet. Summ was not taught in schools, but Ella had learned it at her grandfather's knee.

"Where did you get this?"

"A Yalyishman visited Zann a few months back. They had a private meeting for a bit before Zann got to screaming and hollering. Threw the man out on his katooey. Wouldn't go along with whatever it was the man wanted, and wouldn't tell me a thing about it.

"A few weeks ago, the man comes back. I guess trying to convince Zann one more time, but he didn't even let the fella in the house. Wouldn't speak to him. Had me go tell him that if he ever darkened our doorway again, Zann would shoot him where he stood." She fidgeted with her teaspoon. "That scrap of paper fell out of his pocket."

Ella raised a brow. "Fell out, huh?"

Mayzi shrugged. "I grew up on the streets of Portside. Might have learned to pick a pocket or two." She didn't seem ashamed of that at all. "Wanted to know more about the man that got my husband so upset. It isn't like Zann to fly into rages, you know? His temper's more . . . subtle. Tiny cuts not one big chop. But something about this Yalyman got his craw up and I wanted to know what. But I couldn't make sense of that writing, and that paper was the only thing he had in his pocket."

A smile fought its way to Ella's lips. She admired Mayzi's audacity. "These are addresses. One to the billiard hall where your husband has his meetings and one is somewhere in West Portside."

Mayzi looked disappointed. "Oh, is that all?"

"Did you show this to anyone else?"

"No, don't know many Yalyfolk. None to trust at least. Don't want Zann to know—he hates my meddling." She gave a sad smile. Then flagged down the serving girl for the bill.

"When you find the baby . . ." Mayzi teared up again and shook her head. "There's good in Zann, too, you know. Just because he shouldn't be a parent doesn't mean he's all bad. We had good times. And if that baby is brought up right, nurtured and loved, he'll be something. He'll have the good parts of his father in him."

Ella reached for her hand and squeezed. "I'm sure he will."

Mayzi sniffed and nodded. Then left a handful of coins on the table and disappeared out the door.

Ella took a deep breath, her heart opening to the woman. The scrap of paper in her hand burned a hole in her palm.

She wasn't sure why she should care about a strange Yal-yishman visiting Zann Biddel. But somehow it felt important. There was little chance that this related to how she could find her nephew, but still, it tickled at her brain. So many threads tied events and people together. Kess, Syllenne Nidos, Zann Biddel. Could she unravel enough of them to lead back to her nephew?

CHAPTER TWENTY-THREE

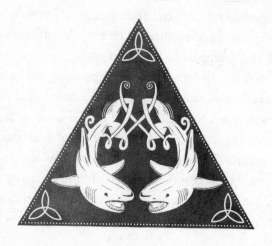

When the Master of Sharks met his beloved, he longed to gather all the roses of the world for her.

His sister, Eagle, warned that tenderness can be a tortuous touch.

—COLLECTED FOLKTALES

Jack stood outside Jasminda's door, gathering his courage before knocking rapidly. His breathing grew shallow as the seconds ticked by. When the door finally opened, he schooled his features, attempting to hide his wonder. She was radiant in the outfit she'd worn at dinner. The gorgeous golden dress highlighted the color of her skin and made him want to feel its softness. Her hair was tamed somewhat, but still wild, gorgeous, and free, like her. But her eyes were red-rimmed from crying.

That phantom ache above his heart flared again. He rubbed at it unconsciously. She studied his movement, worry creasing her forehead. He swallowed the lump in his throat and bowed low, causing her to take a step back.

"Excuse me, my lady, but you inquired as to the completeness of my healing. I . . . I fear I may have reinjured myself and wondered if you would be so kind as to inspect it for me."

She tilted her head up at him, her brow furrowed. He was afraid she would shut the door in his face at so flimsy an excuse. Instead, she took another step back, allowing him entry. She turned on her heel and headed to the fireplace where a chair had been dragged over quite close to the flames.

"Are the palace physicians not up to the task, Your Grace?" She motioned to the chair; he sank into it.

"They are the best in the land."

"I'm having trouble singing here. There are too many people. But I can take a look." The bag she'd brought from home lay on the floor, and she crouched, retrieving her jar of balm. She approached him, her focus solely on the spot beneath his clothes where the wound had been. When her eyes finally met his, something passed between them, but she firmed her mouth into a frown. "That will have to come off," she said, motioning to his covered chest.

He unbuttoned his coat and laid it aside, then undid his dress shirt and slid out of it. Her focus never left his chest the entire time. When he'd disrobed enough, she knelt in front of him, one hand resting on his thigh, the other gently prodding the newly healed skin.

"What makes you think you've reinjured yourself?" she said, voice full of accusation. "Your Grace," she added, yanking her fingers away.

"Because it hurts. Just here." He pulled her hand back, holding it in place against his heart. "And don't call me that. I'm still Jack."

Her lips trembled, the pools of her eyes swam with tears. "No, you're not just Jack anymore. You never were."

She again tried to draw her hand away, but he held on tight, grasping the other, as well, and bringing them up to meet. He stroked her silken skin and lifted her joined hands to his lips, kissing each softly then placing a palm on each side of his face.

"I'm sorry, Jasminda." He squeezed his eyes shut, unable to take the pain evident on her face.

"What are you sorry for?"

"For not telling you. For being unable to be just Jack for you. Trust me, I never wanted any of this."

"Why not?"

"My elder brother was groomed to rule. I was never as smart or accomplished as he. Never as good at all of this." He waved around the lavish room. "Most of my childhood was spent in barracks, training for the army. I don't believe I'll ever feel like a prince, not on the inside. I should have told you . . . I just couldn't bear to."

Her thumbs skimmed his cheeks, and she slid out of his grasp to brush his forehead, his chin. A finger grazed his lips, causing him to shudder.

She kept hold of his face but rose from the ground and sat on his knee, leaning her forehead to meet his. He wrapped his arms around her waist and held her tight, never wanting to let go.

"I don't know what to do with you," she whispered, stroking his face, her lips a breath from his own. "I cannot keep you, but I cannot turn you away."

Jack nudged her head up and drank her in. When her gaze dropped to his lips, he leaned forward, capturing her mouth. They kissed tentatively at first. He allowed her to explore, touching her lips softly to his, then with more pressure. Eventually, she gripped the back of his head tighter, her mouth hungrily attacking his. Her taste was so sweet, the scent of her slowly driving him crazy. He pulled away, but she leaned in, not letting him go.

"Last night I . . . Perhaps we should slow down," he said, shifting her in his lap, not wanting to scandalize her with his growing need. She would likely require time to trust him. He couldn't push. It was enough that she was in his arms again.

Her chest heaved. She sat atop him, eyes still closed, kiss-swollen lips slightly apart. "Slow down?"

"Yes, darling. I may be a prince, but I'm only human." That night at the base he'd lain awake, convinced every nerve ending in his body was connected to the place where their hands had touched. Now, she was so much closer and he was having an even harder time holding himself back. "I don't want you to feel pressured."

She dragged her hands through his hair, igniting sparks of pleasure that rolled down his spine.

"I want you to be certain . . ." He sucked in a breath as she ran her fingers down his chest, then up again. She ducked her head and kissed his collarbone. He did not trust himself for much longer.

"Jasminda." He groaned.

She shifted her knee ever so slightly, rubbing against his straining crotch. "Yes?" She smiled wickedly, her mouth edging closer to his nipple.

"You're killing me."

"Then let it be a warm death," she said, hiking up her skirt so that she could fully straddle him.

Sitting on his lap, she delighted in his unmistakable desire for her as it settled between her thighs. She should be appalled at her forwardness. The rich, city girls he was used to were probably far more demure. Even prettied up in a fine gown after a fancy bath, Jasminda would never be like them. But he had come to her. He wanted her. It was not possible, and yet here he was.

Jack's skin burned hot beneath her hands. The contrast of hard and soft made her fingers long to stroke him everywhere.

He stilled her hands. "Jasminda, are you certain?" The heat in his eyes was tempered with concern.

She nodded. "I would like to have this with you." Unspoken was the reality that this could well be her only chance. He could be her lover. Perhaps not for more than this one night, but if that was all she had, then she would take it and hold it close in her memory forever.

"You have done this before, I would imagine." She laughed at his sheepish expression. "Handsome soldiers are not the lonely sort." She pressed a kiss to his forehead, nose, and lips, then brought his hand to her breast and trapped it under hers. "You can show me."

"But I've . . . I don't want you to think . . ." He shook his head. "It was different before."

She sat back, dropping his hand, her skin rapidly cooling. "Am I so different?"

"You are. In every way."

Her mind raced as doubts swarmed. She drew away and moved to stand, but he wrapped his arms around her.

"Jasminda, don't mistake me. You are like nothing I ever thought possible. Like no one else I have ever met. And I am glad of it. You are remarkable."

She did not want to feel the joy his words inspired, the resurgence of hope within her. Nothing had changed. He was still a prince and she a farm girl with the wrong skin color and too much magic. Tonight was just a night. But as his arms tightened, pressing her against him, her heart threatened to revolt.

He kissed the shell of her ear, her jaw, her chin. "I will show you, if you will show me."

"Show you what?" she whispered as his tongue tickled her neck.

"Your secrets."

"I haven't any secrets."

He focused on her other ear, tugging on her lobe with his teeth. She shivered, the tiny motion sending a spark all the way to her toes.

"Your body begs to differ." He stood, lifting her easily. After she settled on her feet, he leaned in for another endless kiss. Molten longing pooled between her legs.

"There is sylfimweed in the kitchens, I trust?" she asked.

"I should think so with the number of soldiers I reprimand for being found sneaking out of storerooms with maids." He placed a hand on her belly. The thought of having his child was not something she could entertain at the moment. Yet another fanciful idea to quell. She would go to the kitchens in the morning to obtain the herb.

Jack frowned as he pressed against her stomach. Thinking of half-breed bastards, no doubt. Before she could reassure him that she had no such designs, he kneeled and placed a kiss over her navel through her dress. She froze. He reached down to the hem of her dress, then slid his hands underneath to caress her ankles and legs. Her breath hitched. She needed the damnable dress off. Now.

Fumbling with the strap wrapped around her bosom, she found the end and gave it a strong tug, causing most of it to unravel. Jack watched with rapt attention as the dress loosened and eventually gave way, leaving her top half bare and only a thin silken slip covering her bottom half.

His eyes traveled up her body to meet hers. Never breaking their locked stare, she walked backward to the four-poster bed overtaking the room and sat facing him. He rose and prowled in her direction like a cat ready to pounce. A shiver rippled through her as he caressed her legs, hands sliding under her slip, running up her thighs, pulling the material up to her waist.

"No knife?" He sounded disappointed.

"It didn't match the dress."

He worshipped her body with his tongue, pressing kisses every place he could reach. Hands on the curves of her bottom, he spread her legs wider, settling his weight between them. Jasminda arched up, wanting more but at the same time longing to touch him, too. She freed her arms from her sides and slid her hands down his back, digging her nails into his flesh when he did something particularly delightful with his tongue or fingers.

Their remaining clothing came off with haste. The feel of the silken material sliding across her skin, followed by Jack's lips, set her nerve endings ablaze. When she stroked him, his eyes closed on a hissed breath. She loved learning him, changing the pressure and monitoring his reaction as she squeezed and caressed.

He cupped her face and kissed her silly once again. She wrapped her legs around him, urging him to keep going, to never stop.

"Jack," she cried. "Please."

With permission granted, he eased himself into her. A sharp, stinging sensation accompanied the feeling of being stretched wide. She strained as he pushed farther inside her and focused on his face inches from her own. The discomfort was expected, and tempered in large part by her excitement.

"Are you all right?" he whispered.

She kissed him in response. "What happens now?"

"Now I start moving, but I want to be sure not to hurt you."

She wriggled against him, delighted by the fullness of his invasion of her body. Jack grimaced, the tension of not moving evident in the veins bulging in his forehead and neck.

"You're not hurting me," she said and kissed him again. This seemed to break his tenuous control and finally he gave her what she wanted.

Their dual rhythms harmonized as they flowed together. She ran her hands down his back and even lower, wanting to push him even deeper inside her, wanting to hold all of him with her body. When he sped up his pace, she matched him, and a curious feeling arose, like the scent of rain before a thunderstorm. It spread and grew, radiating outward from the center of her until she was inundated by the driving storm.

And then the lightning struck.

Jasminda came completely apart. She screamed but wasn't

aware of it until the rawness in her throat brought her back to reality and the beautiful tempest that felt like it had lasted a lifetime slowly faded away.

Her breath came in short bursts, and Jack was doing little better. His face was flushed and sweat dripped from his hair down to his chin. He gave her a look of pure tenderness and peppered her face with more kisses. When he moved to get off her, she clutched him to her more firmly.

"No, not yet."

He rolled them onto their sides, still intertwined, still one. Jasminda wiped the sweat from his brow and kissed him everywhere she could reach.

"Jack."

"Yes, my darling?" he said, breathless.

"Just . . . Jack," she said and smiled. He brought her even closer, kissing her until they both had to stop to catch their breaths again. She locked her legs tighter around him, determined to imprint this moment not just in her memory but into her skin, her bones, her soul, and her Song.

Sometime later, Jasminda reveled in the feel of Jack's fingers winding through her hair as they lay in the enormous bed. "I have something for you," he said.

"What is it?" She grinned and he beamed down at her, appearing lost for a moment. Then he shook his head as if coming out of a fog and stood, crossing the room to his discarded jacket.

Jasminda appreciated the view of his strong back and the muscles working in his legs and lower. He turned to find her staring and flushed, his face and chest growing red.

"Am I not supposed to look?" she asked, saucily.

He shook his head and returned to the bed, a thin, rectangular box in his hand. Gathering her again into his chest, he held the box out. She brushed her fingertips across dark blue velvet emblazoned with Elsira's crest and looked up at him questioningly.

"Open it."

Gingerly, she plucked the box from his palm and lifted the lid. A shiny gold medal winked up at her in the dim light. A five-pointed star with the profile of a man wearing a crown at its center hung from a wide blue and gold ribbon. Around the man's head circled the words *IN FEAST AND IN FAMINE WE SUSTAIN*.

"It's the Order of the Grainbearer. Elsira's highest honor for service to the crown." Jack's voice was full of pride.

Jasminda's heart stopped beating. "For me?"

He squeezed her shoulder. "You saved my life. This is just a token, but you deserve it."

"But . . . but . . ."

"There's generally a nomination process and months of paperwork and a fancy ceremony, but I didn't want to wait for all that. I may do away with it entirely from now on. I just went into the storage room where they keep these and got one for you."

Her mouth gaped open.

"Don't worry. It's official. I signed you into the registry myself."

She snapped her jaw closed but a minute passed before she could form words. "Thank you."

"I suppose I should call you Dame Jasminda now." He smiled and bowed. She lay her head on his chest again, admiring the finery of the medal. On record as having been of service to her nation. A lump grew in her throat.

Somewhere, a clock struck midnight.

"You know, it may be easier if . . ." Jack trailed off. Jasminda lifted her head, not liking the tone of his voice.

"If what?"

He stroked a hand across her jaw. "I don't want them to make your life here miserable. There will be questions, speculation . . . gossip. About us." Worried eyes searched her face.

The tiny light that had flickered to life in the center of her chest faltered. But she'd known. When he'd showed up at her door, she'd known. When she'd let him in, and when she'd chosen to go down this path, she knew where it would lead and where it would not.

"So what would be easier?" The question fell from her lips on a whisper. She must not have done enough to mask her feelings for he pulled her closer, tightening his grip around her.

"If we remain discreet." His voice wavered. That tiny wobble stole the strength from her growing hurt. It was not exactly a rejection, but the reality was clear. He could never truly be hers. He belonged to the people now, and the people were fickle masters.

"You are right," she said to his chest, then pressed a kiss there to show she bore no ill will about the state of affairs. She did not. If her heart broke the tiniest bit, it was only because she had allowed it to grow weak and sentimental. That would never do.

She sat up, pulling herself out of the fortress of safety his arms provided. "This is no one's business but ours. We don't ever have to speak of it again, if you'd prefer."

"No, that's not what I . . ." He reached for her but she pulled away, turning to sit on the edge of the bed with her back to him.

"You should probably go. You will be missed if you leave it until morning." She wished she had something to cover herself with. There were robes in the great wardrobe hulking in the corner of the room. She'd peeked in it earlier. All she had to do was walk over there and retrieve one, but she did not trust her shaky legs.

Tears formed in the corners of her eyes, and she pushed them back. She tried to force that same will into her legs to push her to stand, but just when she thought she'd found the strength, nimble hands enfolded her waist, sliding her across the bed. Jack turned her over until she was on her back with him straddling her, his face inches from her own.

He kissed her. She closed her eyes involuntarily and lost herself in it. Even if by some miracle she found someone to kiss again, it would never be like this.

"If you want me to tell the world I will," he said. "I will call for a press conference on the steps of the palace and shout your name from every roof and balcony." He placed kisses down her jaw, pausing to nuzzle the crook of her neck and inhale deeply.

She threaded her fingers through his hair, so short now there was barely anything to hold on to, and pulled his head up so she could peer into his eyes. "Don't be ridiculous."

"I don't want you to think that I . . . that I care what anyone else thinks. I just don't want it to be harder for you than it has to be."

"All right." A quiet acceptance of an unavoidable fact. "What have you said about my presence here?"

He settled onto his elbows, still on top of her, and her center warmed at the press of him against her.

"You are my honored guest. You saved my life at great risk to yourself, and are welcome to stay as long as you like." He grasped a lock of her hair between his finger and thumb. "I will erase the debt. Your taxes. I would have done it anyway."

She shook her head and looked around the room; even in the dark, its finery was visible. "I don't want to owe you any more than I do already."

"You owe me nothing—"

She hushed him with a finger across his lips.

"I will not allow you to lose your home," he said around her fingers.

"I don't intend to. I'm going to lodge my appeal in person tomorrow at the Bureau of Taxation. It's my last day to do so, and my case is solid."

"I know it is. I'll have Usher, my valet, assign you a driver. You can go and get it cleared up."

"Thank you." She smiled, battling the sadness that kept creeping in from the corners. The clock struck the quarter hour.

"You really should go and get some sleep," she said, smoothing a finger across his brow. "Can you discreetly get back to your rooms?"

He sighed, rising to a knee. "I can use the back passageways. There are secret corridors throughout the palace too narrow for the servants to bother with. I used to hide in them as a child." He reached for her. "How I wish I could stay beside you the whole night."

She did not give voice to all the things she wished that would never be.

He stood, finally, retrieving his scattered clothing and dressing. Jasminda admired each of his body parts as they were hidden from her view. When he looked at her one last time, she glimpsed a well of pain inside him she had never seen before, one that tugged at her in a new way. And it made it all the more difficult when he kissed her good-bye and walked out the door.

CHAPTER TWENTY-FOUR

A woman seeking wisdom climbed to the top of the Mistress of Eagles's hilltop home.

Why is it a drunken man may fall from a tree and walk away perfectly well, but a sober man will break his bones? she asked.

Eagle replied, Why is a blind man not scared of the dark? The price of knowledge is often fear, and fear loves destruction.

—COLLECTED FOLKTALES

West Portside wasn't somewhere Ella would choose to go at night. Or even on a particularly cloudy day. No, if you couldn't manage to avoid visiting at all, bright sunshine was the only way to go. She wasn't even really sure why it was called "west" as it was at the northern tip of the neighborhood.

Here, the shore was too rocky for ships to berth. Warehouses, brothels, seedy apartment buildings, and taverns were clustered on filthy, narrow streets. The worst poverty in the already impoverished area was on display. She gripped the handle of her shael, hidden in her bag, as she walked, but no one paid her any undue attention.

The address Mayzi had discovered appeared to be a tavern, though the wooden sign over the door had faded into illegibility. It swung, cracked and chipped, from a rusted chain. She had a moment's hesitation. Maybe this was a bad idea. Should she wait or bring someone along with her? But who? Her only confidantes were either on the other side of the country or elderly.

She looked over her shoulder. The street was empty. No sign of the tail she suspected she still had.

It was midmorning, certainly not a tavern's busiest time. Reasoning she would be all right, she squared her shoulders and pushed her way through the creaking door.

More bodies than she'd expected were scattered around the space. A weathered bar jutted out into the middle of the room with a ragged woman behind it, pouring ale into a cloudy glass. She did a double take at Ella before setting the drink down for her customer.

"No talk of dreaming now, eh?" the barmaid said approaching.

"Dreaming?" Ella asked.

"I know how you lot like to get on. Just keep it simple and civil in here. Nobody wants to hear any talk of religion in these parts."

Ella looked down at her plain blue dress—the oldest and most worn one she owned. It was faded and nearly threadbare, nowhere near the deep color of women of the Sisterhood. And her hair was covered in a kerchief, not their customary topknot. She'd dressed as simply as possible, so as to not draw attention, but even her old work clothes were finer than what most of the tavern's patrons wore. And among the few other women in the place, she was the youngest and healthiest. She stuck out worse than a wolf among sheep.

"I'm not here to preach. Don't worry. Do you get many Sisters here?"

The barmaid sniffed and lifted a shoulder in a noncommittal way. Ella sat at the bar and ordered an ale. The woman raised her brows, but pulled the drink without further comment.

"When was the last time you saw . . . someone like me here?" Ella asked. At the barmaid's unfriendly squint, she hurried to add, "I just want to make sure to spread the word that this place is off limits for . . . outreach." She took a sip of the warm ale and smothered a grimace. It was watered.

"Few weeks back. She didn't order a thing."

A customer at the other end of the bar hailed her and she bustled off. Ella picked up her mug and wandered into the dark interior of the tavern. A few lanterns shone in corners, but if there were windows, the curtains had been drawn tight, so tight that no light broke through. The heavy gloom made this a great spot for clandestine meetings.

She was following her instincts. The Sisterhood wasn't known for proselytizing. Were they changing their patterns or was there another reason a Sister would come to a place like this or was the barmaid just mistaken? Ella didn't really believe in coincidences. Kess had some connection with Zann Biddel, who'd been visited by a Yalyishman, who at some point must have come to this tavern. Where, possibly, at least one Sister had apparently been seen. What had Mayzi stumbled into?

Ella headed to the back corner, one where the lantern barely even hit. She had to squint to see her drink in her own hand. She sat at the table, making the mistake of touching its sticky surface. Rags and cleaning solution must be in short supply here.

From her vantage point, she had a view of the entire room, though she would be nearly impossible to see. She looked around, startled to find the table next to her occupied. A reedy old man sat facing her, his back to the room. His bronze skin melted into the shadows, but his eyes were bright. She could just make out the darker lines of swirling tattoos on his face that marked him as a Raunian.

He bent over his table and sipped his drink.

"Pardon me," Ella said, leaning over. "Are you a regular here?"

The man nodded. "Been coming to Tecla's place for nigh on twenty years now. Breakfast after I get off work." He pointed to the plate in front of him. Ella wasn't sure she'd trust any food from this establishment, but she nodded encouragingly.

"You chose the best spot in the house." He grinned, revealing several missing teeth.

Ella smiled back. He seemed like a lonely old man, happy enough for some company.

"Do you work on the docks?" The tavern was pretty far from the shipyard, but Raunians were known as master seamen. Also, master pirates.

"No. I'm an import-export man." Another grin. A smuggler

then. "Ran afoul of the king of Raun a while back. But there's plenty of money to be made in Elsira." He waggled his brows.

She raised her glass to him then took another sip of her watery ale. She must not have hid her disgust for the man laughed.

"Tecla isn't exactly known for the quality of her spirits."

"Don't tell me—people come here for the decor?" She waved a hand around. He chuckled.

"You could say that. Dark corners and short memories here." He tapped his head. "Old Nir never forgets a thing, though. I remember the price I paid for a shipment of bullion when I was a lad of nineteen. Blessing and a curse, it is." He dug back into his breakfast.

"So you do business here?"

"Aye. Many a deal's been struck at these tables."

"Ah, that must be why religious types are unwanted. The barmaid, when I came in she mistook me for a Sister. Can you imagine?"

"Fair amount of women come through. Don't know if they're sisters or not."

"No, I mean, women of the Sisterhood." She motioned to her head as if to mime a top knot.

Nir snorted. "Oh, them. Not done up in their robes or any-thing. But I seen a sharp-faced woman come in here a time or two, sit where you're sitting now. Had that haughty look about her those Sisters take on."

"Was she young? Exceptionally pretty?" Gizelle's visit to the jail came to mind. If Syllenne was in any way involved with whatever was happening at this tavern, she might have sent Gizelle to do her dirty work.

"No. Older. Looked like she was always smelling something foul, that one."

Ella's breath caught. "Silver hair with streaks of red just here?" She motioned to her temple.

"Aye, could be her."

Would the High Priestess herself have come to this dilapidated tavern?

"I wonder who she could have been meeting."

Nir opened his mouth to answer but then thought better of it. "I mind me own business, I do. That's the smartest thing for a body to do."

"Right you are. Best way to stay out of trouble." She sipped the ale, which didn't get any better the longer she drank it. At least she didn't have to worry about getting tipsy.

Nir glanced over at her a few times.

"The thing is," Ella said, "It is unusual, don't you think? A Sister showing up here. They hold themselves so high and mighty, kind of like kings and queens, you know? Acting as if they're half a step from the Prince Regent himself. Meddling in the lives of regular folk."

Nir nodded his head.

"I mean, what cause did your king have to run you out of your own country?"

"None," he said solemnly. "It was a travesty of justice."

"I'm sure. A man like you just trying to make a living."

"I work hard," he piped in. "I don't cheat them who don't cheat me. Not too badly at least. A man's gotta survive."

"Exactly. And these Sisters and their secret meetings. Sounds like it'll end up bad for someone. Probably some regular person like you or me."

Nir frowned. "Didn't see what cause a Sister would have to meet with a burly Yalyman anyway. A Summ, if I'm not mistaken."

Ella's chest fluttered with excitement. "Couldn't have been about religion."

"Nay. I came in as the woman was leaving. Looking smug as a snail tucked in his shell. After she left, the Yalyman pulled out one of those contraptions they favor over there. Like a telephone, but without the wires. Spoke into it like he was talking to someone on the other end."

Ella nodded. The communicators were common in Yaly. Elsirans were so afraid of change they didn't use most of the technology that other places relied on.

"He said some words in some other language. Not regular Yalyish, I speak that well enough. Maybe some Summ dialect. I have a good head for languages. Speak eight myself. And like I said, I remember everything I hear. What the fella said sounded like *Aniwa utapet it bulala aritanar.*"

Ella sat up straight. "Can you say that again?"

The man repeated the words, and she swallowed. Her hands shook and she released her mug, sliding her palms across the sticky tabletop without even noticing.

"Strange times we live in, missy. Better believe they're gonna get stranger." He wiped his mouth on the edge of his shirt and pushed his chair back. "I'd best be on my way. Time doesn't sleep, but Old Nir needs to. You take care now."

"You, too." Ella stared without seeing as the old man rose and limped off.

Her eyes had finally adjusted to the darkness enough to see what his breakfast was. A few crusts of toast, the remains of runny gruel, and boiled eggs. One had been cracked open, but a whole one lay on the plate, uneaten.

St. Siruna.

She stood on shaking legs and left the tavern, her heart a hummingbird's flutter.

The words he'd spoken were indeed in the Summ dialect. One that was close to being lost. She hadn't heard it spoken since she was a child, but had spent enough years with Paw-Paw to understand the words. They sent a chill through her.

The woman will help us kill the prince. That's what the Yal-yishman had said after the person who might have been Syl-lenne Nidos left the tavern.

Kill the prince.

Notices of Prince Alariq's sudden and tragic death were everywhere. Ella cared nothing for Elsiran royalty but could not escape the fact that the leader of the land was dead. In an accident—a freak storm several nights ago. Was it really murder?

She checked over her shoulder to find a bulky figure half a block down. Scrambling to go faster, she tripped over her own feet, speed walking through the streets, more certain than ever that she was being followed. The words of the Yal-yishman were a thundercloud in her mind, threatening her with heavy consequences. Why did she go to the tavern alone?

She increased her pace and the following footsteps did as well. Breath racing, Ella turned down a street at random, fear clenching her heart in its grasp as the sound of heels crunching on gravel followed. She pulled her shael out from her bag and gripped it tight, testing its weight in her palm.

Once again, she wished she believed in prayer.

CHAPTER TWENTY-FIVE

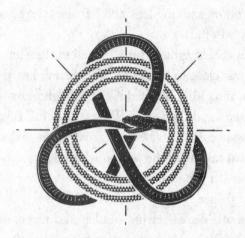

And what of justice? the lawman asked the Mistress of Serpents.
Justice is a beautiful woman, who when courted by nu-
merous suitors, chooses whom to wed by having the men draw
straws.

—COLLECTED FOLKTALES

The memory of Jasminda's touch still shivered across Jack's
skin. He could swear her scent suffused the air. He breathed
deeply, fortifying himself as the Council Room filled with
grumbling men.

"What is the meaning of this?" the Minister of Finance
said as he stalked in sulkily. "How dare you summon us so
early?"

Jack bristled at the man's tone, but held his tongue. Years

of commanding the army had accustomed him to a certain amount of respect. Who would have thought that being the Prince Regent would afford him less? But in the eyes of these men he was a less-than-suitable alternative to his brother, Alariq.

A Council meeting had been on the schedule for the afternoon, yet as soon as Jack had entered his office, still riding on the bubble of elation after leaving Jasminda's room, he had been brought swiftly back down to earth. He'd asked his secretary to move the meeting to first thing in the morning. "We will begin once everyone arrives," he said curtly. No trace was evident of the good humor he'd had only an hour before.

When the last minister appeared, Jack took a deep breath. He opened the folder before him and pulled out a curling sheet of paper.

"I received this early this morning. It appeared in my offices. And when I say *appeared*, I mean it popped into existence in midair right over my desk."

Gasps came from around the table. Jack cringed recalling how he'd plucked the page from the air, feeling the residual vibrations of Earthsong on the single sheet.

"It pertains to the True Father's terms for peace."

Another round of gasps and murmurs resonated.

Jack ran his fingers across the letter. He had read it over and over again and could almost recite it by heart. He peered at every shocked face around the table, then repeated each word.

"It has come to the attention of the beloved leadership of the Republic of Lagrimar that preparations for war are being made by the Principality of Elsira. While We assert Our right to pursue the protection of Our people against the ambition and reckless dominance of all outsiders, We acknowledge that a peaceful and permanent solution to the many years of strife between our lands would be advantageous.

"Our offer is peace in exchange for the immediate return of every Lagrimari within the borders of the Elsiran principality. Our people are Our greatest resource, and it is within Our right to negotiate for their safe return to home soil.

"The entire power of Our crown is united behind this generous offer of peace. If Our people are returned within three days, a guarantee will be made to honor all current borders in perpetuity for the length of Our reign and to immediately cease and desist in any actions that may be deemed by the Principality of Elsira as acts of war.

"In witness whereof We have hereto set Our hand the eighth day of the tenth month this five hundred and twelfth year of Our reign."

Silence descended. Jack released the paper and let it fall back onto the table.

"The refugees," Minister Nirall, Lizvette's father, said under his breath.

"Yes," Jack replied. "He's promising to abandon whatever scheme he has for destroying the Mantle if we return them."

Zavros Calladeen, Minister of Foreign Affairs, leaned forward, not meeting Jack's eyes. "But why all of a sudden? Of what military value are they?"

Nirall shook his head. "Women, children, old men. Some of the children may have powerful witchcraft, but would that prompt the offer of permanent peace?"

"Perhaps this is a blessing from the Sovereign. After all, these *refugees*"—Pugeros, the Minister of Finance, spat the word out like he would a rotten bite of food—"are already

straining the Principality's coffers. With this year's abomina-
ble harvest *and* the increase on import tariffs out of Yaly, we
are already facing difficult financial waters. The latest debacle
with the king of Raun means an even more dire situation for
our economy. We simply cannot afford to provide food and
care for the refugees for too long. At most we could support
them for a few weeks."

Jack was incredulous. "Then we take out a loan." Guffaws
sounded from around the room. He raised his voice. "And we
work to educate the people on why ejecting political refugees
is not only a callous move but is fundamentally un-Elsiran.
We would send these women, children, and elders back into
the grip of a madman?"

"Your Grace is surely not suggesting that we destroy what's
left of our economy and plunge ourselves further into debt for
a handful of savages?" Pugeros asked.

Jack slammed his hand on the table. "What of our honor?"

Calladeen's voice was low and measured. "Honor is not
about doing what is right in a vacuum of consequences. Honor
is doing the hard thing and letting history determine your
legacy." He quoted words Alariq had said many times. Jack
wanted to punch him in the face.

"There is international precedent," Stevenot said. "We are
under no obligation to burden ourselves with their care."

"This is not a financial question, gentlemen, but a moral
one," said Nirall. A former professor and the Minister of Education and Innovation, he was most often the voice of compassion and reason. "They are fleeing a brutal dictator. We
must treat them the same way we'd treat our own women and
children. There must be a way to find enough resources to care
for them all."

"Minister Nirall." The timbre of Calladeen's voice resonated as he addressed his uncle formally. Calladeen, the youngest on the Council save Jack, owed his position as Minister of Foreign Affairs not to his uncle's influence but to his own keen intelligence, politicking, and ruthless ambition. "I visited this camp the Sisterhood has erected, and much as I would like to feel sorry for these refugees, I am moved by something less like pity and more like suspicion to see them crossing our borders in such increasing numbers."

"Surely, you do not suppose that those miserable creatures could be spies? I'm told they practically kiss Elsiran soil when they arrive," Nirall replied.

"Never forget their witchcraft," said Calladeen. "This Earthsong they possess is dangerous. What is to stop them from bringing down a violent storm or a rockslide or a fire?"

Jack simmered just below a full boil. He'd never understood what Alariq saw in Calladeen. "Earthsong saved my life. On more than one occasion. Like anything else, its bearer determines whether it's a weapon or a blessing. Now is there a chance there are spies among them? Certainly. But does that mean we turn our backs on all those seeking aid?" Jack shook his head. "A Lagrimari man is the only reason the coming war is not a surprise, unlike every other breach. Instead of treating them as enemy agents, we should be trying to learn from them, gaining additional intelligence, and working together to find a way to stop the True Father."

"That is a naive way of looking at things, Your Grace," Calladeen said haughtily. "The Lagrimari are not tacticians. Additional intelligence has never defeated them. Superior force, training, and discipline have done that for nearly five hundred years."

Jack bit his tongue, recalling the Fifth Breach veterans' story. Intelligence and tactics had indeed won the day fifty years ago. Not even the Council knew the truth of what really ended that war. Nor were they likely to believe him if he told them. "Things are changing, Minister Calladeen. My time embedded with the enemy showed me that. We cannot be so arrogant."

Calladeen seethed. If he thought he could intimidate Jack with a stare down, he was wrong. While these men may be superior politicians, Jack was no stranger to conflict. And he would not back down from a battle.

He ground his teeth together. "And what makes you think the True Father would keep this promise of peace? What confidence do we have in his word?"

"We have negotiated peace treaties before," Pugeros said.

"And they have all been broken. Whether in five years, fifty, or one hundred, there is always another breach!" Jack stood suddenly, his heavy chair sliding against the floor with a groan. "He wants out of that Sovereign-forsaken desert he's been stuck in. That hasn't changed. What happens when we return the refugees and the Mantle falls anyway? He will be that much more powerful before he comes to invade us. We have no leverage here."

"It is a risk," Stevenot said thoughtfully.

"A great one," said Nirall, adjusting his spectacles. "We will need time to consider the ramifications. We have three days to decide. Let us table this for the moment to give it the proper reflection." He looked to Jack for confirmation. But Jack shook his head.

"There is nothing to consider. We are honorable Elsirans. Let's start behaving as such. I want the latest budget audit on my desk this afternoon." Pugeros visibly paled. "We will find the funds to care for those seeking refuge in our land. No excuses."

Jack's pronouncement was met with withering gazes from almost every seat at the table. He didn't care what they thought, he just wanted it done.

He moved toward the door, needing to get out of the airless room and all of the closed-minded intolerance. Perhaps Alariq would have dealt with the situation more diplomatically, but Jack was a soldier. He gave orders and they were followed. Couldn't these men see that if they gave in to the True Father's demands, they would not be so unlike him? Jack couldn't—he *wouldn't* allow Elsira to sink into unfeeling barbarism. He'd thought the war was against a foreign enemy, when really he just may have to save his land from itself.

"Lady Oola, are you ready to begin?" My cousin Vaaryn stands in the center of the amphitheater that is the Assembly Room. Rows of benches spiral around him, filled with the other children of the Founders. He is aged and stooping, the eldest of the Thirds. Next to him, spine as rigid and unyielding as his face, sits my beloved Eero.

When I shudder, Yllis squeezes my hand. I stand, all the heavier for the weight pressing against my heart, and force myself to look upon my twin.

"Eero, son of Peedar, second-born to the ninth child of the Founders, what say you to the crimes of which you are accused?" My voice sounds strong, but inside I quiver from nerves. The closest relative of the accused must stand up for him in Assembly, but I do not want to be here, not as observer, judge, or as his Advocate.

"My only crime, sister"—the word is a sneer falling from his

mouth—*"was being born Silent in a world of Songbearers."* He is not chained or bound in any way and crosses his arms in front of him defiantly.

I clear my throat and take a breath, still amazed at the cruel way he speaks to me now. *"Your crime is the kidnapping of Sayya, Fourth descendent of the Founders. Do you deny this?"*

He looks straight ahead, his gaze boring into the wall. *"As a Third descendent, I see no reason to dignify this proceeding with a response."*

I swallow. *"As you well know, only Songbearers are counted in the line of descendents. The Silent are not—"*

"Did you not gift me part of your Song, sister? Does that not make me a Songbearer?" The accusation in his voice cuts me. There are so many feelings swirling inside—anger, pain, despair, even hatred. The person before me cannot be my beloved brother. He simply cannot be.

I step closer and Yllis rises beside me, lending his support, as always. *"You are not a Songbearer, and it was my mistake to use that spell. I take responsibility for that. Because I love you and would do anything for you."*

"Anything?" The venom in that one word burns.

"Anything but give you more of the power you abused. You forced me to cut you off by your actions."

"I was innovating, the way the Cantors do."

"You set things out of balance. Earthsong is not to be used for better prices in the marketplace or to cheat at cards. You cannot ruin a crop because a farmer insulted you." Tears well even as the anger rears its head. *"And you cannot steal a girl away from her bed at night and attempt to force her to gift you her Song!"* I do not ask the question I want, whether he has actually found a way to take power from someone. The fact that he tried with Sayya must

mean that he has discovered some new way—a way that does not require Earthsong.

A shiver rolls through me. I force myself to fulfill my role as Advocate. "You have heard the accusation and evidence presented against you. And as you have not denied it, now is the time. Unburden your conscience."

He shakes his head, and a smirk crosses his face. "You all think you can continue to subjugate us. That the Silent will continue living as second-class citizens for the rest of time. Sayya made me believe that she cared for me, but when I offered for her she could not bear to wed a Silent. And now my own sister forsakes me. This Assembly is a sham. If you want to judge me of a crime, then have my peers judge me. Why are there no Silent in the Assembly? Why must we make do with the scraps of life while Songbearers reap all the benefits?"

"What are you talking about, Eero?" I crouch down, near enough to look into his eyes, yet far enough so that he cannot reach out and strike me. The fact that I even think this is a possibility is sad proof of how much has changed over the past two seasons. Last summer he was the other half of my heart, but by the time the leaves fell from the trees, he had become my enemy.

"There are no Silent in the Assembly because only a Songbearer can read a man's heart, can know the truth buried within. How can a Silent judge? What scraps has life given you? We ate at the same table all our lives. What inequities have you suffered, brother, that makes you hate us so?" My voice cracks on this last sentiment.

His eyes harden but still he does not look at me. His jaw is set, and his body may as well be made of stone. As his Advocate, I cannot use Earthsong to determine his state of mind, but as his twin I would never need to.

Yllis pulls on my shoulder gently, and I allow him to lead me

back to my seat. *Vaaryn struggles to his feet and calls upon Cadda,*
Sayya's mother and Advocate, to have the final word.

"It is so rare for us to hold one of our own in judgment; crime in
our land is so infrequent. The guidance of the Founders steers us
toward mercy." Her voice is soothing and calm. "Though my daughter
was troubled greatly by Eero's actions, she was not harmed. We ask
for his captivity so that a Healer may give him the aid and comfort
he so obviously needs."

Eero snorts and rolls his eyes.

Vaaryn stands before Eero, and suddenly my brother's expression
freezes. He rises into the air, his arms locked to his sides, his legs still
bent in the sitting position. For criminal proceedings, a random
sampling of nine Assembly members serve as judges, communicating
using Earthsong to make their decision. Eero floats for a few mo-
ments until Vaaryn speaks again.

"The Assembly agrees with the recommendation of Cadda. It is
decided that Eero, son of Peedar, will be delivered to the Healers,
who will tend to his mental instability until a time wherein he is
determined to again be in his right mind."

"Be it so," the Assembly says in unison.

I do not want it to be so, but I cannot change reality. I watch
my brother float away and wonder when I will see him again.

CHAPTER TWENTY-SIX

The Master of Bobcats faced down an enemy with far greater numbers proclaiming, Woe unto he who trusts the odds. For he is defeated before he is begun.

—COLLECTED FOLKTALES

Jasminda saw Rosira in the daylight for the first time as the town car she rode in rolled through the streets. She reached the city center more quickly than she would have liked. The government offices were housed in a sprawling building of white marble that straddled three city blocks. Its architecture was similar to the palace's with arched windows and carved columns. Only a great dome sat at the center of the government building, and its copper roof had corroded to green long ago.

The auto pulled to a stop in front of a set of grand steps

leading to one of the building's many doors. The driver—a friendly man with sparkling eyes—had assured her this was the correct entrance to the Tax Bureau. Now Jasminda swallowed nervously, smoothed out her skirt, and began to climb.

Earlier that morning, Nadal had arrived with a stunning array of clothing for her to choose from, with hemlines ranging from a respectable midcalf to an eyebrow-raising above-the-knee. Beading, sequins, and tassels adorned the collection. But Jasminda had chosen the simplest frock, navy blue and stylishly loose-fitting, with a waistline that grazed her hips. Now she wished she'd selected something fancier, something that screamed, *I'm staying in the palace and am the very close acquaintance of the Prince Regent.*

Inside, she crossed the lobby to the information desk. The woman seated there peered curiously above the rim of her spectacles, but directed Jasminda to the property tax office without further comment. After traveling hallways only slightly less convoluted than the palace's, she located the proper door. The office's tiny antechamber was a waiting room. Though the hour was early, already three people sat in the wooden chairs lining the walls.

Jasminda scanned the small space and spotted a clipboard sitting on the open half door leading to the inner office. She added her name and took the seat farthest from everyone else. The two men and one woman couldn't seem to take their eyes off her. She sat up straight, determined to ignore their scrutiny.

A portly security guard ambled by and did an almost comical double take. "Oy," he called. "What are you doing here?"

"I'm here to see the Eastern Manager about my property taxes," Jasminda replied coolly, maintaining eye contact. The guard tilted his head, gaping at her like she'd grown horns.

"You have papers?"

She pressed her lips together and handed over her citizenship documents.

A harried-looking woman appeared in the half door and called a name from the clipboard. One of the waiting men stood and was admitted into the office.

The security guard inspected the papers and stared a bit longer at Jasminda, who looked straight ahead, sitting up tall. Eventually, he passed them back, muttered something unintelligible, and sauntered away. What could he do? She wasn't breaking any laws and despite all appearances, she *was* a citizen.

It was an hour before her name was called.

"Jasminda ool-Sareefour?" The clerk pronounced the words as if speaking around marbles in her cheeks.

Jasminda stood and marched to the door. Everyone else had been let in without comment, however, the clerk made no move to grant her entry.

"What are you here for?" the woman asked, eyeing her up and down. Dark auburn strands escaped from her messy bun.

Jasminda bit back an exasperated sigh. "My case number is Y7033. I've appealed my tax judgement in writing and was told that the only option was to come here and appeal in person. You see, we never received—"

"Wait here," the woman said brusquely, then turned to rummage around in the large file cabinet behind her. She retrieved a folder and riffled through it for a few moments before her gaze shot back to Jasminda.

"I'm sorry, I can't help you. Only the Director can hear in-person appeals and he's not here today."

Jasminda chanced a connection to Earthsong to test the

woman's statement. The press of the city made her stumble in place almost drunkenly as the energies pressed into her from all sides. Thousands upon thousands of people so close by. She barely managed to keep hold of the connection and sense the woman before her.

Lying. Or rather, hedging. Confident that she was doing right, but still scared. It was confusing. But Jasminda gathered her file had been marked somehow.

"When is the Director expected to return?" she asked through clenched teeth.

"Oh, I don't know. It may be some time." Another lie.

"Just enough time for my window to appeal to close? Today is my last day."

The woman blinked and slammed the file closed. "I can't help you."

Almost the truth. She wouldn't help, that was clear. Jasminda released Earthsong and fought the urge to sag with relief. She turned away, then back again, an idea forming in her mind. The clerk was pale, her eyes wide and frightened.

"I don't suppose the Director knows a man named Marvus Zinadeel, does he?"

The woman swallowed nervously. "Y-yes. They have lunch together once a month." She narrowed her eyes. "Why?"

Jasminda snorted and turned on her heel. She strode through the government building, her steps echoing on the marble floors. At the town car, she was ready to wrench open the door in anger, but the driver beat her to it.

"Do you know a merchant named Zinadeel?" she asked him.

He seemed surprised, but nodded. "Yes, miss. He owns several department stores in midtown."

"Which is the headquarters?"

Fifteen minutes later, she stepped in front of Olivesse's, a three-story monstrosity in the middle of the bustling merchant district. Mannequins wearing the latest fashions filled the windows. An irrational burst of pride zinged through her to see that the very dress she wore was currently displayed, only in sea-foam green.

It reminded her that she did have allies. At least one, and he was a fairly important one. But she could do this on her own. She was not a leech and would not earn any of the gossip sure to follow in her wake. Before she could second-guess herself, she went inside.

In all her life, she'd never seen so many clothes in one place. She'd thought the wardrobe Nadal had procured was fine, but this was unimaginable.

She fought to hide her amazement as she walked down the center aisle, passing racks upon racks of clothing. Her fingers itched to reach out and explore the fabrics. Silk and chiffon, lace and linen. This was the true wealth of her family. This was what Mama had walked away from to live in their little valley, which suddenly seemed like it was on the other side of the world, not just the country.

A sprightly sales woman approached, her forehead lined with uncertainty. "Is there something I can help you with?"

"Where is the owner's office?" Jasminda asked.

With a bewildered look, the woman pointed her to the back of the store. In moments, Jasminda stood in front of Marvus Zinadeel's secretary, who appeared just as flummoxed to see her as everyone else she'd encountered this morning.

"He doesn't know I'm coming so I'm certain he hasn't given

you any excuses as to why he can't see me," Jasminda said. "I'll be going in now."

"But—but you can't—" The secretary stood, however, Jasminda towered over the diminutive woman, glaring at her fiercely. She flinched, allowing Jasminda to smoothly step around her and open the great mahogany door to her grandfather's office.

The interior was all dark wood, somber, heavy furniture, thick hand-woven rugs, and bulky brocades. The intercom crackled to life as the secretary's warbled voice announced the arrival of an unwelcome visitor.

Jasminda stopped short just inside the door, her confident forward motion arrested by the sight of the man before her.

He stood, cutting an imposing figure in his tailored suit. His hair had gone white at the temples but retained its reddish-blond color on top. He was handsome in a distinguished, distant way. Tall and lean and more intimidating than she'd imagined.

"Grandfather?" she said, her bravado falling away under the intense scrutiny of his golden eyes.

"Jasminda." His face was inscrutable. He leaned against the side of his highly polished desk and crossed his arms, looking her up and down. Finding her lacking.

She took a few more steps but stopped, not wanting to stand too close to him. She didn't bother to greet him properly, and he made no move to do so with her. With effort, she steeled her spine. "I went to the Taxation Bureau to lodge my appeal in person this morning, but it seems I won't be allowed to."

His expression didn't change, but something in his eyes flashed.

"I believe you and the Director are quite chummy. Perhaps you have some insight as to why he will not be able to hear my appeal."

Zinadeel's eyes burned into her. "Can't say that I do. Best take it up with them if you have some complaint."

This would be a test of wills then. "And what of this document you want me to sign?" She produced the folded and crumpled paper from her pocket. It had gotten soaked in the rain and then dried out and was overall a bit worse for the wear.

Zinadeel tracked the paper with his gaze. "What is there to discuss? It is a generous offer. You should be speaking with my solicitors at any rate. They handle these types of affairs."

"But I wanted to talk to you in person, Grandfather. I have questions." Gathering her strength, she strode forward and sat in front of him, perching gently on the very edge of one of the two chairs facing his desk. A deep furrow appeared in his forehead, but he walked behind his desk and sat.

"Well?" His voice was suspicious. Unyielding.

"I know that Papa contacted you after Mama's death." She wasn't sure if she imagined the wince he gave. This was the man who had cut Mama off two decades earlier without a word—was it possible he felt some regret?

"And I myself wrote to you on numerous occasions over the past two years. Yet you did not see fit to respond until now. The first time I hear from you is mere months after the first time I heard from the Taxation Bureau. Twenty years without a tax bill, can you imagine?"

She forced herself to smile. "And then, out of the blue your *generous* offer arrives, which would provide enough to pay this sudden debt. I am very curious why that is. Can you enlighten me?" She sat primly, hands clasped on her knee.

His frown deepened. "Is it not obvious why? I am a respected man. I am running for city Alderman in the spring. My daughter Eminette's poor decisions reflect back on me, on all of us. I am doing my duty as head of this family by trying to mitigate the unsuitability of her choices."

Jasminda held her face very still. "So you want me to accept hush money to never reveal your daughter's transgressions?" She shook her head. "You cannot erase my mother from this world. She loved my father, and I am the result of that. It happened and your money cannot destroy it."

Zinadeel snorted. "Money is a great motivator. It makes people forget. Or remember, depending on which is convenient." He peered down at her, sizing her up. "What do you really want?"

"I want to know the true reason you offered me this deal."

"I've told you." He waved his hand impatiently.

She shook her head, watching his brow descend.

"And where do you expect to live once your little farm is sold at auction *tomorrow*, hmm? What will you do? How will you eat?" He gave her a self-satisfied smirk. "If forty thousand isn't enough, how about fifty? Is your sense of nostalgia worth fifty thousand pieces? Eminette is dead, she can have no opinion on the matter."

Red stole across her vision. She gripped the arms of the seat to keep her limbs still. "My parentage isn't for sale."

"Everything is for sale. It's just a matter of negotiating the proper price. Your home and your life for mine. It is a fair exchange, I should think." His shrewd gaze seemed to cut right through her. "Or have you some other option?"

She thought of Jack. He had offered to pay off her debts, and then what? Would that make her the whore the soldiers whispered of? She shivered at the thought. That was nearly as bad as renouncing her mother and taking *this* man's money. But she was well and truly stuck.

She stood. "I will not make this easy for you," she said through gritted teeth.

Her grandfather chuckled maddeningly as she stalked out of the office, past the wide-eyed secretary. The timbre of his amusement echoed in her ears as she left the store without another look at the fine clothing or beautiful things.

Back at the town car, the driver rushed to open the door for her.

"Back to the palace, please."

She didn't look back as they pulled away.

A knock at the door made Jasminda jump. She scrubbed away the stubborn tears that had escaped, despite her best efforts, and approached.

"Who's there?"

"Miss Jasminda, it's Usher."

She relaxed and opened the door, glad to see him. His gray head of hair and kind face were welcome sights. That morning he had led her through the palace to the vehicle depot to meet her driver. Usher held Jack's trust, and hers by proxy.

"The prince requests your presence."

Surprised at the summons, she followed. Usher led her through the bowels of the palace, down many steep staircases, each older than the last. Here, the original stone walls and floors had not been plastered over or carpeted. Kerosene lamps instead of electric shone dimly, lending an acrid tinge to the cool air, though to Jasminda's mind, torches would not have been out of place.

"This is the oldest part of the palace, Miss Jasminda. It is used exclusively by the Prince Regent."

Something odd brushed against her senses. The energy of this place was overwhelming. The hallway in which they stood ended with a door. Usher pushed it open with some difficulty and motioned her through. Giving him a quizzical look, she stepped cautiously then gave a yelp when her feet slid down.

The floor was like a bowl; the inside of the room a white sphere with the door hanging in the middle. Candles glowed eerily from little alcoves notched into curved walls made of no material she could fathom. Everything was smooth and white, but the shadows from the candles flickered gloomily.

Jack knelt on one knee at the bottom of the bowl, underneath a long, white capsule floating in midair. The smooth, seamless surface of the capsule was made of the same strange material as the walls. The object resembled an elongated egg, about six feet in length. It hovered courtesy of an ancient, intensely powerful spell that tingled the edges of her senses like static electricity.

Jack rose, facing her as she found her footing and gingerly stepped down the concave floor. Exhaustion wearied his features, but his expression brightened at the sight of her. She slid into his arms, and he held her so tightly she could scarcely breathe. But she did not complain.

"Are we where I think we are?"

Jack lifted his head, looking up at the floating capsule. "The resting place of the Queen Who Sleeps."

She stared in awe. "But this chamber is sacred. Can I be here?"

"Not even the Sisterhood may come down here—only the Prince Regent and those closest to him." He took her hand and pulled her directly underneath the Queen's encased form, then led her to kneel with him. "We come to seek Her counsel and wisdom, to pray for the knowledge and strength to lead in Her stead."

She wrenched her gaze from the smooth surface of the Queen's tomb. Not a tomb, for She slept only, and it was promised that She would awaken.

"Being here, does it spark any insights into the visions?" Jack asked.

She stood and walked the length of the Queen's encasement, staring up at it. A crushing sense of defeat teetered at the edge of her awareness. She shook her head. "This place is full of power, but I don't know. It's not like anything I've seen."

Shame for her weakness and the little progress she was making with the caldera filled her. She relayed what she'd seen to Jack—Eero's trial, him being taken away for treatment. "I wish I could go faster. I'm sorry." She sank down to the ground, and Jack came to sit next to her.

"I know you're doing your best. I'm not trying to pressure you, just help." He grasped her hand, but the worried look never left his face.

She ran her fingers through his somewhat disheveled hair. "Something's wrong. Something new."

His shoulders sagged. He told her of the letter from the True Father and the terrible demands.

Tears once again stung her eyes at the thought of all it had taken for the refugees to make it to Elsira in the first place.

Only to be sent back . . . It was unthinkable, but she knew too well how little value a Lagrimari life held here.

"What will happen?"

"I have three days to ensure the Council doesn't make a grave mistake."

Jasminda shuddered. If only she could make more progress. She would try again now if her Song wasn't still depleted from this morning's vision and her trip downtown.

Nothing was going right. The auction was tomorrow and she was no closer to saving her farm or awakening the Queen. Jack was lost in his duties. She was glad he hadn't asked about her visit to the Taxation Bureau. She didn't want him to offer his aid again.

Relying on him and his princely connections would be lovely. But where would she turn when this dream dissolved back into reality? Even now he was not really hers, and if she grew to depend on his care, on his help, then she risked so much more when it was over. More than she could bear.

Lost in thought, Jack's expression was dark.

"They will come around," she said, leaning against him. "They have to."

Jack snorted. "Those old men are so stubborn and callous and they have little respect for me." He sighed. "What if I can't save the refugees?"

Jasminda didn't know what to say. Odd that they both felt so powerless, she the only one for whom a magical object worked and he the prince of the land. But they battled forces much more powerful than they. She could only hope those forces wouldn't win.

CHAPTER TWENTY-SEVEN

*Said the Master of Jackals to the soldier, A victorious warrior
fights for one of three things: a righteous cause, a broken heart,
or a noble death.*

—COLLECTED FOLKTALES

"It's just a simple request." Zaura's voice grated on Benn's
nerves.

"There's nothing simple about it," he replied.

"You're telling me you can't spare one little, tiny translator."

"Since that translator is a human being and there are only
a handful of Lagrimari willing to translate, then no, I can't
spare one. No matter how little he may be."

She grumbled, following behind him ready to press her
case. Benn spun around to face her. "Listen. I've got twice

daily transports of refugees heading to Rosira where the Sisterhood is trying valiantly to feed and house them all. With so little support from the Council, it's laughable. The High Commander is now the Prince Regent with the problems of an entire nation to sort out. He's doing his best, but there are roadblocks at every turn. One of them being the language barrier. Every settler we have willing to work with us after decades of mistreatment at Elsiran hands is a blessing. I realize that your research is important but—"

"The Lagrimari people are fascinating," Zaura interrupted, as if she hadn't heard him. "I've already outlined enough material for at least three books on my initial observations alone. A pity more aren't Earthsingers. Their magic is similar to a form of mysticism I studied when I was in—"

"Lieutenant!"

Benn ran a hand across his forehead, so grateful for the presence of the private approaching him, he fought the urge to give the young man a hug.

"Telegram just in for you, sir."

"Thank you, Private." He frowned and unfolded the scrap of paper. And the world stopped.

Benn knew what it was like for his bones to shatter. He'd been standing on the street corner one moment, waiting for the constable to turn the dial on the traffic semaphore and change the sign from STOP to GO. The normal city noises prattled around him. He was fourteen and invincible in the way that teenagers always are.

The street sign changed. He stepped off of the sidewalk. A young groom at the stable across the street lost control of the not-quite-broken-in colt he'd been trying to wrangle into his stall.

Benn heard a sound like the roar of an ocean wave before it crashed down on the shore. The collision was imprinted on him. Seared into his skin like a brand. Though the physicians and his family would dispute it later, he recalled the impact of the hooves. Remembered being tossed into the air, flipping over three times, landing on his back. The horse coming down across his legs. He didn't pass out until much later. Long after the sound of the ocean stopped braying in his ears, like the cries of some poor injured creature.

And so he knew how it felt to fall apart and need to be put back together again piece by piece. And it was happening again. Fissures formed throughout his skeleton as his shaking hand dropped the telegram on the floor.

Zaura had been chattering next to him, but her mouth shut abruptly. She crouched to grab the discarded paper and read it aloud. "Seamonster, I need you."

She flipped it over as if expecting something more on the back.

Every possible horror that could have befallen Ella ran through Benn's mind. Dully, he recognized that she'd been at least safe enough to send the telegram. But then abject terror stoked his blood until it raced through him, bypassing every organ. Was it the Sisterhood again? Were they threatening her with more than just deportation? If anyone touched a hair on Ella's head he would burn every temple to the ground.

Home. He needed to get home. How could he get home?

"You need to sit down, son," Zaura said, forcing him into one of the chairs in the hallway.

He raised a shaking arm to check his wristwatch. The express bus had already left for the day. He would have to take a four-wheeler and drive back, though he might get court-martialed for it.

He popped up. "I need to go."

"All right," Zaura said reasonably.

"Now. Ella needs me."

"Ah." She eyed the telegram again. "Well then you should definitely go."

"Right." He turned to the right, then to the left, flustered. He organized logistics for thousands of men, why could his brain not work out how to get home to his wife?

"How are you getting there?" Zaura asked.

He blew out a breath in exasperation and began walking toward his office. That's where he'd been headed initially before the telegram. He'd be able to think there.

"I don't know," he said. "But I have to leave now."

"How about I drive?" Zaura said.

He stared at her. She looked very serious. She even held out her hand as if expecting him to place keys in it.

"Drive what?"

"One of the vehicles you have sitting around here will do, I'm sure." She shrugged.

"You can't steal an army vehicle."

She grinned. "I've done it before. Who's going to stop me?"

"Any soldier on the base."

Zaura scoffed, waving off his concern. "You all may be good at fighting, but you're shite at stopping an old woman with determination."

"Zaura, this isn't something that can happen. There are consequences. I'll handle whatever comes my way but—"

"Nonsense, boy. I'm a special guest of the prince. Well, the former prince, but I think it still counts. I've got diplomatic immunity."

Benn wasn't sure that applied here, but she was already heading down the hall. He sped after her, his much longer legs still needing to work to catch up. She raced outside and over to the vehicle depot where lines of autos and trucks waited in the overcast afternoon.

She went from vehicle to vehicle, peering in the window until she found one that suited her. "Checking the fuel levels," she said.

Smart. He wouldn't have had the presence of mind to think of that. Why waste time fueling up if he didn't have to?

Wait, was he really considering this?

"Where are the keys?" she asked.

"I'm not giving you the keys."

From her shorter height she shouldn't be able to stare down at him, yet she managed. "You're in no condition to drive, young man. You can barely walk in a straight line. Now do you want to get home to your wife or not?"

He swallowed. Then led her to the key shed and picked up the keys to the vehicle she'd chosen.

Before he could second-guess this lunacy, she'd grabbed them from his hand, climbed into the auto, and started the engine. He leaped into the passenger seat, still closing the door as she raced off. The base went by in a blur as she drove with the pedal all the way to the floor.

"How fast are you going?" he asked, as they swerved around a group of geese crossing the road.

"By my recollection it's a fourteen hour drive to Rosira."

"Yes."

"I plan to get there in ten."

She pressed the accelerator and his stomach dropped.
"I'd like to get there alive."

Zaura just cackled and raced off into the dying light.

With Zaura behind the wheel, driving faster than a leaping sailfish, she and Benn made the trip from the base to Rosira in under eleven hours. Including one stop for fuel. It was a feat Benn had no desire to ever repeat. She did not let Benn drive, saying she didn't trust his emotional state. Which he found mildly offensive. He was not having an attack of the vapors, for Sovereign's sake; his wife had sent him an urgent telegram pleading for help.

And as a way to distract him from the photoplay running in his head of all the disasters he imagined befalling Ella, Zaura told stories. Tales of the places she'd traveled and some of the unbelievable things she'd witnessed.

At first, Benn would have preferred she focus on the road, but she'd informed him in no uncertain terms that, "I can very well do more than one thing at a time, young man. I once scaled Mt. Genellac to interview the last member of a dying tribe of mountain dwellers. Spent three weeks building an aerie on the side of a cliff while communicating only in hand signs."

And so he'd listened. Zaura's life had truly been fantastic. She'd lived in places he'd barely even heard of and had rubbed shoulders with the elite from around the world. And yet she lingered on the stories and legends of commoners more so than kings.

Benn had never left Elsira—like most Elsirans, he'd always balked at the idea of going elsewhere. What more could you want? They had wonderful weather, vibrant cities, beautiful countryside. Traipsing the globe was for other folk; Elsirans loved their land above all. There was a sort of innate superiority that had been bred into them. Ella had teased him about it before, good naturedly, but hearing Zaura's tales made him wonder—was it possible he was missing out on something?

Though according to her, much of his own culture had somehow passed him as well.

"What do you mean you don't know the Cavefolk creation story?" Zaura asked, incredulous.

"It's just . . . that's not something I've heard of before." He knew of the Cavefolk, of course. They were the original inhabitants of Elsira, from a time before recorded history. They'd dwelled in the mountains when Elsira had been a harsh and unforgiving terrain, a rocky desert that barely supported life. And then the Founders arrived—the Lord and Lady from some distant, unknown land who transformed Elsira into the lush, abundant country it was today.

They and their descendants ruled for millennia, years of peace and bounty. His grandmother had regaled them with tales of the children of the Founders. He'd loved hearing of the wisdom of the Mistress of Eagles and the courage of the Master of Jackals.

The Queen Who Sleeps was last in their line, but She was assailed by the Betrayer and cast into a deep sleep. Her last act was to create the Mantle, protecting her people from the worst of the True Father's awful power.

In the driver's seat, Zaura grumbled under her breath about substandard education, but then began the story. "A spirit escaped from the World After where the dead from many planes of existence merge into the single, eternal flame. But this spirit resisted the flame and found the land, where it formed a body from red clay and water. The bright rays of the sun caused the body to harden and crack, so the spirit fled underground. To beat away the loneliness, the spirit fashioned a companion from stone and the water of its own body, now red from the clay, and this was the blood.

"The spirit breathed life with the words of creation and became the Breath Father. The companion was the Mountain Mother. The father was death and spirit. The mother was life and matter. From their embrace, emerged the Folk of the caves.

"When the weight of the earth became too heavy and the threat of the sun too fierce, the Mountain Mother cut her stone skin allowing the blood to dry and crust, then bent her back forcing it through the confines of the earth and into the sky. And so the eastern mountains were born.

"The Breath Father, after having witnessed the growth of the first children of the Folk, decided to rest. And so he settled on either side of the mountains and allowed his body to crumble, freeing the spirit once again to return to the flame."

Outside the vehicle, the countryside passed in a verdant smear. "Is that story going in your book?" Benn asked.

"I don't know. I haven't met an Elsiran yet who knows it."

He turned to her. "Then how did you hear it?"

"Came to me in a dream," she said, then downshifted as the road narrowed. He would have followed up with one of the many questions that sprang to mind, but they all dissolved when the vehicle crested a hill to reveal Rosira and the ocean beyond in the distance. "Dreams are funny things," Zaura was saying. Benn tried to ignore the speeding of his heart as he got closer to home.

"You lot have built a whole faith around them, wishing and praying for certain dreams while ignoring the rest. Why is it that only the Dream of the Queen is prized in Elsira?"

Benn was only half listening. "Because of what She sees," he said. "What She knows. She can tell you what step to take for good fortune, or to avoid some horror." He had prayed to the Queen many times during the trip west—mostly to save them from Zaura's driving. "She told my great aunt Noora that the man she loved would return from the war and she shouldn't marry the baker's son."

"And what if Great Aunt Noora had married the baker's son? What then?"

"I don't know. She wouldn't have been happy, I guess."

"Was she happy?"

Benn turned at her arch tone. "I don't know. She died before I was born. What's your point?"

Zaura shrugged. "No point. Just questions. I ask questions and write down the answers. Leave the speculation to others."

"Somehow I doubt that."

"If I were the kind to opinionize, I might wonder why you didn't go home as soon as you knew your wife had been arrested."

His throat constricted. "Sovereign knows I wanted to, but I . . . I have a duty." The excuse sounded meager to his own ears.

"Duty? To the military? What about your duty to yourself?"

He'd thought she would mention his duty to his wife, so her question stumped him. "What do you mean? I accepted the commission. The army tells me where to go and how long to be there for. That's part of what I signed up for. Ella—"

His heart spasmed. "Ella knew. She always supported my dreams."

"And your dreams are what?" Zaura's eyes never left the road.

"Staff General. Youngest Staff General." Saying those words aloud didn't bring the feeling of anticipation they once did. They sounded hollow.

"And Ella, she wants to be married to the youngest Staff General?"

Benn deflated. "I'm sure she doesn't care at all." He rubbed the bridge of his nose.

"What does she care about?"

He breathed the word more than spoke it. "Me."

Zaura hummed. They'd reached the outskirts of Northside.

"There's an old saying among the Wakia people in Ecresh. 'The ravines are full of men who jumped to their deaths with food in their bellies but no love in their hearts.' In their case it's true. Highest suicide rates in the hemisphere."

She left that little gem floating in the air between them, remaining quiet for the rest of the ride. Benn gave directions to his apartment, and as the city he'd lived in for most of his life flew by, something clicked together inside him. It was like he could feel Ella's presence over the kilometers that still separated them. He'd had his priorities out of order. That much was clear.

But if Ella was safe and unharmed, he'd never make that mistake again.

CHAPTER TWENTY-EIGHT

What can I do to gain favor? asked the tax collector to the Master of Jackals.
Marry well.

—COLLECTED FOLKTALES

The newspaper cartoon displayed a baby with a shotgun in one hand and a scepter in the other, a crown of bullets sitting askew on his head. On one side, grotesque caricatures of Lagrimari refugees gobbled food from huge bowls, while on the other, waifish Elsiran farmers split a single loaf of bread.

An editorial on the same page detailed Prince Jaqros's plan to starve his own people in favor of the refugees. It dredged up the swirling chaos surrounding his mother's emigration after his father's death—she had renounced her citizenship before fleeing the country. Those had been dark days.

Of course the reporters did not mention his father's mistreatment—that was a secret no one knew. The damage the former Prince Regent had caused with words and occasionally with fists. How Jack hadn't been able to protect either of them. How the light had fled his mother's eyes until she'd had to leave. Jack's fingers dug into his palms at the memory.

Today's newspaper article reported "no confidence that the offspring of a woman who many consider a traitor to her country could effectively rule." His recent reckless undercover mission and subsequent disappearance were laid out. He was young and headstrong and prone to rash behavior.

Jack slammed the paper shut and tossed it to the ground. Usher stooped to pick it up, smoothing the folds and placing it neatly on the bureau.

"What happens if I abdicate?" he said, seriously considering the idea.

Usher sat next to Jack in the armchair in front of the fireplace, a finger to his lips in thought. "Your second cousin Frederiq is a lovely boy, but a twelve-year-old Prince Regent would fare little better in the press, I'm afraid."

Jack groaned. "The Council would run that child ragged and rule unchecked. Sovereign only knows what manner of damage they'd cause if left entirely to their own devices." He rose and leaned against the mantelpiece. "I don't know what to—"

His secretary knocked on the door then stuck her head in when he replied.

"Minister Nirall for you, Your Grace."

Jack sighed. "Show him in, Netta. Thank you."

Nirall entered, his normally jovial face grim. Jack forced a warm greeting and bid him to sit.

"You've seen today's paper, Your Grace?"

"Unfortunately."

"What passes for journalism these days is offensive," Nirall said with a sniff. He shook his graying head. "However, this refugee business has the people on edge."

"And they blame me? For failing to turn away these threadbare women and children? Is that what the people are saying?"

"Your Grace, the people simply want to know that their Prince Regent and their Council hear their voices and have their best interests at heart. They're afraid helping the refugees is taking away vital resources from our own people."

"And the rest of the Council has concern for their interests? Giving in to the True Father's demands is madness." Jack shook his head. "If we could only get more of them to see reason . . ."

Jack closed his eyes, wearied of the task in front of him. Whenever he dropped his lids he saw Jasminda's face smiling back at him and the thought soothed him. The cares of the world disappeared in her arms; how he longed for nightfall and the comfort of her touch.

"What do you think Alariq would have done?" he asked.

Nirall exhaled slowly. "He would have examined all sides of the issue very carefully. Measured them twice to cut once."

A hint of a smile cracked Jack's bleak face. "My brother would have measured them no less than four times. That's why he was a good prince."

Nirall leaned in, resting his elbows on his knees. Round spectacles and a gray-streaked goatee in need of trimming gave him a professorial air. "Alariq was also very good at deflecting."

"How do you mean?"

"Sometimes, when people are up in arms about something, they need their attention to be redirected elsewhere."

Jack frowned. "What could redirect them?"

Licks of fire reflected in the man's spectacles, setting his eyes aglow. "The people have been displeased over the shortages for some time, but the royal wedding was going to be the perfect distraction. The right mix of glamour and austerity, of course, but an event to capture the public's imagination all the same."

With a sigh, Jack slumped farther in his chair. "I'm sure that would have done the trick. It's too bad they could not have wed. I hope Lizvette's spirits are not too low."

"She's quite well. And she would still make a very fine princess." Nirall's gaze held Jack in its grip.

He was dumbstruck. Several moments passed before he could respond. "You can't be suggesting . . ."

Nirall reached for Jack's arm. "Our two families are still a good match. A strong princess will go a long way to improve your public perception. A wedding, an heir, it would be—"

"That is ludicrous!" Jack stood. "Lizvette loved my brother. How could I . . . It would be extraordinarily inappropriate, not to mention in very poor taste. I'm not sure how you could even think such a thing."

Nirall stood and bowed his head. "I did not mean to offend you, Your Grace. I was simply trying to offer a potential solution."

Jack backed away. "The title Minister of Innovation fits you too well. But this is outlandish. I could never do such a thing to the memory of my brother, nor to Lizvette."

"You could honor him by maintaining his legacy. He chose my daughter for a reason, and you and she have always been friends. I do not believe the idea would be as unappealing to her as you think."

Jack held up a hand. "Please stop. I do not want to hear any more of this. I cannot."

"Forgive me, Your Grace. I won't speak of it again." Nirall bowed formally and took his leave.

Usher shut the door and came to stand by Jack's side.

"Has everyone gone mad, Usher?" When he did not respond, Jack looked over. "What? You can't think that lunacy makes sense?"

"Alariq was popular with the people. He had the luxury of waiting to marry. An unpopular man is aided by a well-loved wife."

"Don't spit platitudes at me, old man. How could she be well loved, jumping from one brother to the next?"

"Your grandmother did the very same thing to much regard when her first husband died. The people like continuity."

"The people are idiots."

Usher set a hand on Jack's shoulder. "I'm sure the feeling is mutual."

Jack scowled and shrugged off the contact. "I do not love her."

"Many things will be required of you in your new position, young sir. Unfortunately, falling in love is not one of them."

Jack's gaze fell upon the newspaper. He stormed over to the bureau, snatched up the offending sheets, and threw them into the fire. He rubbed his chest watching the pages burn; the spot just under his shoulder where he'd been wounded had suddenly begun to ache. Or maybe that was just his heart.

"What's your name?" Jasminda asked her driver—the same one as the day before—as the town car curved through the streets. In the rearview mirror his eyes were a sparkling shade of green. She'd never seen eyes that color.

"I'm called Nash, miss."

"Have you lived in Rosira all your life?"

He chuckled. "Oh no, miss. I'm Fremian. I've been here . . . going on thirteen years now. I reached master status in the Hospitality Guild, and when I passed my Level Ones—that's the exam—I had my pick of positions. Most go to Yaly, but I've always liked living by the sea. I started in the resorts up north and let me tell you . . ."

Nash certainly wasn't short on conversation. During the short trip, he told how he came to Rosira following a young lady who had eventually relented and agreed to marry him. Nothing in his manner indicated any suspicion or distaste for Jasminda.

"Nash, I'm sorry to interrupt, but are there many Fremians in Elsira?"

"Not so many, miss. A few servants in the palace and at the premiere vacation spots, some professors at the university, too, but the immigration laws are strict. Down in Portside, you'll see folk from every corner of the globe working the ships, but they're prohibited from entering other parts of the city."

Nash's native Fremia was a land that valued knowledge and excellence above all else. They had the best schools and universities and offered elite training in everything from art, to science, to warfare and hospitality. Around the world, no one was better at what they did—no matter what it was—than a Fremian.

"And do your people have any . . . opinions on the Lagrimari?"

He gave her a knowing smile. "Fremia has always been neutral, miss. We stay out of the conflicts of other lands."

Just outside the city limits, Nash turned onto a rough path cut into the dirt, and drove another half kilometer or so before stopping. A miniature city lay stretched out ahead, made up of orderly rows of white tents with oil lanterns strung up on poles to form the perimeter.

Nash turned in his seat to face her. "It isn't like here. So many people from all over the world come to study back home, we're used to differences of all kinds. It must be hard living in a land with so much sameness that any deviation at all stands out."

She nodded but couldn't find her voice to respond. Nash sobered, then straightened his hat and exited to help her out of the vehicle.

"I shouldn't be too long," she said.

He tipped his hat to her. "Take as long as you like, miss."

The warm feeling she had from her conversation with Nash faded slowly as she approached the refugee camp entrance. Soldiers milled around, at odds with the nearly half a dozen women of the Sisterhood busily unloading supplies from several trucks.

Jasminda had come to find Gerda and tell her and the others what she'd learned so far from the caldera. Perhaps the elders could provide some guidance, but at the very least, she wanted to update them. She twisted her hands, dreading disappointing the Keepers with her lack of progress, when her attention was captured by two people on the other side of the vehicles.

An Elsiran man and woman stood arguing. The woman was clad in the blue robes of the Sisterhood. The man was slim and rather short, wearing a black suit and cap similar to Usher's. He looked like a driver.

Jasminda could not hear the words of the dispute, but the man's motions were emphatic. However, the voice rising with emotion was high pitched. When both turned, Jasminda's breath caught. The fellow was really a woman, dressed in male clothing. But what really caught her eye was the face of the Sister.

With her golden auburn hair tied in a topknot the way all Sisters wore it, her topaz-colored eyes, and straight nose peppered with freckles, she was the spitting image of Mama. The only thing that kept Jasminda from crying out and running into the woman's arms were the burn scars across her left cheek and jaw extending down her neck.

Jasminda drew closer until she could hear better.

"Clove, *please.*" The Sister's voice was lighter and breathier than Mama's. Jasminda almost didn't trust her memories. There was no way two people could look so similar.

The shorter woman gave an exasperated sigh. "You promised you would be there, Vanesse. I needed you."

Vanesse. Jasminda knew that name. Her mother had spoken it often enough. Jasminda had even tried addressing her letters to Vanesse Zinadeel when those to her grandparents kept being returned unopened. But her mother's sister had not responded, either.

Aunt Vanesse.

Her only proof was a first name and a face nearly identical to her mother's.

"I wanted to be there," Vanesse was saying, "but Father needed me at his presentation. He insisted."

"You are a grown woman," Clove said. "You can tell him no." Vanesse's hand went to the burn on her face self-consciously.

Clove sighed, her shoulders lowering. She reached up and caressed Vanesse's cheek, right over the scar in a very intimate way. Vanesse leaned into the touch before pulling back sharply, her eyes scanning the area. She caught sight of Jasminda and froze.

Clove looked over her shoulder, her gaze glancing off Jasminda. Her expression was dejected.

"Can we talk about this later?" Vanesse asked. Clove shrugged and shuffled off to a town car parked at the end of the row of the military vehicles.

Vanesse sniffed, watching Clove walk away. Then she turned and slowly headed toward where the other Sisters were working. Her eyes were downcast as she passed Jasminda.

"Your father is a beast," Jasminda said, unable to hold her tongue.

Vanesse jumped and stared at her as if she was crazy for her outburst. "You speak Elsiran." She looked at Jasminda more closely. "How do you know my father?"

Jasminda held the older woman's gaze. "He is my grandfather." She stood tall, daring her aunt to deny her. For a moment, Vanesse just stared mutely as if not comprehending what she was seeing.

"Jasminda?" She let out a gasp, almost a sob, and rushed forward, wrapping her arms around her niece. Jasminda was frozen in place as Vanesse crushed her. "I can't believe it. You look so much like Eminette," her aunt whispered into her hair.

"No, I don't. But you do." She found the strength to wrap her arms around the other woman and hold on as Vanesse continued to squeeze.

When Vanesse pulled back, tears streamed down her face. She cupped Jasminda's cheeks. "No, I see her in you. Your chin, your forehead." She stroked each part as she mentioned it, and the tears continued. They welled in Jasminda's eyes also.

Vanesse released Jasminda and wiped at her eyes, sniffling. "Come, let's sit." She motioned to a log lying in the grass a few paces away. They settled in next to one another, and Jasminda studied the burn scars marring her aunt's cheek and jaw. Her left ear was mangled as well.

Vanesse touched her face and dipped her head. "Your grandmother did that."

Jasminda's jaw slackened as she struggled to comprehend a mother burning her own child. "Was it an accident?"

Vanesse snorted. "No. I was sixteen and she caught me with"—she looked over toward where Clove had disappeared— "someone she thought unsuitable." Jasminda could imagine her grandparents would find another woman unsuitable.

"Emi had been gone for four years, sending us letter after letter. Mother and Father would burn them, so I started going for walks to meet the post carrier so I could read them." Her voice hitched. "Mother had told everyone Emi died of a fever out in the Borderlands, but Emi had written letters to her friends telling what really happened. Our parents were incensed. So when it looked like I was going to end up an embarrassment, as well . . ." Vanesse's gaze lengthened. She stared across the makeshift car park toward the expanse of tents, lost in the memory.

"When she came after me with the oil, I thought she wanted to kill me. She doused my bed and then lit the match before I even knew what was happening. Said she wanted to make sure no one at all would steal me away from her. No one would want me. I would never shame her the same way my sister did." Vanesse's hand fluttered near her face, never quite touching her scars.

Jasminda's breathing was shallow. A tear escaped as she took in her aunt's misery. "And your father? What did he say?"

She sniffed. "'All actions have consequences.'" Her voice was deep in an imitation of Zinadeel.

"But the Sisterhood. How could your parents support you joining a group that aids the settlers?"

Vanesse straightened and wiped her eyes again. "The Sisterhood is respectable. The Queen has shown us Her blessing many times. Providing for the less fortunate is something that brings honor to the family. The irony that Emi met your father while in the Sisterhood is perhaps lost on them. Or maybe they just believe that I'm too ugly to be a temptation."

Vanesse dropped her head. "I'm sorry I haven't been there for you. My parents are very . . ." She searched for a word, her eyes clouding.

"You're afraid of them," Jasminda said, growing cold as a guilty look of assent crossed her aunt's face. She could not fault the woman. How would she feel if she'd been burned by her own mother for falling out of line? Her grandmother must have a tenuous hold on her sanity to do such a thing. And she knew firsthand how intimidating her grandfather was.

"How did you come to be here? Where are you living?" Vanesse asked, appearing truly interested.

Jasminda allowed herself to revise her opinion of her aunt and told her of the events leading her to Rosira—leaving out the caldera and her exact relationship with Jack—and of visiting her grandfather. Vanesse listened to the story, her horrified expression growing with each twist and turn.

"You must be careful of Father. I believe he's capable of anything," she whispered, shivering a little. Any lingering anger Jasminda had held toward the woman dissolved into pity. The family Jasminda had known was kind and loving. She'd never once feared either of her parents and couldn't imagine doing so.

Vanesse grabbed Jasminda's hand and squeezed. "I hope that we can get to know one another. I would very much like that."

"Me, too." Jasminda's heart lightened at the thought of having a family again.

"There's a place we can meet where no one will see. Though you may have to invest in a good-sized cloak, or perhaps some face paint so you're not recognized."

Whatever else Vanesse said was lost to the rushing in Jasminda's ears. Her aunt could only get to know her in secret. Hidden corridors, cloaks, and face paint. Late-night rendezvous and secret trysts. Was there no one who would bring their acquaintance with her out into the light of day?

She pulled her hand out of Vanesse's grasp and stood on shaky legs. "I'm supposed to meet with some of the refugees now. I have to go."

Someone else's secret. Someone else's shame.

She left behind the question on Vanesse's face and the call of her name on the woman's lips.

CHAPTER TWENTY-NINE

How may I gain power? asked a servant to the Master of Bobcats.

Bobcat replied, A man who seeks power believes he can control his kite in a furious gale. A man who has power, releases his string.

—COLLECTED FOLKTALES

Jasminda wasn't certain of how to find the elders. Each tent she passed was identical to the next. Fortunately, the camp was rather small.

Within a few minutes she stumbled upon Rozyl, Sevora, and the other two Keepers from the mountain. Jasminda dreaded asking Rozyl for anything, but she had little choice.

As she approached, a ripple of unease charged the air. The

Keepers had their faces to the sky, as if they were listening to something.

"What's wrong?" Jasminda asked. No one answered.

She reached for Rozyl, brushing her arm to get the woman's attention. Her fingers merely glanced across Rozyl's skin where she'd pushed up her sleeve. But a violent press of Earthsong rose and slammed against Jasminda like a physical shove. She couldn't separate herself and was plunged directly into the flow of Rozyl's connection to Earthsong.

Jasminda cried out, suffocated by the maelstrom of energies of so many people around her. Pain, white and hot, lanced through her body, blinding her. Somehow she had linked to Rozyl's power, and it felt like being crushed into paste. Suddenly, a filter emerged between her and Rozyl's Song, like a window shade pulled down to hide the glare of the sun. It muted the volume of the energy, and the vise around her chest loosened.

She was still uncomfortable but could now pick out details in the Earthsong surrounding them. The nearby soldiers—tension rippling through them, fear and distrust pulsing along with the blood in their veins. The despair of the refugees, the hope and the hopelessness. Their heavy hearts and minds.

Finally, she was able to tear her hand from Rozyl's. She coughed and gasped, relieved to break the connection. Rozyl regarded her with disbelief.

"Don't you know better than to touch someone when they're linking?" Rozyl said, looking at her like her hair was made of spiders.

Jasminda realized that Sevora had been holding Rozyl's other hand. "I-I didn't realize—"

"And why did you not shield yourself?"

"Shield?" So that must be how Earthsingers coexisted in large numbers. Jasminda shook her head. "My father was the only other Earthsinger I knew. He did not teach me." She wondered what other lessons she had missed.

"Your Song is so weak," Rozyl spat.

Jasminda cringed and wrapped her arms around herself. "My brothers could not sing at all."

"I don't know why it must be you," Rozyl said with disgust, and took off down one of the wider paths through the tents, the others on her heels, their disapproval evident.

"I don't know what just happened, but I didn't ask for it, either. I didn't ask to be the only one the caldera will work for," Jasminda called out, racing after Rozyl's quick steps. The woman continued to snub her, and soon they emerged at the camp's entrance where a crowd had grown. The Keepers disappeared into the throng of people.

Still shaking from the unexpected force of the link, Jasminda strained for a better view of what had captured everyone's attention. "What's happening?" she whispered to a woman cradling a sleeping baby.

"I think they're holding back the rations."

Jasminda moved to the front of the group to verify. Vanesse and two other Sisters stood near a line of soldiers arguing with the captain. At their feet were crates of rice, potatoes, and vegetables.

"You cannot keep rations from these people. I won't allow it," a gray-haired Sister said.

Jasminda approached. A few other refugees broke away from the crowd and drew nearer to the soldiers, as well.

"Is there a problem delivering the rations, Captain?" Jasminda said.

The man looked at her sharply, evidently surprised at her command of Elsiran. He glanced at her dress, obviously expensive and so different from the threadbare fabric covering the refugees. She'd not seen this man before, and he probably had no idea of her identity, but he could plainly see she was different than the rest.

"This witchcraft will not be tolerated," the captain said.

Jasminda crossed her arms and stood her ground. "Exactly what witchcraft are you referring to?"

The man glowered at her. "That." He pointed an accusing finger at the first row of tents.

The field on which the refugee camp had been built was covered in brittle, end-of-the-season grass shedding its green for the impending autumn. But each tent in the row had a bed of blooming flowers before it—grouped into different colors.

White desert lilies graced one. Red bristlebrushes another. A golden flower she didn't recognize blossomed in front of a third tent. Before their eyes, green stalks shot through the dry earth of another canvas structure and opened, revealing brilliant purple petals.

"Flowers?" Jasminda asked, unable to keep the derision from her voice. "You're afraid of flowers? Something to brighten the landscape and bring a little joy? What is wrong with you?"

The man's face hardened. "It's evil. The whole lot of you *grols* are evil." He spat, aiming at Jasminda's feet. The Sisters raised their voices in protest.

A boy of about twelve came to stand next to her. She recognized him as the child who'd aided the settlers in Baalingrove. On her other side, two settlers regarded the confrontation warily.

Outrage overcame the pain of the words she'd heard so many times before. "You have no right to withhold the rations, Captain. Not for something so innocent. Do you not have orders to feed these people? Where is your honor?"

The captain's face contorted. "You'll not speak to me of honor, witch."

"Just leave the food here. We'll carry it in ourselves." She moved toward the nearest crate. The boy at her side approached as well.

"Stay back. Don't come any closer." The captain's hand hovered near the pistol strapped to his waist.

Jasminda stilled, but the boy kept moving, not understanding the captain's command. In the space of a heartbeat, the captain pulled his sidearm and pointed it at the boy. The entire line of soldiers drew their rifles on the gathered refugees. The Sisters, startled, took several steps back.

"No!" Jasminda screamed. In Lagrimari, she shouted, "Stop!"

The boy looked over at her, brows drawn. His eyes glittered, warm and golden brown, lighter than most Lagrimaris'. His face still held the roundness of youth, but those enchanting eyes were hard.

The child took another defiant step toward the food. Somewhere close by, a woman screamed, "Timmyn!" He tensed, hearing his name, then took another step.

Time slowed as Jasminda shook her head and opened herself to Earthsong, struggling to work out the shield technique she'd witnessed Rozyl use during their unexpected link. It worked just enough so that the other energies weren't screaming in her head, drowning out her thoughts and severing her connection, but she was far from proficient. The soldiers' emotions were a whirlwind of fear and aggression. Too far gone to be soothed by Earthsong, even if she'd been strong enough to do so.

She reached out to Timmyn and found the well of pain to be deep. He was in a place beyond hearing. *You don't have to prove anything,* she wanted to tell him. *We will not let you starve here. The prince would never allow it.* Her helplessness crushed her as she felt his hurt.

When the shot rang out, Jasminda lost her connection to Earthsong. She grabbed at the air in front of her, too far away to catch him as Timmyn fell backward onto the ground. A deep-crimson stain ballooned across the fabric of his shirt. Jasminda looked up at the captain in horror. His face was an emotionless mask.

She fell to her knees. Her breath came in short, shallow bursts. Tears blurred her vision. She vaguely registered a group of refugees taking the boy away to be healed. Through the fog she heard Vanesse speaking. Her words were just a jumble of sounds that didn't penetrate. Time ceased to exist. All she could hear was the crack of the gun and the thud of Timmyn's body hitting the earth, over and over again.

The Assembly Room grows quiet as all eyes focus on me. Their expectant gazes draw me back to the present. My mind had been aloft, far from this room and out in the early summer sunshine, feeling the waves gently lapping at my feet. That is how I wanted to spend my birthday, at the sea, as I always have before.

I straighten my shoulders and regard the room. Every face holds a tension it never has held before. And it is all my fault.

"All here are agreed?" My voice is low. I speak out loud as has

been the custom during Assembly for the past half a millennia. I will not give in to the paranoia of so many of my cousins gathered here, afraid of eavesdroppers.

We are agreed, *murmur many Songs against my consciousness.*

"Today is the first day of my twenty-first summer. I am the youngest Third. Vaaryn, you are two hundred years my elder. Your leadership has been unblemished. I am untested. Is this really wise?"

When Father, the last Second and the youngest son of the Founders, passed into the World After, Vaaryn assumed his responsibilities in the Assembly. The idea of leadership passing to me was unfathomable.

"Yes, dear cousin," Vaaryn says. "I am not much longer for this world. It is best that the youngest should lead us."

Most Thirds lived only a few years past their two-hundredth birthday. Fourths less than that, and Fifths barely made one hundred. The Silent were old at seventy.

"But it is because of me that we face war with the Silent. It is because of me—" I choke on the words as a sob rises to my throat. Yllis is there with an arm around me, steady and stable, my rock in the storm.

Yllis's mother, Deela, rises. "So it must be you to lead us through. We have lived in peace for hundreds of years with the guidance left by the Founders, but perhaps it has been too easy for us. We have never been challenged in this way before."

"Eero and those who follow him have poked at a sore that has been dormant for a long time," Yllis says. "The Silent have no voice in the Assembly. Their parentage is not claimed. If it was not Eero now, it would have been someone else in the future. It is not all because of us."

He wants to take more of the burden of Eero's fate away from *me, absolve me of some guilt, but it is mine to hold. Yllis developed the complex spell, which allowed me to share my Song with my twin, but I was the one who used it. Who kept using it and ignored the truth for too long—giving Song to the Silent would cause them to go mad. The Silent were so for a reason.*

"Very well," I say. "I accept. So be it. See to it."

It is as if the Assembly takes a collective breath. "Be it so."

And with three little words, I have been made Queen.

CHAPTER THIRTY

Beware the Master of Monkeys. He would sell you the night as a cloak for the sun.

—COLLECTED FOLKTALES

Ella's heartbeat matched the rapid patter of her feet as she walked down the street. Weak morning sunlight battled through the gray overcast sky. A bad storm was coming.

The hair parlor didn't open for two hours but she'd been unable to sleep in, exhausted though she was. The walls of her flat seemed to be closing in on her, so she'd gotten dressed and headed out, thinking the fresh air would do her good.

But now fear compressed her lungs. Every few steps had her looking over her shoulder. That man in the straw hat—was he following her? She sped her steps and ducked into an alley, scrambling for breath.

Her hand never left the interior of her bag where she clutched the shael in a steely grip.

The man in the straw hat walked past, oblivious.

Ella sighed.

The day before, after leaving the tavern, she'd pulled her shael on an unsuspecting old vagrant woman out walking her dog. She'd apologized profusely, but the paranoia hadn't abated. The fear had caused her to reach out to Benn with a frantic telegram. One she now regretted.

He hadn't answered. Had he even received it? It wasn't like her to panic, she'd been on her own for a long time, since she was thirteen and sent off to boarding school. She'd done all right, managed to figure out adolescence without any guidance from her sister and mother. She'd gotten into university, managed the grants and scholarships that covered her living expenses. Taught herself how to negotiate the rent on her first apartment, fend off unwanted advances from a professor, pay her taxes.

But she wasn't sure at all how to handle the knowledge that the High Priestess may have had something to do with Prince Alariq's death. Nor deal with the consequences such knowledge could bring.

Crossing the Sisterhood was one thing when it was just herself and her nephew. But stealing an infant was nothing compared to regicide. Was the group really powerful enough to help murder a prince?

She was probably overreacting. The idea was preposterous. Why would Syllenne want to kill the prince? Why would a Yalyishman? It was all so unlikely. Prince Alariq had been respected, fair and just by all accounts, or at least as much as a prince could be, she reckoned.

Perhaps the old Raunian had heard or remembered wrong. But what was the chance he'd misheard words so precise? She'd wracked her brain for other meanings—maybe a homonym or a speech impediment could have accounted for what he'd told her.

A squeaking creature scampered behind her in the alley, startling her. She really needed to pull herself together. When she walked back onto the sidewalk, a neighbor called out a greeting. She waved, trying to look cheery and not betray the terror churning inside.

Foot traffic was heavy this morning. She was surrounded by a sea of people and could not shake the feeling that she was being watched.

Another glance over her shoulder. Half a block behind her, a small face dipped from sight, popping behind a delivery truck. Ella had seen that child before.

Street urchins were common enough. The children ran around unsupervised, often causing mischief. Ella knew better than to keep anything of value in her pocket, and her bag was always clasped and close to her side.

She turned in the direction of the telegram office, wanting to check in and make sure she hadn't missed Benn's response. Minutes later she emerged empty handed, struggling to bury her disappointment.

He was busy, she knew he was busy. But she'd hoped . . .

The same small boy, dirty cheeks and curly auburn hair, was still a half a block behind her. This time staring up at a display window as if fascinated by the selection of women's shoes. Ella narrowed her eyes.

She fished a peppermint from her bag and approached the

boy, slowly, but before she'd taken more than three steps he took off down an alley.

Ella knew Syllenne Nidos must be having her followed. She'd imagined large, burly men in dark suits with hats pulled down over their eyes—then again maybe she'd read too many tenthpiece novels as a girl. It was much more likely the High Priestess had hired cheap, inconspicuous labor. The kind who was small and could disappear from sight easily.

If Ella had wanted to have someone followed, she would use such a resource as well. Clever.

She continued down the street slowly, coming to a stop before the bookshop, admiring the display of magazines in the window. A few coins later, she exited the shop with a brown paper bag holding the latest issue of *Captain Fineen's "Don't Tell Your Mother"* magazine.

She stopped at the little park on the corner of 40th and Earl, sat on a centrally located bench, and began to read. *"Don't Tell Your Mother"* was well-known for its raunchy jokes, cartoons, and illustrations. Even street children with no education would be tempted by its contents.

She scanned the pages for several minutes before abandoning the magazine on the bench and moving to the intersection. As the crowd waiting to cross the street grew, Ella glanced backward.

The boy hovered over the bench, and then the magazine disappeared as if he'd performed a magic trick. Ella smiled.

Her next stop was the baker's. Five hunnies bought her a bag of day old cookies. She stood in front of the bakery, crunching on yummy chocolate chip goodness. In the mirror of the auto parked next to her, the boy's reflection crept closer.

He was so focused on the cookies, mouth salivating, that he didn't notice when Ella spun around and grabbed him by his ear.

"Ow!" he exclaimed.

Ella grinned while passersby looked down at the filthy boy with some disgust.

"Lemme go!" he yelled.

"Not a chance. We're going to the candy shop."

That shut him up.

One bag of licorice later, she and the boy sat on the same park bench. He proved he really was a magician by making a half kilogram of candy disappear. She felt a little guilty for plying him with sugar, but desperate times and all.

"What's your name?"

"Iddo," he said around a mouthful of cookie.

"And why are you following me, Iddo?"

Crunch. Crunch. Crunch.

She sighed. "How much are you being paid to follow me?" He looked up with guilt in his eyes. This boy couldn't be more than ten.

"Yes, I know someone is paying you. If I match it, will you tell me?"

He couldn't have been paid much given the way he was sucking down those cookies like he hadn't eaten in days. Still, he had some loyalty to him. Ella was impressed, but also perfectly willing to administer a little guilt of her own.

"Did *they* buy you sweets and a rude magazine?"

"You didn't buy me a magazine!"

"So that magazine hidden in your shorts is what, an illusion?"

He looked down, then at the bag in his hand, and shrugged.

"All right. A lady sometimes comes by the old garage where my crew hangs out. Offers a haypiece a day to keep track of people who she says. She uses my crew and some others, too."

That was pretty decent money for a street child. Definitely enough to buy at least fleeting loyalty and more than she could afford to match.

"What did this lady look like?"

Iddo's face took on a dreamy expression. "Like the sun if it was a woman. Eyes so bright they nearly glowed."

Judging by his dazed appearance, he'd had a run-in with Gizelle.

"Have you followed other people for her?" she prodded.

"Aye." Another cookie disappeared into his mouth. "There was a man who looked like he could work on the docks, but wore a proper suit, like a whirvy. Foreigner."

"Yalyish?" Ella asked. The boy shrugged. "What did he look like?"

"Dark skin. Mustache. Tall."

He could be Summ-Yalyish. "Anyone else?"

"That fella who holds meetings at the billiard hall. Always trying to hand out books to people."

Zann Biddel.

"And his lady friend." The boy shrugged. "That's all."

"You mean his wife?"

"No, we know Mayzi. She's good people. Always with a smile and a hunny fer a lad when she can spare one. No, this was his doxy."

Ella tensed. "What did she look like?"

He squinted as if trying to remember. "Sorta like ya. But older. Hard eyes. Not kind like yours. But she hasn't been around in a long time."

"No." Something small and sharp clawed at her from the inside. She fought the burning behind her eyes. "She won't be around again."

"Funny one, that. We followed her and she followed that billiard hall fellow. Before she became his lady friend, that is." Iddo yawned.

Well that was interesting. Kess had been watching Zann Biddel before they became involved. And the Sisterhood had watched Kess.

A doxy. Though Iddo's crude language had stung, the fact that he even knew of such things made her chest ache even more. "You've probably seen things you weren't meant to see. Grown-up things."

He shrugged again. "Seen a lot, miss."

"I'm sure you have. Did you follow me yesterday?" Ella whispered, fear cooling her skin. If Syllenne knew she'd been to the tavern, that could mean even more trouble.

"It was me who was sposed to, but I took sick. Ate a bad sandwich and had the skids."

Though she hadn't heard that term before, she'd gathered what he meant.

"And did anyone replace you?"

"No. I didn't tell no one. Everyone knows not to eat Old Nik's meat, not if ya don't want an extended stay in the privy, but I did it anyway." He shook his head looking very aggrieved with himself. Ella held back a laugh.

"But you're feeling better today?"

"Right as the river," he said, smiling, showing off a mouthful of surprisingly bright teeth. At least he'd obtained some dental care at some point. Which reminded her.

"You need a bath, Iddo."

He sniffed himself. "Water shut off in our building last week. Mum's tried calling the landlord, but he's nowhere to be found."

"Why don't you come back to mine and get cleaned up? Then you can have a proper breakfast."

He looked surprised and then grinned. "Don't need breakfast," he held up his bag of dwindling cookies, "but I wouldn't mind a bath."

They headed back to her flat, some of the tension draining from her shoulders. If Syllenne didn't know Ella had been to the West Portside tavern, then she couldn't suspect what Ella had learned.

She was almost feeling normal again as they came up to her street. Then a frenzied voice called her name and nearly forced her out of her skin.

"Ella!" Benn yelled, barely waiting for the vehicle to come to a stop before jumping out and racing down the sidewalk.

Ella turned, hand on her heart, eyes wide with fright. Then her face changed, morphing into recognition, surprise, disbelief. Her mouth moved, making the shape of his name but no sound came out.

Benn's heaving chest nearly collapsed. He rushed forward and embraced his wife, patting her for injuries. Tears streamed down his cheeks as he took a step back to verify that she was whole, healthy, here with him.

He scooped her in an embrace and squeezed, turning her around and around. "You're all right, you're all right."

Her arms came around him, grounding him back to earth. "Yes, I'm fine. W-what are you doing here?"

"Your telegram scared the pants off of me."

In his arms, she became rigid. "Oh, saints forgive me. I didn't mean— I'm so sorry. I just wanted to talk to you. I was so scared, I . . ." She pulled back, looking into his face, then her eyes caught the attention they were getting on the street. "Come inside." Her smile warmed him, but there was still tension in her gaze.

She took his hand in hers and led the way to their building's door. Then called out, "You, too, Iddo. You still need that bath."

The dirt-encrusted boy who had been steadily creeping away from them stood still, looking guilty.

"This is Iddo. Iddo, this is my husband, Benn."

The boy nodded. "Sir," he mumbled, before staring down at his shoes.

"Taking in strays," he leaned in to whisper.

"Something like that." Ella looked at the child fondly.

Behind him a throat cleared. "And this is Mistress nyl Herrsen," he said, moving aside to make room.

"Zaura, please." The woman stuck her right hand out and she and Ella shook hands, Yalyish style.

"I've heard so much about you. I can't believe you came all this way, as well." Ella seemed to be vibrating with mortification and tension. She took another look around their surrounds. "We'd better get upstairs before . . ."

Benn pulled open the door to the building. "Before what?"

She bit her lip, but didn't answer.

They all climbed the steps and entered the small flat. Ella hustled Iddo off to wash with a litany of instructions Benn thought the boy was old enough not to need, then she came back into the main room looking flustered.

"Did you drive straight through the night? You must be tired and hungry. Can I offer you anything to eat or drink?"

"Some tea would be lovely," Zaura said, polite as you please from her seat at the kitchen table. Benn had never heard her sound so civil before. For a moment, he wasn't sure she was the one who had spoken.

"Nothing for me," Benn said at his wife's questioning look. He supposed his normal bodily responses like hunger and thirst would return, but for now his entire being was devoted to discovering the source of the urgency in Ella's note and the fear in her eyes. He thanked the Sovereign for her safety, but something was obviously very wrong. Why hadn't he come home before?

Ella put the kettle on to boil and stood for a moment at the stove. She startled when he placed his hands on her shoulders and gently turned her around.

"What's happened? What was the telegram about?"

She swallowed. Then looked around as if to make sure no one else was hiding in their tiny apartment. "I think . . ." She blinked a few times, then visibly steeled himself. "I think Prince Alariq was murdered."

The gas of the stove hissed, and water ran in the washroom. Iddo was singing to himself, his voice charmingly off-key.

Ella took a stuttering breath. "And I think . . . High Priestess Syllenne Nidos is involved."

Blindly, Benn reached behind him for a chair and was vaguely aware of Zaura pushing one in his direction. It screeched across the floor before resting against the back of his legs. He sat heavily, then, after a moment, pulled Ella down onto his lap.

"Start at the beginning, seashell."

She nodded. She told them first of how Iddo and his crew had been following her along with Zann Biddel and Kess. Of how Biddel's wife had visited her. Of the paper the woman had lifted from the Yalyishman and Ella's visit to the tavern. Her bravery should not have surprised him, yet it did.

"Are you certain that's what the old Raunian said?" Benn asked. "*The woman will help us kill the prince?*"

Ella nodded. "He seemed to have a very good memory and a natural ability for languages. He pronounced everything perfectly."

"Raunians tend to have better recall than most people," Zaura added. "No papers or pencils in their primary schools. Everything is memorized." She tapped her head.

"And you don't think he was trying to trick you in some way?"

Ella pursed her lips. "No. I don't. I'm usually a good judge of character. I believe he was telling the truth."

"But why would the Sisterhood want Prince Alariq dead?" Benn couldn't fathom such a thing.

"Not all the Sisterhood, just Syllenne. At least, I think so. I'm pretty sure the average rank and file Sister would have wanted no part in this. And I don't know why." Ella's voice was miserable. "I wish I did."

The kettle screamed just then, and Ella jumped up to turn off the heat. Benn set out two mugs for the women and took the kettle from her to pour before settling Ella back on his lap. They only had the two chairs, plus he just wanted her as close as possible.

"So, let's lay this all out," he said. "The Sisterhood set a watch on Kess, one of their own, and at the same time, set a watch on Zann Biddel?"

Zaura leaned forward. "It's not uncommon for people in power to be wary of other groups coming up, those with potential to impact them. The Dominionists might be small now, but they've already grown quickly in Yaly. Only a decade ago there were a mere handful, now there are tens of thousands there."

"All right, so Syllenne wants to keep an eye on them," Benn reasoned. "But not just with street children, she sends one of her own to get closer?"

"If Kess was in Syllenne's inner circle," Ella said, "then she could have been assigned to spy on Biddel."

"Probably dig up some dirt on him," Zaura offered. "You say his wife told you he stepped out on her before. Maybe that was Kess's way in."

Ella looked horrified. "So Syllenne had Kess . . . seduce him? To get dirt on him?"

Zaura spread her hands apart. "What better blackmail fodder than an affair he'd rather keep quiet? Him being the leader of a nascent religion and all."

Ella shivered.

"What about the baby?" Benn asked.

"A mistake, maybe." Zaura said, shrugging.

"Or maybe she had real feelings for him." Ella's voice was small. "Maybe she just wanted a baby—she was thirty-seven. I have a hard time believing she would be so callous as to seduce another woman's husband, though. Then again, I didn't know her as an adult. She could have been controlled by Syllenne. And we still don't know why she was exiled to Sora." She looked up, hopeful. "Maybe Kess had a change of heart, and went against Syllenne."

Benn squeezed her gently. "Maybe."

She smiled weakly and sipped her tea.

"So while he's being watched by the street children," Benn said, "Biddel is visited by a Yalyishman with some kind of scheme. And assuming it's the same man that Syllenne met at the tavern, that scheme would have been to kill the prince."

"But Zann refused," Ella said.

Benn squinted. "Why would the Yalyishman approach him in the first place?"

"Dominionists come from Yaly," Zaura said. "So how did Zann Biddel learn about them? Who converted him? I'd think that whoever introduced him to the sect in the first place felt they had some hold over him, or was trying to exert power over him. What other connection could a fisherman in Portside have with anyone from Yaly?"

"That makes sense, I guess," Ella said. "But even though he's converted to their religion, I don't think he'd hold any allegiance to a foreigner. From what his wife said, he's a nationalist through and through."

Zaura swirled her tea cup. "So the Yalyishman is thwarted in whatever he wants Zann to do for him—which may or may not be killing the prince. He goes back to try again and Zann won't let him through the door, but sometime between the first and the second visit, he gets the address of the tavern."

"And if we believe it was him who was meeting with Syllenne Nidos at the tavern," Benn said, his head beginning to hurt, "then she agrees to help him kill Prince Alariq. This makes no sense. Involving herself in such a plot would be beyond foolish and dangerous. Someone in her position?"

Zaura shook her head and pointed at him. "Imagine you are one of the most powerful people in Elsira, save the prince. And some other group believes they can kill that prince. Those would be quite the allies to have in your corner, would they not? If they failed, who would ever believe you were a part of it? It would be preposterous. You'd lose nothing either way."

Benn was stunned into silence. The sound of little Iddo splashing and wailing his heart out was really the only thing tethering him to reality. That and Ella's warm body against his.

"Sisters have unfettered access to the palace," Zaura said. "No one would have questioned their presence."

It was so unlikely, but still . . . possible.

"If any of this is true, we have to tell Jack," Benn said.

"But we have no proof. Do you think he'll believe us?"

Benn frowned at his wife. "He trusts me, we've worked together for years. If they're willing to kill one Prince Regent, who's to say they won't kill again?" He shuddered with concern for Jack. "And now that we know exactly how dangerous Syllenne Nidos is, it's more important than ever to find the baby."

Ella's eyes were worried. He rested his head on her shoulder and squeezed her tight.

"I think I have an idea," she said.

Whatever it was, he was here to help. He wouldn't let her down again.

CHAPTER THIRTY-ONE

*The Master of Monkeys told his betrothed, I will steal for you
the juiciest fruit from my neighbor's tree.*

*When he returned, he found the neighbor's cape stuck in
the window, and his love nowhere to be found.*

—COLLECTED FOLKTALES

BEDLAM STRIKES REFUGEE CAMP

An attack by Lagrimari refugees on Elsiran military
personnel resulted in the shooting of a young refugee.
Witnesses say the refugees had been threatening violence with their magic, causing the soldiers to respond
with force.

Tensions have been high in the camp, which was es-
tablished by the Sisterhood to answer the refugee crisis

impacting Elsira. The influx of foreigners through reported cracks in the Mantle has been a hotly contested
issue. Many are unhappy that the Prince Regent seems
to be allowing unfettered immigration by these unknown persons.

Jack crumpled the thin newsprint in his fist. He knew very
well there had been no attack by the refugees. The evening
papers had gone from printing gossip and long-ago scandals
to outright lies.

News of the incident had enraged Jack the moment he'd
heard. The captain had been arrested immediately, and while
the boy had made a full recovery due to the camp's Earthsingers, Jack was resolved to court-martial the offending officer.
A decision that would no doubt be met with opposition.

The door to his office opened, and Usher stepped in. Faint
music filtered in from the hallway.

"You will have to at least make an appearance, young sir."
Usher stood looking reprovingly at him.

"I don't know why they didn't cancel the bloody thing.
Now is no time for a ball."

"Third Breach Day falls on the same day every year. They
cannot cancel an entire ball because the Prince Regent is in a
foul temper."

Jack stood, rolling down his shirtsleeves and buttoning
them. "Don't I have the right to be in a temper when unarmed
children are being shot? When this entire country seems to
have fallen victim to lunacy? At what point, I ask you, am I
permitted to be upset?"

Usher picked up Jack's discarded formal dinner jacket and
held it out for him. He slipped his arms through and focused

on working up some joviality for the ball he was being forced to attend. It wouldn't do for him to scowl his way through, giving more fodder for the papers. Only one thing would truly make him smile, though.

"Is she coming?" he asked, unable to keep the hope from his voice.

"Would it be wise for her to?"

Jack's shoulders slumped.

"She would prefer not to be at the center of any undue attention. Isn't that what you agreed to?"

"I know, I know. It's just . . ." He sighed and checked his appearance in the mirror. He looked tired, older than he had even a week ago. For a moment, he had an inkling of how this position could have turned his father into a brute. Jack could feel his edges hardening. The bit of himself that he'd always held back when he'd been in the army, that person he would have been if he'd been born to a baker or a farmer had always remained inside him, catching the odd glimpse of sunlight in stolen moments when he hadn't had to flex his muscles as the High Commander. But that hidden self was now being choked. The only times he could seem to breathe anymore were when he was with Jasminda, and even then they had to remain hidden, secret. He couldn't acknowledge anything true about himself, and he was afraid it was changing him.

He stalked down the hallways toward the cacophony of the ball. The ballroom had been decorated, somewhat garishly, in orange, the color of Third Breach Day. Each of the seven breaches had a holiday attached to them, initially as a memorial for all that had been lost in the wars, but more recently it was just an excuse for a celebration. None were as lavish as the yearly Festival of the Founders, where all work ceased for three days, but each Breach Day was commemorated by excessive decorations in the color of the holiday and a palace ball for the aristocracy.

Jack entered the corridor outside the rear of the ballroom where a dozen butlers were organizing trays of appetizers. The lead butler did a double take and rushed over, admonishing him, in the most respectful way, for being in the servants' hall. Jack brushed off the man's request to stop the band and make a formal announcement of the Prince Regent's arrival.

"I just want to watch for a bit," Jack said. "I promise you can announce me once this dance is finished. I'd hate to interrupt." The butler's obsequious expression barely hid his displeasure at this interruption to the normal order of things, but he backed off, allowing Jack to peek through the curtains separating the hall from the ballroom.

This was the vantage from where he'd watched these events when he was too young to attend and still longed to. The elegance, the glamor—long ago he'd found them fascinating. Now all he wanted to do was escape.

The band played one of the up-tempo, syncopated melodies that had become popular of late. Couples on the dance floor marched back and forth to the beat of the music. He wasn't the best at these modern dances but enjoyed them more than the tamer, boring classic steps.

A delicate fragrance reached his nostrils, and for a moment, his heart rose in his chest. But the light feminine scent wasn't Jasminda. He turned to find Lizvette standing next to him.

"How did I know I'd find you hiding back here?" she said, a smile on her lips. There was still tension around her eyes, but Jack knew that would take time to fade.

"What can I say? I'm terribly predictable."

She stepped to him, linking an arm through his and peering out at the crowded dance floor. "Perhaps consistent is a better word."

"Yes, I far prefer that. And I'm not hiding. I'm biding my time."

She chuckled and pulled him toward the doorway. "Come, Your Grace. There is no time like the present. And yes, I would love to dance."

He barely masked his grimace and followed her out past the bewildered lead butler just as the band finished the current song. The man scampered up to the microphone on the bandstand and rushed through the recitation of Jack's titles at top speed as all present bowed.

Jack suppressed a groan as the band started in on a tame, traditional melody. He danced the long-practiced steps with Lizvette, holding her stiffly. Just beyond the dance floor, glass doors opened to the terrace and gardens beyond. A cool breeze filtered in, reminding him of his time in the mountains.

He could almost imagine he was holding Jasminda. They had never danced, though. Perhaps he would have a phonograph delivered to her rooms so he could hold her against him and feel her heartbeat as they moved in time to the music. The thought loosened the tension that was binding him. He would dance a few more songs then steal away to be with her.

"My father came to see you, did he not?"

Jack tuned back in to the room, almost having forgotten it was Lizvette he held. "Ah, yes. He told you about that. I'm sorry he had to bother you with that business. Don't worry. The thought never crossed my mind."

She grew stiff beneath his fingertips. "Would it be so bad?"

Sad eyes blinked up at him, and he missed a step, nearly bumping into a burly man dancing inelegantly beside him.

"What are you saying?" He was barely able to get the words out through his shock.

"I know the press has been harsh . . . with everything about your mother and this dreadful business with the Lagrimari. I just . . . Well, perhaps Father is right. Perhaps I can help."

Her face was open and hopeful. He couldn't sense any guile there, but her words were madness.

"What of Alariq? His memory?"

She lowered her head. "I will always hold Alariq's memory dear. He was truly one of a kind. But wouldn't he want you to be at your best advantage? I think he would want this."

Jack snorted. "My brother would not so much as let me borrow a pair of his shoes, much less his future wife."

"Alariq is dead." Her voice was clipped. "And I am not a pair of shoes." The eyes staring up at him were full of hurt.

"Of course not, Lizvette. I didn't mean to say . . . I only meant that . . . Wouldn't Alariq have wanted for you to find love again? Happiness? Not just sacrifice yourself to aid my popularity."

Her expression melted as she looked up at him. "Love?" She said the word like it was a curiosity, some foreign species of fruit that had appeared on her table. Her hand on his arm squeezed gently, then turned into almost a caress. Discomfort swirled within him. "Do you not think something could grow? Here?" She placed a hand on his heart.

The music stopped, and the other couples on the dance floor clapped. Jack drew away from Lizvette, from the unwelcome pressure of her hand on his chest, and turned to give polite applause, as well. He used the moment to gather his thoughts. She was in mourning, perhaps confused. He and Alariq were not much alike, but perhaps she was only grasping for the last threads of him left. He'd known her his whole life . . . at least he thought he knew her.

He bowed to her. "Thank you for the dance." Ignoring the question in her eyes, he rushed off the dance floor to stand near the doors leading to the terrace. The collar of his shirt constricted like a noose. He longed for fresh air to breathe.

"Your Grace," a voice called out behind him. He turned to find a cluster of men from the Merchants' Board regarding him expectantly.

He could see now how the conversation would go: a few minutes of pleasantries, how lovely the ballroom was decorated, how fine the musicians. Then, possibly a round of complaints when he inquired after their families—a son too enthralled by the weekly radio dramas for their liking or a daughter being courted by an unsuitable beau. Then, far too quickly, they would get around to what they really wanted to talk to him about. Some favor or request, with just a nudge so that he recalled how useful their support was and thinly veiled threats of the damage that would take place if that support were withdrawn. Nothing overt, but enough pressure exerted on any joint could eventually cause a break.

The men wrangled from him a promise to consider a proposal to reduce worker wages. He didn't tell them that as soon as the plan escaped their lips he did consider it . . . and found it untenable. No, he smiled and nodded, shook hands, and wished them back to wherever they'd come from as quickly as possible. Just when he thought the Queen had finally smiled upon him and the conversation had reached its death throes, a rotund character called Dursall spoke up.

"Quite a shame what happened to that little *grol* boy."

Jack's jaw clenched at the epithet.

"Well, with so many of them there, something like that was bound to happen," a wine importer named Pindeet said.

"I don't know," said Dursall. "I don't suppose a *grol* is any more likely to commit violence than, say, an Udlander. If they were brought up in a proper environment, I'd think you could almost entirely erase their more barbaric tendencies." The gathered men nodded in agreement. "Speaking of which, what's this I hear of a Lagrimari woman staying in the palace?"

Jack chose his words very carefully. "She is Elsiran. Born of a settler and a woman of the Sisterhood."

"Quite unusual," Dursall said. "But it proves my point. Perhaps it is in large part due to the gift of half her parentage, but from all accounts she is well-spoken and well-groomed. I daresay almost fit for polite society. How do you find her, Your Grace?"

Eight pairs of eyes were trained on him. He tasted each word on his tongue before allowing it to leave his mouth. "In truth, I don't know her that well. In the handful of times in which I've made her acquaintance, I've found her to be quite . . . acceptable." He swallowed.

The conversation continued for a few minutes but was impossible for him to follow. He regretted the words as soon as they'd left his mouth, but what was he to say? To mention that he was in a constant state of longing for her touch, that a day without seeing her was incomplete, that she was the most fearless and impressive woman he had ever encountered would have been more than these old hogs needed to know.

He was about to slip out to the terrace when an elderly woman dripping in diamonds, the wife of a former Council member, stopped him to attempt to wrangle an invitation for her *very eligible* granddaughter to the next state dinner. Jack looked longingly at the doors to freedom before plastering on a smile.

CHAPTER THIRTY-TWO

*Eagle warned Horse: Tread with caution and tranquility,
the ground ahead is full of brambles.*

*Horse shook off the warning saying, Watching your feet is
a sure way to bump your head.*

—COLLECTED FOLKTALES

The pounding of rain against the window left Jasminda anxious and on edge. The storm had caught up with her. Each drop of water held untapped menace and eroded whatever sense of calm she'd held since that night at the Eastern Base.

Her emotions were raw, not just from the arrival of the True Father's storm, but from her sleepless night.

The evening before, she'd watched the ball from the shadows of the terrace. She'd merely wanted a glimpse of the festivities and to see Jack in his finery once again. Hiding amidst the billowing folds of the curtains, she'd felt like a ghost, as though her existence was mere myth.

Her heart had leapt when Jack had come so near, almost close enough to touch. But she'd also been close enough to overhear what he said to those aristocrats, how he'd called her "acceptable." The words echoed in her head, seizing her heart in an icy grip. She knew she wasn't being fair, she understood his evasion, but nothing about this situation was fair, nothing about her life had ever been.

He hadn't come to her that night, either. Usher had brought her a note with Jack's apologies. Urgent matters of state kept him away.

Now she sat in the palace's Blue Library, books spread around her, trying to concentrate. She forced herself to focus on the book in her lap—Elsiran history. Wanting to start at the beginning, she'd pulled down dozens from the shelves, growing more and more uneasy with each one she read. The history before the war was treated like a fairy tale or a parable. Tales of the Founders were little more than children's stories written for adults. There were no dates, no names or locations—just stories of wonder and generosity from the esteemed Founders and whimsical folktales about their offspring.

Even the fates of the Lord and Lady were never mentioned, only that leadership eventually passed to one of their descendants, the Queen Who Sleeps, who continued their wonderful work. Then, inevitably, each book would contain a short and very vague passage on her betrayal by the True Father and the spell he cast that placed her into an endless sleep. A sleep that could only be broken when he is sent to the World After. His true identity or where he came from were never touched upon. Nor were his motives.

It was as if history and myth had intertwined somehow, and vital facts had been lost or obscured. And now she was beginning to understand the truth through the visions. Nothing in the recorded histories could disprove what the caldera showed. And the emotions she felt when she was Oola, the Queen, were all too real. Every sorrow, every bit of angst and guilt and fear became hers, and lasted long after she came back to herself.

The time between the visions was shortening, as well. This morning she'd seen a brief vision of Yllis asking Oola to marry him. It was not the first time he'd asked, and she again denied him. Her emotions had been unstable—finding her brother and restoring peace to their land had been all she could think about—but her Song sensed Yllis's frustration and pain. The vision ended abruptly, almost in the middle of a thought, and Jasminda hoped she would be strong enough to try the caldera again later that night.

She looked up from her spot on the floor and stifled a gasp to find Lizvette standing before her, willowy and elegant in a cream-colored gown.

"I didn't mean to shock you. Please forgive me," Lizvette said.

"No, I'm sorry. You haven't been standing there long, have you?"

"No." The generous way she smiled made Jasminda think that wasn't precisely the case.

Jasminda rose and tiptoed her way out of the prison of books she'd created, motioning to a set of chairs at one of the study tables. Lizvette perched in her seat, back straight, hands folded neatly in her lap. Jasminda copied her pose, but her body didn't take to it naturally.

Lizvette looked around. "I never come in here. It's so odd that I've lived in the palace all my life and rarely take advantage of its resources."

Jasminda shrugged. "It's easy to take things for granted. Hard to believe that what seems permanent can ever be taken away." She sank in her seat like a deflating balloon.

"You have had a great many losses?" Lizvette's body was rigid, but her voice kind.

"I've lost everything. Everything I've ever had." Jasminda snapped her back straight again and refused to give in to the melancholy. "But I'm sure you don't want to hear about my sorrows."

"I cannot imagine what it must be like."

"You've had your share."

Lizvette's only response was a thinning of her lips. Jasminda opened herself to a trickle of Earthsong, becoming better at shielding each time she tried. Lizvette's emotions swirled in a storm of grief and longing. Surprised at their strength and depth, Jasminda lost her hold and the connection slammed shut. The other woman's placid, controlled face hid a maelstrom of pain.

Jasminda's heart went out to her. "Would it . . . help to talk about him?"

Lizvette's eyes widened, and her hands clenched in her lap.

"Prince Alariq?" Jasminda prompted. "It's said talking about our departed ones keeps them alive in our hearts."

Lizvette released her hands to the arms of the chair and took a deep breath. "Oh, Alariq. Yes. I mean, no, thank you. I . . ." She smoothed out the fabric of her pristine dress and smiled. "I came to see you to give you a warning. I'm afraid it might not be safe for you here in the palace. Things are becoming quite strained with public opinion regarding the refugees. Jack is doing his best, but he faces heavy opposition."

Jasminda's slippered foot tapped the floor as tension seeped into her limbs. "You think someone will harm me?"

Lizvette's long neck stretched impossibly longer. She stood and crossed to the shelves, holding the most recent newspapers. "Have you seen today's paper?"

When Jasminda shook her head, Lizvette brought it over, smoothing the pages on the table.

MYSTERIOUS LAGRIMARI WOMAN HAS PRINCE IN A TWIST

His Grace, the Prince Regent has tongues around the palace wagging with his reported admiration for a young half-breed Lagrimari woman. Miss Jasminda ul-Sarifor, age and birthplace unknown, is a guest in the palace and has received the royal treatment. Records show that she was awarded the distinguished Order of the Grainbearer in a secret ceremony. Miss ul-Sarifor apparently saved the prince's life shortly before his coronation, though the details of the rescue have not been forthcoming.

Prince Jaqros has turned down the social invitations of several lovely young women in the Elsiran inner circle, purportedly to further his relationship with the exotic and interbred ul-Sarifor.

Her stay in the palace is said to be ongoing, and

while officials are tight-lipped as to the true nature of her relationship with our new, young prince, our eyes and ears remain open.

"*The Rosira Daily Witness* is not much more than an extended gossip column," Lizvette was saying, though the oceanic roar of blood rushing through Jasminda's ears made it difficult to hear. A bubble of despair burst in her chest as she read the headlines and scanned the other articles. She pushed the paper away, not wanting to see any more.

Lizvette's eyes were glassy, her face sorrowful. "The press has always bothered him. They've never cut him any slack. Ever since his mother's emigration. And now it's worse than it was then." She clucked her tongue. "She was too young and possibly too delicate for the demands of palace life. It broke her."

Eyes the color of dying embers singed Jasminda. "He needs to be seen as strong. He needs to fill Alariq's shoes and be loved by his people and not hated. Do you understand?"

Jasminda nodded, fighting the approaching tears.

"Father says if he marries well, he can put these troubles behind him."

Cold fingers gripped Jasminda's heart. Lizvette's head lowered as she stared at the carpeting. A chilling knowledge bit Jasminda. She reached out for Earthsong again, this time prepared for the woman's hidden emotions. The longing pervading her was not a futile thing as it would be for a departed lover. It was vibrant, vigorous, and full of life.

"Are you in love with him?" Jasminda asked, her whole chest numb.

Lizvette blinked, momentarily taken aback at the question.

A crack of vulnerability broke through her poised demeanor. In an instant, it was gone. She rose. "I only offer you advice. Please be careful. It would break him if anything happened to you."

She left the room in a cloud of soft perfume, completely extinguishing the cooling cinders of hope still clinging to life inside Jasminda.

She was unable to focus on the thick and dusty books any longer. A build-up of pressure sat on her heart, searching for an escape valve.

She pushed the restlessness down, determined not to allow the foul power threading through the rain to affect her again. Though she had not set foot outside since the storm had struck the city early in the morning, its repulsive energy penetrated the palace walls.

Her stomach grumbled; it was long past lunchtime. Thinking it best to avoid as many people as possible, she decided to locate the kitchen herself. No need to bother Nadal when she was perfectly capable of the task.

However, her confidence in her ability to manage the often crisscrossing, often dead-end passageways of the palace had been optimistic at best. Swiveling her head back and forth at the T-shaped intersection in which she stood, she fought against the rising tide of hopelessness. The events of the past days rooted her where she stood. She feared she would never find her way again.

"May I be of assistance?" a deep voice purred behind her.

Jasminda turned to find the unpleasant man who'd practically dragged Lizvette away from her at that first dinner watching her from a doorway. Tall and broad shouldered, he had unusually dark hair and a precise goatee. But he stared at her as if she were an item in the display case of the butcher's shop.

A surge of anger flared inside her at his self-important expression, tempting her to grab hold of her Song. She took a deep breath to release the tension and shook off the tingling in her limbs. The storm was playing its tricks again. "I don't believe we've been properly introduced. I am Jasminda ul-Sarifor." She held out her hands, challenging him to greet her properly.

"Zavros Calladeen, Minister of Foreign Affairs." He ignored her outstretched palms but bowed deeply. The bow was more formal than the pressing of hands and indicated a higher level of respect, but she got the sense he found it distasteful to touch her.

"I was searching for the kitchens," she said.

"Are your servants inadequate?"

"Not at all. But I'm the independent sort." She tilted her chin higher, with each breath battling the desire to give life to her rage and wipe that haughty sneer off his face. She could rattle the ground beneath his feet or pull the moisture from the air and soak him where he stood. But she held herself very still—on the edge of a knife blade of control.

"Allow me to escort you." He offered his elbow, though his expression made her think he meant to jab her with it.

"Oh, that's not necessary." Spending another moment in his company might just tip her over the edge.

"I must insist," he said. "You never know when there may be unsavory characters around." He spread his arms to indicate the potential villains lurking about, but the only unsavory person here was him. "I'm sure our Prince Regent would never forgive me if harm were to befall you."

"I appreciate your concern for my welfare, but I am in no need of escort from you."

He quirked an eyebrow. "You have had a stimulating few days here, I'm told."

She remained silent, practically vibrating with tension.

"The incident at the refugee camp? I hear you were quite near the action."

She gripped the fabric of her dress in tight fists to stop the shaking of her hands. The images flooded her, only serving to heighten her building fury. "If by stimulating, you mean horrifying, then you are correct. That soldier had no honor, shooting a child."

Calladeen drew uncomfortably close. Her Song slipped free of her grasp, reaching for the well of Earthsong, filling her with the vibrant energy. Her shield came up effortlessly.

"You feel the Prince Regent is acting honorably in subjecting the captain to a court-martial that could result in his execution?" he asked.

A spell escaped her, lowering the temperature in the hallway. Her voice was layered with ice when she responded. "That captain would have killed the boy for no reason if there had been no Earthsingers present. The prince is doing the only honorable thing."

Calladeen shivered visibly in the rapidly cooling corridor. "Such a shame that honor is not the most important quality in a leader. Leadership is about making hard choices and not indulging one's every whim. For example, bringing home a stray pet is not in line with effective governance."

Jasminda narrowed her eyes as the space between them chilled so drastically she could see her breath in the air. "Say what you think you need to say to me."

He pulled his collar closer to his neck as he pinned her with an accusatory glare. He must know it was her doing this. Satisfaction unfurled within her, warming her blood. She smiled cruelly as he took a step back, a tinge of fear leaching some of the contempt from his expression.

"Your presence is a problem," he said. "You make him weaker. Unfortunately, Jaqros is the only prince we have. He is not strong enough to survive the scandal of an attachment with you. He needs a princess the people can rally around, not some mongrel whore installed in the palace."

The crack of her hand against his cheek echoed across the marble floors. She had never slapped someone so hard before. She had never slapped anyone ever. But the bubbling madness inside of her applauded. Her Song surged, seeking other ways to retaliate.

Calladeen smirked, crystals of frost gathering on his goatee. Jasminda took a deep breath, vibrating with energy seeking an outlet.

"Zavros." Jack stepped into view from behind Calladeen. The prince was all warrior now, face cut from stone. His voice was low and deadly, forcing the taller man backward a step. "If you ever so much as look in her direction again, I will personally ensure your eligibility for the Order of Eunuchs. If you have a problem with me, you bring it to me. You do not speak to her. You do not look at her. As far as you are concerned, she does not exist."

Calladeen's eyes widened.

"Now get out of my sight."

The man lowered into a hasty bow before fleeing down the hallway.

The ferocious rage that had built inside Jasminda deflated

with a pop. She released her Song and the hallway warmed instantly.

Jack reached for her. She longed to fall into his arms but instead took a step back. His forehead crinkled in confusion. "Are you all right?"

Shaking her head, she took another step away from him. She didn't trust herself, and as glad as she was to see Jack—glad that he'd intervened before the storm pushed her even further—the pain building within her came rushing to fill the space the anger had occupied.

"I caught the tail end of what he said." Jack looked angrily toward the direction Calladeen had taken. "You know I would not let anyone harm you. You're too important to me."

"Me? Important? I thought I was merely acceptable." The words flew from her mouth, a final, bitter assault from her stung pride.

Understanding dawned on his face. "You heard that last night? You know I didn't mean—"

"Shh. Someone may overhear. Voices carry up here, don't they?" She motioned along the long, resonating hallway.

Jack took another step toward her, but she motioned him to stop, shaking her head. "Please don't."

With a final look in his pleading eyes, she turned and fled. His expression was burned into her memory, but she had to escape. She didn't want to be near Jack with the storm's venom running through her veins.

Eventually, a passing servant stopped and, at her request, directed her to the vehicle depot. Lunch could wait. She had to find Nash.

CHAPTER THIRTY-THREE

Horse trotted into a briar patch. She struggled savagely to free herself but the thorns dug in deeper.

Eagle passed by saying, Avoidance is always preferable to escape.

—COLLECTED FOLKTALES

"That's the place?" Ella asked, pointing to the four story, gray and brown structure, which looked even more drab in the steady rain. A tangled web of electrical wires entered the building at the roof, and the wooden porches on every level had once been painted with bright colors, but now were peeled and cracked.

"Yes, miss," Iddo said. "That's where we go to collect our payments and give the reports. Third floor." They stood inside the vestibule of the post station across the street, taking refuge from the relentless storm. Iddo's eyes tracked the street with a focused energy rare in one so young.

"And the woman who hired you. The . . . beautiful one," Ella cringed internally to describe Gizelle as such, "she's the one who pays you?"

"Always her. She holds the purse." Iddo wore the new shirt and trousers Zaura had bought him. Clean and in fresh clothes, he was barely recognizable as the scamp she'd caught following her the day before.

"Thank you for your help," she said, pulling a tenthpiece from her purse and offering it to him.

"No charge, miss," Iddo said, grinning. "Mum said I can't take no money from ya after all ya done. She's right grateful."

She ruffled his hair. "Go on then, and don't get into any trouble."

"Me? Trouble?" He laughed as he wrenched open the door and sped off, pulling another disappearing act.

Ella pushed into the main lobby of the post station and stood at the front window, pretending to read the flyers tacked onto the bulletin board. There weren't any restaurants or cafes on this street where she could sit and watch the building. It was a mostly residential area with row homes, apartment buildings, and the odd shop or two.

She loitered there long enough to have read every posting on the board twice. It would be suspicious for her to stand here much longer. But just as she began to turn to leave, the door to the building across the street opened and a woman emerged. Iddo had told her that his contact had worn street clothes and hadn't looked like a Sister. Still, Ella had half expected women clad in blue robes to be hovering about. However, the woman who came out wore a drab, green dress, much like Ella's own.

She crossed the street and passed just in front of the post station, giving Ella a glimpse of her face under her hat.

Ella pushed her way out the door, nearly tripping over her own feet. "Berta?" she called out.

"Miss Ella!" Berta smiled brightly at her and reached out for a hug. They stood under an awning, the rain a steady slap on the tarp above. "How are you?"

"I'm doing well. How's the baby? Step in here for a moment." She tugged her client into the vestibule again, out of both the rain and the direct sightline of the windows of the building she'd been watching.

"Oh, the little thing is growing like a weed. Lungs like out of tune bagpipes, he has. He's with my ma now. And my hair's still looking lovely, thank you very much." She beamed and turned her head from side to side. "Just as easy to keep up with as you said, even with the weather."

"I'm so glad to hear it. What are you doing up this way, I thought you lived down by Shepherd's Square?"

"Oh, we do, we do. Just coming from my part-time job." She angled her head across the street.

"Berta, you're not back to work already?"

"Only a few hours a day. My midwife contacted me a few days back about a woman looking for a wet nurse for her nephew. The poor child lost his ma in the birthing and can't tolerate cow's or goat's milk. It's only a few hours work a day, so I got up off my arse and came down. The pay's too good to pass up. Four pieces a day!"

Ella struggled to mask her shock. She blinked rapidly and sucked in a breath. "H-how lovely. And so sad for the poor child."

"Aye," Berta shook her head, then leaned in. "And did you

hear about the poor lad over at the refugee camp? Disgraceful. If it wasn't for my Lanson's job with the Engineering Corps, we'd go back to Fremia where people are civilized."

Ella clucked her tongue in agreement, the disconnect between her mind and body growing. On the outside, she stood chatting about the news of the day, as if her world might not have just broken open, while inside, she was desperate to reroute Berta to the topic she'd left behind so quickly.

"What kind of monster shoots a child like that?" Ella heard herself say. "I don't believe for a moment that boy attacked a soldier. I know we aren't getting the full story there."

"Not likely. Elsiran papers aren't worth the pulp they're printed on. A couple of homegrown dockworkers got into a shouting match with some Fremian sailors this morning about the whole thing. Bet you twenty pieces the papers will be calling it a riot."

Ella smiled despite herself. "They'd kick the lot of us out if they didn't need university trained scholars and guild-level workers. But never let them admit a foreigner can do something better."

Berta snickered.

"I'm sure we even nurse their children better," Ella said, tugging the reins of the conversation. "That baby up there, is he Elsiran?"

Berta shook her head. "I don't think so. The aunt is as Elsiran as they come, but the baby, he's got such dark eyes. And a funny little cap she insists he keep on his head all the time. Fussy child. They say it's just the colic, but I think he knows his mama's gone."

Grief punched at Ella's chest even as she vibrated with hope. "What a shame." Her mouth formed the words while her mind raced ahead. "I-I have a friend who's also nursing. Any chance they need more help?"

"Well, they have two wet nurses that I know of. Could be they'd like a backup, in case one of us can't make it. No ice-box in the apartment, so they can't keep milk for long when we bottle it. Tell your friend to go up there to the third floor and ask for Raynna."

"Oh, I'm sure she'd be so grateful. Thank you, Berta. What does Raynna look like?"

"Middle aged, curly hair."

Not Gizelle, then. But there was little doubt in Ella's mind that the baby was Kess's. "Thank you again, Berta. I'll tell her. You'll be back here tomorrow?"

"Yes, in the afternoon. It was so good to see you, Ella. Not sure when I'll be back to the hair parlor, but I've been telling all my friends about you."

They said their good-byes and the woman hurried off down the street. Ella looked back at the apartment building, a plan already forming in her head.

CHAPTER THIRTY-FOUR

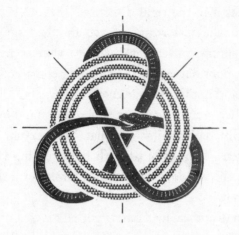

The Mistress of Serpents came upon a man sleeping by the riverside. In slumber, all are powerful, she thought. But awake, we are trapped by our memories of liberty.

—COLLECTED FOLKTALES

Somber men in dark suits with even darker expressions lined the streets. A few women were scattered among the group, as well, many waving hand-painted picket signs with slogans like *WAGES NOT WITCHCRAFT!* and *FEED THE PEOPLE NOT THE REFUGEES!*

Jack's motorcade wound its way back to the palace. He had spent the afternoon fulfilling a guest appearance Alariq had scheduled at the Export Council. Smiling and touching palms and glad-handing bigwigs and fat cats was not how he'd wanted to spend his day. And now, it seemed, the poor were having their say as well.

He did not begrudge the people their anger, if only they would focus it in the right direction. They needed someone to blame for the misfortunes of late, and the Lagrimari refugees were simply convenient. But the asylum seekers had not caused the poor harvest or the shipping embargo. And their absence could not fix them, either.

A smaller group of refugee supporters standing closer to the palace lifted his spirits somewhat. Not everyone in his land was so callous. Then a woman with a sign reading *WHY NOW?* rapped on the window as the limo slowed for a sharp turn. Yes, why now?

Back in his office, he'd barely gotten his coat off when his secretary ran up out of breath. "The Council called an emergency meeting an hour ago, Your Grace. They're voting."

"Voting on what?"

"I'm not sure, You Grace. They wouldn't say."

"Thank you, Netta." Jack straightened his suit coat and rushed to the Council Room. He opened the door and six faces regarded him. Some shocked, some guilty, and several entirely too smug.

"What is the meaning of this?" he asked, dropping heavily into his seat. The Council could meet as long as a quorum had been reached, but to do so without the Prince Regent present was unheard of.

"Your Grace," Stevenot's eyes were wide and round, "the people are demanding action. We could not afford to wait."

"Action?" Jack's brows raised.

"Yes, we've received a petition with well over two thousand names."

"And what do all of these people want?"

Calladeen leaned forward, hands clasped in front of him. "To eject the refugees from Elsira."

"We have already voted," Pugeros added.

Jack held himself very still, reining in his ire. "I see you've been most efficient, doing so without the added burden of my presence."

"It was urgent." Calladeen's voice was a rumble.

"The terms the True Father demanded," Nirall said, looking a bit green. "We've agreed to them."

"You bloody well haven't," Jack roared.

"We had to. Public safety is at risk. There was a riot down in Portside this morning." Nirall's expression was apologetic.

"You are falling right into his hands! This is what he wants. I will not let you do this. I will veto."

"And what happens when news of the True Father's letter gets out and the people learn that we had a chance for peace and did nothing?" Pugeros asked.

"How would word of the letter be made public unless someone in this room does so?" Jack peered at faces gone suddenly blank. "You threaten to reveal classified national secrets to get your way?"

Calladeen spoke. "The Council vote was unanimous, Your Grace. The only way to veto would be to invoke Prince's Right and dissolve this body."

A hush fell across the room.

Jack fisted his hands on the armrests. *Unanimous?* Not even Nirall had seen reason. So that was why they'd felt so confident holding the vote without him. Jack's veto would have stood if even one Council member had dissented, but Calladeen was correct. In the history of Elsira, only one other prince had invoked Prince's Right. That ancestor of his had been branded a tyrant and beheaded in a coup. With the enflamed emotions of the populace being what they were, Jack could not expect his fate to be any different.

The meeting continued around him, wrapping up. The ministers gave him a wide berth. Jack was certain his anger could be felt, radiating off him like waves of heat. He hoped it singed everyone it touched. He had been outmaneuvered, and deftly so. These men wouldn't have dared do this to his brother, box him into a corner in this way.

The wood grain of the table was smooth against his flattened palms. The voices of the men faded as he studied it.

Here he sat in the chair his brother had occupied. And his father. And his grandfather and great-uncle. A member of the Alliaseen family had been the Prince Regent since the loss of the Queen. The blood in his veins was noble, royal. That was supposed to mean he possessed the best qualities of an Elsiran.

And yet he had lost.

The refugees would be sent back to a life that was not a life. Back to die. He could not save them, any of them.

His mother, gone without a word. His brother, determined to pilot that wretched airship, no matter how foolish. Jasminda, harassed by a member of his own Council. The press nipping at her heels.

He was unworthy of the crown, the responsibility, the power. Even unworthy of the woman he loved.

She had walked away from him in the hallway earlier as she should have. She'd been in pain—pain he had caused. His heart splintered.

What would his legacy be? Would the pages of the history books be kind? Or would they only remember him for dooming hundreds of innocents? For the loss of an entire nation?

This illusion of peace would be short-lived.

The True Father would destroy the Mantle—perhaps tomorrow or next month or next year. And what then? Being right would not save his people.

The knots in the wood of the table kept their silence, though they stared back at him in accusation. He did not blame them.

War.

Silent versus Songbearer.

Blood in the streets.

Silent outnumber Songbearers more than ten to one, and while Eero has not turned them all against us, he has managed to bring many more than I ever imagined over to his side.

I always thought he was able to wrap me around his finger because of my weakness for him, my love. But it is a talent of his. He is charming. When he talks, people listen. They believe and trust him. They follow him, taking up arms against their neighbors, rending our land in two.

Our Songs make us fearsome foes, though Earthsong cannot be used to kill. But none who have felt the energy of a million lives strumming in his or her veins can rejoice in sending any living creature to the World After.

Early on, we healed any Silent harmed in an attack. The Assembly believed this would bring them to our side. But it did not. I cannot understand if the Silent are jealous of our Songs or fearful of them. The truth likely lies in a combination of the two.

Swords clash. The Silent fight through the rain and ice, the mud-slides and fire. They are pelted with rocks, tumbled with earthquakes, but they persist.

It is within the power of the Songbearers to entirely unmake the land from the fabric of its being, in the same way that we do the reverse, creating a beautiful landscape where once a desert stood. But we think of the future—a future of peace.

Eero knows my weaknesses. He knows me too well. I should never have been made Queen to lead the fight against him. I am the last person that should have been chosen.

Yllis studies with the Cantors day and night. His guilt is an anchor around his neck. It pulls him away from me. I have not allowed him to answer for his part in the scheme to help Eero sing. And I have not agreed to marry him. How could I with things the way they are? I thought I was protecting him by accepting all the blame, but that and my repeated refusals of his marriage offers have changed things between us.

The hurt in his eyes when he looks upon me cuts deep. So deep I do not believe I have a heart any longer. My heart was never my own. It belonged more to the ones I loved than to me.

War.

It drags us under.

It tears us apart.

CHAPTER THIRTY-FIVE

*A traveler stood at a crossroads, uncertain of which way to go.
The Mistress of Frogs whispered in his ear, Just as lightning transforms the tree into cinder, so does doubt change progress to stagnation.*

—COLLECTED FOLKTALES

Jack padded into Jasminda's chamber well after midnight, unsure of what his reception would be. His heart was weighed
down by heavy chains and the only thing that could lift his
spirits was her—even though she would be well justified in
refusing to see him.

She was still awake, sitting by the fire, staring pensively
into the dancing flames. He approached with halting steps. She
looked up, eyes shining with unshed tears, and Jack dropped
to his knees.

"The servants are gossiping something fierce. Is it true? The refugees are being sent back to Lagrimar?"

A great hollow space opened in his chest. He nodded.

"Oh, Jack." She collapsed against him. He exhaled the breath he'd been holding since he'd seen her last.

"I have prayed to the Queen, but She has given no counsel. I do not think I hold Her favor."

"Jack," she whispered, wrapping her arms around him and drawing him closer. His body relaxed, at home with her in his arms. "You are a good prince. You are selfless and fearless."

His head dropped. "I am constantly afraid."

She grabbed his chin and tilted his face up. "But you rise above it."

He smiled grimly. "Even you are too good for me."

"Nonsense," she said and pressed her lips to his. He kissed her back greedily, holding her head firmly in his grip.

"I'm so sorry about earlier," she said. "I wasn't myself."

"No, I'm sorry."

She brushed her fingers across his lips. "I have no right to change the rules we both agreed upon."

He shook his head. "I don't want there to be any rules for us. I just wish . . ." He squeezed her tightly to his chest again, not sure even of what to wish for. A different world, a kinder one.

He rose and lifted her so that he could sit in the chair with her on his lap. He rubbed circles into her back, noting the tension in her muscles.

"What will happen to me?" Her voice was empty as an echo.

He shifted so he could peer into her eyes. Misery suffused the beauty of her face. "Jasminda—"

"Half-breed. Mongrel. That's what the papers say, right? I do you no favors by staying here. And didn't the True Father's letter say every Lagrimari must be sent back?"

Jack's lungs compressed as if he was at the peak of a mountain sucking in air too thin to quench his need. "You are not Lagrimari."

"Am I not?" Her eyes were almost wild. "I may have been born in your land, share half your blood, but I'm not one of you. I'm not one of them, either. I don't belong anywhere, Jack."

"No," he said, voice steely. "No, you belong with me." He held her tighter, his chest vibrating with the racing of her heart.

"For how long? How long until you must find an acceptable princess? One that you need in order to regain the people's trust? We were only ever going to be temporary."

He crushed her to him and stroked her soft, springy hair. "Are you saying you want to leave?"

"No."

"Then—"

"But I cannot stay."

He shook his head rapidly, desperate to jostle a solution into his brain. "If being prince is good for anything, then I should get to be with the woman I love." He pulled away and clutched her hands to his chest. "Do you hear me? I love you."

Saying it out loud took the edge off the panic building at the thought of her leaving. "You are strong and intelligent and fearless and beautiful. I had never even hoped a woman like you existed. I love you, Jasminda."

Tears traced her face. "I love you, too. You must know that. You are my whole heart, Jaqros Alliaseen. My whole heart. I never thought I would . . ."

She looked away, and he wiped her streaming cheeks.

"Do you want to know what I saw, in that awful test to find the cornerstone?" Jack's voice sounded hollow to his own ears.

Jasminda looked up, eyes wide. They hadn't spoken of their visions. He had no wish for Jasminda to relive whatever horrors she'd seen, but now he felt the need to tell her.

"I saw my land in flames. My people dying in the streets because of my failure. And I saw you." His voice cracked. "I saw you being carried away from me. Ripped out of my arms, screaming."

She cupped his cheeks, tears filling her eyes. She kissed him softly, first on his lips, then his cheeks, eyelids, nose, forehead, before returning to his mouth.

She was so gentle it made him anxious. He did not deserve such tenderness. He deepened the kiss, grabbing hold of her waist and stroking her side. The tightness she'd held melted away as her arms came around his neck.

Jack lifted her and carried her to the bed. She kneeled on the mattress as he stood devouring her mouth with needy kisses. She slid her palms down his chest and began working on the buttons of his shirt. Her expertise at removing men's clothing had grown, and she had the shirt hanging open and the trousers pushed to his knees in record time.

As he was undoing the ties of her dress and sliding it over her head, a blade of awareness sliced into him. Jasminda was soft and pliable, her body receptive to his touch, but something was different. There was a distance present between them that had never been there before, even as she discarded her slip with a seductive smile and lay back, inviting him between her thighs.

He needed to erase the space separating them, to bring them back in sync. Trying to show her how much he cherished her with his hands and lips and tongue. She panted and cried out his name, begging for more, but he held off, bringing her to the brink of climax, then easing her back down, ignoring her protests. Her limbs shook with need, they were skin to skin, and yet she was not close enough.

She guided him inside her. The indefinable sensation of sinking deep within her was so much more than lust. The gentle rhythm of their lovemaking sped up to a pounding beat as he fought to chase away the nagging worry, guilt, and fear. She loved him. She would stand by him in this dark time.

He drove into her, spurred on by her nails digging into his back and her shrieks of pleasure. Losing himself in her skin, her scent, her cries, he could almost outrun the gloom of what was to come.

Afterward, she lay in his arms, stroking his skin, not seeming to mind the sweat and stickiness after so much exertion. He held her tightly against him, as tight as he dared without crushing her. For even though she had been right with him the entire evening, a voice in the back of his head told him she was slipping away.

CHAPTER THIRTY-SIX

A merchant set a trap for the thief stealing from his wagons at night. In the morning, he found the Master of Monkeys caught in the snare. Forgive me, the merchant cried, for I did not know it was you, my lord.

Monkey, once free, praised the man for his cleverness. For it is not every day, he said, that I am beaten at my own game.

But when he had left, the merchant found his shelves bare and all his goods were gone.

—COLLECTED FOLKTALES

Iddo knocked on the door to the third floor apartment. Ella thought he had quite a commanding knock for such a small boy. From her place halfway up the stairwell to the fourth floor, she heard the creak of the door opening, but not what was said between him and whoever answered. If all went to plan, Iddo should be telling Gizelle that he'd seen Ella going through the 35th Street Gate into Rosira proper. Apparently, the children were to alert the woman immediately if that happened. *So they can have me arrested and deported within the hour,* Ella thought.

Iddo must have done his job because swift footsteps approached the stairwell. Ella crouched below the railing, then sneaked a peek between the bars to see a bronzed head rushing down the steps. She caught a glimpse of the side of the woman's face as she descended. Iddo whistled, following more slowly. Once she heard the slam of the main door below, Ella emerged from hiding and strode down the hall.

She knocked much more cautiously than Iddo had and waited a moment until the door cracked open, revealing one suspicious looking eye.

"Mistress Raynna?" Ella said. "I'm the wet nurse. Berta sent me in to take her place today. She's coming down with a cold. Didn't want to pass it on to the little one." In reality, members of Iddo's gang of child mischief makers had been tasked with slowing down Berta's progress today and prevent her from arriving on time. It was a shame to make her miss out on the income, but Ella would just have to find some way to make it up to the woman.

The apartment door opened a fraction wider and the possessor of the mistrustful eye, who Ella supposed must be Raynna, looked her up and down. She was short and round with thinning coils of hair and an upturned nose. Ella smiled and stood patiently under the scrutiny.

"Four pieces a day, right? To nurse?" she prompted.

Raynna shut the door abruptly in her face and several

chains scraped against the wood. Were they expecting trouble? Finally, the door opened again and she was let in.

The flat itself was dreary, furnished with only two hard chairs and a table in the main room. The cracked walls were in need of paint and the small kitchenette in the far corner lent the space a desperate air. Through a doorway lay a bedroom with a single bed and crib as its only furniture. If the Sisterhood wanted to give the appearance of a regular home, they were doing a poor job of it. Though for four pieces a day, they could expect the women working here to overlook it.

Raynna stood with her arms crossed, hard gaze never leaving Ella.

"In here?" Ella pointed to the bedroom. Raynna grunted and Ella brightened her smile before heading inside.

The baby was asleep and swaddled tightly in a yellow blanket, only his little face visible. Ella rushed over to pick him up. She was about to pull off the cap covering his hair when she felt a stare burning into her back. She turned to find Raynna glaring at her. The woman moved as silent as a spider.

"I hate to wake him," she said, cradling him to her chest. "Maybe I should express my milk until he wakes up."

Raynna grunted. "I'll get the bottle."

Left alone for the moment, Ella looked for a place to sit. There were no chairs of any kind in the room. She supposed the wet nurses sat on the bed, though if it belonged to Raynna that seemed a bit personal. Still, with no other options, she sat on the stiff mattress. Raynna reappeared with a bottle, funnel, and nipple and lay them down next to her, then stood by the door as if she was going to watch the process.

Ella smiled and with her free hand began to undo the buttons of her dress. This was going to get very awkward, very fast if the rest of the plan didn't go off as designed. She just had to keep up the charade long enough for—

A knock sounded at the door.

Raynna's perpetual frown deepened. With the street urchins coming and going for their pay and to give updates on those they were following, this place must get quite a bit of traffic. Still, Raynna seemed none too happy about answering the door.

Once the woman was out of sight, Ella jumped into action. She pulled a length of fabric out of her bag and folded it into a sling. Then she drew up the corner of the baby's little black cap to verify his hair color. Pale strands of fine white hair were plastered to his head. She tugged the cap back into place and tied the sling around her, strapping the baby to her chest. Then she wrapped a heavy, knitted shawl around herself, to hide the bundle from sight.

Thank the saints the child didn't awaken. Instead he seemed to snuggle against her chest, and a shot of warmth went through her.

Ella crossed to stand behind the bedroom door and peeked out into the main room. Through the crack, she watched Raynna and her new visitor. An old woman, stooped over and gripping a cane, talking loudly as if she was hard of hearing. Zaura was right on time.

"I tell you, the leak is coming through to my place downstairs," she said, adding far more creak to her voice than was there naturally. "I need you to check your sink, missy."

"Nothing is leaking here!" Raynna yelled.

Zaura grumbled and pushed her way in, past a startled

Raynna, and headed to the sink in the corner of the apartment. With a glance behind her at the bedroom, Rayna followed.

Iddo had told her the space was tiny—still, it was even smaller than Ella had anticipated, making her task all the more difficult. The women's backs were to her as Zaura spun the faucet handles, turning the sink on and off and on and off again. Ella tiptoed toward the still open front door. She hadn't noticed any creaking floorboards on her way in, and could only hope her steps were light enough. As the two women bickered about the plumbing, Ella slipped out.

She grasped the precious bundle to her and sped down the steps, clutching the shawl with her free hand. Down the two flights and out the front door into the driving rain. She lifted the shawl to cover her head and moved quickly down the walkway to the sidewalk. Scanning the street for threats, she didn't even breathe.

Foot traffic was light here making it more difficult to blend in. Raynna may have noticed her absence by now, or maybe not—Zaura had been eager to play her role and Ella didn't doubt the woman could find ways to keep Raynna distracted for a quarter of an hour at least.

Ella was almost home free.

Down the street, on the corner, Benn stood next to the hired taxi—an auto, not a carriage. He waited in the rain with the car's door open, one arm reaching for her as she approached. Ella's racing heart began to settle, then she glanced in the window of the grocer's she was passing. A telephone booth was positioned right in the window. The woman with the receiver in her hand looked familiar.

Ella's heart regained its rapid pace. Gizelle stared at her through the glass, only a dozen paces away.

The Sister's eyes widened with disbelief. Ella's chest felt like it was on the verge of collapse. She picked up her pace, aware of the gaze tracking her, and ran to Benn. One arm protectively covered her nephew, the other pumped as she gained speed.

She leapt into the taxi screaming, "Drive!" Benn hopped in beside her and slammed the door. The car took off and Ella looked behind her, out the tiny rear window.

Gizelle had run onto the sidewalk. She stood there soaked to the skin, unmoving, watching them drive away.

The wave of fear receded as the woman became just a small dot in the distance. Against Ella's heaving chest, her nephew was a warm presence.

Shivering from the adrenaline rush, the rain, the fear and the relief, Ella broke down and cried.

CHAPTER THIRTY-SEVEN

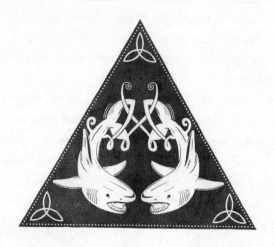

The Master of Sharks visited a merchant dealing in rare and precious gems. How much of your profit do you give to the poor? he asked.

Why should I share the fruit of my labor? the merchant responded.

Shark replied, The gem that is most valuable, is the one shining upon the most people.

—COLLECTED FOLKTALES

Jasminda awoke alone. It was just as well. She would rather remember Jack as he was last night, holding her close, whispering how much he loved her. The vision he'd spoken of chilled her. She hated that she was going to make a small part of it a reality, but she had no other choice. Her love for him would do him little good in the long run.

She located her dress, the one she was wearing when she arrived. It had been washed and pressed and was the only thing she truly owned here. She also strapped a serrated knife, nicked from her dinner tray, to her thigh using a garter.

Though her heart was fracturing, it was time for her to go back home. She would continue to unlock the secrets of the caldera for as long as it took to gain answers. Once she knew more, she would contact the palace, but in the meantime she needed to find a way back east.

The palace hallways were quiet. Jasminda managed to locate the office nearest the vehicle depot and asked for Nash. Within a few minutes he appeared, a newspaper tucked under his arm. With a nervous glance to the paper, she wondered what today's story was.

"Is it done?" she asked.

"Yes, miss." His keen green gaze never strayed from her. "An account has been set up at the Royal Elsiran Bank. I have the deposit slip—"

She waved her hands to stop him. "I don't want to know how much. It was enough for the taxes and to buy back the land?"

He nodded. "And then some. The dealer's eyes nearly bugged out of his head when he caught sight of your Order of the Grainbearer medal. Very rare they are. It brought in a tidy sum."

"Well, you keep the rest. I—I don't want it." Her fingers twitched remembering the feel of the soft velvet case and cool metal. Jack's cautious smile as he'd given it to her. It was done. On her terms at least. Her grandfather could take his shame-laden contract and swallow it whole for all she cared.

Rebuilding the cabin on her own would be slow, but she would manage it. What did she have if not time? A wave of dizziness swept over her at the thought. "I need to get out of here."

Nash's face softened. "Of course." He led her to the door, picking up a large, black umbrella from a stand full of them and protected her from the driving rain as they stepped outside. Though there was a steady torrent, Jasminda was calm. The storm's power over her had always required a catalyst— her anger. When she was collected and even, she could stay in control. So leaving now was doubly necessary before something else sparked her rage.

Just as she and Nash reached the row of town cars, rapidly approaching footsteps caused her to turn. Four Royal Guardsmen marched up, splashing across the pavement, stiff and imposing.

"Miss," one of the Guardsmen called as she backed toward the auto. "I need you to come with us."

She had never before been summoned by the Royal Guard. Usher had brought messages from Jack, but he'd never sent anyone else. She cast a glance at Nash, whose brow was furrowed, before turning and following the Guardsmen back into the palace.

Despite the large umbrella, her dress was soaked from her few minutes outside. She shivered, following the men through the halls to a wide doorway. They descended a staircase, wet steps squishing on the stones, then followed a hall leading to another staircase. At the end of a sparse hallway, a fifth Royal Guardsman stood before an elaborate brass gate that he unlocked as they approached, before ushering them through. Jasminda froze when the iron bars of the dungeon cells came into view.

"What is this about?" she asked, whirling around.

The door to a cell hung open, and the Guardsmen all stopped walking, blocking every direction except into the cell.

"I'm being arrested?" Her gaze darted around the small space, sparse but clean. "By whose order?"

The young, bland Guardsman did not look at her as he spoke. "Miss, by order of Prince Jaqros you are remanded here for your own protection."

"My protection? From what?"

"Please, miss," he said, pointing to the cell.

"Why am I here? Why won't you tell me?"

"Miss Jasminda," a familiar voice said. Usher stepped out from behind the row of Guardsmen. "There has been a threat made against you. He doesn't know who to trust. He's trying to protect you."

Fear stole the strength out of her budding anger. Lizvette had hinted as much the day before, but an actual threat turned her blood cold. "Then perhaps I would be safer elsewhere. He should just let me go."

With no other options, she stepped inside the cell and shuddered as the door clanked shut behind her.

"He is not strong enough to do that." Usher stepped to the bars and slipped a thick, warm blanket through a gap. Jasminda accepted it, lay down on the thin cot, and cried.

That is impossible, *Vaaryn says through his Song.*

Then how would you explain it? *Deela, Yllis's mother, replies. She, Vaaryn, and I sit in the Great Hall. There are still loyal Silent working as servants here, but there are no doubt also spies for the other side, as well. No important conversation is held out loud any longer.*

No Songbearer would gift Eero their Song. There are only two who even know the spell. *Deela looks at me, and I shrink a bit more inside.*

So you believe he has actually learned to steal Song from a bearer? *Vaaryn's forehead wrinkles in disbelief.* That would be . . .

A disaster, *I finish. But it must be true. Eero is singing again. Through the window, the battle for the skies is clear. Only hours ago, the placid, clear day was interrupted by sudden, unnatural clouds. Songbearers on the front lines had to fend off tornadoes, hurricanes, snow, and ice all afternoon.*

Who has he stolen from? *Deela says.*

I shake my head. We are still accounting for all of the Song-bearers in the city.

Will all the Silent want Songs now? *Vaaryn wonders.*

I frown, considering. I do not think he will want to share. My brother was never generous.

How do they still follow him? Do they not find him a hypocrite? Especially when his demands are for a separate land for the Silent. *Deela's face is so like Yllis's, even more so when working out a difficult problem.* He has split us apart and wants to make it official, by creating a land just for them, yet he steals the Song of a Songbearer.

His gift is winning the hearts and minds of others, *I say.* Logic is not always required for that. And as for his demands, perhaps we should give him what he wants.

Vaaryn's rheumy eyes go wide.

Hear me out. If we take the abandoned land east of the mountains, we could reform it and rebuild, just as we did this land, *I say.* We could leave the west to the Silent and rebuild to the east.

I let them mull over my suggestion for a while. The thought of leaving my home sickens me, but this war must end.

We must bring this to the Assembly, *Deela says.*

I nod, certain I can convince them.

At least once he is separated from the Songbearers, he will not be able to steal what the Silent do not possess, *Deela says, seeming to be reassured by this.*

Eero has already stolen so much from the Silent—their peace, their stability, their future—but I keep these thoughts to myself as we take our leave.

Yllis finds me before sunset as I pace the floors of the Great Hall, awaiting updates from those on the front lines. He is rumpled and creased, his hair is lopsided, but he is as beautiful to me as ever.

"You must come with me," he says. I startle at hearing his voice aloud, but I am so grateful he has spoken. He leads me to his office in the laboratory of the Cantors.

"I think I have found a way . . ."

"Do you think it wise to speak?" Though I love to hear his voice, I, too, have been seized by the paranoia affecting the other Songbearers.

"You, too, Oola?" He pins me with a withering glare, one I must grow used to seeing from him. What once was soft and cherished between us is now all hard edges. "No Silent are allowed within the walls of the Cantors."

"Very well. You think you have found a way to do what?"

He points down to his leather-bound notebook. Tight handwriting fills every page, obscuring the color of the original paper.

"I have studied everything we have on the ancient ways of the Cavefolk. They are Silent but manage to harness a vast power different than Earthsong—from a different source. Just as powerful but not as limited. Cantors have long used the Cavefolk techniques,

but only with Earthsong. They have never attempted any of the more robust spells because they all require one key ingredient." His finger stops below one word, written boldly, traced over and over.

Blood.

I meet Yllis's eyes, which gleam in the lamplight.

"With blood magic, we can create a spell to silence any Song," he says.

"Blood magic?" I shake my head and step away. "We cannot."

He steps toward me, his eyes on fire. "We must."

"No, there is another way." I tell him of the plan I shared with the others. "What he wants is his own land. The war will end once we give him this."

Yllis stares at me for a long while and shivers run up my spine. "You were always blind when it came to him."

"What do you mean?"

For a moment, the hard shell he's constructed around himself cracks, and I see a glimpse of the man I fell in love with. Yllis moves closer to me, placing his hands on my shoulders. "He wants what he has always wanted: power."

I shiver. Both from the truth of his words and his close proximity. "So this spell . . . how does it work?"

"It is a binding spell to prevent connection with Earthsong."

"And we will need someone's blood?"

His eyes darken, and he nods. "Let me worry about that. Link with me, and I will teach you the spell."

His hand is the same as I remember. Warm and big, it swallows mine. I hardly get to relish the feeling of his skin when I'm thrown into his link. The feel of the spell sours my tongue, but I commit it to memory.

CHAPTER THIRTY-EIGHT

A wise man asked the Mistress of Eagles, How can I hear the
voice of the Divine?

All voices are the Divine, she answered.

But what of those speaking evil?

Eagle replied, Evil is heard with the heart and not with
the ears.

—COLLECTED FOLKTALES

Anneli's house was really no place for a baby. But considering
Ella couldn't go back to her apartment, it was the safest place
she could think of. Though as she stood in the crowded parlor, surrounded by waist-high stacks of papers, books, and
magazines, holding a bawling infant gearing up for his next
ear-splitting shriek, she questioned her choices.

They'd only been there a few minutes and the infant had awoken as soon as they'd arrived. Benn had gone immediately back out to the grocer's to fetch supplies—namely something the child could eat. According to Zaura, a certain strain of terryroot, boiled to a broth then cooled to room temperature provided nutrition compatible with an Udlander's sensitive stomach. Centuries of not eating meat made their constitutions very delicate.

"Breast milk from meat eaters is probably what's got the little man so upset," Zaura said, waggling her finger in his face. "His diapers are probably wretched as well."

Ella supposed she should check the diaper, though there had been no foul smells from that direction as of yet.

"I hope this won't disturb the neighbors," she said as the baby continued to wail.

Anneli sniffed. "Houses on either side are empty. Never got new renters in after the last ones left. Quieter that way."

Ella gaped. "You own the houses on either side of this one?"

"A couple more down the block as well. My Henrik was always a fan of real estate." Then she shuffled off into the back to the kitchen to scare up some supper.

Ella rocked the child and cooed at him. Sung a half-remembered lullaby from childhood, but nothing seemed to calm him. He was still wrapped up snugly in his blanket, only his head visible. Maybe he was too warm, or wanted more freedom for his limbs. She set him down to unwrap him just as Benn banged on the door.

"I've got it," Zaura said, rising to let him in.

Her husband entered dripping wet from the unceasing rain. He removed his shoes in the entryway and raised the grocery bag. "Managed to find the terryroot. How's the little one?"

"Still upset."

"Well, hopefully having something in his stomach will calm him."

Zaura took the bag. "I'll brew up the broth. Should be ready in a tick."

"All right Master Large Lungs, let's get you unwrapped, shall we?" Ella peeled away the blanket, freeing his tiny limbs. Smiling at the unique scent of baby that made her think of mornings on the farm and flowers in bloom, she stroked a finger down his little arm. And her vision whited out.

Ella was somewhere dark and warm. She couldn't see anything around her, just a solid blackness spreading out forever.

She spun around, holding her arms out. And then there was Kess, grown-up Kess, but looking healthy in a way Ella hadn't seen her. Rosy cheeked with glistening eyes brimming with tears.

"Kess?"

Her sister turned toward her voice, but didn't seem able to see her.

"Ella. You're the only one who will get this message." Kess's voice echoed a bit, like it was coming from much further away than where she stood.

"The spell is tied to the blood. Mine, my child's, yours. It was dangerous, but the only way. When I knew . . ." She stopped, tearing up. "When I knew I wouldn't make it to see my son reach even one day old, I put everything I had left into this spell. I wanted a record of what I've done. All my mistakes."

She looked down as a tear escaped her eye. "One day he will want to know who his mother was. And he should know. The good and the bad. It may be too late for the prince, but the rest of it—I can go to the World After unburdened. I can do what I should have done a long time ago.

"Ella, you must protect him. I cannot. Syllenne will want to use him. She'll want to hold him over his father's head as bait. As proof of the secrets better left hidden. And now I've placed another secret in his blood, but it was the only way. You have to believe me. I hope one day you both will forgive me for it." She sniffed.

"If Syllenne finds out what I've done, he'll never be safe. If she manages to take control of the palace . . ." Kess shook her head. "I've left you my memories. You'll know what to do with them. I don't know how much you remember about those spells PawPaw used to do, the ones that made Mother so upset. But I couldn't stop thinking about them. After I left home, I went east and spent years learning blood magic and then many more trying to forget. It's a terrible power. And it was never meant to be used this way. Objects can be made to hold memories, but then anyone's blood could unlock them. The only way to make sure that you alone could access my memories was to tie them to my own blood—the blood we share— and to his. Those who bear the blood need only touch the object of the spell to unlock it."

Her body shuddered with a sob. "I know I've been a terrible sister. I've done many things I regret, but I love you, Ellie. And make sure he knows I love him, too. Give him a good, strong name. I'm so sorry."

And then she was gone. Ella was thrown into a vision—a memory. She was Kess, younger and skinny and in a forest somewhere. She sat next to a withered old man using a wicked blade to cut into his own heavily scarred arm all while muttering in a foreign tongue. Blood magic.

Ella blinked and she was in a temple standing before a slightly younger Syllenne Nidos as the woman spoke about loyalty and sacrifice.

Ella just got glimpses, but soon learned that she could sift through them. Navigate them. Years flew by, years of memories. Kess camping outdoors, on a ship rocking on rough seas, hiking through mountains. Standing before a temple in Elsira. Talking with Gizelle, who must have only been a teenager. It was chaotic, but just as she was beginning to truly get the hang of how to pause and really explore the images flying by, she was wrenched away.

She gasped, coughing in Anneli's front parlor. Benn held the child, staring at her with concern in his eyes. Zaura stood over her, an empty cup in her hand. Ella's face was wet. Zaura must have thrown water on her.

Ella blinked, adjusting back to the present and reality. Then she peered at the baby. The tiny cut from where Kess had sliced him marred his forearm. It didn't appear to have healed at all over the course of the week.

PawPaw's words came back to her like a slap in the face. "Everything has a cost. Even love."

In the kitchen, Ella hunched over the mug of tea in her hands. Benn sat across from her at the table, still holding the fussing infant. He'd quieted enough to drink broth from the bottle, but then had immediately began to cry again.

She'd tried touching him once more and been thrown back

into the visions until Benn had forcibly pulled her away. Any skin to skin contact would push her into Kess's memories. Had her sister known this would prevent Ella from caring for her nephew? From changing him or bathing him?

A knock sounded at the front door, and Ella popped up. She followed Anneli to the hallway with Benn and Zaura close behind her. Anneli peered out the glass at the side of the front door.

"Friend of yours?" she asked gruffly.

Ella craned to look over her head and smiled. She threw the door open to reveal Mayzi on the doorstep standing under an enormous umbrella.

"You came!" Ella exclaimed. She moved aside to let Mayzi enter, but Benn blocked the woman's way forward, holding the crying child protectively against his chest.

"You invited her here?" he asked, eyes narrowed with suspicion. "How do you know this woman, Ell?"

"She's . . . the baby's . . . stepmother. Sort of." Ella shrugged. "And yes, I called her."

Benn reluctantly moved aside.

"Zann didn't try to stop you, did he?" Ella asked.

"No, he was mid-speech when I left. Eyes on a pretty shop girl in the front row." While her tone was jovial, her face was heavy with pain. Then she focused on the baby in Benn's arms and her smile returned, turned up bright.

The baby chose that moment to let out another wail. "Can I hold him?" Mayzi asked.

Benn looked ready to say no, but Ella prompted him with a nod. The longing in Mayzi's face was so familiar. Reluctantly, he handed over the infant. Who quieted immediately.

Everyone stared in disbelief.

Mayzi cooed, making funny faces and smiling. It transformed her face, erasing the hard edges. They were all transfixed.

"Well, let's get some tea in you," Zaura said finally and head back to the kitchen. They all followed.

Benn turned to Ella, while keeping an eye on Mayzi, who stood rocking the baby. "What's going on?"

She leaned into him, whispering. "His blood holds the proof we've been looking for. And if Syllenne ever found out, it would be his death sentence."

Benn melted with concern. "So we take him away. We can go to Fremia, or maybe Yaly. Somewhere he won't stand out so much with that hair. And somewhere Syllenne can't reach us."

Ella stared up at him, openmouthed. She blinked over and over, like a skipping record, but the rest of her body felt far away. She couldn't possibly have heard what she thought she did.

"What?" he asked, eyes wide.

"You would leave Elsira?"

His expression of concern turned into one of chagrin. He dropped his head and sagged his shoulders. "Of course. I would do anything for you."

She fell into the chair behind her with a thud. "But your job. Your dream. You can't just leave it, after all the work you've done to get there."

Benn dragged a chair close to hers so they were knee to knee and took her hands. "I've been an ass. And I consider myself very lucky that you've put up with me for so long. I'm sorry, Ella. The fact that you would ever think I'd put my job before you . . ." He shook his head. "Well, what else would you think?"

Misery shadowed his gaze. "I thought I had to prove something—to the world and to myself. But none of that matters. I understand that now." He squeezed her hands tighter. "If we need to leave to protect him, then that's what we'll do."

Ella's chest was full enough to burst. It felt like she'd swallowed the sun. Tears kissed her eyes and she gasped for breath around the explosion of joy in her lungs. Benn drew her into his arms. She sat on his lap, burying her face in his neck.

A knot loosened within her, one she hadn't realized had kept her trussed for a long time. It had tightened slowly over the years, cutting off her air and circulation. She'd had to numb herself to the pain of being alone. To the feeling of abandonment, of not quite being enough. She knew Benn loved her, and she'd tried to be happy with what she had. Ella had always made do. She only realized how heavy the burden had been now that it was lifted.

She imagined herself and Benn and the baby—a little family in a cottage somewhere. They could go back to Sirunan, or maybe one of the larger commonwealths. She would have the quiet home and loving family she'd barely allowed herself to dream of. It could be perfect.

Her arms tightened around Benn. But was leaving Elsira the way? Living while constantly looking over their shoulders? Always afraid that one of Syllenne's goons would track them down and discover their secret? How long would that perfect little picture last until it was shattered? And how could she physically care for her nephew? She couldn't touch him at all without blanking out into one of Kess's memories.

With a deep breath, she sat up, uncertainty whirling within. Zaura and Anneli were whispering in the corner, their silver heads bent together. Mayzi still played with the infant, delight brightening her face.

"It's just like I thought. Looks like she has the magic touch," Ella said.

Mayzi swung the infant around, gibbering baby talk and eliciting gurgles from him. He'd only ever cried when any of the rest of them held him.

"What made you think he would take to her?" Benn asked.

Ella couldn't quite say. She'd been struck by the notion that Mayzi needed to be there. Before she knew it, she'd been asking the operator to dial the billiard hall. It was almost as if someone else was guiding her actions.

Mayzi spun around again and bumped into the bag of remaining groceries on the counter. The few items left in the bag were jostled. A can fell out, and the box of eggs tipped over. Two rolled off the counter before anyone could stop them.

Ella almost didn't need to look to know what she'd find on the floor. One egg had broken, spreading its yoke on the black and white tiles. But miraculously, one egg landed completely whole.

St. Siruna. It looked like her champion hadn't abandoned her after all.

She pulled her hands from Benn's and stood, staring at the sign on the ground. "All right," she said. "I'm listening."

CHAPTER THIRTY-NINE

The Master of Jackals waded into the sea and found a fish floundering in a forgotten net.

When he went to free it, the fish responded, Leave me be.

Said the Jackal, Don't you want to be free?

The fish replied, I do not trust you not to eat me. I will take my chances with the will of the ocean.

—COLLECTED FOLKTALES

The young maid standing in Jack's office sniffled and wrung her hands. "No, Your Grace. I would never let anyone else in Miss Jasminda's rooms. Never." Red-rimmed eyes overflowed with tears. "I always saw to her myself, just as Usher asked."

Jack sighed and paused his pacing. "And you have no idea how anyone would have gotten hold of this?" He pointed to the low table where the beautiful, delicate, golden gown Jasminda had worn her first night in the palace lay. It had been found, slashed and partially burned, outside the doors to the Prince Regent's office suite.

"No, Your Grace." The girl shook her head violently, took another look at the gown, and burst into a fresh round of sobs.

"All right, all right, Nadal," Jack said, motioning for Usher to comfort her. "I believe you. But you haven't heard anything from the other servants?"

She leaned into Usher and quieted. "Some of them have been cool toward me since I wouldn't gossip about Miss Jasminda with them. I haven't heard anything."

Jack dropped roughly onto the couch, nervous energy rattling through him. He answered the question in Usher's gaze with a nod, and the man led Nadal away, returning a few minutes later alone.

"She's going to hate me," Jack said as he rubbed his burning eyes, wishing he could rub away the weariness and the heartache. "She has every right to. But she's in the safest place in the palace. Almost anyone could have sneaked into her rooms. Any person in this palace could mean her harm."

Usher clucked his tongue; Jack looked up. "What?"

"You should go to her, young sir."

"Was she really leaving?" Jack sank down, every bone in his body feeling twice its weight.

"It appears so," Usher replied, apologetic.

Jack groaned, closing the lid on the emotions that threatened to spill out at the thought of Jasminda's absence. A horrifying idea struck him. "Mother often talked of wanting to leave. I would hear them arguing . . . Father would never let her." He scrubbed a hand over his face. "I'm just like him, aren't I? I will never be able to escape the shadow of his cruelty."

He stood and walked to the terrace doors, looking out at the city stretching before him and beyond, to the endless waves of the ocean, turned dark and ominous, churning from the force of the storm.

Usher came to stand by him. "You are nothing like him."

Jack rested his forehead against the cool glass. The weather outside matched the agitated whirlwind inside him. "Then why do I feel like the villain here?"

The buses with the refugees were now on their way toward the border. By this time tomorrow, they would all be back across the mountain. Only the Queen knew what their fates would be, but Jack could guess. He chuckled mirthlessly.

"What have I done, Usher? The woman I love in the dungeons. Allowing the refugees to be sent back. What does this make me?"

"It makes you a prince."

"And what is that worth when I can't save anyone?"

The darkness in his heart was in danger of overtaking him. He rubbed his chest as if he could massage the broken organ from the outside. "I must go to her. Either she'll forgive me or she won't. Besides, I don't want her staying in the palace any longer than necessary. You've gotten in touch with Benn's wife? Asked if Jasminda can stay with her down in Portside until I can figure out who's responsible for this?"

"I'm working on it. We'll find a safe place for her." Usher's reassuring voice was a balm to Jack's soul.

"All right. Thank you." He cast another glance at the ruined dress; anger beat a rhythm inside his chest. "I can't fail her, too," he rasped, nearly choking on the words.

Usher clapped him on the shoulder and squeezed. Some days the only thing keeping him upright was the man's presence.

He gave Usher a sidelong glance. "How do you stand me, old man?"

"I don't really have a choice, now, do I?" Usher said with a droll smile.

Jack shook his head and left for the dungeon, feeling even more guilty for keeping Jasminda locked away a moment longer than necessary. He had wanted her safe while he questioned the servants, but the task had taken longer than anticipated. As he entered the outer chamber leading to the cells, the guards snapped to attention.

"Captain," Jack said. "It's time to let her out."

The captain's eyes widened. "L-let her out, Your Grace?"

"Yes, open the cell. I'll take her with me."

The captain's gaze darted to his fellow guard, rigid beside him, then back to Jack. "B-begging your pardon, Your Grace, but she's already been let out."

Jack stilled, every muscle in his body tensing in alarm. "I gave explicit orders that the young woman was to be held here until I ordered her released."

"Yes, Your Grace."

"Then by whose authority was she released?" Jack roared.

"Yours, Your Grace." The captain held out a folded letter, stamped with the official seal of the Prince Regent. Jack snatched it from his hands and read the contents, instructions to release Jasminda to the custody of the letter's bearer.

He motioned for the guard to open the door to the cells and strode through, needing to see for himself that Jasminda was really gone. A blanket lay neatly folded on the cot inside an empty cell.

He spun back to face the captain. "Who brought this note?"

"A servant, Your Grace. A maid. I didn't know her."

"And you thought I'd send a maid to retrieve someone from custody?"

"The letter bears your seal, Your Grace."

Jack turned away, trying to tamp down the rage boiling in his bloodstream. At its edge was a cold fear. Whoever had stolen Jasminda's dress and destroyed it had wanted to send a message to Jack. They must have taken her, as well. Would they really harm her? All to punish him?

One person had clashed swords directly with Jasminda recently. Someone who could gain access to the royal seal. Jack's breathing came in short spurts as he exploded from the dungeon, racing up the stairs three at a time.

"Where is Minister Calladeen?" he growled to the young man at the main Royal Guard station.

"He's in his offices, Your Grace."

A red haze swallowed Jack. His whole body quivered as he stalked down the hall and slammed his way into the offices of the Minister of Foreign Affairs. A startled young secretary yipped in alarm when Jack stormed into the inner office.

Calladeen stood, eyes wide.

"What did you do?" Jack demanded.

"I don't know what you're talking about."

Jack marched across the room until he was nearly nose to nose with the man. "Where is she?" he yelled. Calladeen shrank back, leaning almost comically away.

"Where is who, Your Grace?"

"Don't play games with me, man. Where is Jasminda?"

Calladeen placed two hands up in a motion of surrender and stepped away from the wall of anger radiating from Jack's body. Jack clenched and unclenched his fists, waiting for the moment when he could release his frustration in a flurry of violence.

"Your Grace, I swear by our Sovereign, I do not know."

Jack's glare was ruthless, and the man seemed genuinely afraid. Jack held up the letter. "You did not forge this message from me ordering her release?"

Calladeen plucked the letter from Jack's hand and read it over, a frown pulling down his mouth. "No, I did not. But I do recognize the handwriting."

Jack had paid little attention to the curling script of the letter. "Whose is it?"

Calladeen's sharp face grew pensive. "Lizvette's."

The caravan of buses rolled across the country as the wet day darkened into a tempestuous, thundery night. Rain pelted the metal of the bus's roof so hard it sounded like hail. Jasminda sat near the front, handcuffed to a bar running under the window.

On the bench across from her sat Osar, squeezed together with a woman and two smaller children. All the mothers held their children close, blanketed in fear and sadness. The refugees had taken a risk in trusting their Elsiran neighbors, and they had lost.

Jasminda felt her own loss acutely, the loss of Jack and now her freedom. The cold metal bit into her skin when she jangled the chain connecting the cuffs. The soldier sitting in front of her craned his neck, glaring at her. She narrowed her eyes at him, hardening her stare until he turned around.

She'd thought being locked in the dungeon would be the worst this day would hold. She was wrong.

While imprisoned, she had mulled over the latest vision from the caldera while waiting for Jack to appear and explain himself. Then the clank of keys approaching had made her sit upright.

A young maid appeared outside her cell with two Guardsmen in tow. The door opened, and the girl motioned Jasminda forward. She stood, shocked the Guardsmen allowed the maid to lead her away.

"Did Jack send you?" Jasminda asked as she was passed a hooded cloak, large enough to cover her face. "Where are we going?"

"There's a car waiting for you, miss."

"To take me where?"

"We must hurry," the girl said, leading her through the servants' passages at a rapid pace.

The last vision had left Jasminda's Song depleted, so she could not test the maid's emotions. Jack would not have allowed her to be released to just anyone, though it was odd that he'd sent a servant she didn't know instead of Nadal or Usher. They soon arrived at an outer door. Just under the overhang, protected from the driving rain, Lizvette waited with an unfamiliar driver and vehicle.

Jasminda froze. "Jack didn't send you, did he?"

"It isn't safe here for you," Lizvette said, scanning the area as if a ruffian would spring from the bushes at any moment.

"Who wants to hurt me?"

"Please believe me. This is for the best." Lizvette wouldn't meet her eyes but nodded at the driver before turning away. "Do not harm her."

The burly man narrowed his icy gaze and approached. Fear spurred Jasminda into action. She spun away and ran, but the driver reached out a long arm and grabbed her. She kicked and flailed, but her shout was muffled by his large hand covering her mouth. A pair of handcuffs clinked as the metal slid across her skin.

He manhandled her into the backseat where another man, who she hadn't noticed before, waited. In the brief moment when the driver removed his hand from her mouth, she gasped for air to scream but a gag was stuffed between her lips and tied around the back of her head. She continued thrashing, but the second man held her in a crushing grip. The driver took his seat and slammed the door. Jasminda struggled to look out the window, seeing only Lizvette's retreating form disappearing into the palace.

Jasminda writhed and twisted, but the fellow holding her had arms of iron. Deciding to save her strength, she relaxed her body. Stealthily, she inched her skirt up to reach for the serrated knife strapped to her leg. She removed the blade and twisted again, preparing to slam it into her captor's thigh. The driver's gaze flicked to her in the rearview mirror, and he wrenched the steering wheel, swerving the car on the rain-slicked streets and knocking the knife from her grip.

Her captor growled and smashed her head against the window, momentarily blacking out her vision. She stilled as her wits returned and rested her head against the glass to cool the pounding.

Lizvette's betrayal shouldn't have been as shocking as it

was. The woman's coy warnings the day before had been for what? To simply mask her own desire to do Jasminda harm?

As the car wound through the city, the storm pounded away. Once again Jasminda was relieved her Song was exhausted. She would cause no destruction now. Her head swam as the auto made a turn onto a muddy road that led to only one place.

The camp was in chaos when they arrived, stopping just past a line of waiting buses. The man holding her, whose face she still hadn't seen, pulled her from the auto. Cold rain sliced through her dress, numbing her. Rage roared inside with no outlet.

Dozens of Sisters stood before her, arms locked together, dresses plastered to their skin, topknots unraveling, attempting to form a human barrier between the soldiers and the refugees. The Sisters repeated a prayer over and over, asking the Queen Who Sleeps for protection.

Starting at the end of the line, the soldiers pried the Sisters' hands and arms apart as the women's prayer grew louder. Mud lapped at their ankles and more than one man and woman slipped and splashed in the muck.

Behind the Sisters, refugees lined up solemnly in rows, waiting to board the buses, resigned to their fate. However, some would not go quietly. A handful screamed and wailed, planting themselves on the ground and refusing to move.

As the soldiers broke through the resistance of the Sisters, they also handcuffed protesting refugees and held them under armed guard before forcibly placing them on the buses. The man holding Jasminda transferred her to a young soldier who dragged her over to the group of restrained refugees and pushed her to the ground. Water and dirt oozed into her boots and coated her dress. Four men trained their rifles on the group.

Jasminda shivered. She angled her head down until she could pull the gag from her mouth, then sucked in deep breaths, surveying the turmoil around her.

A white-haired general barked orders, instructing his men to ensure every Lagrimari made it across the border. No exceptions.

"What if they won't go?" a lieutenant asked.

"Shoot them."

Jasminda's shivers turned into uncontrollable shaking. Those weren't Jack's orders, but it didn't seem to matter. Screams and cries filled the air.

Among the protesting Sisters was Aunt Vanesse, who spotted Jasminda and broke away from the others to rush to her side. She was distraught, wet hair caught in thick tangles down her back, her blue robes covered in mud.

"Oy!" Vanesse hailed one of the officers and pointed to Jasminda. "She is not a Lagrimari. She is an Elsiran citizen."

The lieutenant looked at Jasminda askance and raised his eyebrows. "Do you have proof of that, Sister?"

"You have my word as an Elsiran. This girl's mother was my sister," Vanesse pleaded.

The lieutenant shrugged. "Even if that were true, we're under orders." He looked Jasminda up and down again. "How Elsiran can she be if she looks that much like a *grol*?" He shrugged and stomped away.

Vanesse screamed, and Jasminda reached for her hand, clasping it in her bound ones. They were both icy cold. Vanesse fell to her knees, sobbing, but a strange calm had fallen over Jasminda. Her anger had changed, transforming into a bitter sort of pity that coated her tongue.

"We both know I don't really belong here."

"No. You're all I have left of Emi. I will find someone who will listen. You don't belong over there, either." Vanesse shuddered. "We can find a place for you. I promise." She squeezed Jasminda's chilled hands.

"Do *you* even have a place here? A way to be who you really are? With the person you love?" Jasminda's voice had an edge to it that she hadn't meant to put there.

Vanesse reared back as if slapped. Her mouth hung open. "What do you know of that?"

"I know that I love someone I can never be with. Not openly. And I thought stolen moments would be enough, but they're not. I don't want to be a secret, hidden away, never allowed to see the light of day. I don't want to be a liability. I want to be a treasure."

Recognition lit within Vanesse. "You *are* a treasure. I'm sorry that you haven't felt that way." She placed her palm on Jasminda's cheek, then leaned forward to kiss her forehead.

"I wanted to tell you—I discovered why Father needed you to sign those papers. It wasn't just because of his run for Alderman." Vanesse sniffed, regaining her composure to brush a sodden chunk of hair from her eyes. "Emi had a trust fund worth hundreds of thousands. Seven years after her death, if unclaimed by her legal heirs, it would go back to our parents. Father had a large investment go badly, and this shipping embargo has hit his business hard. He had his eye on Emi's money and wanted to be sure it was uncontested. If you had signed . . ."

"I would have given up my right to an inheritance I never even knew of," Jasminda said. Her mind spun.

Vanesse nodded. "I didn't know all the terms of the trust before I started looking into it. But I—I claimed the bequest in your name. The money is yours if you want it."

Something split inside Jasminda's chest. The warmth and love from her aunt gave her the push to drive out the lingering bitterness. Emotion clogged her throat as she felt freedom from the rain. It was a moment before her voice returned. "Thank you, Aunt."

"There is no need. It's what Eminette would have wanted." Vanesse dropped her head. "I envied her courage in grabbing what she desired out of life. I envy it now." Another Sister called her name, and Vanesse stood jerkily. She pointed to the ground. "This injustice will not stand."

"Aunt, if you can get a message to the prince . . ." Jasminda said. There was little chance that Vanesse could get through to Jack in time. An unknown woman, even one of the Sisterhood, was unlikely to receive an audience with the Prince Regent.

Vanesse's brow furrowed, but she nodded. "I will pray for us to meet again." And then she was gone.

After another half hour in cold, wet misery, Jasminda was herded toward a bus with the others. A soldier pushed her roughly into a seat and locked her handcuffs around the bar, securing her in place.

Rozyl tripped up the steps, a soldier at her back. The two locked eyes. "I guess you're one of us now," the Keeper said, her lip curling. The soldier shoved her toward the back of the bus.

Jasminda pressed her head against the fogged window and

slumped in her seat. Vanesse's revelation beat against the impossibility and danger of her situation. If she could get out of this, she could start over, rebuild.

But the caldera was heavy in her pocket. Besides the obvious lack of appeal of being forced to live in a land she knew nothing about, she could not allow the stone to fall into the hands of the Lagrimari. She needed a plan, but didn't know where to begin.

Through the windshield, the headlamps illuminated only a few feet ahead of them. The rest was inky blackness, rain tapping a staccato beat on the roof. The driver took to the radio, inquiring as to whether they would be stopping due to the hazardous conditions. The only response was static.

The True Father's storm flooded the countryside, turning the lush, fertile farmland to swampy lakes of woe. It had tracked her this far, and now here she was, bringing the caldera directly to the enemy.

She had to protect the stone—with her life, if necessary.

CHAPTER FORTY

The Mistress of Horses quarreled with an astronomer over the shape of stars in the sky.

What you see as a fine lady dancing, Horse said, I view as a stampeding herd.

—COLLECTED FOLKTALES

Lizvette's only movement came from the rise and fall of her chest as she breathed. She didn't move so much as an eyelid to blink. She sat rigid in the chair, hands clasped neatly in her lap.

Jack, on the other hand, was all motion, pacing the floor of the sitting room in the Niralls' residence suite. "Where is she?" Gravel coated his throat.

"On a bus with the other refugees."

He dropped his head into his hand. "Why?"

"It was the best place for her."

Jack spun to look at her. "And that was your decision?" His supposedly healed wound throbbed angrily, as though the grief and pain were trying to claw their way out through his chest. He wrenched open the door and ordered the Guardsman outside to radio the refugee caravan and pull Jasminda off the bus.

"And was it you who destroyed her dress?" He resumed his pacing.

Her head shot up, eyes wide. "Her dress?"

"Her gown, ripped and burned and left in front of my office today."

Lizvette blinked slowly and took a deep breath. "That wasn't me."

"Do you know who it was?"

She notched her chin up higher and stared straight ahead.

Jack made an exasperated sound and crouched before her, careful to maintain his distance. "Tell me."

A single tear trailed down her cheek. Her jaw quivered. "I think it was Father," she whispered.

"Nirall?" Jack reared back on his heels, almost falling. He braced himself with a hand on the floor and shook his head. "I don't understand."

Her hands were squeezed together so hard, the tips of her fingernails had lost all color. She shook her head and another tear escaped her eye. Those were more tears than Jack had ever seen her shed in her entire life. She had always been a stoic child, never screaming or crying, not even when injured. Everything kept bottled up inside, even now.

Her whole body vibrated as if the strength it took her to remain composed had run out and pure chaos reigned underneath her placid exterior. She was at war with herself. Jack could see it plainly. Her distress stole a measure of rancor from his anger.

"Vette, we have known each other all our lives. You must tell me."

Her jaw quivered, but she nodded, darting a glance at the closed door. "He wanted me to be the princess. I suppose it would make up somewhat for me being born a girl. Alariq was kind, but he never held my heart."

She looked at him pointedly, and his stomach sank in understanding. He opened his mouth, unsure of what to say, but she continued. "When Alariq died, Father didn't miss a beat. He was determined to be the grandfather of the next Prince Regent, no matter what it took. Jasminda was an obstacle, but one that worked in his favor. If you would not choose me of your own free will, then he would give you a push."

"What kind of push?"

"Feeding information to the press. Giving them fodder for the fire. Presenting me as the solution."

"And you went along with this, Vette? Why?"

She swallowed and brushed away the wetness from her cheeks. "I never wanted to hurt you, and I certainly never wanted to see her harmed. But Jack, you are the Prince Regent of Elsira. You must marry well. Your wife is not just for you; she will be the princess of the land. Did you really think there was a future with her? It's for the best that she leave now with the others."

Jack shot to his feet as the ache in his chest seemed to spread to his whole body. His hands pulled at the short ends of his hair, searching for a release from his frustration. "Lizvette, there is no future for me without her."

"So she should have stayed here, hidden away for the rest

of time so you could sneak into her chambers? And then what? What about when you need an heir? She's to be content being your mistress while you sire the next prince with someone else?"

"You had no right! Not to decide her fate. Did she get on that bus willingly?"

Lizvette turned her face to the fire. "I gave explicit instructions that she was not to be harmed."

Jack leaned against his desk, imagining Jasminda fighting tooth and nail against whatever hired thugs Lizvette had acquired.

"Did you think of what it must have been like for her?" Lizvette looked down to her folded hands. "If one day, someone ever loves me, I would hope they would scream it from the rooftops." Her smile was brittle.

Jack fell onto the couch and slumped down. Lizvette was right. In a perfect world, he would have shouted his love for Jasminda from every window in the palace . . . but the world was far from perfect.

A knock sounded at the door, and a Guardsman entered.

"Your Grace, radio communication with the refugee caravan is down due to the thunderstorm. We're unable to contact them."

"Then send a telegram to the Eastern Base and keep trying the caravan. I want to make sure she doesn't step one foot inside Lagrimar."

"Yes, sir." The Guardsman spun on his heel, readying to leave.

"Wait." Weariness lay over Jack like a blanket. He looked at Lizvette and sighed. "Take her to the Guard's offices for questioning. The charge is kidnapping. And arrest Minister Nirall, as well."

Lizvette stood and brushed her dress off, her sad eyes relaying an apology. Jack's head fell to his hands as the weight of the crown grew even heavier.

As Lizvette Nirall was led out of Jack's office, Benn's sense of unease grew. Her head was down instead of in its usual state, pointed toward the sky, and guards surrounded her. She still maintained the majestic bearing he'd always observed from afar, but something was off. In fact, the entire palace was drawn tighter than a bowstring and held under the same strain. He wondered where the arrow was pointed.

Jack's valet, Usher, walked past quickly, his brow heavily furrowed. He didn't notice Benn sitting in the guest area, waiting for an audience with the new Prince Regent. Netta, Jack's secretary, shrugged when Benn tossed her a questioning glance. Her aggrieved expression said, *You don't want to know.*

Generally, Benn had open access to Jack, but that was when his boss had merely been the army's High Commander. Now, not only was Benn AWOL from his post at the base, Jack had taken on a massive new responsibility and the transition did not appear to be going smoothly.

Netta waved him forward with a free hand even as she seemed to be talking on two different telephones at the same time.

"Commander?" Benn called out from the doorway. Jack sat on the couch in the center of his office, hunched over. He looked up, bleary-eyed, hair rumpled.

"Benn? What are you doing here?" It was obvious he hadn't slept well, maybe in days. Sweet Sovereign, what was this position doing to him?

"I had an emergency, sir. Ella needed me. I didn't have time to get leave approved." Benn crossed to sit beside him. "Are you all right, sir?"

Jack's eyes were bloodshot. "Jasminda is on the caravan with the refugees. They're being sent back to Lagrimar." His breath was shaky. "I've mucked this all up."

With everything happening with Ella and the baby, Benn hadn't fully processed the snippets of news he'd heard about the refugees. But now, images of the faces of the people he'd met, those desperate souls fleeing brutality and hopelessness, flashed in his mind. And Jasminda was with them? Going back to Lagrimar? Jack's weary tone and mood made more sense.

Burdening him with news of his brother's possible murder now would be cruel. Especially since they still had no proof he could share. Ella had spent more time with Kess's memories, which had revealed no further plot against Jack, so the prince didn't appear to be in any danger at the moment.

"What can be done?" Benn asked instead.

"I'm not sure. I'm trying everything I can to get Jasminda back—as for the rest . . ." He spread his palms, looking down at his hands. "History will remember me as the man who failed hundreds of refugees. It will paint me as cruel—I'll be the one who lost it all . . . I've given my life to duty and what has it gotten me?"

Somewhere in the room a clock ticked off the seconds. Jack's labored breathing grew more ragged.

"You love her, don't you?" Benn said. "Jasminda."

Jack sat up straight, his lost expression turning decisive. "I do."

"Love has a cost." Ella had murmured something like that today. It wasn't the first time he'd heard her say it, but it was probably the first time he'd really understood.

"What do you mean?" Jack asked, expression blank.

Benn turned toward him. "My duty to my country—I've been holding fast to it since I was fourteen years old. You for even longer. I thought it was the most important thing. The foundation for the rest of my life. I was certain." He made a chopping motion with his hand for emphasis. "Love has cost me that certainty. I thought I could love Ella without changing. But that's impossible. And she suffered for it. I had to give up parts of myself in order to gain something better."

Jack looked down at his hands again, clenching and releasing them. "So, you're saying I have to give up something to get Jasminda back?"

"You might have to jump off a ravine with a heart full of love." Benn frowned. "Or something like that. And what I'm really saying is that I need to resign my commission in the army, effective immediately. I can't be deployed hundreds of kilometers away any longer. If my service record is closed dishonorably as a result, then so be it."

He stood, searching Jack's face, waiting for his response. Resigning had been a spur of the moment decision, but it felt right. He had to let go in order to grab on to the future.

Jack stood as well, a cloud over his face. "War is coming, Benn. The Mantle will fall very soon, I'm certain of it. There won't be any avoiding the battle we'll face."

"I know, sir. But I need to fight my battles some other way. I can't sacrifice my family to do it any longer."

Jack clapped him on the shoulder with a sad smile that barely curved his mouth. "Instead of resigning, why don't you transfer to the Royal Guard? I still need you, but you'd be working from Rosira, and not the Eastern Base."

Shock froze him for a moment. "Are you serious? What about my injury?"

"There's no Staff Corps in the Guard, but there are administrative roles. We'll find a way to utilize your talents here, I'm sure of it."

"I'll have to talk to Ella, but I thank you." There was so much uncertainty with their future plans. He couldn't commit to anything without knowing what she wanted to do.

"I can't lose my people, Benn." Jack squeezed his shoulder then stepped away. "Not now, when there are so few I can trust."

Benn nodded, touched by Jack's faith in him.

Jack sighed deeply. "Now I have to go badger the Comms team about stopping that bloody caravan." He marched across the office, then stopped at the doorway, looking over his shoulder. "You came here to resign? That was it?"

Benn shifted on his feet, avoiding the prince's gaze. "There's another matter—but it can wait until after this crisis is over."

Jack peered at him for a moment before appearing to accept this. And then he was gone.

CHAPTER FORTY-ONE

Said the astronomer to the Mistress of Horses, And what of when the stars fail to shine?

Horse replied, The day the stars forsake the sky is a day not worth contemplating. For it will be our last.

—COLLECTED FOLKTALES

"There is too much interference, sir." The communications officer flipped a switch, testing yet another connection.

"What kind of interference?" Jack asked, peering over the man's shoulder.

"It's very unusual, but we're not able to contact any unit east of the Old Wall." Static could be heard through the man's headset.

"So the entire northeastern sector of the country is radio silent?"

"Yes, sir. No telephone, two-way, or cable communication is operational. They're all down."

Jack rubbed the back of his neck. "It's almost as if this were intentional."

The officer looked up, startled.

Jack did the math in his head. The caravan was too far along for vehicles to catch up with it, and there was no way for him to contact anyone who could get Jasminda to safety. Panic threatened, but he beat it back through force of will.

He banged his fist on the table, and the young officer jumped. "Blast it! I would need wings to get to her now," Jack murmured, then stopped short. His gaze rose to the ceiling.

The airship.

Alariq's pride and joy. And the cause of his death.

It was still there on the roof of the palace. After the crash, technicians from Yaly had come to repair it. Jack had wanted the thing removed, but hadn't yet gotten around to ordering it.

The idea was risky, too risky to even be contemplating, but what was the alternative? Jasminda trapped in Lagrimar? Forced to work in the mines or the harems or worse. She could be killed. He could not save the hundreds of refugees, much as he wanted to, but the life of one woman, the woman most precious to him, could he not even save her?

The airship was the only way to get to the border fast enough—maybe even beat the caravan that had left hours earlier. However, it was this precise situation, flying in a rainstorm, that had killed his brother. Jack had called Alariq foolish . . . Who was the fool now?

A sacrifice, he thought grimly. *Perhaps what I'm giving up is my sanity.* He stalked out of the communications room and into the small office the army maintained in the palace.

"I need an airship pilot. Immediately," he told the soldier on duty.

"Sir, the army doesn't have any ships or pilots. The airship was a gift to Prince Alariq from—"

"Yes, I know all that. But there must be someone in this city who can pilot a bloody airship. Find the ambassador to Yaly. It's their invention, he must know someone."

The sergeant rushed to stand, confused but determined.

"Your Grace." A Guardsman appeared in the doorway. Jack whirled around to face him. "There's a woman here from the Sisterhood. She's been raising quite a ruckus for some time now, saying she needs to speak with you."

Jack sighed. "Now is not the time."

"Your Grace, she's saying it has to do with Miss Jasminda. I thought you might want to speak with her."

Jack peered more closely at the Guardsman. He was the same fellow who'd escorted Lizvette to questioning. Tension gripped Jack, and he nodded. "Take me to her."

They'd kept the woman in the main lobby of the palace, and Jack could hear her voice from two corridors away.

"I will not stand down, and you would do well to keep out of my way, sir. I refuse to leave this palace until I have seen Prince Jaqros!"

"Sister," Jack said as he approached. The woman startled and spun around, gracing him with the tiniest curtsey possible before rushing to his side. A Guardsman reached out to stop her approach, but Jack brushed him off. "What can I do for you?"

"You can stop a great miscarriage of justice, Your Grace. My niece, a citizen of Elsira, despite all appearances to the contrary, was chained and forcibly placed on a bus headed to Lagrimar with the refugees. She does not belong there and I—"

"You are Aunt Vanesse," Jack said. The woman stopped, stunned. He should have recognized her at once, but his mind was scattered in a million directions. How many Sisters had burn scars on their faces? "Jasminda told me about you."

She looked confused, but the determination in her eyes burned bright.

"Please, come with me," he said, leading her toward his office. "I have been trying to rectify that situation, believe me. But I've been stymied at every turn."

Jack stopped at his secretary's desk. "Netta, I want you to check in with the palace regiment every five minutes for an update on their search for an airship pilot."

Netta nodded and picked up the phone.

"An airship pilot?" Vanesse said, squinting at him.

"Yes. I fear that is the only way to get to her before the caravan reaches the border. My brother had the only airship in Rosira and pilots are in short supply."

"Your Grace, I have a . . . a friend, who can drive just about anything. She's competed in the Yaly Classic Air Race the past two years flying speed crafts. If there's anyone who can pilot it, she can."

Jack stared, speechless, before breaking into a grin. He picked up the startled woman and spun her around, only putting her down when her small fist began beating against his back.

CHAPTER FORTY-TWO

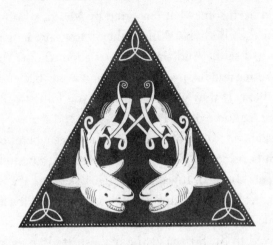

A young woman spurned by her lover asked the Master of Sharks about courtship.

Pretty words and compliments make the heart sing, Shark said, but a golden tongue may hide sharp teeth.

—COLLECTED FOLKTALES

Ella followed the small figure running down the street in front of her, even going so far as to splash through the same puddles. Her galoshes and rain slicker, borrowed from Anneli, kept the worst of the rain away. The old attorney was remarkably well provisioned for someone who only left her house twice a year.

The little girl ahead of Ella turned down a narrow side street, one which the street lamp failed to penetrate. Ella was suddenly aware of all the dangers these street children faced.

Iddo's little gang were wiser than their years and bore the confidence that came from youth, but they were still just children. Anything could happen to them alone at night.

She'd been somewhat reassured by Mayzi, who was confident in the children's skills. "They know the dangers," the woman had said. "And they're smart about them. They may seem carefree and happy-go-lucky, but it's only because they're still resilient. If they weren't out with you tonight, they'd be out there for some other reason."

Mayzi had told her of the gaps in the fence where you could slip from Portside into Rosira without crossing a gate and having your papers checked. It was still a huge risk—one she was glad Benn hadn't been there to try and talk her out of. She left after he'd gone to the palace to speak with the prince. But as Ella had prayed to St. Siruna at the makeshift altar she'd set up in Anneli's front parlor, a calm had overtaken her. This path she walked, she did not walk alone.

The little girl Iddo had sent waited at the dead end where the fence blocked off the street. She pointed a small arm toward the fence post, where the chain links had separated leaving a small opening. It was child-sized, but Ella could squeeze through.

"Thank you," Ella called out. The girl waved then disappeared into the wet darkness.

Benn's offer to leave Elsira with the baby reverberated in her head. It was selfless and loving and made her heart swell. But it also made her uneasy. She would do whatever it took to protect her nephew, but Kess's memories had revealed much about Syllenne's ruthlessness. And it was clear to Ella that the High Priestess had to be stopped.

Kess had seen it all go down. After receiving the report of

the Yalyishman's first visit to Zann Biddel, Syllenne had tracked the stranger down. She'd pretended to be an associate of Biddel's, one willing to hear him out. And so they'd met at the tavern.

He'd called himself Alban and nearly left when Syllenne sat down, correctly supposing her to be a Sister, though she was dressed plainly. Sisters did have a recognizable look about them, even out of robes. Kess had been observing on the far side of the room but unable to hear. Syllenne had debriefed her afterward.

It had taken more than one meeting for Syllenne to gain Alban's trust. And even so, he would rather have dealt with Biddel. But after being shunned a second time, he finally agreed to entrust Syllenne with his true mission. Whether he knew he was eliciting help from the head of the Sisterhood or whether he thought he was talking to a lackey was unclear. But shining bright as crystal was the fact that Syllenne had absolutely agreed to the plot and lent her resources to its execution.

Kess had protested. She was used to Syllenne's ambition, her quest for power and influence, but could not condone murder.

Prince Alariq was not a malleable man, but he was fair. He didn't think very highly of the High Priestess and was not easily swayed by her, and Kess admired him for it. And for her refusal to participate, she was exiled to Sora and told that her baby was to be utilized to keep Zann Biddel in check. The child's very existence undermined the Dominionist values of family and honesty. Kess's baby would be at Syllenne's mercy and this was too much for her to bear.

And now, if Ella fled with what she knew, what further horrors would the High Priestess ordain?

Ella was just a hairdresser. A failed printmaker and taxi driver and a dozen other things. She was not important. Then again, Syllenne was the daughter of a potato farmer. And she had helped kill a prince.

People could change.

Elsira itself was also a land of great contradiction. Ella was not truly welcome within its borders and yet it was home. More home than Sirunan where she'd grown up, more home than Fremia where she'd gone to school. Certainly wherever Benn was would be where she belonged, but she loved Portside—the people, the life, the energy. What would happen to her friends and neighbors and co-workers with Syllenne left unchecked? How could she live with herself if she had the means to change things, but was too afraid to try?

The temple loomed ahead, ominous in the gloom. Ella pulled her rain hat down over her ears and trudged forward, toward it. A few others were entering through the main double doors, bulky bedding under their arms, ready for another night in which they might receive the sought-after dream.

Inside the sanctuary, Ella retreated to a dark corner. It was late, but Iddo had one of his crew tailing Syllenne, and had sworn she was in the temple somewhere. Perhaps she was in her office? That was the logical first place to look.

The office door was just off the main space, but as Ella approached, it opened and Gizelle exited, looking piqued. Before the door closed behind her, Ella could see the room was empty. Gizelle walked around the perimeter of the sanctuary, passing close by Ella, who dipped her head, hoping her hat and coat shielded her. It must have worked; Gizelle paid her no attention as she stormed past.

She entered a side door, which Ella recognized as the stairwell from her previous visit. After waiting several minutes, Ella stepped into the open area, walking carefully around sleeping worshippers, and then knelt, hopefully inconspicuously, near the middle of the sanctuary.

Far above her, the balconies of the upper floors and their strange carvings looked down on her. And at the very top, two figures, cloaked in shadow, stood at the railing.

Ella climbed the steps slowly, chanting a silent prayer. At the top she paused, listening for voices but heard only silence. She peered around to the open space and found Syllenne, alone at the balcony, standing perfectly erect.

"Did you need anything else, Gizelle?" Syllenne called out softly without turning.

"I do need something, Your Excellency."

Syllenne spun around, her blue robe billowing from the movement. Her eyes flared then narrowed as Ella stepped into the light.

"What do you think you're doing here?" she bit out, voice as sharp as her features.

"I understand why you like it up here." Ella looked around. She'd had plenty of time to examine the balcony when she was here before, but now it looked different. Not so intimidating. Beautiful in its own way.

"Where is he?" Syllenne asked.

Ella looked up at her guilelessly. "Where is who?"

A pulse ticked in Syllenne's jaw. "Where. Is. The. Baby?"

"Oh, you mean my nephew?" Ella tilted her head to the side. "You assured me that the Sisterhood were looking after him and that I had nothing to worry about. Do you mean to say that you don't know where he is? You've lost a week-old infant?" She placed a hand over her heart as if appalled.

"Don't play games with me, girl." Syllenne took a menacing step forward. "I know you have him. Do you need another reminder of my influence and reach? Perhaps another few hours in a prison cell? Or a trip back to the land of your birth?"

"If something happens to me tonight, not only my attorney, but my husband—the personal assistant to the Prince Regent, I'm not sure if you were aware of his position—well, they'll know exactly where to look." She held the older woman's eye. "And wouldn't you like to know what I've already told them?" Syllenne's nostrils flared.

"And besides," Ella continued, "given your influence and reach, my nephew cannot possibly be the only thing you have on Zann Biddel."

Syllenne's head jerked sharply. An eyebrow rose, and then she cracked a humorless smile. "Why, Mistress Farmafield. I have misjudged you." She looked irritated at this discovery. "Your sister led me to believe that you were a bit dull. Flighty. Kess and her secrets." She sighed. "I will miss her dearly."

"And yet you sent her away."

"I thought a few months in the Borderlands would sharpen her back into the tool I needed. The silly fool fancied herself in love. Couldn't see what that classless fisherman who thinks himself a prophet was turning her into. Allowed herself to fall pregnant because she was sentimental. She'd lost her edge." Syllenne shrugged. "She wasn't supposed to die."

Ella had a difficult time reading her, and Syllenne's affect gave little away. But Kess's memories had revealed a close relationship between the two—before her sister's change of heart. Kess had been Syllenne's right hand, privy to every scheme and plan. It stood to reason the High Priestess would miss her in her own way.

"So, what do you want? In exchange for the baby. You've proven yourself an interesting adversary. I'm willing to consider a negotiation."

Ella raised her eyebrows at the faint praise. "If it's dirt on Zann Biddel you want, I'm sure you'll find more. My nephew—he isn't your last opportunity. Biddel has many faults to exploit. And what I *want* is for you to leave me alone. Leave my family alone. And my friends. No more threats. No more arrests. We're no one to you. Just forget about us."

Syllenne sniffed. "I have not gotten to where I am because of my short memory."

"You do realize," Ella said, taking a step closer, "that others remember things as well? The conclave, for instance, the one that resulted in your ascension to your current position—they have memories, too."

"Do they?" Syllenne sounded smugly dubious.

"Yes, and though up until now their fear of you has trumped all else, that will not always be the case. Time does much, it allows bitterness to grow and fester. It loosens tongues."

Ella leaned forward as if sharing a secret. "In fact, I'd imagine that with a little effort, the memories of many whom you've crossed could be coaxed into greater clarity. All it would take is for one of them to speak up."

Syllenne stiffened. "The word of one disgraced Sister is not enough to hold any merit against me."

"What about ten? Or twenty?" Ella spread her arms apart. "What about those who no longer wear the robes? The ones who left the order entirely? There are many places in this country where the name Syllenne Nidos inspires not just fear, but anger. Given the proper inducement, I wonder which will win?"

"Who have you been talking to?" Syllenne's eyes narrowed.

"Did my sister tell you that I was a very good listener? That my memory is good as well. And people have a tendency to open up to me." She shrugged. "It's the strangest thing. Been happening since I was young. Virtual strangers will treat me like an old friend. Before now, I haven't had a real reason to hone that particular skill set. But things change."

She smiled and stepped back. "Leave my family alone, and we won't have to have this conversation again."

The High Priestess's expression could have frozen a well through and through.

"Nod if you understand," Ella said, frost in her voice.

With a jaw clenched so tight she may have cracked a tooth, Syllenne tilted her head a fraction.

"Pleasant evening, Your Excellency. I'll see myself out." She turned on her heel and left, feeling Syllenne's glacial stare on her back. She'd been careful not to reveal anything that only Kess would have known. Let Syllenne believe that Ella had caught the ear of a disgraced Sister. Have her put her resources toward plugging those leaks. Ella had a wealth of information to use to bring Syllenne down.

All she needed was time.

CHAPTER FORTY-THREE

On the occasion of their parents' deaths, Bobcat gathered his brothers and sisters. Let us put away petty things, he said, and rejoice in our kinship. For the day is not long off when our good-byes will multiply.

—COLLECTED FOLKTALES

The buses lurched to a stop where the paved road ended, not far past the entrance to the Eastern Army Base. Beyond loomed the border, deceptive in its ordinariness. Grass of the foothills gave way to the Breach Valley, a nondescript stretch of rocky dirt. The hills on either side veered up sharply, transforming into jagged mountains towering overhead. All seven Mantle breaches had occurred here.

The only other visible indication that one country ended

and another began were the hundreds of Elsiran troops and vehicles gathered with weapons drawn, pointing toward an equal number of Lagrimari troops on the other side. Bullets could not pierce the Mantle until it was breached, but both sides were intent on their standoff.

The rain had ended sometime during the night. Perhaps the storm had done its work. The caldera was nearly back in Lagrimar, after all. Early morning sunshine broke through the gloom. The refugees filed off the buses silently to huddle together amidst a sea of soldiers.

On one side of Jasminda stood Osar; Rozyl was on the other. The only words the Keeper had spoken had been to ask whether Jasminda had the caldera on her. After she'd affirmed it, Rozyl had not left her side.

Across the border, rows of Lagrimari stood at attention. A familiar face at the front of the line made Jasminda's breath catch.

The soldier stepped forward, smiling broadly. "By order of His Majesty the True Father of the Republic of Lagrimar, I, Lieutenant Tensyn ol-Trador do hereby declare this a day of peace. My brothers and sisters, I welcome you home."

Lieutenant? He'd had a promotion then. Jasminda grew sick to her stomach to see the man's smug grin. She stood in the middle of the crowd of refugees, but hunched down anyway, hoping he wouldn't see her.

Tensyn raised both hands over his head and paused dramatically before clapping them together. An earsplitting crack rent the air. The ground shuddered, rolling and shaking, throwing everyone off-balance. From the direction of the army base, an alarm sounded.

"Breach!" shouted an Elsiran.

"Breach!"

"Breach!"

The word was repeated, the message passed along, as the Elsiran soldiers hunkered down.

The armies appeared evenly matched in numbers, though the Lagrimari weaponry was visibly old. They bore muzzle-loaded, single-shot rifles at least fifty years out of date. Many had bayonets or swords, as well. Jasminda eyed the Elsiran soldiers nearest her, noting the far more advanced automatic rifles with coils of ammunition at the ready. Tanks were spaced evenly along the border, with smaller armored four-wheelers bearing giant rifles and larger weapons that looked like cannons or grenade launchers. The Lagrimari had no vehicles, but the barrels of huge wheeled cannons sat on the front lines. Elsira's superior economic power and technology was unquestionable. But the Lagrimari had one advantage the Elsirans couldn't buy.

The wind grew from a gentle breeze to a gale within the blink of an eye. Jasminda's hair whipped back, the force of the wind stinging her eyes. It died down after a few breaths. But thick clouds exploded into existence on the Elsiran side. They swirled and raged unnaturally, then shuddered as deadly sharp icicles shot down. The ice stopped in midair a hand's breadth from their heads, then crackled and fell apart, dusting the Elsirans and refugees in a layer of snow.

The army's Earthsingers were taunting them.

Movement at the top of the lower foothills drew Jasminda's attention. Lines of additional Lagrimari troops came into view from behind the hilltops on either side of the flatland of the breach area. They marched over the hills, descending across the border between the lands.

"They've done it," Jasminda whispered. "They've destroyed the whole thing. The Mantle is gone."

Within minutes, the number of Lagrimari soldiers more than doubled, vastly outnumbering the Elsirans. Jasminda spotted Tensyn leading his men across the former barrier. An Elsiran general marched forward to meet him.

"There is no need for losing life this day. I will address my brethren," Tensyn announced in broken Elsiran. The general reluctantly stood aside as the lieutenant approached.

"Listen close," Tensyn said in Lagrimari. This seemed to be a cue for all the refugees to sit down. Jasminda settled on the muddy ground with the others. "This day is a joyous one. The Mantle, which unfairly trapped us for so long, is now demolished."

A cheer went up among the Lagrimari soldiers. Tensyn drank in the applause, before raising a hand to silence the men. "I am pleased to welcome all of the lost souls back to the open arms of the Fatherland. Your presence will help us usher in a great peace. However, before your return, there is something His Majesty requires. One of you holds an artifact that has great significance to our blessed leader. A red stone, smaller than my palm." He raised his hand over his head. The Elsiran troops nearest him followed his movement with their rifles, but he paid them no mind.

"The stone must be returned before your homecoming may begin."

Jasminda's chest tightened. Though it must have been her imagination, the caldera in her pocket seemed to hum to life. She flexed her fingers, eager for a weapon of any kind, a way to fight through the terror and escape.

Tensyn paced the length of the tightly gathered crowd of

refugees. "To underscore the importance of compliance with any and all beneficent requests of His Majesty's, I will return one of you to the World After every minute the artifact is not within my possession."

He pulled his pistol from the holster at his hip and pulled back the hammer. The general closest to Tensyn pulled his sidearm, as well.

Tensyn chuckled. "I will harm no Elsiran. This is between me and my countrymen," he said in Elsiran. The general nodded but continued pointing his own gun at the lieutenant.

Tensyn produced a watch from the pocket of his crisp uniform, and though Jasminda was at least three dozen paces away, she could feel each tick of the clock like a beat inside her chest.

The minute that passed felt like the longest of her life, until it ended and Tensyn grabbed a random refugee from the crowd. Gray hair, a stooped stature . . .

Gerda.

Jasminda gasped. When Tensyn lifted his pistol to the old woman's head, Jasminda hurtled into motion. Her body acted without thought, but she struggled against an immovable object while trying to rise and get closer to Gerda. She looked down to find hands wrapped around her waist, squeezing painfully, holding her in place. Wrenching her neck around, she stared into Rozyl's hard eyes, wet with unshed tears. But her face was implacable. Jasminda turned back around. Through the crowd, Gerda met her gaze and gave an almost imperceptible shake of her head. Jasminda slammed her eyes shut.

The shot rang out.

"No!" Jasminda's scream echoed in the wake of the gunshot,

reverberating off the mountain peaks. Many things could be healed with Earthsong, but a close-range shot to the head was not one of them.

Rozyl didn't let go, tightening her hold and forcing Jasminda's head down.

"Someone has something to say? The location of the artifact perhaps?" Tensyn's voice was self-satisfied. Nausea swept over Jasminda. Her empty stomach heaved, but nothing came out. The Elsiran general looked horrified, but made no move to stop the executions.

The clock continued to tick, and Jasminda couldn't watch another person die. She couldn't be responsible for the death of one more innocent.

This time Tensyn pulled a young girl from the crowd, out of the arms of her shrieking mother. Jasminda slackened her body; Rozyl's grasp weakened slightly. Taking advantage, Jasminda broke out of the woman's arms and shot to her feet.

Tensyn's gaze landed on her, recognition widening his eyes. Jasminda opened her mouth to confess. Before she'd taken a breath, Rozyl shot up beside her.

Turwig was next, moving faster than a man of his age rightly should. One by one, the other Keepers she'd met in the cave and at the camp stood, and even Lyngar, a man she'd suspected of having no emotions whatsoever, had tears in his eyes as he looked at Gerda's lifeless form sprawled on the ground.

Tensyn blinked, peering from one Keeper to another. "The artifact. Who has it?"

"I have it," Rozyl called out, her voice strong and clear.

"I have it," Lyngar said.

The statement was repeated by every Keeper standing.

"I have it," young Timmyn said, taking to his feet. Other refugees, children and mothers, the young and the elderly, all stood, proclaiming to have the caldera. Most of them had no idea what they were even admitting to, but Jasminda was moved all the same. She had thought she'd known misery and heartache since the loss of her family, but she had nothing on these people. She'd also thought she truly understood love, but the actions of the other refugees humbled her.

They were all in this together. This group of strangers were acting as one with her. Standing together in the face of almost certain death. Tears streamed down her cheeks, and she swiped them away.

The lieutenant pursed his lips, searching the crowd until he found Jasminda. He looked ready to speak, when a ripple of movement behind him caused him to turn.

CHAPTER FORTY-FOUR

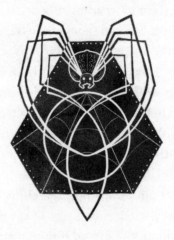

Now Spider was more crafty than any of his brothers or sisters. And he was the only one who wept not a single tear when his parents met the World After.

—COLLECTED FOLKTALES

The row of Lagrimari soldiers parted to reveal a solitary figure. Jasminda could only stare as dread cooled her skin.

Weak sunlight glittered off a jewel-encrusted mask covering the face of a man walking across the field. No holes for eyes, nose, or mouth were visible—just a covering of multicolored precious stones obscuring his entire head. A heavy tunic lined with even more jewels flowed nearly to his ankles. He walked across the ground as if laying claim to the land. As if he had already conquered everything he surveyed.

His approach was endless, his paces measured. The thousands gathered were silent; not even a bird call interrupted the quiet.

With a flick of his wrist, two dozen refugees before him went flying through the air and crashed in a heap on the ground. The Elsiran army appeared frozen in place. Jasminda was unable to tear her gaze from the force of nature that was the immortal king, but vaguely registered some barrier separating where she stood from the Elsirans around her.

Noise reached her ears slowly, as if muted. A jeweled glove jerked, and another swath of refugees went flying. A sickening crunch of bones accompanied them and low moans rose.

Jasminda's lip quivered. Now, none stood between the True Father and her. Though she could not see his eyes, she felt his attention on her. He knew she carried the caldera.

He tilted his head to the side, regarding her. "What is this?" His voice was nothing like that of his younger self. Hollow and raspy, it was the sound of death.

Jasminda flinched.

"Yllis truly was innovative. He trapped his entire Song in the stone you carry, girl." The True Father laughed, a sand-papery sound that rippled down her spine. "So much power. A Song unmatched by any alive today. Give it to me and you *may* live."

Hot tears escaped Jasminda's eyes. Her body shook. A tunnel had been formed out of ice or wind or pure magic, perhaps all three, Jasminda couldn't be sure. On the other side of it the Elsirans raged, blurry and ineffectual. Their weapons fired into the swirling tunnel walls, but did not penetrate.

She and the refugees, along with a handful of Lagrimari soldiers, were trapped in this cage with a madman. So this was his power, tainted and bitter.

"No." Her voice was soft amidst the immense twisting power surrounding them.

The True Father inclined his head. That was the only warning she had before she was ripped from the ground and tossed into the air. The earth came back to meet her; this time the crunch she heard was from her own bones. Pain was delayed for one blissful moment, then her entire body ignited.

The king's power lifted her again, only to smash her down just as cruelly. White-hot agony lanced her. Deafening screams rang in her ears. It took a moment to realize they were her own. Then, in a flash, she was healed and standing upright.

She wobbled on noodley legs, searching for support and finding none. The other refugees lay on the ground around her, many broken and bloodied, watching with wide eyes. Jasminda took a deep breath—not nearly enough to sustain her.

The True Father laughed again. "Who are you to defy me, girl? A child with barely enough power for me to take. An insignificant whelp, yet you dare utter the word 'no'?"

He turned in a circle as if to ensure everyone was watching. "Though perhaps I should thank you." He tilted his head to the side. "Your attempt to shore up the Mantle's cornerstone with your negligible power amused me. And there is so little left that I find entertaining."

Guilt shrank Jasminda's chest.

He drew closer. "You thought to use the stone you bear against me? Or do you wish to lash out with your feeble Song and do something to stop me?" He laughed—the brittle sound turned her blood to ice. "Now give me the stone and you may die quickly."

Jasminda trembled. She could not stop him from taking the caldera but she would rather die, as slowly as it took, than give it to him. "I know who you are, *Eero*," she said, fighting the quiver in her jaw.

The True Father froze. Once again, unseen eyes raked over her skin. "I have not heard that name in a long time."

This time, he dragged her into the air slowly. He stepped closer until he was directly beneath her, his head tilted up. "I think I would prefer to never hear it again."

Her skin constricted, squeezing tight against her muscles. The air surrounding her compressed, bearing down until her bones cracked, one by one. Her throat was crushed before she could scream. The pain went on and on. She lived inside it until she was certain she had passed out. But the impact of the ground on her shattered body rattled her. He'd dropped her.

Jasminda's skin was a bag of bone shards. She could not move. Drawing breath was nearly impossible. A whistling sound escaped her lips when she tried to fill her lungs. They must be pierced with slivers of her ribs.

"Get the stone," the True Father's death-like voice rasped. Apparently, he would not deign to get his bejeweled gloves dirty. She was vaguely aware of hands pawing her, and not gently. The pain on top of pain made little difference. She could not draw enough breath to cry out.

As the seeker mauled her, something brushed against her outstretched hand. Earthsong buzzed at the edges of her senses. Was this someone trying to heal her?

Somehow, she managed to agonizingly lift her eyelids, but closed them again immediately. She'd fallen next to Gerda's lifeless body. Jasminda forced herself to look upon the old woman. Gerda stared back sightlessly, her neck twisted at an impossible angle. Jasminda's vision blurred.

The Earthsong prickling at her was insistent. A link wanted

to form. She could barely think but opened her Song to it—
perhaps it would aid in the healing, though she knew in her
heart it was too late. Even a strong Singer would need far more
time than Jasminda had left in this world.

Whoever was searching her pockets stopped suddenly. The
warm presence of the stone left her. They'd found it. Now, it
was too late for everyone.

Gerda's blood pooled, inching toward Jasminda's face.
Soon it would mix with her own. Had the old woman's sacrifice been in vain?

A memory tickled her mind. The spell Yllis had taught
Oola in the last vision. A blood sacrifice.

The link opened between herself and whoever the persistent Earthsinger was—Osar, she recognized the feel of his
Song belatedly. Some part of her skin must be in contact with
him, though numbness had begun to erase her pain. He offered her control of the link and his powerful Song.

Jasminda startled at the feel of every heartbeat of every
person nearby inside her body. She breathed with the breaths
of thousands. Insects burrowed deep under the ground came
into crisp focus. Every blink of every eye was loud as a camera's shutter. She sensed the True Father's spell, the tunnel of
wind and water separating the Elsirans from them. She could
see how it was made, perhaps even copy it. She filed the
knowledge away.

Instead, she centered her attention on the ground beneath
her and reached for the memory of Yllis's spell. With her en-
hanced power, she could almost taste Gerda's blood mixed
with the dirt and sand. Jasminda twisted the energy of Earthsong, mixing it with the woman's lifeblood.

Power swelled within her as she wove the threads of the

differing energies together. The spell came to her as if channeled from another mind—in a way it had been. The complex fabric of intermingling energies was nothing she could explain, but she sang the spell as if possessed.

When she was done, her eyes blinked open again. Gerda's face was now peaceful before her. Underneath them, the ground had become glassy and smooth. Dark as midnight, it extended all around, like fast-spreading molasses. Though she couldn't see more than a few paces in front of her face, she could feel it. The earth beneath them had been transformed to the polished rock surface of the caldera. Just as in the caves.

The True Father's strange tunnel barrier died.

Osar's small face dropped between hers and Gerda's. The little boy watched her grimly.

The smooth surface beneath them echoed with the residue of magic that required death. There was something unnatural about it that made a shiver go up her ravaged spine.

The True Father roared. The sound was filled with anger, frustration, shock. Chaos erupted and his scream cut off in a strangled cry. Emotions beat against her, but Jasminda's vision was narrow. She blocked it all out.

The ground is like the caves now? Osar asked in her mind. They were still linked, his mighty power under her control.

Yes, no one can sing. Jasminda wanted to laugh, but her entire body was numb. *No one but me.* She couldn't even feel her lips.

The caldera? she asked.

Osar's face disappeared and the chaos surrounding her intensified. She sensed him motioning to Rozyl, communicating with gestures. Via the link, Jasminda watched through Osar's eyes as Rozyl rose from the ground and broke into a run. She leapt into the air to tackle a figure with his back to her. Tensyn.

Rozyl brought him down effortlessly and wrenched the stone from his grip. She walked back over to Jasminda and kneeled before her, placing it in her hand.

Though Jasminda could not feel the weight of the caldera, she didn't need to. The vision came anyway.

This is good-bye. The last time I will see my brother.

We have given him everything he wanted. We stand at the border of what will now become two lands, two peoples. Songbearer and Silent, separated for all time.

Once Yllis's barrier spell falls into place, there will be no crossing—those were the terms of the treaty. That stipulation was put in by our side. Many Songbearers have grown weary of the fighting. It is against our nature. Some feel if they never see another Silent, it will be for the best.

Already I miss the way things were, but this was my decision and I must stand by it.

"Will you embrace me one last time, sister?"

The odd, smooth bracelets adorning Eero's wrists hold the magic of Yllis's binding spell. The blood magic that ensures Eero doesn't use whatever stolen Song may be left inside him. He can cause no further harm before the Mantle is erected.

His eyes shine, and I see the boy I once knew within them. One last time could not hurt.

I step closer. My arms wrap around him. We came into this world together, and I thought we would stay that way forever.

A sharp pain pierces my side. I pull back from him and stare at the dagger sticking out from between my ribs. I gasp up at him in horror, but Eero's face is a mask.

I reach for Earthsong, trying to knit the wound, but something is wrong. My Song is weakening, slipping out of my grasp like a wisp of smoke. I breathe in, and in some more, but the breath never makes it to my lungs. Eero whispers a string of foreign words, and I fall to the ground.

Everything goes black.

Voices call my name.

One voice.

Yllis.

"Oola! Oola! Please come back to me. My love, please."

He begs and pleads, apologizes and bargains.

I try to go to him but am locked in place. My breath is gone, and I am separated from my body.

Three archways loom before me. The widest leads back to my body. Another leads to the World After.

But the third calls to me, though narrow and ominous. I step through it, sealing my fate.

The World Between is a smoke-filled antechamber full of endless images of the living. Neither here nor there, it is vast and lonely, only grazed by the living in their dreams. Some believe all dreams take place here.

For me, it is a nightmare.

From here I bear witness to my body on the ground. Eero smashing the bespelled bracelets. He is full of my Song, stolen from my last breaths.

Yllis gives a great cry. He gathers a swell of Earthsong and sings the spell to create the barrier between the lands. The cornerstone engages and I feel its power pulsing through the energy.

Eero steps away from his Silent followers, over to the band of astonished Songbearers. Yllis is too focused on his spell to notice. The barrier slams into place, leaving him holding my body on one side with the throng of Silent and Eero, bursting with my Song, on the other with the rest of the Songbearers.

This was his plan all along.

He never wanted to be shut up alongside the Silent forever. He merely wanted to have an inexhaustible supply of Songbearers to steal from.

Eero stands at the barrier, expression smug. "Worry not, Yllis. She is not dead. She will awaken at any moment and live quite a fine life without her Song. She will know what it is like to be me."

Two archways still stand behind me, the one leading to the Living World pulsing brighter than the sun. Calling to me. Pleading with me. I am being given a choice.

Eero's look of triumph changes to a frown. "She will awaken," he says, a tremor invading his voice.

Yllis growls and pulls my body closer.

Eero tries to move forward, but the barrier stops him. He beats against the invisible wall with a fist. "Oola! Oola!" he screams.

Both archways dim and begin to fade. I must make my choice quickly.

If I go back to the Living World, I can resume a life without my heart. The World After holds no appeal, though Mother and Father are there. How can I face them with what I have done to Eero?

Here, in the World Between, I may watch. That will be my punishment.

Justice finally served for my crimes.

I will watch.

The archways fade and disappear.

I watch Yllis bear my body back to the city and cut a chamber into the mountains to house me. Above the chamber, the Silent construct a magnificent palace.

Yllis chooses a loyal Silent to rule. A young man of character and honor, Abdeen Alliaseen, to lead the people in the absence of their Queen.

Yllis makes Alliaseen promise to ensure that history is kind to me and bears no recollection of my fault in the start of the war. He spends weeks, months, years locked in his laboratory, scouring the libraries of the Cantors, searching for something. Doing what he does best, studying magic.

I watch on the day he finds what he has been seeking. He chants words in the ancient tongue of the Cavefolk, words I don't understand. He takes the pendant bearing my father's sigil, the one I always wore around my neck, and cuts himself, spilling his blood over it. He calls for Alliaseen, who, when asked, spills his own blood on the sigil without hesitation, binding the spell. The blood congeals and the magic grows, encasing the pendant in a bloodred stone.

Blood magic will do what Earthsong cannot.

Blood magic may be broken only by those who bear the blood.

Yllis journeys back to the barrier he created and crosses it, using another bit of magic.

He gathers those unafraid of standing against a now impossibly powerful Eero. Those who want to learn to fight. Songbearers are peaceful by nature, but these men and women have been broken. They become something new. He crafts the words of a promise to me, one these new soldiers vow to keep.

I watch as my beloved Yllis wages war on my beloved brother, and I watch when Yllis is slain. Eero is too strong, and the stolen Songs have twisted his mind and made him far more ruthless than even the broken Songbearers.

Yllis dies with the stone in his hand.

His final spell traps his own Song in the stone.

The Keepers of the Promise are supposed to take the stone, cross the border, and present it to the prince, whose touch will unlock the magic. But the Keepers he commanded to hold back and stay safe, rush in seeking revenge. None survive the battle.

The stone sits where it lies. Yllis's gift to me, his whispered spell to bring me back to my body and gift me his own Song, lies under the rubble of the fallen city as his body turns to bones.

The archways are long gone now.

If they were here, perhaps I would pass into the World After to be with him. To thank him for trying to save me.

But being with Yllis is not punishment enough.

So I watch.

For a very long time.

Sometimes, a dream will find me and pierce the loneliness.

But more often, it is endless agony. Standing by watching while the centuries pass.

And now, Jasminda, you have heard my story. Judge me for my faults if you must. But you bear the only evidence of Yllis's love for me. His Song is in your hands.

Release it.

Release me.

It is time for me to end this.

CHAPTER FORTY-FIVE

Beseeched a new father to the Mistress of Eagles, Bless my baby, for her mother died in childbirth.

Eagle replied, Your loss is like a volcano's flow which increases the land. New worlds are born out of destruction.

—COLLECTED FOLKTALES

Jack gripped the edge of the seat as the airship descended from the clouds. What he saw on the ground below was mystifying. Judging by the presence of Lagrimari troops, the Mantle had already been destroyed. But where he'd expected a battle to be raging, there was relative calm.

The Lagrimari sat in even rows on the ground with Jack's troops maintaining the perimeter. Had they surrendered? Could that be possible?

No enemy guns had been drawn, there were no environmental disasters as in the Seventh Breach. What was going on?

Clove set the ship down at the edge of the gathered crowd. "That was some bloody fine piloting, Clove," he said, clapping the woman on the back.

"Thank you, Your Grace!"

Flying through the vicious storm had been just as difficult as he'd imagined. They'd been bandied about by the wind and rain, and nearly struck by lightning twice. But Clove was unflappable, gripping the steering wheel with bloodless hands and navigating them safely through.

With a nod to Vanesse, who had insisted on coming as well, Jack opened the carriage door and tore across the ground, intent on finding Jasminda.

Several soldiers approached him. The base's high general, Verados, was in the lead. "Your Grace, the enemy has surrendered."

Jack looked on, incredulous. "How is this possible?"

"They lay down their weapons as soon as this witchcraft began." He tapped his foot and looked down. Jack peered at the strange, hardened ground.

"It's like the caves, Your Grace."

He turned toward the familiar voice to find Rozyl standing at the edge of the group of soldiers. He motioned her forward, and the men let her pass.

"No one can sing on it?" he asked.

She shook her head solemnly. "No one but Jasminda."

He opened his mouth to ask about her, but Verados cut him off. "The True Father has been captured. Once he was rendered powerless, his troops dropped their weapons. It was just a matter of bringing him into custody."

Jack's eyes widened. "Where is he?"

Verados motioned toward the base.

The king could wait. "Where is *she*?" he asked Rozyl. Her expression was grim. "Take me to her."

Rozyl turned on her heel and marched over to a group of refugees. They sat in a spiral around a prone figure in the middle. Jack's heart stuttered when he recognized Jasminda. He tore through the group to kneel at her side. "They can't heal her?"

"Osar is linking with her. She's controlling his Song but won't heal herself." Rozyl's voice was bitter. "She says she needs to save the power."

He turned back to Jasminda, his stomach clenching at her condition. All of her limbs were twisted at strange angles and her eyes were barely open.

"Jasminda, my darling, I'm here. I'm going to get you off this blasted thing so they can heal you up, all right?"

She lay impossibly still, her eyelids the only movement. Osar sat by her head, stroking her hair. The boy looked up at him pleadingly, then looked to Rozyl.

"He says she wants you to stay with her."

Jack glanced at Osar, who'd never spoken a word. "Of course I will."

"She knows how to awaken the Queen. But there isn't much time."

Jack's pulse sped. "What do we have to do?"

"Take her hand."

Her hand lay palm up, and though her fingers were mangled, the caldera was held loosely in her grasp. He stared at the rock, the way it lay in her ravaged hand.

"Please." Rozyl's voice was a whisper.

Jack's heart broke. Jasminda was so weak. If this was what she wanted, he would do it. He whispered a kiss across her lips, not daring to press against her and cause more pain, then closed his hand over the caldera.

Searing pain shot through his body, as if being pulled apart one organ at a time. He might have screamed out loud, he wasn't sure, but the burning agony was like nothing he'd ever felt. His blood was on fire, it burned bright and hot. Then it was gone.

Breath returned to his lungs. He was once again kneeling on the glossy surface of the unnatural ground, next to the woman he loved as she slipped further and further away.

An explosion of light above his head blinded him. He squinted against the small fireball, which rivaled the sun in sheer brilliance. It grew brighter, shining with a white-hot glare before disappearing.

In its place, a figure floated, wrapped in ivory fabric. Her skin shone gloriously. Dark, curling hair swirled around Her head, blown by a nonexistent breeze. She moved like liquid, spinning and stretching. She righted Herself and hovered before Jack, dark eyes piercing him with intensity.

He swallowed and lowered his head in deference.

The Queen had awoken.

CHAPTER FORTY-SIX

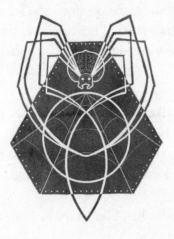

Spider squabbled with his brothers and sisters over their parents' inheritance.

I am most deserving, he said, for being the youngest, I had them the least amount of time.

One by one, the others grew exhausted by the discord. Leaving Spider standing alone in a prison of victory.

—COLLECTED FOLKTALES

The normally tingling buzz of Earthsong was an earthquake against Jasminda's consciousness. She was no longer linked with Osar, but another Song shook her to the core. The swelling force pulled her under, leaving her sputtering, coughing, gasping for breath.

She could now fill her lungs completely. Feeling came back

to her body. Her bones were in their proper places, her body whole again.

A warm solid hand rubbed her back in gentle circles. She focused on the feeling, the comfort, and leaned into a familiar embrace. Hands stroked her head, her face. Lips brushed her forehead. She wanted those lips someplace else so she rose to meet them.

Jack.

His kiss was like air to her. She breathed him in and held him there inside her, never wanting to exhale. His arms tightened around her, and he pulled his lips away. She whimpered, wanting to keep kissing him. On his chuckle, she opened her eyes.

His smile undid her. She stared at him, drinking in the beauty of his features.

"I thought I'd lost you," he whispered.

"I thought I'd lost me as well."

His expression shuttered, and he blinked back tears. He pressed her to him again, wrapping his arms around her as she became aware of her surroundings.

Shell-shocked refugees—healed of their injuries—rose from the ground, staring in awe at a point behind her. She pulled away from Jack, craned her neck around, and nearly fell backward.

Floating above them was Queen Oola, ethereal and beautiful, fierce and overpowering. Jasminda gaped at the Queen's familiar face. Looking at the woman was like looking into a mirror.

Something hard jabbed Jasminda's closed fist. She uncurled her fingers to reveal a bronze pendant bearing the Queen's sigil attached to a thin metal chain. The caldera surrounding the pendant was gone, burned away by the awakening spell.

A hush of quiet descended. The refugees began to kneel. Jasminda climbed off Jack and kneeled as well, bowing her head.

"Jaqros Alliaseen. Jasminda ul-Sarifor." The Queen's voice rang out, rich and thick as raw honey. "Rise."

Jasminda darted a glance at Jack; both of them stood on wobbly legs. Power surged along her skin as she and Jack were gently lifted into the air and drifted over the heads of the awe-struck crowd. The spell released her a handful of paces away from the Queen. The difference between Her power and the True Father's was night and day.

Queen Oola floated down until She was almost at eye level. The pendant in Jasminda's hand seemed to transfix Her. Jasminda held it out in offering. The chain lifted into the air and settled around Her neck, where it belonged.

Jasminda tugged at her mother's pendant, the same spidery sigil of snaking, curved lines around her own neck. The Queen's mark.

"I owe you a gratitude for awakening me," the Queen said. "You must bow before no one."

Jasminda's Song flared to life. The slow trickle of her weak capacity for power enlarged, and she was engorged with a rush of Earthsong. She struggled to catch her breath as the sensation shot through her. It was like being in the link all over again: everything around her sharpened into focus. She gasped as pure energy pulsed inside her. Her Song expanded, stretched, changed. Grew larger and more powerful—a raging river, with white-capped waves shuttling over its banks.

This was different from what Oola had done for her brother, who'd had no Song to enlarge. This had the feel of permanence to it.

Jack caught hold of Jasminda's hand to steady her.

"Your Majesty," she said, inclining her head. "Why me?"

Queen Oola drew closer, Her dark gaze peering deep inside Jasminda as if seeing her very soul.

The power gushing within her made it hard to concentrate, but Jasminda stared at the pendant resting against Queen Oola's chest to bring her thoughts into focus. "Why was I the only one affected by the caldera? Why could no one else see the visions?"

Queen Oola's expression did not change, but Her eyes lightened and a breeze lifted Her hair. *Blood magic may be broken only by those who bear the blood.*

"Whose blood? Mine? I'm sorry, but I don't under—"

"Prince Jaqros," the Queen interrupted, out loud this time.

Jasminda wanted to push for answers, but Queen Oola had effectively ended her inquiry. She looked around. Every eye in every direction was glued to the Queen.

"You are the rightful ruler of this land." Oola turned to Jack.

He deepened his bow. "I rule only in your stead, Your Majesty."

"You are loyal and true, as is your beloved." She swept Her gaze to Jasminda, who still vibrated with her new, incredibly powerful Song and a head full of questions. "I will abdicate my throne to you. To both of you."

Gasps sounded. Jasminda's own heartbeat pulsed rapidly. She held onto Jack even tighter.

"My gift to Jasminda is the strength of Song she will need

to be queen. Use it well. My wish is for you to unite the people as they once were. And rule. Well."

She ascended over the heads of the troops, toward the place where the two lands met. "This border is no more." Her voice carried, strong and clear. "Singer and Silent will live as one. So be it. See to it."

"Be it so," said Jasminda under her breath. She could barely think for the questions swirling around in her head. Could it really be true? She and Jack together as king and queen?

Oola rose higher into the air, surveying the land and the people. A disturbance among the Elsiran soldiers caught Her attention, and She hovered, staring at the sea of men.

"What is it?" Jasminda asked. Jack shook his head. They pushed forward through the gaping onlookers, following Oola as She floated closer to the buildings of the base.

Standing before one of the four-wheelers, surrounded by guards, was the True Father. Eero. His hands were bound before him and his mask was still in place, but his head was tilted up, clearly looking at his sister.

Jasminda tapped into the maelstrom of emotions surrounding her and struggled to parse them out. The strongest by far were from Oola—pain, shame, anger, heartbreak, and finally, relief. Oddly, Jasminda could sense nothing from Eero. His emotions were a vast emptiness. Were he not standing directly on the caldera, she would have thought he was blocking her Song somehow, but perhaps he had no feelings left after centuries of tyranny.

Oola lowered Herself before Her twin until Her feet hovered over the ground. The Queen reached for him and ran a finger across his grotesque mask. Jasminda once again pushed forward, drawn toward the two as if by an invisible chain.

Having spent so much time inside Oola's head, worry blossomed within her at the Queen's reaction.

"You have returned," Eero rasped.

Oola winced at this new voice of his. "I have come back for you," She said.

They spoke quietly, just for the two of them, but Jasminda made out their words.

"You came back to take from me what is mine," Eero said.

Oola dropped Her hand. Jasminda was now close enough to see the tears welling in the Queen's eyes. Her worry grew.

"I came back to right my wrong." One tear broke free and streamed down Oola's cheek. "What have you done, brother?"

She reached for his mask and pulled it off his face. A silent shudder went through those on both sides.

None alive had seen beneath the mask he'd first donned centuries ago. Subjugation and misery had altered the collective memory, and the Lagrimari had forgotten their leader was not an Earthsinger like them. They'd forgotten why he preyed on them and stole their power.

The jeweled disguise fell from the Queen's fingertips. Beneath it, Eero's face was unchanged from the young man Jasminda had seen in Oola's memories. He looked Elsiran still, with haunting golden eyes and ginger hair.

The shock of the crowd was oppressive. It slammed into Jasminda, forcing her to throw up a shield against the assault. Murmurs filled the air as Lagrimari and Elsirans alike took in the two. The beloved Elsiran Queen and the hated Lagrimari dictator. Neither were what anyone had expected.

"Will you embrace me one last time, sister?" Eero's words echoed those he'd spoken before betraying his twin all those years ago. Jasminda froze.

Oola's emotions sharply changed. Guilt came to the forefront; Her resolve to right Her wrong was slipping away under the weight of the familiarity and love She still felt for Her brother. The metal band of his shackles snapped—the whisper of a spell from Oola.

Eero's amber eyes held a warmth that did not correspond to the emptiness inside him. Oola could not sense it, She had always been blinded to him, just as Yllis had said, and even now, *even now*, as Jasminda observed, She continued to be so.

Jasminda needed a way to get through to Oola, to make Her see Her brother for what he really was.

Your Majesty. Jasminda thought a message, the way she had with Osar, the way the Earthsingers of old had. *He is not the boy you knew any longer. You must not allow him to sway you.* If the message had gone through, if Oola had heard her plea, the Queen gave no acknowledgment. Instead, Her self-condemnation seemed to grow.

Jasminda trembled. History could not repeat itself again. "We have to help Her," she whispered to Jack.

"Help *Her*?"

Jasminda never took her eyes off Oola. They'd thought Her a goddess, but She was a woman, a woman with a broken heart who had nothing left in this world. A woman caught in a vortex of pain.

"She can't do it. Even after everything . . ." Jasminda wrung her hands. She, too, knew heartbreak. She, too, knew loss. But somehow Oola had allowed those emotions to overtake Her resolve, and now She faltered when She needed to act.

"We have to stop him before he harms Her."

Jack's expression was incredulous, but he nodded. The True

Father was now bound from using Earthsong by the caldera, and if Oola's feet touched the ground, She'd also become powerless. But in the final vision Jasminda had seen through Oola's eyes, Eero had then, too, been bound by Yllis's blood spell. The bracelets on Eero's wrists had been calderas with a similar spell against using Earthsong. But those bracelets had not stopped him from stealing his sister's Song. To do that he must have used pure blood magic, Jasminda surmised. And blood magic had allowed him to destroy the calderas.

If the True Father were to access Earthsong now, there was no telling the amount of damage he could do.

Jasminda strained to remember the words Eero had spoken after he'd stabbed his sister, words Oola had not understood for they had been in the tongue of the Cavefolk. They invoked the blood spell, and if Eero used it, so could Jasminda.

She reached out to the soldier next to her and pulled the knife from his belt. The man looked up in surprise, but at seeing the Prince Regent, held his tongue. Jack's gaze was questioning, but he made no move to stop her. Jasminda squeezed the knife's handle and moved closer to the standoff between the twins with Jack on her heels.

Oola's face clouded in misery. Jasminda circled around Eero and approached him from behind. The king's shoulders stiffened, but he did not turn. Instead, he took a step closer to his sister and wiped the tears from Her face, then wrapped his arms around Her waist.

With a yell, Jasminda ran forward and plunged the knife into his back, then whispered the string of words that would bring him to the brink of death and release his Song.

The stolen Songs inside him catapulted at her, their attack

violent. She kept a hand on the knife but her knees buckled under the onslaught. The Songs were tainted; they battered ruthlessly. Her connection to Earthsong flared as her own Song fought back. Like a virus infecting her, the stolen Songs wore away at her shield, dragging her under. They were oily, slick with a layer of malevolence from their former host. Jasminda took them on, having no other option, but feared she would not survive the struggle.

Her knees hit the ground. Blackness swept over her vision.

Suddenly, another Song brushed against her consciousness. Oola was trying to link with her. Jasminda gladly gave up control of her Song, and the practiced strength of Oola's immense power took over. The Queen funneled the stolen Songs away from Jasminda. Her hand, still clutching the knife impaled in Eero's back, was covered by Oola's. Blood ran down Jasminda's arm.

Using the same spell Yllis had discovered to trap his Song in Her pendant and create the caldera, Oola manipulated the energy to force the stolen Songs into the knife before pulling the blade from Eero's back. The sickly taste of blood magic fled Jasminda's tongue as the Songs were imprisoned.

Oola pulled both their hands away, and the knife clattered to the ground, the blood on it spreading, hardening, transforming into the red stone of a caldera.

Oola released their link, and Jasminda fell back, gasping for breath. Jack was there behind her, propping her up, his arms buoys in the whirling sea, keeping her afloat.

Eero crumpled to his knees screaming, his brittle shell pierced at last. Jasminda slammed her shield into place as the man's emotions sprang free of their bonds. She did not want to experience the suppressed feelings that five hundred years of ruthless brutality had forged.

Oola's tearstained face stared blankly at Her brother's weeping body. Her attention moved to Jasminda, eyes heavy, but grateful. "It is done," She whispered, then shot into the air, soon becoming a dot against the sky.

CHAPTER FORTY-SEVEN

The Mistress of Frogs intervened in a feud between two brothers. Family is a two-bladed sword, she said. It must be maneuvered expertly to avoid injury.

—COLLECTED FOLKTALES

The gates were open. By order of the king, the Portside gates were now open once a week and anyone could enter Rosira on that day without being asked for their papers. It would take a while to change the law permanently—many Elsirans were up in arms about this small step—but Ella grinned as she watched the crowd at the Bishop Gate vie for a step into formerly forbidden territory.

She, however, was headed in the opposite direction. Wooden planks creaked beneath her feet as she walked down the piers until she reached a large steamer ship with a line of passengers waiting to board. She moved past the people and their luggage until she stood at the edge of the platform, staring out at the vast, dark sea.

She hadn't ever liked ships. The voyage from Fremia to Elsira had been unpleasant. Beset by seasickness, she hadn't enjoyed the tiny bunks in the overcrowded steerage section, which were the best accommodations she'd been able to afford. Being young and excited for an adventure had made the journey bearable, but she was not eager to board a large ship again.

The cloudless sky was a gift after days of pernicious rain. She tilted her head up, allowing the sun to warm her face, and breathed the crisp, fresh air. For the first time in a long while, she was truly at peace. It was a feeling she didn't want to let go of.

Behind her, a frantic mewling sounded, followed by a happy gurgle. Ella spun around, smiling broadly. Mayzi stood there, the tightly swaddled bundle in her arms in motion, fighting against the blanket wrapped around him.

Mayzi's hair was cut, curled, and dyed a platinum blond. With her dark sunglasses and new belted dress, she looked like the star of a photoplay. The new look suited her, if Ella did say so herself. That hair was some of her best work.

"Are you ready?" Ella asked.

"Ready as I'll ever be. But . . ." She removed her sunglasses, revealing a worried expression. "Are you sure? Really, really sure?"

Ella reached for the baby, careful not to touch his skin and be thrown into another vision. Somehow, Kess had managed to embed a lifetime's worth of memories into his blood. Ella had seen everything having to do with the Sisterhood and Syllenne, and while she was eager to learn more about her sister's travels before arriving in Elsira, the child's safety was paramount.

She stroked her nephew's covered head, smiling down at him.

"Where I'm from, Mayzi, we have different gods. They're not like yours. They won't ever wake up and walk among us, but they can make themselves heard. Now that I'm listening, I know what I'm supposed to do. My path is here, in Elsira. I can't be his mother, but I know that you can. I believe he was meant for you."

The infant started to fuss—the only one who could hold him without him crying was Mayzi. Ella passed him back to her and he quieted immediately.

"See?"

Mayzi shook her head.

"He'll never be safe here," Ella said. "I think I bought us some time, but Syllenne won't stop looking for him."

"But why?" Mayzi asked. "She doesn't need him. Why can't she leave well enough alone?"

Ella shrugged. "She's used to getting her way. She knew a lot about Kess, and one day she'll figure out what those dying words were. We can't take that risk. This is the right choice— as long as you're sure you want to leave."

"Oh, I'm sure. I love this little one like he's my own. And if Zann found him . . ." Her haunted expression reinforced Ella's certainty.

"What did you decide to name him?" Ella hadn't felt that it was her place to name the child. Let his mother do that.

"Uthar. It means 'well loved' in Udlander." Mayzi smiled. "And that he is."

Ella touched the little arm covered by the blanket. "He certainly is." Sadness edged her conviction. She was doing the right thing, even though it was difficult.

"When you get settled, send a telegram. Use the code Anneli gave us."

Mayzi nodded. "I will. She's already gotten in contact with some friends of hers who will help us out. We'll be all right."

"Are you worried about Zann?"

Mayzi twisted her mouth. "Zann is right where he wants to be. People hanging on his every word. I'm sure he'll replace me quickly. And he'll never know where we are."

The low tone of the ship's horn blew. It was time for them to go.

"Well now," Ella said. "Don't worry, we'll see each other again." She kissed the little black cap covering his hair. The wide world would be more forgiving of his differences than Elsira could ever be. And he would have a loving mother. In some ways, Mayzi reminded her of Kess. She thought Kess would approve.

"Safe journey," she called out as Mayzi and Uthar made their way up the gangway and into the ship. She sent a silent prayer up to St. Maasael, champion of travelers and sailors. *To the merciful Unknown who created all worlds, allow your champion to guide their steps. May the wind blow true, the horse ride straight through, and the dark corners of the passage be lit by you. Amn.*

Ella waited until the sailors drew in the ramp and the ship finally pulled away, plumes of smoke rising from its stack.

Then she turned around and started for home. She had a priestess to take down after all.

CHAPTER FORTY-EIGHT

Jackal stood at the edge of the world to watch the eclipse of the sun. Though the light was obscured, it shined bright enough to blind.

—COLLECTED FOLKTALES

THE QUEEN HAS ARISEN

Week-long Celebration Scheduled Across the Land
Elsira Enters New Age of Hope

The shortest Breach War in history ended only hours after its commencement, and the faith of thousands of Elsirans was renewed when our beloved Queen awakened from Her five centuries of slumber. Details are still coming in at this time, and we still do not know what prompted this miraculous resurrection, but a source from within the Sisterhood stated that magic was almost certainly involved . . .

QUEEN OF DECEPTION?

Reactions to Her Appearance Shock Many
[Continued from page A1]

One witness to the awakening, speaking on the grounds of anonymity, shared his displeasure with the revelation of the Queen's physical appearance. "To think, we'd been praying to a *grol* this whole time. I just can't believe it." Others call such statements blasphemy. Syllenne Nidos, High Priestess of the Sisterhood, decried the "false believers," saying, "Those whose faith was built on any assumption of the Queen's appearance must search their hearts and remember all of the blessings She has provided to so many. We must work together to heal the years of false thinking, both about magic and those who bear it."

Temple attendance has surged in the days following the Queen's awakening, though so has defection from the religion that many are now calling a cult. Attendance is rising at gatherings of Dominionists, a tradition that originated in Yaly and boasts a growing membership worldwide.

Jack tossed the newspaper aside and ran his hands through his hair. He rose to pace the floor of his office, his gaze skating back and forth to the clock on the wall. Finally, Usher pushed through the doors and closed them, leaning back.

The man was out of breath and for a moment, Jack felt bad. Usher was not a young man, but he'd insisted on completing this task himself.

"Did you get them?"

Usher's expression was grim for a moment, before bursting into a smile. "Yes, both of them." He brought his arms from behind his back to reveal a velvet box in each hand. Jack was familiar with the long, blue case in Usher's left hand. It held Jasminda's medal, reclaimed from the unscrupulous dealer who would dare try to sell such a thing on the black market.

But the medal didn't concern Jack much. What he was really interested in was held in Usher's right hand. Jack snatched the smaller box and headed for the door.

"Thank you," he called over his shoulder in response to Usher's chuckle.

Jack slipped into the side corridor and over to the unused back passageways. He didn't want anyone stopping him in the hallways just now. His patience was paper thin and he needed to get this done as quickly as possible.

The hidden paths he'd discovered as a child proved very useful. He slipped into the Blue Library unseen by all, including the room's sole occupant.

Jasminda sat amidst a heap of books, as was her way. She'd mentioned earlier that morning that she was researching the rules of succession for Elsiran monarchs. She took the prospect of being queen very seriously and was overwhelmed at all the knowledge she felt she needed to be a good ruler.

Jack wasn't worried about her, though. It would be a challenge to be sure, but one she was well suited for.

The days ahead would be difficult; the collective wounds

on both sides were deep. But Queen Oola seemed confident the gap could be mended. They'd already taken the first small steps.

The True Father was locked in the dungeon; Lizvette was under house arrest in her rooms, facing the possibility of exile; and her father, Nirall, had not been seen since the day of the breach. An arrest warrant had been issued for several counts of treason, but Jack did not expect the man to turn up anytime soon.

The monarchy had been secured in Jack and Jasminda's possession by Oola's word, but Jack needed to say a few words of his own.

He approached Jasminda from behind. She looked up, cocking her head to the side. With a burst of magic, she shot into the air and flew into his arms. The impact of her body against his was a little too hard.

"Oompf," she said, crashing into him. She smiled sheepishly as she clung to him. "I'm still getting used to this."

Jack chuckled, holding her tight before releasing her. Much as he always wanted her in his arms, he needed his hands free for this task.

"Do you forgive me for putting you in the dungeon?" he asked.

She pursed her lips as if thinking about it. He was afraid he would never hear the end of it and vowed to ask her once a day for forgiveness. "If you forgive me for trying to run away."

He dropped his head. Her leaving still caused a phantom pain in his heart, but he did forgive her. He kissed her to make sure she knew. And there was one thing he could do to ensure she'd never leave again.

He opened the velvet box he carried and dropped to one knee. Jasminda's eyes widened and her lips began to tremble. He presented her with a traditional Elsiran engagement ring of two interlocking bands engraved with her name and his in curling script.

"Jasminda ul-Sarifor, will you marry me?" He brought her hands to his lips. "Will you love me? Honor and protect me? Rule with me? Be my queen? Repair the damage of the two lands with me? Grow old with me? Have children with me? Make this world a better place with me?"

She swallowed, and Jack held his breath. The moment stretched on until he wasn't sure he would be able to remember to breathe in this lifetime.

"Of course, Jack. Of course." Her smile was bright as she slipped the ring onto her finger.

Jack pulled her into his arms as they fell back onto the library floor. He vowed to never let her go again.

Benn waited outside Jack's office for the return of the Prince Regent. He wasn't sure if his tale of magic and memories would be believed, but given everything that had happened over the past few days in Elsira, he thought he had a decent chance.

And Jack needed to know what had really happened to his brother.

Before she'd left, heading into Lagrimar even as wave after wave of Lagrimari was leaving that country, Zaura had given him a bit of advice. "A predator at the top of the food chain doesn't often feel the need to look behind him."

He'd mused on this for the past couple of days, but wasn't

quite sure what she'd been trying to say. How did that relate to his situation?

The buzz of activity in the hallways quieted. Benn looked up to find everyone around him frozen, looking wide eyed at the procession that approached.

At the center of a group of Sisters stood the Queen Who Sleeps, regal and beautiful and terrifying. Benn swallowed as She drew closer. Electricity charged the air. She was a magnet and they were all bits of metal, flying toward Her.

At Her right side walked a thin, older sister, with tinges of red at the temples of her silver hair. The High Priestess was in deep conversation with the Queen, leaning in toward Her, a self-important light brightening her face.

Benn sat back in his chair, locked into place as the awe of beholding the Queen in the flesh mixed with the horror of Syllenne Nidos being so close to Her. Fear for what this could mean for Ella and for Elsira as a whole filled him.

The Queen turned Her head and then Her sharp, dark gaze was on him. Holding him in place as pins and needles poked at his skin. He could not take a breath for one long moment.

Then Her attention moved away and the entire entourage was gone, disappearing around the corner.

Slowly life came back to the hallway. Phones rang and typewriter keys clacked. Benn inhaled deeply and gripped the arms of his chair.

Even if Jack believed him, Benn had no idea what came next. All he knew was that Elsira would never be the same.

EPILOGUE

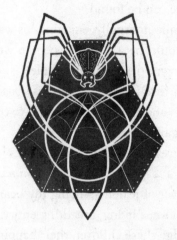

Spider, suspicious of the sun, kept to the shadows.

—COLLECTED FOLKTALES

The desert stretches out before me, bleak and brown. Lives have been scratched here into the dirt, but the misery of my people echoes. It reached me in the World Between and it reaches me still.

The Elsiran soldiers have taken the capital city of Lagrimar. Their motorized transports cut across the country, inspiring awe and hope in those they pass. Word of my awakening has traveled with them. I ride upon the wind, crossing the vast distance in almost no time at all.

As I fly, dark heads tilt up and dark eyes rise to me. I block out their awe and fascination, their reverence and wonder. Block them out until I locate the one I seek.

He stands at the entrance to the city. His power a brilliant star outshining a sea of flickering candles.

Your Majesty. His thoughts reach me, cautiously. Not a smidgeon of awe can be found.

Darvyn. I smile internally, enjoying his wariness. Quite a lot of trouble could be avoided if people were more wary. Though for Darvyn, trouble is inevitable.

He has been through an ordeal these past weeks—one I did not foresee—and there are more tests to come. For I have need of him. Again.

You must go west, I tell him. He clenches his jaw. *You will aid the new king and queen, Jaqros and Jasminda.* I force myself to numb the sliver of jealousy slicing my heart when I think of them—their love, a living, breathing entity, taunts me. But I cannot begrudge these children their happiness.

No. I need to find her. His thoughts turn to his own tattered heart. To the woman who owns it.

Sympathy and sentimentality are like quicksand. I cannot allow them to pull him under as they did me.

Now is not the time for you and her. I owe the new queen a debt, and it must be paid. Family is all that matters now. And it is high time Jasminda's family came home.

His eyes bore into me coldly. I call the wind to me and rise into the air. He will help.

I will give him no other option.

ACKNOWLEDGMENTS

To the readers who rolled with me the first time around, you have my eternal gratitude! I hope this iteration of Jasminda and Jack's story makes the waiting more bearable.

This book was conceived after a week-long writing workshop where my creative mind was torn apart and put back together again. The next year I went back with the opening chapter to have the process repeated. Huge thanks to Junot Díaz, Marjorie Liu, and both my VONA crews—your voices made me a better writer.

Thank you to my editor, Monique Patterson, for bringing me on this amazing journey. You offered me an unexpected detour that terrified me, but you have been the best possible guide. And immense thanks to everyone at St. Martin's Press for all the hard work that made this possible.

To the BCALA and the librarians who saw something relevant in my fantastical love story, I'm forever grateful. And to my agent, Sara Megibow, whose enthusiasm knows no bounds, thank you for ushering me through this process.

Thanks to Danielle Poiesz, who first polished my words, and James T. Egan, who designed an amazing package for them to live in. To Quinn Heraty, my fabulous lawyer, thank you for shepherding me through unfamiliar terrain. To Kaia Danielle, the best signal booster ever, and Kara Stevens, who helped keep me accountable: y'all rock. And to everyone at The Muse Writers Center, thank you for lighting the match.

To Ines Johnson for being my favorite human, and Cerece Rennie Murphy for being relentlessly reliable.

To Paul, who's made of the same star stuff as me, only upside down and backward, thank you for carrying me across the finish line and supplying the missing pieces. To my father, who won't see this but I know is someplace where he can feel it, and my mother, who sees everything, thank you for always supporting my dreams.

And to Jared, thank you for believing in me and for lifting the heavy stuff to make space for me to write. I love you.